# PROLOGUE

*New York City*
*Duke and Jane's apartment*
*Six weeks before the wedding*

t is a truth universally acknowledged that a romantically minded modern woman probably has her wedding planned on Pinterest. As a romance novelist engaged to a dashing billionaire, I was no exception. From the perfect venue (Kingstag Castle in Dorset, England) to the perfect dress (Monique Lhuillier), I had everything all picked out. And I had an amazing wedding planner, Arwen Kilpatrick, to make it a reality.

Now I just needed to count down the days until my dream wedding with the love of my life, Duke Austen.

"Look, our invitations have arrived!" I eagerly opened the box and lifted one out, admiring the heft of the paper.

"Better not let the gossips get ahold of one," Duke murmured as he slid his arm around my waist and kissed my neck.

"Although now someone will have to spend hours licking envelopes."

"If we'd just gone with Paperless Post ..."

"You and your Internet-y things. I'm a traditional girl. We're going to have a proper wedding with proper paper invitations."

I held it up.

*Jane Sparks and Duke Austen request the honor of your company at their wedding on August 26th at Kingstag Castle, Dorset, England*

"Isn't Kingstag Castle perfect?"

"Yes. And private. Just you, me, our closest friends, and family."

I turned and wrapped my arms around him, standing up on my tiptoes to kiss him. I had found the perfect guy for me. We were going to have the perfect wedding for us.

I was all set to lose myself in this kiss when the phone rang. It was our wedding planner. I ignored it and Duke laughed softly and we kissed some more. Then the phone rang again. This time, I picked up.

"Hi, Arwen! Great news! The invitations arrived. You have bad news? What?"

I sat down on the couch, pressing the phone to my ear.

"Okay, I'm sitting."

Duke, looking concerned, came and sat down next to me, and tried to eavesdrop on the terrible, horrible news Arwen was delivering.

"It burned down?! But Kingstag Castle has been standing for eight hundred years! It survived the Wars of the Roses!"

Duke let out a low whistle. What followed was a very distressing conversation in which I learned that a fire had broken out in the kitchens and spread from there. Many of the public rooms had sustained damage that would result in a year of extensive repairs and renovations. A year!

This was a disaster. I hung up and burst into tears.

No one who saw Duke Austen would assume him to be a billionaire, or one of the most influential people in the tech world. To me, "billion-

# AT THE SUMMER WEDDING

# AT THE SUMMER WEDDING

## SHOCKING, UNPREDICTABLE, AND UTTERLY ROMANTIC

MAYA RODALE     KATHARINE ASHE

MIRANDA NEVILLE     CAROLINE LINDEN

THE LADY AUTHORS

ISBN-13: 978-0-9860539-4-8

Originally published as AT THE BILLIONAIRE'S WEDDING

*The Best Laid Planner* © 2014 Miranda Neville

*Will You Be My Wi-Fi?* © 2014 P. F. Belsley

*The Day It Rained Books* © 2014 Katharine Brophy Dubois

*Prologue* and *That Moment When You Fall in Love* © 2014 Maya Rodale

Cover Design © 2022 Erin Dameron-Hill / EDHGraphics

Published by The Lady Authors

# CONTENTS

aire" conjured images of distinguished men in suits. But Duke was a rogue all the way. He wore, as a uniform, broken-in Levis and free T-shirts that revealed his muscled arms and chest. His hair was mussed up. And when he smiled—he had a smile that made good girls like me desperate to do bad things.

They didn't call him the bad boy billionaire for nothing.

He might not look like a hero, but oh, he was.

As I was crying over the death of my dream wedding, he pulled me close and said, "It's okay."

"It's not," I sniffed.

"We'll find another castle or big fancy house." As if they were just littering the countryside. Well, they probably were. But ...

"Everything will be booked."

These things were booked out well in advance. I knew because I had reserved my castle a year ago. There was no way we'd find another place that would be beautiful, luxurious, could accommodate our guests (who had already received their "save the date" requests), and be private enough (so the media wouldn't find out or get in and cause problems on the special day).

"I'm sure there's something out there," he said, proving that though he was a tech genius, he was oblivious to the ways of Bridezillas. "Let's see what we can find. I have an Internet-y thing that might help."

"What is it?" I asked.

Duke took my hand and led me to his computer.

The Internet-y thing was Google. He typed in "English country house weddings."

A million results came up and Duke started visiting all the different sites and making phone calls to England. I shuddered to think of his phone bill after two hours of this.

"You're booked?" he asked. Again. "Bummer," he said. Again.

I sighed and wondered about Vegas ...

"No availability? Just curious—how much money would make you have availability?" Even Duke, who was perpetually good-natured, finally started to get frustrated at having the same conversation over and over.

"I think you have called every ancestral house in England that hosts weddings," I said wearily. Then, adding sarcastically, "Surprisingly, they are all booked for every Saturday in August. Now we have to cancel our wedding."

Duke took my hands in his and gazed into my eyes.

"Nothing is going to stop us from getting married," he said. "Nothing is going to stop me from giving you the wedding of your dreams, okay?"

See: hero. My hero. I decided to have faith that this would somehow work out.

Duke seemed to be looking at something on the computer screen behind me.

"What's that one?"

I glanced back. "Brampton House. I actually really like it, but it's not even open yet."

"Like hell it isn't," he growled, reaching for his phone. "What's the number?"

I told him, he dialed. A conversation ensued. Duke paced. There was talk of renovations, the number of rooms, our need for privacy, and a huge check if it was all done in time. Duke hung up, turned to me, and said, "We're having our wedding at Brampton House."

"What?!"

"It's a beautiful old ancestral house that's being converted to a hotel which we can have exclusively for the week for all our friends and family. Best of all, since it's not open yet, it's unlikely the media will think that our wedding might be there. I know you were worried about keeping everything on the DL."

"But we haven't even seen the place yet! You can't spend a fortune on a place you've never seen."

"Do you want to go now?"

He wasn't joking.

"I have a book due and you have a new product launch. We don't have time to see it and from what I overheard, it sounds like he'll need every minute to get it ready in time."

"We'll send Arwen," Duke said. "She's sharp as a tack. If she thinks it's a suitable location, our wedding will go ahead as planned. And let's not tell anyone where it's going to be."

"It's perfectly dreamy," I said, throwing my arms around Duke. "Nothing can go wrong now. Absolutely nothing."

*Duke Austen and Jane Sparks request the honor of your company at their wedding on August 26th. Please join the happy couple for a week of festivities and celebration ...*

# THE BEST LAID PLANNER

MIRANDA NEVILLE

# CHAPTER
## ONE

Arwen Kilpatrick steered the world's smallest car along the world's narrowest road, peering through the swishing windshield wipers and praying she wouldn't meet another vehicle. Not daring to use her phone while driving on the wrong side of the road— especially a road so narrow it possessed only one side —she made a mental note: *helicopters*. Duke and Jane's wedding guests couldn't be expected to arrive in cars smaller than the smallest Chevy ever. A nonstop helicopter shuttle would add cachet and each passenger would be presented with a miniature picnic basket: a split of Dom Perignon, Brazilian brigadeiro chocolates, and maybe little pots of caviar. Too messy: tiny caviar-stuffed blinis. Did they make blinis in England? If not, she'd fly someone in from New York to do it. Or Moscow.

Drunk with the power of an event planner with an unlimited budget, she barely jammed on the brakes in time to avoid a head-on collision and promptly stalled the engine. When the airport car rental place had only a stick shift available, she had dealt. She'd driven a tractor on her parents' farm until she'd run over a pig at the age of fifteen and they took away the keys. She knew gears and clutches. Sort of.

A man in a mud-caked Jeepy-looking vehicle waved his hands. From his gesticulations she gathered she was supposed to back up to let him pass. She messed up the clutch and stalled again, twice. Assaulted by waves of jet lag she leaned her forehead on the steering wheel, then jerked backward when the horn blasted.

The other driver had left his vehicle and banged on the side window, his temper no doubt exacerbated by the rain dripping off the brim of an ancient rain hat. She let the window down six inches.

"What's the matter?" he asked, reeking exasperation.

"I'm having trouble shifting with my left hand," she said, refusing to admit it was the clutch—and her four-inch heels—giving her grief.

"American," he replied as though it explained everything and not in a good way. "Look here, you'd better get out and I'll back your car to the passing place."

Not wishing to arrive at Brampton House looking like a drowned rat, she scooched over to the passenger seat, getting her pencil skirt caught in the gear stick. "Get in," she said sharply when he appeared mesmerized by the sight of her thighs. *Dirty old man.*

Okay, not old. And wet rather than dirty. While he folded a long body into the tiny car, started the engine, and traveled a hundred feet backward with effortless competence, she observed that he was in his early thirties and handsome in a hunky, James McAvoy kind of way.

"You were driving too fast in the lane," he said. "You should slow down and look out."

"I was doing twenty." Arwen crossed her fingers. She hadn't been watching the speedometer, neither was she sure if they used miles or kilometers in England. "It shouldn't be legal to have roads this narrow."

"Try talking to the County Council about it," he said.

"I suppose it's why your cars are so tiny."

"They get the job done and don't waste petrol."

She owned a hybrid herself, but if he wanted to make stereotypical assumptions about gas-guzzling Americans she wasn't going to contradict him. Plus he looked comical with denim-clad legs almost hitting the dashboard, and kind of cute.

Reaching a spot where the road was slightly wider, he stopped and got out of the car. After a step or two toward his own vehicle, he came back. "Do you want me to turn it round for you?" he asked, leaning in through the open door. "This road only leads to Brampton and the house isn't open to the public at the moment."

"Thanks but no thanks." Arwen resisted the urge to tell him to mind his own business and stop dripping water in her car. The guy had the nerve to stand in the rain, an eyebrow raised, probably waiting for her to return to her seat. No way was she giving him a flash of her panties.

"Are you sure?"

"Quite sure."

"Pity," he said. For a moment stormy eyes glinted with something more than annoyance.

"What?"

"Never mind. There's a wider road back to the village. Turn right at the Brampton gate." He closed the door and stomped away. Seconds later he revved up his disreputable vehicle, which needed a new muffler, sending up a shower of mud as he passed. More than twenty miles an hour she'd bet. Or kilometers. Arwen's first encounter with the Brampton natives was not encouraging. Still, even scolding sounded better from a deep voice with a British accent. Of course they all had lovely accents and some of them were villains: Benedict Cumberbatch as Khan; Richard Armitage as the Sheriff of Nottingham; Alan Rickman in almost anything. His voice was up to that standard.

Resisting the distraction of British vowels and cheekbones, she slowed to a crawl for the last half mile. A set of impressive stone pillars and a discreet sign marked the entrance to Brampton House, Country House Hotel. It had rained on and off most of the way from the airport, but as she drove through the open gates a beam of sunlight opened a crack in the clouds and illuminated a vision in honey-colored stone and glass. Arwen, who had organized weddings in every available mansion within easy reach of New York City, had never seen a more beautiful house. Seventeenth-century with later additions, she remembered from the history on the hotel's rudimentary website. Things had looked desperate when Jane's first choice of wedding location fell through at the eleventh hour. But even in the short time available, Arwen could do something spectacular here, a celebration that would be talked about in every magazine on the country. Her name would be in *Brides, Town and Country, People...*

First she had to make sure that Brampton House, newly converted to a hotel, was up to the standards required of a wedding venue for America's newest tech billionaire and his bride. Going to her high-school reunion in Pennsylvania and reconnecting with Jane Sparks was the biggest piece of luck of Arwen's career in the competitive world of event planning. Luxe Events was not going to blow the opportunity. At the gate she stopped to take a photo and texted it to her partner Valerie, then called her, ready to babble about how gorgeous the place was and rub Val's nose in it, just a little bit, for having to stay in New York to complete the arrangements for a routine wedding at Tavern on the Green.

Nothing. Her phone showed one dot, which faded before her eyes into No Service. The photo hadn't gone either. She hoped this was merely a dead spot. If not, the hotel had better have damn good Wi-Fi.

Clouds parted further as she drove down a tree-lined avenue bisecting impossibly green fields to the crunchy gravel approach to the house. An epic flight of stone stairs, wide enough to photograph the wedding party and all the guests, led to a huge front door. Not a single vehicle spoiled the dazzling historic panorama and Arwen had been told to proceed to the east wing. Glancing at the sun, she turned left and drove around the side of the house to discover a more utilitarian elegance. Several cars and vans were parked in another graveled area. On one side was the main house, at right angles to a separate building entered by an archway with a picturesque clock tower. The look was spoiled by a huge pile of dirt sitting forlornly next to an abandoned backhoe. Whatever excavation Lord Melbury had going would have to be finished and cleaned up in time.

Following the instructions in Duke's assistant's e-mail, she knocked on an already open door into the house. "Hi there!" she called, peering down a long broad corridor, hung with hunting prints opposite a long row of hooks holding coats, hats, etc. Shoes and boots, several dozen pairs, were lined up on the floor, punctuated by occasional tennis rackets and fishing rods. Not very hotel-like, but this was the family's residential quarters. Since no one responded to her calls, she stole gingerly up the corridor feeling lame at every "hello" and so rattled she almost tripped on a tall black leather boot that had broken ranks and fallen into her path. She'd entered a freakin' Lord's stately home without permission and felt like they might put her in the Tower of London or something.

*Come on, Arwen. You're a tough American professional woman and this is nothing but a glorified mudroom.*

She took a deep breath. "Anyone here?"

"This way." She followed the soft female voice into the biggest kitchen she'd ever seen. At the far end an elderly woman stirred something in a pot resting on a massive black stove, possibly as old as the house.

"Hello, dear," she said. "What are you looking for?"

Nothing could be less alarming than this sweet little old lady with perfect short gray curls and a pink floral apron covering her white blouse and gray skirt. "Are you Mrs. Thompson?"

"Call me Nanny."

"I am Arwen Kilpatrick. Call me Arwen," she said, relieved at this evidence of informality. "I'm here about the wedding," she added when Nanny looked puzzled. Was it possible that Duke Austen's secretary had failed to call and announce her arrival?

"We were expecting a Welshman called Owen," Nanny said. "But I'm sure you'll do just as well. American, are you? Americans have such funny names. Is Arwen a family name?" Nanny was not apparently an aficionado of J.R.R. Tolkien.

"My mother's maiden name." Her usual lie. She had always hated being named after an elf. Since she had parents who didn't believe in marriage, the concept of a maiden name played to her personal fantasies.

"Would you like a coffee?"

Arwen eyed a big jar of instant on the pine table that dominated the center of the room and shuddered. "Thanks, I picked up Starbucks at the airport. Would it be okay to see my room and freshen up?" Even traveling first class—thank you, Duke Austen!—she felt grimy after the overnight flight.

"Of course, dear. Follow me."

Her room was gorgeous, all antique furniture and faded chintz in blues and yellows that picked out the colors of the wallpaper, a Chinese pattern of bamboo, lotus flowers, and birds. She tested the mattress on a canopy bed out of a costume drama and found it eminently nap-worthy. If the guest rooms in the new hotel were like this it would be perfect. Those New York and Silicon Valley hipsters were going to get a taste of real class. The bathroom was a couple of doors down the hall, but Nanny assured her there were no other guests and she had it to herself. She plugged in her laptop and phone, using three-pin adapters bought at the airport, and noted a couple of bars of Wi-Fi. Hopefully she'd get better signal elsewhere in the house. She'd better. Internet service was more important than bathrooms to tech guys.

She had no complaints about the spacious bathroom with the biggest stand-alone tub she'd ever seen. The showerhead was hand-held but gleaming silver, the hot water plentiful. She washed away all traces of the flight as she wallowed luxuriously and planned her *I am a kickass wedding planner who takes no prisoners* outfit: jeans, Tory Burch jacket, and the Valentino flats she'd found on deep sale. Heels would be preferable to lend her gravitas and height, but she was in the country and walking on gravel in stilettos was not for sissies.

Time to work, but first the hair.

Plugging her travel hairdryer into another adapter, she turned it on and was rewarded by a whir, an explosion of ominous sparks, and silence. Crap.

Then she noticed the light on her laptop charger had gone out. She'd blown a fuse.

*Nice start, Arwen.* Her stomach lurched. The reason she'd come to Brampton was because a kitchen fire had damaged Kingstag Castle, Jane's first choice.

She tore down to the kitchen in a panic, her head filled with a vision of the headlines:

**_Historic Mansion Burned to the Ground_**
**_American Wedding Planner Blamed_**

Nanny, unfazed by wet hair and her flimsy Chinatown robe, assured her that someone called Harry, who was ever so handy, would fix it and offered her a glass of sherry while she waited. What the hell. This was a good moment to break her rule about not drinking at lunch (or technically before lunch). The old lady sat her down with a beautiful cut glass decanter and a matching glass. The sherry was dry but tasty and Arwen felt the tension ease out of her. Despite its size, the room was comfortable and welcoming. She could imagine half a dozen small children with milk mustaches sitting around the old table, munching on cookies.

"Do you know if there's anywhere in the house I can get cell service? Mobile phone service," she added when Nanny looked blank.

"Harry will know," Nanny replied, lifting a gigantic pot from the scary black stove.

"Do you need help with that?" Arwen asked. "It looks awfully heavy."

"I can manage." Nanny drained something that looked suspiciously like cauliflower into a huge colander in an enamel sink almost as big as the bathtub. Everything in the place was on a monumental scale.

"Is there anything else I can do?" she said, once assured that Nanny wasn't going to collapse under a tsunami of boiling water.

"Thank you, dear, but I won't make you work when you've only just arrived. Relax and enjoy your sherry." Arwen took another sip, which wasn't a good idea since it inspired a crazy desire for sleep.

"I'd like to look around the facilities." That was a really hard word to pronounce. "Fa-cil-it-ies," she repeated. "Is Lord Melbury here?" Although she didn't suppose the lord of the manor would concern himself directly with a wedding planner.

"He and Lady Melbury are abroad."

"Who's in charge of the hotel?"

"Harry can answer all your questions. He'll be in for lunch soon."

A wonderful old clock surrounded by an amazing collection of copper molds read twelve thirty. Arwen set down her empty sherry glass and rose to wobbly feet. "I'd better go back upstairs and get dressed," she said.

. . .

Harry glanced in his rearview mirror and wondered if he should have stayed to make sure the pretty girl in the white Vauxhall managed to get her car in gear. He hated being rude, especially to pretty girls, and this one was particularly attractive. For a moment his predicament had faded behind the urge to chat her up, find out what she was doing in the narrow lane, a shortcut used by very few. Once she was out of sight his black mood descended again.

He took several deep breaths and tried to empty his mind of the morning's cock-up and achieve inner peace. It was his own fault for trying to run the excavator himself. Fed up by the nonappearance of the workmen for a third day and anxious to get the trench dug so they could run the gas line to the new catering kitchen, he'd managed to bugger the fiber optic cable bringing high-speed broadband to serve the entire hotel. It turned out you couldn't patch that kind of wiring together with electrical tape. Who knew?

Then he'd learned that Duke Austen had sent a man called Owen Kilpatrick to look the place over before he wrote the gigantic, heart-stopping check, the monumental bonus for opening the hotel early for Austen's wedding to Jane Sparks.

Instead of spending a happy morning pottering around with heavy machinery, he had to go into Melbury and persuade British Telecom to restore Internet service to Brampton House immediately. It was going to take no small degree of charm and groveling to get the capricious gods (i.e. telephone company employees) to hurry up. And the charming and groveling had better be good because this Owen fellow would arrive at any moment and nothing was going to amuse the representative of an Internet billionaire less than a total absence of Internet.

Two hours later, the Land Rover threw up showers of gravel as he screeched round the corner, any semblance of inner peace shot to smithereens by his total failure to make the servants of British Telecom see reason. What the hell was he going to say to Kilpatrick? Lie through his teeth, he supposed.

In the kitchen, Nanny was laying the lunch at the big pine table he'd known all his life. A bubbling cauliflower cheese sat on the AGA but thank God she'd got out a decent bottle of claret. Dear Nanny. The revolution in British food had passed her by and she cooked as if they were still in the nursery. He supposed it was lucky she hadn't made Welsh rarebit, since she was convinced that Duke Austen's representative from New York was Welsh.

"Oh good, you're back, Harry dear. We have a blown fuse in the Chinese bedroom."

He groaned. "It would happen to Mr. Kilpatrick." They'd assigned him the best spare room.

"Such a surprise, dear. He's not Welsh at all."

"Fancy that."

"He's not a he either. It's Miss Kilpatrick and she's American."

Harry had a nasty feeling about this. "Tall and blond?" he said hopefully.

"Oh no. Quite small with lovely shiny dark hair. Pretty."

Just as he feared. He'd yelled at Duke Austen's representative and ogled her legs and he wasn't sure which was worse. Bloody bloody hell. On the bright side, if he could bluff his way through the current crisis he wouldn't mind getting to know her better. "Tell me what happened, Nanny. From the beginning. I want to know everything she said."

"Nothing very much, though she seems a nice girl. I offered her a nice cup of Nescafé but all she wanted was a bath."

Harry shook his head to dispel a sudden image of Miss Kilpatrick's legs draped over the edge of the bathtub. "Did she ask about the Wi-Fi?"

Nanny shook her head. "The poor girl was so upset when she came down in her dressing gown with her hair wet. She plugged in her American hairdryer. There's no electricity in her room."

"Bugger. Let's hope it's only a fuse." The main house had been rewired for the hotel conversion but the family quarters weren't quite finished. There was quite a lot that wasn't quite finished and Miss Kilpatrick needed to be kept in ignorance. "Doesn't the woman know that American and British electrical systems are incompatible?"

"I'm sure I don't know." Visits to foreign parts had never impressed

Nanny. Her idea of abroad was a nice holiday in the Isle of Wight. "She was ever so sorry. I told her not to worry and you'd have it mended in a jiffy."

"Sorry was she?" Harry had an idea how he might turn the situation to his advantage.

"You be nice, Harry. Accidents happen. Change that fuse and bring her down to lunch."

Whistling optimistically, Harry grabbed his tool bag and headed for the Chinese bedroom, with a small detour via the estate office where he unplugged the wireless router. It wasn't as though it would do any good, power or no power.

From the little he'd seen of her, Miss Owen—was that really her name?—Kilpatrick was a strong-minded young woman not afraid to argue. He needed to put her on the defensive. If she was still in her dressing gown—a short one, please God—all the better.

She was. And sprawled on her stomach on the Chinese counterpane, fast asleep, as he discovered when she didn't answer his knock and he assumed she must be in the bathroom. Feeling a bit guilty, Harry had another look at the legs that were just as good as he remembered. Piously, he refrained from trying to peer beneath the red silk robe that hardly covered her bottom. He bet her little bum was just as shapely as her limbs. She stirred on the bed and wiggled it. Since he'd rather not compound the bad start to their acquaintance by being caught leering like an elderly rake, he found the hairdryer on the floor next to a plug, fished out a screwdriver, and got down on his knees to remove the socket cover.

SOMEONE WAS in the room and Arwen felt a breeze up her ass. Suddenly quite awake, she rolled over and tugged at her robe, covering her behind but baring her boobs. Luckily he wasn't looking. The man, Harry she presumed, was on his knees fiddling with the plug and revealing several inches of skin between a black T-shirt and low-hanging blue jeans. Not to mince words, he was showing butt crack. Crack of mighty fine butt.

Harry, the handyman who knew everything, was tall and lithe

with intriguing hints of strength beneath the tee. And what a fabulous butt. The hips were slender, but the glutes well developed, doubtless by constant manual labor in the service of his noble overlords.

Arwen's notions of the British aristocracy were vague, gained from reading about the royals in *People* magazine and, more recently, in Jane Sparks's historical romance novels. She was fairly sure they didn't have much real power anymore, but she kind of enjoyed imagining this hunky guy shaking off the shackles of oppression and stringing up his cruel masters from streetlamps. Although that, she remembered from an old movie version of *A Tale of Two Cities*, was the French Revolution. She'd majored in Environmental Studies at Emory, with an undeclared minor in the history of party-giving.

Or perhaps he just worked out a lot, a boring explanation compared to the vision of him swinging a sledgehammer under the whip of a supercilious aristocrat in jodhpurs and a monocle. Or were those Nazis?

Time to shake off the jet lag fueled lust and move into intimidating professional mode. Pity she was wearing a crumpled silk robe selected because it took up very little packing space.

"Ahem." She staggered to her feet and knotted her sash, tightly. As she coughed again, Harry stood up and turned.

"You! You were leaving," she said stupidly.

"Yes I was, and I came back. I happen to live here."

She inventoried a set of features that made her understand what chiseled meant: prominent brow, straight brown hair, blue eyes, the high cheekbones she'd noticed even under the shadow of the world's least stylish rain hat, and lips that quirked attractively.

"What do you do here exactly?" She found it hard to believe such a scruffy guy was related to a lord. His T-shirt had a paint stain in a place that drew attention to the possibility of pectoral muscles to match his fine ass.

"This and that. I'm supposed to show you round so that you can finalize the plans for Mr. Austen and Miss Sparks's wedding."

"*If* I decide Brampton House is suitable."

"I understand Miss Sparks fell in love with the history of the house.

And of course Brampton is regarded as the finest example of late seventeenth-century domestic architecture in England."

He was right, of course. Jane was crazy about the place, even more than she had been about the fire-damaged castle. "Mr. Austen is determined that his fiancée gets the wedding of her dreams and it's my business to make sure it doesn't turn into a nightmare. It's what I do and I take it very seriously. I haven't had an unsatisfied bride yet."

He flashed white teeth in his perfectly shaped mouth. "I call that excessive devotion to duty."

"Nothing is too much trouble to make her day perfect," she said, lowering her eyelids. "After the confetti, however, I generally turn the matter over to the bridegroom."

"What about him? Have you had an unsatisfied bridegroom? I find it hard to believe."

"I've never *had* a bridegroom. Always a wedding planner, never a bride." Oh my God she was flirting with the handyman, or whatever he was. How unprofessional could she get? "And that's the way I like it. This isn't getting us anywhere, Mister ..."

"Just Harry."

"Well, Just Harry. Can I dry my hair now?" She put her hand up and discovered frizz.

"Not with that hairdryer. I'm afraid it'll be good for nothing but the dustbin after the jolt it took."

"Oh my God, my laptop!" The orange charging light was on again. "Will your damn electricity fry that too?"

"Computers and mobiles are fine with an adapter. They take very low voltage. Anything with any power and you have a problem."

Arwen grabbed her phone. *"No service,"* she said. "How am I supposed to make calls?"

"I can show you places in the grounds that get signal."

"And no Wi-Fi bars, either. Surely you have internet."

"Of course we do. Brampton is a country house hotel with all modern conveniences."

She fiddled with her settings, then thrust the phone at him. "Look. Nada. No Wi-Fi."

Harry gave an exaggerated sigh. "I was afraid of that. The wiring in this part of the house is very delicate and I'm afraid your blown fuse may have disturbed the router signal."

"Really? I've never heard of such a thing."

"You're not in America now, Miss Kilpatrick. Things are different here." He launched into a long explanation about bandwidth and watts and amps and volts that turned her head to cotton. "So you see," he concluded, "you really mustn't blame yourself. There was no way you could have known that a humble domestic appliance like a hairdryer could cause so much trouble. I'm sure it won't take more than a day or two to recover."

Great. She hadn't burned the house down, but the way Harry the Handyman was carrying on she'd done the next worst thing.

Since Arwen set a high premium on doing things right the first time, apologizing for mistakes was one of her least favorite activities. "I'm sorry," she said. "I hope this won't happen if one of your hotel guests makes a similar mistake." Being mad at herself made her bitchy and being bitchy made her more mad at herself.

"Not at all. Everything's new over there, as you will see when I give you a tour after lunch. You'll feel much better after some food." He smiled with friendly condescension. "Let me fetch you an English hairdryer so you can get ready. I'll be back in a tick."

"Don't bother." Her hair was a lost cause unless she washed it again. And lunch sounded wonderful, even if she had to eat it with this hunky oaf. Her stomach rumbled, though she wasn't quite hungry enough to crave cauliflower. Roast beef and Yorkshire pudding on the other hand … "How long do I have?"

"We usually have lunch at one." On the way out the door he turned. "I've never met a girl called Owen before."

"You still haven't. It's Arwen." She spelled it out.

"Ah, the elf. You look more like a pixie."

She acknowledged the remark with a perfunctory shrug. Some days she wished Tolkien had never lived.

"I suppose you've heard that before."

"Two or three hundred times."

"Rule number one: if you want to be original, never joke about people's names." He gave a wicked little smile that made her stomach flip. "I shall be very serious when I call you Elf."

ALMOST HER UNRUFFLED SELF—THERE wasn't anything to do about hair that had gone haywire in the English climate—Arwen joined Nanny and Harry for lunch. She'd have expected a meal served in a formal dining room by a butler, but supposed that wasn't offered when the owner wasn't in residence. She was tickled to discover that even a casual meal at the kitchen table in company with the cook and the handyman merited fabulous old china and silver, huge starched linen napkins, and vintage Bordeaux served in crystal fine enough to shatter at a breath of wind. She sipped carefully.

While the wine was a treat, she was appalled to discover that cauliflower in a thick white sauce was the main course of the meal.

"Delicious, Nanny darling." Harry, who was consuming the stuff hungrily, caught her sideways glance and winked. "Cauliflower cheese is her forte," he explained.

Unwilling to insult Nanny's notion of haute cuisine, or hurt her feelings, Arwen swallowed some of the nauseating concoction while answering questions about what exactly a wedding planner did.

"We hope to have lots of weddings here," Harry said. "We should pick your brain."

"How much I do depends on the bride. Sometimes a girl has been planning her own event practically since the cradle and my job is to make her dream a reality, usually within the bounds of an impossible budget."

"Is Miss Sparks like that?"

"We went to high school together and she was always pretty laid-back. She knows what she wants, but she isn't unreasonable. Still, when you're engaged to a billionaire, your standards are different from a professional woman who needs to squeeze every drop of value out of her hundred grand. Not that I blame my clients," she added hastily. "Weddings are expensive." She could have said a lot more about the demands of outrageous Bridezillas who could leach all joy out of a wedding planner's job. She put on her best tough businesswoman expression, developed to browbeat recalcitrant caterers, florists, and banqueting managers. "This afternoon I would like an in-depth tour of Brampton House so I know I can deliver what Jane wants. I never settle for less than perfection."

Harry looked less than browbeaten. "Are you full or can you find room for some Stilton?"

"Yes, please," she said with fervor.

The cheese and crackers were divine with the wine and the meal concluded with a fruit compote drenched in heavy cream. Apparently low-fat was not a known concept here. Luckily for her chances of staying awake that afternoon, Harry made espresso served in exquisite demitasses while Nanny fixed herself a huge cup of instant. "That foreign coffee's too strong for me," she said. "I like a nice English cup of Nescafé or Maxwell House."

"Are you ready for the tour?" Harry asked. Instinctively she reached for her phone to check email and messages, before she remembered.

"You said there were places I could get signal," she said.

"Bedrooms first?"

"And then the public rooms and the hotel kitchen. I assume your guest won't be fed on meals produced on *that*." She nodded in the direction of the giant black stove.

"And then the Mausoleum. A lovely spot to make telephone calls, with a view that would inspire anyone to eloquence."

"I've always heard that England is full of history but I had no idea the dead were equipped with cellular service."

"I told you Brampton offers all modern conveniences."

# CHAPTER
## TWO

Miss Arwen Kilpatrick had a mind like a computer and the body of a Turkish sultan's favorite harem girl. The first Harry found enviable, the second mesmerizing, and the combination irresistible and frequently distracting from the details of bedrooms and bathrooms and room service. He was confident that the conversion of two stories of Brampton to hotel rooms satisfied the blend of country house elegance and state-of-the-art luxury for which he planned to charge his guests a fortune. But Arwen left nothing to chance. Watching her prod the mattresses and inspect chests of drawers gave him ample opportunity to examine her less cerebral virtues.

"Why aren't there fridges and minibars in the rooms?" she asked, bending down to peer into an empty cupboard.

He dragged his dirty mind from an appreciation of her assets. "May I remind you that we are doing a favor to Duke Austen by opening the hotel early to please the fantasies of his historical romance writing bride?"

"For which you will be well compensated."

"Of course," Harry said. "Without mini-bars, the future Mrs. Jane Austen's wedding guests will be able to imagine themselves in the pages of a Jane Austen novel."

"I saw the Keira Knightley version of *Pride and Prejudice*. Those Bennet girls lived in a pretty filthy place."

"That was Longbourn," he said firmly. "Think of Brampton as Mr. Darcy's house."

"Right, Pemberley. No mud. Will you have footmen in powdered wigs?"

"Unfortunately, it's hard these days to find trained staff prepared to dress that way, especially at short notice." He didn't add that most likely room service would be delivered by local women who would have to be talked out of Gap jeans and into maids' uniforms. "We're still working on finding people but I can assure you that there will be no lack of comfort. Now for the honeymoon suite."

Even the steely-eyed wedding planner seemed impressed by the first Lord Melbury's rooms. In their youth, the current Melburys had furnished them like an eastern souk. All the pseudo-Ottoman drapes and pillows had been tossed out, along with the leaky hot tub. The original gilded plasterwork was restored at vast expense, and the original furniture dug out of the attic and spruced up with the most lavish pseudo-eighteenth-century materials Colefax & Fowler could provide. My Lord's dressing room became a bathroom, complete with a brand new Jacuzzi bathtub. Arwen sat on the edge of the massive four-poster bed and tested it with a delicious bounce. "Good mattress," she said approvingly.

His throat went dry and he turned away so she wouldn't see him licking his lips. *Down, Harry*. This business was too important to blow.

"Okay, I think we're done up here. Now for the reception rooms."

He was happy to see even Miss New York Elf struck silent by the State Rooms. As he pointed out the features of the three chambers he was, as always, awed by their magnificence and reminded why he had chosen to live in this impractical house. Realizing that she wasn't taking in his history lesson, he let her admire in silence.

"Wow," she said in the Gold Saloon. "Just wow. Can we use these? I feel like I should be wearing white gloves to even touch anything."

"It wouldn't do to get too wild in here, but I—we—intend to let them out for formal occasions."

"Am I allowed to sit down?"

With a little bow he offered a Chippendale armchair, part of several groupings of seats arranged around the sixty-foot-long room. "You look dazed. Is it the wonders of Brampton or jet lag?"

"A little of both, I think." She sat down with her back straight, as though frightened to connect with the tapestry back. In her neat black jacket and tidy jeans she seemed like a creature from another planet set down in the seventeenth century. The contrast pleased him. But then pretty much everything about her pleased him.

"Relax. You won't break it. Thomas Chippendale made furniture for gentlemen with giant bellies from consuming large amounts of roast beef and three bottles a day. Does jet lag always hit you hard?" He took the matching chair on the other side of the fireplace.

"I don't know. I've never been to Europe before. I studied environmental science and did my study abroad in Central America."

"We've tried to watch our carbon footprint in designing the hotel. The swimming pool is heated with solar, for example. How does one go from environmental science to party planning?"

Finally accepting that Chippendales were for sitting, she leaned her head back and half closed her eyes. "I was in the middle of a rain forest in Costa Rica waiting for the rain to stop with nothing to read in the camp except a stack of ancient American magazines. I found a feature on Malcolm Forbes's famous seventieth birthday party in Morocco and I was enthralled. I realized I quite desperately wanted to be there with jet planes, and beautiful gowns that didn't smell like mold, and fruity drinks, and above all *dry* desert air, instead of where I was." She paused. "I sound shallow, don't I? It's not that I don't care about pollution and global warming and so on, but I didn't want to devote my life to it. I think I only chose the major to please my parents."

"Oh yes, them. The things we do because of our parents." Damn. He'd left himself open to awkward questions. Not that she'd shown much personal curiosity about him. She believed he was some kind of not-so-glorified lackey and, for the moment, he preferred to leave it at that. "What's the most lavish event you've ever planned?"

"Nothing like the Forbes bash. This one, I hope."

"I remember reading about an Internet magnate holding a Lord of the Rings style wedding that cost ten million dollars. I thought maybe that was one of yours. The name, you know. You have to be the queen of hobbit-inspired parties."

Arwen took his teasing in good part. "That was Sean Parker of Facebook. I'll have you know that I wouldn't touch a Tolkien-themed event, even for the commission on ten mil. *No orcs, ents, or hobbits* is stipulated in my contracts."

"Is Duke Austen's wedding going to cost that much? I do hope so."

"I bet you do. And it's my job to make sure my customer isn't over-charged." She was wide-awake and all-business again.

"I have been duly warned and terrified."

"What exactly is your job around here?"

"I am the representative on the spot of the Brampton Estates."

She rose shakily to her feet and he could see that computer mind going back to work. "I'd better move before I fall asleep. I don't think we can hold the wedding in here. It's a big room but there isn't room for almost a hundred guests to sit down."

"We've always assumed big ceremonies and receptions would be held outside in marquees. Tents, I mean. As soon as you're ready we'll go to the gardens. There are all sorts of possibilities."

She had no trouble seeing them. Harry was awed by the way she envisioned a village of tents and awnings among the terraces, gardens, and lawns that stretched down to the lake from the south front of Brampton. She seemed to be able to calculate measurements in her head, using her phone only to write down a few notes, her small fingers flying over the screen.

"We can make this work. I think the lawn will be best for the wedding itself."

"Risky. It can rain a lot in August."

She nodded. "I'll have a backup plan."

He took a deep breath. That sounded awfully promising. "Are we going ahead with the wedding here?"

"I'm not ready to commit. I'll need to see the kitchen and make a few calls. Where's this cellular hotspot you promised me?" She followed Harry's pointed finger up the hill to the Mausoleum, a domed temple surrounded by an open colonnade that soared above the park.

"That gazebo thing?"

"It's a Mausoleum."

"That's depressing. Can we rename it?"

"If you hold the wedding here you can call it anything you like." Thus ruthlessly tossing out the two-hundred-and-fifty-year history of one of William Kent's most inspired creations. Arwen looked weary at the sight of the steep hill.

"Why don't we call it a day? We have plenty of time tomorrow. You should sit down and rest. Watch telly, read a book, sleep."

"I'm here to work," she said, as though relaxation was a foreign concept.

"No one should work all the time."

"I do. Wedding planners have to be on the job twenty-four-seven."

"Sounds grim." Also what he'd always heard about Americans and their work ethic. "Shall I carry you up the hill?" he said softly.

An absurd offer, for a quarter mile walk, even with a smallish girl in his arms. But she was a smallish girl he rather desperately wanted to get close to. Spending weeks with the wedding planner was another incentive for getting her to agree to Brampton as the site of the billionaire's wedding.

She shook her head. "No need. My calls can wait. Let's take a look at that solar-heated swimming pool."

BRAMPTON HOUSE WAS FABULOUS. Of this Arwen was convinced, after an afternoon touring the house and grounds followed by a disgusting dinner—thank God for Stilton and red wine—and her much-needed and totally comfortable bed. She awoke feeling jet lag free and ready to get to the bottom of any major potential problems before she okayed the wedding.

She found Nanny in the kitchen concocting something dire over the AGA, which she'd learned was the correct name for the monstrous stove, and watching the news on a small television nestling among cookbooks, piles of magazines and antique china on a priceless wooden hutch. Refusing fried eggs and Nescafé, she accepted a container of yogurt—the first syllable rhyming with *jog* according to Nanny—and eagerly awaited the arrival of Harry. Not that she was attracted to the handyman, not at eight in the morning at least, but he was the only one who could operate the espresso machine.

"Have you been at Brampton long?" Arwen asked Nanny.

"I came to Lord and Lady Melbury thirty years ago. I had another job for a while, but H— … but I came back to be cook and housekeeper here five years ago. I'm a pensioner, but I don't think much of retirement. I like to be busy and I don't like knitting. It's a shame we have to turn the house into a hotel, but it can't be helped. It's too big to live in and I never liked seeing it open to the public. All those day-trippers dropping sweet papers on the floors and in the grounds. Don't they teach children not to litter?"

"I'd hate to see people spill things in the State Rooms." Arwen envisioned them as the site of the rehearsal dinner: cocktails and hors d'oeuvres in the Blue Drawing Room, dinner in the State Dining Room, and dancing in the Gold Saloon, which, far from a seedy bar turned out to be the swankiest room in the house. The thought of a bunch of drunken techies in such an environment did concern her.

Nanny smiled indulgently. "Boys will be boys and luckily you can get champagne out of anything. I could tell you such tales of parties they used to have here when Lord Melbury was young and later …" She paused. "Let me just say we've seen some quite wild times at Brampton." Whatever it was she was concealing, she didn't seem to disapprove. Discretion about the family, perhaps.

"Do the Melburys have any children?" Arwen had assumed Nanny was a nickname but perhaps it was an occupation requiring a title, like Doctor or Professor.

"Good morning." Harry's mellow tones came from the doorway. "You're looking rested," he said with a glint of admiration in his blue eyes. He smiled at her in an unsettling way. Flustered, she tried to smooth her thick hair, which was completely insane, either because of the English water or the English hairdryer.

"Bacon and eggs, dear?" Nanny asked.

"Yes please, but first coffee for Arwen. Cappuccino or latte?"

"Latte please." Harry the Handyman was a hero and she could have kissed him right there.

Fortified by caffeine, she was determined to remain businesslike and not be distracted by how cute he looked holding a tiny cup of espresso in his big hand. Her father always said that real men took their coffee black, though he probably didn't have demitasses in mind. "I'd like to see the kitchen this morning. By noon I must find signal for my phone and call my partner in New York."

"Partner?" Harry raised his brows. "What kind of partner?"

"Valerie, my partner in Luxe Events. She'll be coming to join me here nearer to the wedding." Harry looked gratified. "Assuming I decide to recommend Brampton to Miss Sparks and Mr. Austen."

"What can I do to persuade you?"

"Is it your job to persuade me?"

"For the moment, yes. On the financial side Mr. Austen has been conducting his negotiations with the man of business for the Brampton Estates. I'm here to answer your practical questions."

"Like where's the Internet?"

"I expect to have service restored by tomorrow morning." He smiled winningly, but Arwen resisted the urge to be won. Eight in the morning was far too early to be lusting after muscles. And twinkling blue eyes should never affect one's decisions. Time to get tough and ask some hard questions.


Arwen knew how to ask the questions he'd rather not answer. By four o'clock, Harry felt like he'd been put through a wringer. On the plus side, the telephones were working, though not the broadband. It was time to call in reinforcements. He escaped to the estate office, put his feet up on the desk and punched numbers into the thankfully functional phone.

"Mark? It's Harry. I need you to come to dinner."

"Tonight? I love you but I need a bit more of incentive before I make a two-hour drive, especially when I have a hot date."

"You have to come and impress Duke Austen's New York wedding planner."

Mark whistled. "That would be a coup. Those Internet billionaires are vulgarly extravagant, with an emphasis on the extravagant, just the way we like our customers. The press are mad about them so it'll be great publicity. What seems to be the problem?"

"She's mad about Brampton, but she's a bit worried about the level of service at the hotel. I need you to reassure her."

"Tell her the truth," Mark said impatiently. "That the best hotel manager in London has been bribed to leave Claridges's and take over the job."

"I did, but he doesn't start for three months."

"Since you aren't planning to open for four, that's about right."

Harry coughed. "I might have told her we could host this affair a month from now."

Mark's laugh carried the same disbelief with which he'd greeted the news that ten-year-old Harry had a crush on the headmaster's wife. "You've lost your mind. You don't even have a commercial kitchen license."

"I'll see if I can hurry up the inspectors." Hopefully he'd have better luck with the Food Safety Department than with the telephone people. "She already understands that our kitchen staff isn't in place and she'll have to use a caterer. It's guest comfort that concerns her. I told her our brilliant temporary manager comes to us from the Delaville Group." A perfectly true statement. Mark had spent all his university vacations learning the business from the ground up at his family's international chain of luxury boutique hotels. He had a little money and a lot of expert advice invested in the conversion of Brampton House to luxury resort.

"Did you mention that he is your oldest and about to be former best friend?"

"I knew I could count on you. You can get away for a week or two." He could hear Mark grinding his teeth when he told him the dates.

"I'll have you know, my darling, that I was planning to spend my holiday in the south of France soaking up sun with the beautiful people. If I save your cute arse this time, will you promise me sex?"

"Anything but that. I've been trying to be gay for you since prep school and it just won't take. You'll have to make do with Nanny."

"I've been trying to be straight for Nanny since the first time I came to Brampton, but no dice. She doesn't fancy me. If I agree to get into my fast German car and drive to your rescue, promise me she isn't cooking dinner tonight."

"Arwen doesn't like Nanny's food."

"I like her already."

"So I booked a table for three at the Preposterous Pineapple. Eight o'clock."

"Oh God, why? Why not The Bull's Head?"

"Because Ted the landlord always calls me the Honorable Harry in that tiresome way. It won't even occur to Sheila and Carol to blow my cover."

Mark laughed. "Let me get this straight. Miss Arwen the elf doesn't know you are the son and heir to Lord Melbury and the owner of Brampton House?"

"I told you about those ghastly people who came for shooting and kept calling me Lord Harry and one of the wives kept groping me and crept into my room in the middle of the night. After that I told everyone in the estate to just call me Harry—not that they don't anyway—or Mr. Compton if strictly necessary. I think Miss Arwen regards me as His Lordship's odd job man and I'm perfectly fine with that."

"And you want to be loved for yourself. You're such a romantic." Mark knew him far too well. "What's she like?"

"Very bossy. Also pretty as a picture, sexy as hell, and frighteningly clever."

"Darling, she sounds just your type. Does she lust after your brutish proletarian muscles?"

"God, I hope so. No, I don't, not really. This is business and too important to be cocked up."

"Did you really say cocked up? You've been in the country too long, Harry, and you need to get laid. Much better forget this mad idea and come to Cannes with me. There will be slutty Eurotrash to suit every taste."

"I can't. Duke Austen made me an offer I can't refuse and now I must make sure he doesn't take it back."

# CHAPTER
## THREE

Much to Arwen's relief, Harry drove her into Melbury in the Land Rover where they were to meet the hotel manager at a restaurant. His history at the Delaville Group was impressive. Arwen had only had cocktails in the ultramodern bar of the midtown Delaville but she'd recommended it to the out-of-town guests of her wealthier and more sophisticated customers, those who would find the Plaza lacking in exclusivity, and she'd drooled over hospitality magazine pictures of Delaville hotels in Venice and Paris, Rome and Rio among others.

The Pineapple of Perfection, occupying the first floor of a red brick town house, featured scrubbed pine tables, candles, red and white checked cloth napkins, and the hum of English-accented conversation. Delicious smells assured Arwen that Nanny was not doing the cooking. She still had a craving for rare red meat.

A tall woman with a long face and a longer caftan greeted Harry with a kiss on the cheek. "How are you, Harry? I haven't seen you for yonks. Mark is waiting for you on the terrace."

"I've been busy, you know how it is. Sheila, this is Arwen Kilpatrick. She's here from America to see about having a wedding at Brampton."

"How do you do, Arwen?" Sheila said. "Brampton's a marvelous place. Carol and I are thinking of having ours there."

"Congratulations, darling," Harry said. "I didn't know you two had decided to take the plunge."

Sheila simpered, an expression that was odd on her slightly horsey face. "She went down on one knee, the little angel, so what could I say?"

"Do bring her out to our table for a drink, if she has a moment. Sheila's fiancée," he explained to Arwen, "is the cook here."

"What about yours?" Sheila asked. "Boy or girl?"

"I'm the wedding planner, not the bride," Arwen replied.

"Let me know if you need any help catering. We offer a unique menu here."

"I look forward to sampling it. I love the name. How did you think of it?"

"In Sheridan's play *The Rivals,* Mrs. Malaprop uses the phrase instead of the pinnacle of perfection."

"Of course! One of the original malapropisms. I saw that play in college."

"And since the pineapple is an ancient symbol of hospitality, we thought it was ideal."

Arwen was thoroughly charmed. Perhaps she'd hire this couple to put on a pig roast one evening of the wedding celebration. That would be very rural and traditional and make a nice change from the formality of the surroundings.

Sheila led them out to a delightful little back patio scented by a flowering shrub. An incredibly good-looking man, occupying the only table, put down a martini glass and stood to greet them. While Harry's concession to dinner out was an open-necked white shirt tucked into clean jeans and tasseled loafers with no socks, Mark had stepped right out of the pages of *GQ*: tousled blond hair, a perfect scruff, and swathed in Armani from head to toe. The man should be a male model, except that he looked both alert and intelligent. Arwen's mouth watered. What girl could possibly object to dining alone with two such magnificent male specimens? Her sorority sisters at Emory would die of envy and before the night was over they would. First on the agenda was to get a selfie of the three of them and post it on Facebook. She'd already determined that the town of Melbury was not cell-signal challenged.

"Mark Delancey," he said and actually kissed her hand. Normally she'd think it a douche move but she'd forgive anything from such a gorgeous man. "Harry definitely underestimated your charms."

"Did he? That's an ambiguous statement."

"She *is* clever. For God's sake get the girl a drink before she learns all our guilty secrets. The raspberry martinis are excellent."

"They are organic," Sheila said. "As is all our food." She went off to get the drinks.

Arwen was all for organic, locally raised meat. It reminded her of home. "So what's good to eat here?" The question was interrupted by her phone, which made her jump. Even in a couple of days she'd become used to not being constantly interrupted by calls. "I'm sorry," she said, glancing at the screen. "It's my mother. It may be an emergency."

"Arwen, honey, it's Molly." Molly Stanton's voice sounded crackly and distant.

"Hi, Mom." Arwen had taken an early stand against calling her parents by their first names, as soon as she started grade school and discovered no one else did. "What's up? Are you okay? Is Dad?"

"Benjamin is fine. You sound awfully far away? Where are you?"

"I'm in England, visiting Brampton House about a wedding."

"I thought you said Brampton. How funny."

"I did." She couldn't think of any reason why her mother had even heard of Brampton, let alone find her being there either strange or amusing.

"I wanted to let you know we are taking a trip for a few weeks." That was unusual. After traveling the world in their youth, Benjamin Kilpatrick and Molly Stanton had settled on their Pennsylvania farm and rarely budged.

"Where?"

There followed a lot of crackling and a few indistinct words before the phone went dead.

"Everything all right?" Harry said. "You look baffled."

"My parents are going somewhere but I'm not sure where. It sounded like the Isle of Man, but it could have been Burning Man or Afghanistan."

"Not the last, I hope."

"Where's Burning Man?" Mark asked.

"It's a thing in the Nevada desert," Harry said. "Hard to explain."

"Hippies?"

"Exactly."

Arwen was tempted to ask how Harry had heard of an event frequented by devotees of alternative cultures. But she really didn't want to talk about her charming, loving, incredibly embarrassing parents. Time to get serious and grill Mark about his experience. Then she would enjoy dinner and decide which of the pair she'd most like to flirt with. She wasn't a hundred percent sure Harry wasn't gay, Mark too. Possibly together. She'd never heard men say darling so often. She sent Mark an enticing little smile along with her first zinger.

"What philosophy would you bring to ensuring the comfort of a small wedding party while maintaining an atmosphere of informality and ease?"

Mark answered without hesitation. "I see myself as the majordomo of an estate in the heyday of aristocratic power, where My Lord's guests conduct the business of the nation and their private flirtations untroubled by countless servants who cater to their every need while remaining invisible. The titans of high tech are the new nobility. Here's Sheila with your drink."

She decided he was delectable and perfect, and so was the martini.

"Would you like to hear our menu?" Sheila said. "We don't have a printed bill of fare. Our philosophy is a small but exquisite choice of dishes, changing daily according to the whims of the chef and the season. We use local ingredients whenever possible. "

Talking about philosophy did sound kind of pretentious when Sheila did it. Arwen made a mental note to expunge it from her vocabulary unless speaking of Schopenhauer or Nietzsche, which she tended to avoid. She prayed that the chef's whim included something red and rare.

"Because it's unusually hot, Carol has made two salads as starters."

Sheila spoke with all the drama of Emma Thompson accepting an Academy Award. "A lovely quinoa with scallions, broad beans, and dates, topped with wood-grilled pine nuts for crunch. Or you might prefer crispy kale and tofu with shredded coconut and a mango vinaigrette."

Uncharitably, Arwen wondered what percentage of these ingredients were local to southern England. Since she loathed both tofu and kale with equal fervor, she opted for the quinoa.

"Good choice," Sheila said. "So much nutrition. And for the main course may I recommend our signature veggie burger with porcini mushrooms and nondairy creamed cauliflower, served with a pomegranate ketchup and parsnip bacon."

Cauliflower? She was getting a very bad feeling about The Pineapple of Perfection. "Where's the beef?" she asked. Harry and Mark looked guilty, as well they might.

"Where's the wine list?" Harry asked.

"Didn't these naughty boys explain that we're vegan? If you're dying for protein, and I know just how you feel after a long day, Carol will make you a lovely grilled tofu steak with caper salsa."

Sheila had barely left with their order before the men succumbed to hysterical mirth. "You should have warned me," Arwen said. "I was going to hire these women to roast a pig. Oh my God! Tofu!"

"Don't worry," Harry said. "The food really is excellent and I've ordered a good bottle of wine. Sheila's devotion to veganism stops at the wine cellar door."

His charming hangdog grin made her feel a little bit excited, or would if she could be sure he wasn't gay. She asked Mark a few more questions and was soon satisfied that with him in charge she needn't worry about guest services at Brampton. They moved on from martinis and quite delicious vegan snacks to wine and appetizers. She knew she was being played, but these boys were good: far too charming and far too persuasive as they sang the praises of Brampton along with a liberal dose of flattery.

"Arwen has the most brilliant ideas," Harry said. "Her suggestions for tents and lighting in the garden are perfect. She wants something called fairy lights in all the shrubberies."

"Not all, I hope," Mark said. "There's nothing more conducive to snogging than a dark shrubbery. I could tell you stories ..."

"Tact, Mark. And discretion."

"I know Arwen would enjoy hearing about ..."

Arwen wasn't so sure. "You both know the place well."

"I've lived in the area all my life," Harry said. "And Mark has been visiting almost as long. We were at school together. That's why you can absolutely rely on us to make sure Duke's nuptials go off without a hitch."

She took a deep breath, pushed aside her wineglass and swallowed a chickpea. "Stop, please guys. I'm thinking and I can't concentrate with you both telling me how fabulous Brampton is. I've seen it, I've heard you, and I'm convinced."

"So the wedding goes ahead here?" Harry asked.

She raised a hand to silence him and made her brain go through a checklist of salient points, a habit she'd developed over the years. She made written lists too, especially those relating to money and numbers, but she liked to keep the most important stuff in her head where she could retrieve it without constantly checking her computer. The mental exercise often turned up problems she hadn't foreseen. The major issue she could see with Brampton was the lack of a kitchen staff. It simply couldn't be assembled and ready in time, but she'd already agreed that she could hire a caterer for the weeklong affair. The solution gave her far more control over menus than she'd have with an established chef, set in his ways. Which left only one thing.

"You promise there will be Wi-Fi all over the house and gardens?"

"On my honor," Harry said. With his English accent, he sounded like a character in a PBS series or one of Jane's Regency novels. How could she not trust him?

"In that case—"

"Yes?" the men said in unison.

"Yes."

"Great news," Harry said. He and Mark exchanged pleased nods, apparently the British version of a high five. "You won't regret it and I so look forward to working with you."

"One thing. Remember that Duke and Jane want absolutely no

paparazzi. You can't tell anyone whose wedding it is. The guests won't even know exactly where they're going until the last minute."

"Not a problem. I haven't told anyone whom you represent and as far as the staff and locals are concerned, it will be merely the Big Wedding. If I assure them it isn't a film star or anyone they've heard of they won't care."

"Why don't you call Duke now," Mark said, "while we order champagne?"

Instead she called Jane, raving about the beauty of the place and promising a long conversation the next day to start nailing down the details. By the time they'd polished off a bottle of Veuve Clicquot she was thoroughly relaxed and contemplating a working vacation romance. What happens in England stays in England, surely.

A sensible girl—and with her crazy parents Arwen had always had to be sensible—would combine flirtation with a useful contact in an important company in the hospitality industry. Business *and* pleasure. Yes, Mark the Armani-clad smoothie was the better bet, but Harry the hunky handyman was hellishly hot. He raised his glass to her with a lazy smile that gave her the shivers.

As long as they weren't totally into each other, which given her luck was all too possible.

"Arwen darling," Mark said, refilling her glass. "Are you New York born and bred or did you come by your Proenza Schouler black dress the hard way?" He had to be gay. Or maybe English straight men knew designers.

"I grew up on a farm in Pennsylvania and went to college in the south, where I learned to appreciate manicures and catered affairs."

"And wisely moved to New York. Which couldn't you stand: the heat or the crazy?"

It wasn't often anyone realized that the only thing to do when you were a cross between a hippy and a steel magnolia was to move to Manhattan. "You have an impressive understanding of American culture."

"I went to college there. Princeton."

"You too, Harry? Didn't say you were friends from school?"

"Poor Harry stayed in England, where his most interesting cultural experience was going to the pub with a lot of oarsmen."

"Hence his physique."

"He is quite ogle-able, isn't he?"

Arwen's woozy eyes veered from the way the handyman's tanned neck set into his collarbones. "Is that a word?"

"For heaven's sake, Mark." Harry was actually blushing. God, he was cute. But so was Mark. Arwen probed with a stilettoed foot, dodged the table leg, and hit pay dirt with a warm limb. But whose? With whom was she playing footsie? God, her grammar was good.

Harry stood up. Question answered, rather to her disappointment. She should have recognized the touch of Armani against her ankle.

Harry said something about going to the loo and saying hello to Carol in the kitchen. Through the door into the main dining area she saw him stop at a table and say hello to a middle-aged couple. Friendly with everyone, he seemed universally popular.

Mark twinkled at her across the table and gave her calf a rub. "Really darling, I thought you lived in New York. What happened to your gaydar?"

"I don't have one. In college I was voted the Girl Most Likely to Fall in Love with a Homosexual."

"A sign of excellent taste. We are superior beings." He shot his pale pink cuff revealing gold crested cuff links. "Not that I don't enjoy playing footsie with a pretty thing of any sex, but I don't think I'm what you're looking for."

"Are you and Harry ...?"

"Just good friends."

Yes! She gave Mark's groomed perfection a last look without any regret.

The one downside of life in the city was the dating, or lack of it. Admittedly she hadn't given the matter the energy it deserved. On arrival she'd technically still been with her college boyfriend, but the relationship had shriveled on the vine of weekend train rides to Washington, DC, where he worked for a congressman. She sometimes thought his main appeal had been the fact of him being a Republican and pissing off her parents. Since then, consumed by growing her business and pursuing designer clothing on deep discount, she'd had occasional dates and less frequent hookups with a disparate collection of New York professionals introduced by her friends. Being away from home and a little blitzed on champagne made her realize how one-dimensional her life had become.

"Harry's wild about you, you know," Mark said. "Or perhaps you don't since you're clearly a woman of remarkably little perception."

"Really?" She hadn't been sure.

The man in question, tall and fit and rumpled in his casual clothing, returned to the table. "What have you been talking about?" he asked, shooting Arwen a look that warmed her to her toes. "Did I miss something interesting?"

Her chest fluttered wildly, more so than she'd felt in eons. Dormant hormones were on the march. Ambition and common sense seemed to have been replaced by a driving need to get laid.

# CHAPTER
# **FOUR**

I t was a curse to be born with compunction. Honor might be an old-fashioned virtue in the days of hedge funds and the Russian mafia, but Harry wished it wasn't. He hadn't like shading the truth about the readiness of Brampton for a weeklong luxury affair, but consoled himself with the excuse that there was nothing that couldn't be fixed or skirted. He had about a month to make sure the marriage of Duke and Jane went off smoothly.

Making him feel especially guilty was his attraction to Arwen. As he pulled the Land Rover up next to the house, he took a sideways glance at her singing along to Gotye, black skirt hugging her spectacular thighs, short dark hair all messed up and making her look like an elf, whatever she might claim. A very sexy elf. Her decline from no-nonsense, razor-sharp businesswoman to tipsy, completely adorable forest creature wrought havoc with his sense of fair play about professional relationships and secret identities. To tell the truth it was rather flattering to be desired as Harry the odd job man instead of the Honorable Harry, future Lord Melbury.

He opened the car door for her and caught her when she stumbled on the gravel. She was warm and soft and firm. Mark's Porsche had arrived before them but there was no sign of him and Harry guessed that Mark had gone straight to the study to watch television.

"More champagne?"

"Yes, please." Once in the house she walked quite normally, dissipating his fear that she'd fall asleep and ruin the rest of the evening.

"With Mark in the study watching *Mad Men*?"

"Seen every episode."

"In the garden?"

"Are we allowed to drink champagne in the State Rooms?"

"Wait there a second." He left her standing in the back passage among the boots and riding crops and slipped into the butler's pantry to grab a bottle of vintage Krug from the fridge. "Hold these," he said, putting a pair of champagne glasses in one hand and leading her by the other through the great house that he knew so well, the dark passages illuminated only by the rising moon. "Any preferences as to room?"

"The Gold Saloon is my favorite."

"Mine too." He'd always loved Brampton's biggest and most splendid apartment. His pulse sped when he considered ideas he'd first conceived about the room when he was a spotty thirteen-year-old. He found the switch that turned on the ceiling lights, leaving the rest of the room in shadows.

"Gorgeous!" Arwen said, staring at the enormous frescoed ceiling. "I hardly noticed it before."

"It's better seen without distraction. We'll get the best view sitting on the carpet in the middle."

He popped the champagne cork. "To Antonio Verrio," he said, admiring her stretched out on her side like a short-skirted odalisque.

Arwen raised her glass, took a sip, and sneezed. "Now I know why coupe-style champagne glasses are less popular, even if they were modeled from Marie-Antoinette's breasts. Who is this Antonio guy?"

"The painter of the ceiling."

She flopped onto her back and his heart went into double-time. "I'm lying in state," she giggled. "Come down here and tell me what I see."

He lay beside her and gazed at the great painting, so familiar to him yet always fresh. A complex tangle of near naked bodies and swirling fabrics floated against a celestial blue sky, lit by the blazing sun that was echoed in the furnishings of the golden saloon and gave it its name.

"The marriage of Venus and Mars. They are the couple in the center."

"A wedding. How perfect! Most of their guests seem to be underage."

"What's a party without putti?"

She giggled again. "Right, those little angels. I'll suggest them to Jane. Why the wedding theme?"

"The saloon was part of the original design for Brampton. It was built after the Restoration of Charles II, when the family was rewarded for its fidelity during the Civil War. Trouble was, the old manor was in ruins and Lord Melbury almost broke. He found himself an heiress, the daughter of a man who'd made a fortune selling cannons to the other side. The couple built this house from scratch and this fresco celebrated their nuptials, as well as the reconciliation of strife through love."

"That's beautiful."

"Supposedly it was a love match. The Melburys have a history of happy marriages. My … employers, the current Lord and Lady Melbury, have been devoted to each other for forty years."

"I love stories like that," she said with a sigh. "It's one reason I went into the wedding business."

"So you're a romantic underneath that hard-boiled exterior."

"Do I seem like that?" Her voice quivered.

He wanted to kick himself. No woman, however tough, wants to be compared to a ten-minute egg. "I have nothing but admiration for your strength and efficiency. Also your legs."

She was smiling again. "I have a feeling that may be sexual harassment."

"Absolutely. In this room I claim immunity from prosecution on the grounds that Charles II practically invented the crime. More champagne?"

"I'm good. So does that make you one of those rakes that Jane's always writing about?"

The amused lilt in her voice set his heart racing and he answered more seriously than he'd intended. "I've always been a monogamous sort and at the moment not even that." He didn't want to invite questions about his life by explaining that he hadn't had a girlfriend since he moved back to Brampton. Too busy.

They turned to each other for a few breathless seconds, then Arwen looked back at the ceiling. "This room makes me think of the Beistegui Ball."

"What?"

"A fantastic ball given in Venice in the 1950s by a guy named Carlos de Beistegui, one of the great parties of the twentieth century. The guests wore costumes inspired by Venetian paintings. You could do the same thing here."

"Uh, Arwen. Most of these characters aren't wearing much at all."

"True. It would have to be a toga party."

Harry stopped looking at the ceiling and rolled onto his side, propping his head on one elbow so that he could see her face, mysterious and shadowy in the dimly lit room that had, for much of its existence, been seen at night only by candlelight. Thus might his ancestors have enjoyed the centerpiece of their creation. He imagined Arwen clad in colored silks and pearls and hooped petticoats instead of her austere and devilishly sexy black dress. She was laughing and relaxed until she saw him looking and fell silent.

"I've always thought Venus and Mars looked ready to leave the reception and move onto the honeymoon," he said softly.

"They do seem … eager." Her gaze flicked to the ceiling and back to him. Her lips parted. He heard her heightened breathing along with the wild thud of his own heart. He touched her hair, releasing an expensive scent to blend with the acid tang of their wine. Sweeping back the tousled fringe from her forehead, he stroked her flawless skin, traced with wonder the cool taut chin and neck, and let his hand drift downward to her chest, warm and rising lightly beneath his touch.

*Harry, my lad, this is a bad idea and could screw things up.*

Even as he heard his inner voice he knew he would ignore it. His fingers slipped beneath the loose-fitting V-neck of her dress and a crisp lace bra. Her breast was a bit bigger than he expected—Tragedy!—and smooth as silk until he reached the crinkled point of her nipple. She stirred and arched into his touch.

Before it could say another word, he put a gag on his inner voice, kicked it in the arse, and locked it in a cupboard.

HARRY THE HANDYMAN had very handy hands. They were big and slightly rough and her skin liked them a lot. Especially her breasts. Her pelvis too was beginning to twist in anticipation. She was hotter than hell and they'd hardly started. The fact that she was about ready to do it on the floor—although a floor covered with a priceless antique carpet—with a man she'd met yesterday and hadn't even kissed said something.

What exactly did it say? Who gave a damn? Right now her brain was occupied by one problem and one that required neither sobriety nor logic. All she had to do was raise her arms, grab his head, and pull it down to hers, easy as pie. And they were kissing.

When it came to judging a kiss, Arwen considered herself a Justice of the Supreme Court and not one of the boring conservative ones. Harry was going to win his case unanimously, but only after extensive oral arguments.

Yes, the man knew how to kiss, strong and hot, taking no prisoners. Somehow he was on top of her, trapping her with his weight. He made her feel small and sweet and powerless and ready to be taken, dominated even. She parted her legs and thrust her hips upward, feeling denim-cased steel between her thighs.

"Such a deliciously bossy girl," he said against her ear. "You can have whatever you want."

She didn't know what she wanted. Or rather she didn't want to say. She relaxed into the priceless carpet and wondered if she looked like Venus who floated overhead with her mouth open, leering at her brawny Mars, naked but for a helmet and a bit of red drapery.

"I want …" The words stuck in her throat. It must be the historical surroundings that sent decades of progress in women's sexuality out of the window, leaving her weak and wanting like a maiden in a mobcap. "Take me," she whispered.

Harry grinned with wolfish humor and unbridled lust. "Does my lady want her humble servant to attend to her pleasure?" She nodded, mesmerized. He kissed her again, which was just what she wanted, then knelt back and surveyed her with a lazy grin that turned her into a puddle. "Stand up," he said, with a laugh behind the stern words. She teetered on her heels and wondered if they'd damage the carpet. "Leave them on and remove your dress."

When she hesitated he frowned, so she pulled the silk jersey over her head and tossed it away where it caught and hung drunkenly off the back of a chair. His eyes followed it lazily then returned to where she stood in her black lace bra, matching thong, and silver Christian Louboutin sandals. His inquisitive gaze burned into her as he inspected her from head to gold-painted toenails, sending molten lava through her veins. This was the hottest thing that had ever happened to her.

Then he nodded as though arrogantly accepting what he saw and calmly unbuttoned his shirt. Whether from manual labor or hours in the gym, Harry the Handyman was one buff dude. She licked her lips, closed her eyes and moaned.

"Look at me," he commanded.

Not a hardship to obey. She kind of wished he was wearing a tool belt, but the jeans—Levis, not designer—hugged his narrow hips, held by a brown leather belt polished like harness to a high gloss. Dropping her eyes an inch or two lower made her squirm again. She started to ask him if he was going to remove the rest, or if he wanted her to, but he cut her off. "Quiet," he said, "and do exactly as I say."

*Yes please.*

"Do you see that table over there?" He pointed to a desk-sized piece with plentiful gold embellishments. "Walk over and put the lamp on the floor."

Oh my God, he was having her move furniture in a totally historic room. Couldn't he be fired for this? The danger excited her even more.

"Now lean over the table, hands on either side and spread your legs wide."

She obeyed and waited, night air cooling her exposed core. Staring down, her eyes focused on the surface, elaborately patterned in different colors of wood, while her skin tingled in unbearable anticipation. He came up behind and leaned his body against hers, the denim rough and the belt buckle cold against her ass. He unfastened her bra and his hands cupped her breasts, pinching the nipples lightly between his fingers. Her throat was so tight with longing she swore she could pass out. Ordering her to remain still, he played with her for a while, stroking the sensitive area of her ribs and waist, kneading the globes of her ass. The man was magic. How could he tell that his lips and breath on her nape, in the curve of her neck, and across her shoulders would drive her wild? She felt herself wet and swollen and wanting and still all the satisfaction he offered was an occasional finger instantly withdrawn. When she couldn't stand it another second she moaned and he pulled back.

"Yes? Is there something you want?"

"You know there is, damn you."

"All good things come to those who wait."

Not her usual philosophy, but she'd go with it, for now, because the man made her feel great and she trusted him to make her feel even better. Soon.

After some more enjoyable teasing, which reduced her to an inelegant panting, writhing mess, he reached between her legs and held her hard. She almost came on the spot.

"Not yet."

She heard unzipping and condom applying sounds—the genius must have had one in his wallet—and was pushed flat against the surface of the table. He pushed aside her thong, spread her wider and entered, hard. The interval till she exploded could be counted in seconds, but he kept up steady rhythmic thrusts, all the way so his sac swung against her labia, and she came again before he did the same and she felt him collapse against her and soften inside her.

Soon afterward she was curled up on his lap on the big Chippendale chair, her head on his chest, listening to the slowing beat of his heart. She couldn't utter a word and he remained silent for some minutes. "Oh my word," she managed finally. "Oh my word, Harry."

"Is my lady pleased?"

"Are you?"

The way he stroked her head seemed tender. "You needn't have any doubt."

She gave a gusty sigh. "That was fabulous. The best." She tilted her head for a kiss, just a relaxed, intimate exchange of breath. "You won't get into trouble, will you? Having wild sex in the Gold Saloon?"

He grinned like a naughty boy. "Don't worry, no one will ever know. I've fantasized about doing it here for years."

"I'm glad to help you fulfill an ambition." She tugged at her dress, which was crumpled up behind his back. "I'd better get dressed and go to bed."

"Come to my room," he said.

HARRY WOKE UP EARLY, a little past dawn, with the sense of wellbeing that comes from a truly superior sexual experience. Correction: possibly the best night of shagging he'd ever had. Arwen was sacked out beside him, her fists tucked under her head like a child, sleeping the sleep of the just, the jet-lagged, the girl who'd had five orgasms the night before. Tempting as it was to wake her up for another, she might not appreciate being aroused at this hour. Besides, there was something he needed to do.

Pulling on shorts, a T-shirt, and trainers, he grabbed his phone and loped downstairs and set off for a run around the park, the short three-mile route he took when he had too much to drink the night before. He finished with the steep climb up to the Mausoleum and panted while he logged into online banking. It was a bloody nuisance not having Internet at the house, but he'd just as soon not have Arwen see this particular transaction.

Duke Austen had been as good as his word. As soon as Arwen approved the wedding, the massive bonus had been transferred to his account.

The view from the top never failed to thrill him, especially at this hour in summer with morning mist hovering over the surface of the lake, the birds singing like a demented choir, the scent of a thousand flowers sweetening the cool air. And the great house itself, silent, golden, asleep. He could have sold it to a fat-cat banker or to a dreary consortium to make into a conference center, but he couldn't bear to leave Brampton. His father had transferred the estate to him and now he had to make a go of it.

He ought to tell Arwen who he was; she was bound to find out eventually. But it was a lot easier to play the ignorant employee when it came to the awkward questions, and there were going to be more. It was thoroughly irresponsible of him to sleep with Duke Austen's representative and it put her in a difficult position too. No, better go on as they were during the planning phase of this wedding bash. He might even get through the whole event incognito; he'd only visited New York once, for a week, and as far as he knew there wasn't a single tech man, American or otherwise, among his acquaintances.

He was uneasy in his mind, but the other part of his morning routine would help.

Good sex trumps alcohol, Arwen decided, examining her head and finding it clear and her body slack and content. Also alone, which was a good thing. The first waking up together could be awkward, especially when you didn't know the guy well.

Scratch that. Know him at all. She'd gotten drunk and slept with the handyman. Okay, a glorified handyman. But they'd spent about a day and a half almost constantly in one another's company which, she could argue, added up to about six normal dates. Maybe it wouldn't be awkward. Unfortunately if it was, she couldn't just leave and never see him again, or refuse to take his calls—if he called—because she had to work with him in putting together the most important wedding of her career.

The enormity of the situation hit her. She'd committed Duke and Jane to holding the wedding at Brampton, largely persuaded by Harry. She'd drunk too much champagne and slept with Harry.

Oh my God, how unprofessional could she be? Plus, she didn't even know Harry's last name.

His room was very different from the rest of the house and her room in the family wing. The furnishings were sparse and dominated by the king-size bed she occupied. The nightstand was piled high with books: a volume on hotel management, a biography of Dickens, several novels, none of which she had read, and *Start Where You Are* by the Buddhist nun Pema Chödrön. A huge Chinese wardrobe faced her; it could be a Pier One reproduction but she had a feeling it was the real thing. Like the rest of the house, there were pictures on the walls, mostly watercolors and photographs.

Spotting her dress folded neatly—certainly not by her—on a leather banquette, she dashed over and wriggled into it, not wanting to be caught naked in broad daylight. As she searched for her underwear, which she feared might be decorating the Gold Saloon, a sports team photo caught her eye: guys with oars. The members of Trinity College Boat Club were identified, including H.G.G. Compton.

So he was a college-educated handyman with superior upper body development and a name. Who was a genius in bed, and in the State Rooms. That, sadly, was going to have to stop. Their relationship must be strictly business, at least until after the wedding. In search of her own room, she discovered that Harry's job merited his own bathroom and a sitting room with TV, stereo, desk, sofa, and Harry himself, squatting in a perfect lotus in front of the kind of simple shrine one or the other of her parents used when they were in a Buddhist frame of mind: a pair of orange candles and a beautiful jade Buddha on a low table.

He looked round as she tiptoed behind him.

"Sorry. Don't let me disturb you."

"You won't. Not in that way."

"I wouldn't have taken you for a Buddhist," she said, trying to ignore her unpantied state. "Are you vegetarian too?"

"Both in a half-arsed way. The meditation is good for me—keeps things in perspective—and I try not to eat meat for every meal."

"You're not what I would have expected."

"Is that a good thing?"

"I believe it is." Most of the men she knew were so predictable. Maybe Harry's nationality made him seem original and exotic and all Englishmen were such a fascinating mixture of traits.

He unwound his legs and rose gracefully to his feet, giving her an enticing grin. "I haven't said good morning to you, my lovely."

Lovely? She had raccoon eyes! "Morning breath," she murmured, dodging his attempt at a kiss.

"I don't care." He put his big hands on her hips, but she pulled back.

Time to be sensible. At once. Before things got out of hand again. "About last night," she began.

"It was marvelous. Stupendous. The earth shook."

"Harry," she said, resisting the urge to agree. Fervently. "It was great, but it must end. We have to work together and our interests may not always coincide. Let's agree that it was a one-night stand and a happy memory."

"I don't want it to end, darling. In fact, I want to take you back to bed right now." His eyes were blue and soft and smoldery and she wanted to say yes. To hell with work.

She shook her head at such an odd thought. Work always came first. "It would be unprofessional. Besides, I'll be spending most of the next month in London and New York. Our relationship will be strictly business and conducted by phone and e-mail." She gave him a snarky look. "Better get that Internet working, darling."

# CHAPTER
## FIVE

To: Arwen Kilpatrick <ArwenKilpatrick@LuxeEvents.com>
From: Harry Compton <HCompton@BramptonEstates.co.uk>

As requested, I attach a list of tent hire places and wildly expensive caterers. Let me know if I can help since they are all anxious to exploit poor defenseless Americans. I am a great negotiator.
Speaking of which, I would like to negotiate a resumption of relations once Jane and Duke have made it to the altar. I know you've always wanted an English boyfriend.

——————

To: Harry Compton
From: Arwen Kilpatrick

Thanks for the offer, but I always do my own negotiating. Mark is taking me to interview a man described as the Next Gordon Ramsey who may be persuaded to close his restaurant for a week and move his staff to Brampton. I will do my poor best to remain unexploited.

Re. post-wedding activities, I find London surprisingly full of Englishmen. Turns out you are not unique.

P.S. I assume your e-mail is proof of the restoration of Internet service to Brampton House.

———

To: Arwen Kilpatrick
From: Harry Compton

The Next Gordon Ramsey is gay.

———

To: Harry Compton
From: Arwen Kilpatrick

Judging by his hand on my thigh during the interview, I would judge the Next G.R. to be somewhat interested in women. His cooking is divine, with one problem. He has a philosophical objection to vegetarian food. Please send me contact info for The Pineapple of Perfection so that I can order in vegan dishes.

———

To: Arwen Kilpatrick
From: Harry Compton

Glad to hear the bloom is off the Next G.R.'s rose. Speaking of roses, three delightful young ladies from Extremely Costly Florals arrived this morning to plan arrangements. The man from Super Luxurious Persian Tents is here now, measuring the terrace and lawn. Also a team of Dazzling Lighting Designers. Throw in a High King, some Riders of Rohan, and an elf or two and I'm sure you could inch Duke Austen's bill up closer to ten million.

———

To: Harry Compton
From: Arwen Kilpatrick

Bite your tongue. No elves. Also, the Next Gordon Ramsey is in.

———

To: Arwen Kilpatrick
From: Harry Compton

Be still my heart. You used the words *tongue* and *bite* in one short sentence. You are giving me ideas.

Organizing a wedding in a foreign country reminded Arwen of the Ginger Rogers line about doing it backward in high heels. It would have been tough in New York; in London it was a bloody miracle (she was picking up the local vocabulary) what she managed to pull together. She had to admit that daily calls and advice from Mark and Harry helped a lot. Especially Harry.

"Hello, Elf darling." In Harry's voice, even Tolkien was bearable.

"I have news," she said. "I've discovered the Scottish accent. Englishmen don't cut it anymore."

"I trust that simply means you went to see a Gerard Butler film."

"When do I have time to go to the movies? I met this cute Scottish guy while I was waiting for the Next Gordon Ramsey."

"I'm worried about your state of mind if you're falling for random Scotsmen. You need to have some fun. For God's sake, at least make Mark take you to the theater."

"I can't. I spend all day on the Austen wedding, then, when London closes, I get on the phone and deal with my other clients in New York. After a few hours of that I'm good for nothing but sleep." It did sound pathetic. Three weeks in London and she hadn't seen much beyond her luxurious room at the Ritz Hotel.

"I'll catch a train in and take you out," Harry said.

Arwen scrolled though her calendar, and that of the various vendors who'd be requiring Harry's attention at Brampton. "Maybe next Thursday, if I don't have to go to New York."

She prayed Valerie could deal with the latest Bridezilla crisis on her own. Working in London was tough, but a welcome challenge, while she felt no enthusiasm at all for the half dozen New York weddings on their books. As for a date with Harry, that she looked forward to … But it wouldn't be a date. Just a business meeting with entertainment. And maybe benefits?

*Two weeks before the wedding*

ARWEN HAD to go to New York after all—Valerie had sprained her ankle and needed help—and their theater date never materialized. Not only did his poor elf have to make a quick trans-Atlantic trip, she would also return alone, without her business partner to assist her in running the week-long party. He redoubled his efforts to get every-thing ready, not only for his own sake. Unfortunately some things were out of his hands.

The e-mails had been fun and the telephone conversations even more so. Harry had no idea business could be so sexy. If he'd gone into the luxury lodgings trade with any reluctance, extensive communica-tion with a certain wedding planner went a long way to reconciling him to his future as a hotelier. While he looked forward keenly to her return to Brampton in a few days, he wasn't much looking forward to this particular call.

"Hi, Harry." He adored her throaty American voice.

"I have a spot of trouble with the inspectors from the Food Stan-dards Agency."

"Oh my God, you don't have rats do you? Or cockroaches?"

"No rodents or insects. And no inspectors either. Unless I can exert undue influence, they won't be here for two weeks which means the kitchen isn't licensed." The throaty American tones turned into infuriated squawks. "Calm down, darling. I have a solution."

He explained about mobile catering equipment that could be set up in the stable yard: ranges, ovens, and refrigeration, all tying into the main gas line. "We can also use the refrigerators in the hotel kitchen. We just can't cook there."

Arwen had questions, of course, but he managed to satisfy them. "Now I have to break the news to the Next Gordon Ramsey," she said, relatively cheerful under the circumstances. "Luckily I made him sign a cast iron contract."

"If this problem breaks you two up I shall rejoice. The way you've taken this makes me love you even more."

"I've never gotten through an event without one major problem. I'm happy to have this behind us. Hopefully it'll be smooth sailing now."

"I need to talk to you about something else."

"Don't tell me the Internet is out again."

"No, no. It's fast and brilliant." The gods of British Telecom had smiled on him at last and as of today he no longer had to climb up to the Mausoleum to send e-mails. "This is nothing to do with the wedding."

"What?" She sounded intrigued, but Harry chickened out. He'd planned to reveal his identity on their canceled date and he still didn't want to do it on the telephone.

"I'll tell you when I see you. Only a week now and I can't wait."

"Nor can I," she said, sending Harry's confidence soaring. Everything was going to be fine, not only with the wedding.

# CHAPTER
# SIX

All the major problems with this wedding had happened, Arwen decided, or hoped, by the time she went to the airport to meet the happy couple. There had never been anything at all scary about Jane Sparks in high school and objectively there still wasn't. She and Arwen had spoken dozens of times over the past weeks. Still, when your old school friend is about to marry into the Forbes Four Hundred, her wedding is the most elaborate event you've ever planned, and its success can launch your career into the stratosphere, you can't help feeling more than a little anxious. Jane might be easy to please; Arwen wasn't so sure about the bridegroom.

Side by side in the back of the limo during the drive from the airport, the couple exchanged occasional quick kisses and caresses, but otherwise Duke Austen let Arwen and Jane do the talking, not even looking up from his iPhone to answer "whatever you like, babe" when his opinion was sought. But Duke emitted an aura of brilliance and power that was both sexy and intimidating.

"I can't wait to show you the dress," Jane said. "I can't tell you about it now because Duke has a way of listening when you think he's engrossed in something else."

He managed to wink without looking away from his screen. Arwen was dying to find out if the tech billionaire would wear jeans and a T-shirt to his wedding; she'd never seen him in anything else.

What if he didn't like Brampton, she fretted as they drew nearer. Jane was crazy about old English houses and would forgive much in return for authenticity; with Duke, Arwen didn't know. As they reached the narrow road that wound its way to Brampton—not the road on which, deceived by the evil GPS, she'd made her first approach, but one with two lanes that could handle a decent size vehicle—fear of Duke's disapproval gave way to anticipation of seeing Harry again.

Not that their relationship was going to resume while there was business to be done. While covering the thousand details of putting on this event at insanely short notice, he'd managed to make it clear he couldn't wait to get into more than her spreadsheets. Whenever she heard that deep, slightly indolent voice through the phone she would shiver and make herself concentrate on work.

And she succeeded. Harry had better have done everything he'd promised, she thought sternly. If he let her down there would be no chance of sex.

Not that there was anyway.

As they passed through the gates and descended the tree-lined drive to the house, she felt a pleasurable tension. Naturally she couldn't wait to show her wedding couple the truly fabulous arrangements. Jane oohed as the gorgeous house came into view and even Duke pocketed his phone. Arwen wondered, with total irrelevance, if Harry would be wearing his low-slung jeans.

He was, waiting at the main door of the house looking delicious and curiously lordly for a handyman, or property manager, or whatever he was. Harry had a way of seeming at home; something to do with being comfortable in his own body. He'd been comfortable in her body too …

"Jane, Duke," she said, dismissing the disturbing vision. "Let me introduce you to Harry Compton. He's been wonderfully helpful and cooperative in pulling together the arrangements."

"Welcome to Brampton," he said. He greeted Jane first, with a cute bow/nod when he took her hand. "I hope you had a good journey.

We're thrilled to have your wedding here and we've done everything we can to make it run smoothly."

"It's even better than I thought," she replied and Arwen relaxed a little. It was going to take a major problem to kill Jane's infatuation with the place.

Harry shook hands with Duke and turned to Arwen. "Hello there." She stood motionless in the shadow of his body for a second or two, then he kissed her on both cheeks. "I'm glad to see you, Elf," he whispered, and turned his attention back to the others.

As he should. This was business.

Arwen thought she detected an undercurrent of nervousness beneath the slightly reserved courtesy that she had learned during a month in London was normal English good manners.

"Harry has been amazingly helpful. He knows everything about Brampton House." She felt oddly protective of the man she'd come to know and trust.

After a couple of minutes' small talk about trans-Atlantic flights, jet lag, the beauty of the house, and so forth, Mark appeared on the steps, displaying distinct signs of agitation.

"Excuse me, Harry," he said. "There's a telephone call for you."

She wondered what was so urgent that Mark couldn't have taken a message, and why the pair of them had left their guests of honor stranded on the front steps.

"Well, well," Jane said, turning from the spectacular view down the avenue and piercing Arwen with a shrewd glance. "I see you've become quite friendly with the Honorable Harry."

"The English kiss everyone," she replied cautiously.

"Not because of that. From the way he looked at you, I can tell he likes you a lot. How do you fancy being Lady Melbury?"

Arwen stared at her. "Whatever do you mean? He's only the handyman, or property manager, or something. Besides his name is Compton."

Jane laughed. "The Honorable Harry Godfrey-Granville-Compton, son and heir to Lord Melbury. Have you learned nothing from reading my books, Arwen? English lords have different family names from their titles."

*H.G.G. Compton.* The rat bastard. He had to have been laughing at her all this time.

Duke, ignoring this exchange, was staring at his screen. He frowned, shook it, stabbed at it with his finger a few times. "There's no signal here. And no Wi-Fi either."

"Excuse me, Duke," Arwen said, her jaw clenched in a rictus grin. "I need a word with Harry. I'll be right back."

Mark, who was sitting behind the antique desk in the part of the hall set up as a reception area, winked at her and pointed at a door. He knew; rat bastard number two. She found Harry in the small sitting room yelling into a telephone. He concluded by slamming down the receiver with a string of expletives.

"Not so calm now, Your Lordship?" she said.

"Arwen …" He bounded forward then stopped. It was a brave man who dared to placate this particular wedding planner in a rage and Harry seemed to have gotten the message.

"About the Internet," he said. "I can explain."

"You could have given me some warning so I don't look like an idiot in front of my most important clients."

"What can I say?" For a moment he looked so like a golden retriever caught with a prime rib she had the urge to console him. Nor for long, however. Lord Harry had some explaining to do and not just about the mysteries of fiber-optic cable. "It was fine a week ago and went out again this morning."

"You can come with me right now and tell Duke Austen how come he has to climb a hill to check his e-mail and how it's your fault, not mine. And make it good because, unlike me, he understands this electronic crap."

"He's a reasonable man, I'm sure," Harry said. "And why does he need the Internet when he's getting married?" Arwen gave him her nastiest look. "I'll explain," he said quickly. "And there are options, but any good ones will cost so much I'll hardly make any profit on the wedding."

This was not a good moment for him to remind her that he, Harry, was the one making the profit. Not his aristocratic masters. *Handyman, my ass.* He *was* the aristocratic master.

Mark was giving the historic tour of the hall; Jane seemed enthralled while her fiancé continued to stare at his phone as though expecting the universe to right itself and signal to appear at any second.

"Mr. Austen," Harry began.

"Please, call me Duke. Having trouble with your Wi-Fi, I see. Is there anything I can do to help?"

"Probably not. As I told Arwen, I thought I had our problem sorted last week, but it's gone on the blink again. The telephone company says it could recover at any time. Or not." Arwen glared at him, silently fuming at the implication that Harry had kept her informed about the problem when, in fact, he'd never given her the straight scoop.

"I have to be in touch with work," Duke said, clearly on the verge of apoplexy. "I can't stay here. We'll have to leave, Jane."

"I've looked into the possibilities," Harry said. "We could get a mobile satellite connection here within a day or so. Or the dedicated broadband could come back online. Or ..." He went off on one of his technical spiels.

Arwen thought the strain in his face matched her own, as though he had as much at stake as she did. Though if Duke Austen walked, he'd still have his fabulous house and hotel and his *title*; Arwen wasn't sure if her business would survive once the news leaked out of such a spectacular failure. Luxe Events could certainly wave goodbye to any more billionaire gigs.

Then Jane, wonderful Jane Sparks, the best friend a girl ever had, laughed. "Duke, honey, you promised me a Regency wedding and I guess that's what I'm getting. I find it very sweet and romantic that you'll have to pay attention to your bride instead of spending ninety percent of the time with your nose in the phone."

"But ..."

Jane tucked her arm in his and gave him a kiss. "You know everything's fine. There's no reason you shouldn't go all week without checking in at the office." She dropped her voice so only Arwen was close enough to hear. "Remember the hurricane?"

Duke gave his fiancée a scorching look. "I suppose," he said. "And it'll help with secrecy if the guests can't be online all the time."

"As to that," Arwen said, "there's cell signal at the gazebo in the park. We'll fit it out with some comfortable seating and refreshments for when you—and other guests—want to rejoin the modern world for a little while. Otherwise we'll immerse you in the aristocratic country life of old England. As Jane rightly says, nothing could be more romantic. Speaking of romantic, you must see your suite. It's to die for."

"I'll be happy to take you now." Mark inserted himself into the discussion. "I've already sent your luggage up. I thought you'd enjoy putting your feet up with a glass of champagne before touring the house and grounds." He swept them off, leaving Harry and Arwen alone in the hall.

"What can I say?" He gestured hopelessly.

"About what?" The Wi-Fi thing pissed her off, but she was far more upset about the way he'd lied about his identity. "Why didn't you tell me you were a lord? I suppose it amuses you to have sex with the peasants."

"I'm not a lord, my father is. And yes, it amused me greatly to make love to you. And for the record you are about the farthest thing from a peasant I've met. I'm sure Mark could tell me who made that smart little red dress in which, incidentally, you look good enough to eat. I don't name clothing, but I can spot expensive when I see it. Are you sure you weren't amusing yourself by dallying with the lower orders?"

Arwen bit her lip. She hoped she hadn't treated him like a menial, but she had thought of him as some kind of manual laborer, of an elevated kind. He was wearing his usual jeans, with a good shirt, and looked sexy as hell. When he mentioned eating her, she got hot inside.

But she couldn't figure out his motive for presenting himself as a dumb wage slave instead of the owner's son. Had he hoped to influence her report to Duke, somehow? She'd felt guilty about her attraction to him, and worried that she'd let it affect her judgment. It hadn't occurred to her that he was the one doing the manipulating. She needed to consider the possibility from all angles, when she wasn't feeling harassed and upset. Had he given her five mind-blowing orgasms—she hadn't forgotten a single one—simply to keep her sweet about Brampton as the wedding site?

Yet she had agreed to it before she came five times. So perhaps they'd been provided to keep her from noticing any little shortcomings of his hotel, like a functioning kitchen and the freakin' Internet.

"I can't talk about this now," she said. "I have too many things to deal with."

"I got rid of the big pile of earth next to the stables," he cajoled. "And we have a kitchen. The inspectors came yesterday so we canceled the mobile equipment."

"Oh. That's good." The news tamped down her steamy indignation, for a second. "We had that sorted, for God's sake." She was talking like an English person now. "But the Internet?" She almost shouted with exasperation. "And your real name?"

He was looking at her with sincere concern in his blue eyes that she didn't trust. "I messed up, Arwen," he said. "It all started out innocently enough and now I really regret not telling you who I am."

"I must go and see what the Next Gordon Ramsey is doing. I have a wedding to run and no time to spend on screwups."

"Don't you ever screw up?" he asked quietly.

"Not if I can help it."

"How nice for you." He sounded slightly nettled while she was ready to scream like a banshee.

Hoisting her leather tote over her shoulder she stormed off, then stopped at the door and turned. "I can't afford to screw up because I wasn't born a lord. I suppose Mark is a duke or something."

"Uh, his family may possibly own the Delaville Group."

"Good. He should know more about running a hotel than a freakin' English aristocrat."


ARWEN MANAGED to go almost twenty-four hours without exchanging more than a few terse words with Harry. She let Mark handle greeting the guests—she couldn't complain about his skills—while she made final arrangements for the flowers and tents, made sure the Next Gordon Ramsey was installed in the newly inspected kitchen, and avoided his wandering hands. Only when Harry happened to come into the pantry while she was discussing the breakfast menu did she allow the chef to stroke her ass without repercussion.

She stuck her nose in the air when Harry followed her into the hall and waited while she had a few words with Jane's college friend Cali Blake.

"I hear you're a librarian," she said.

"You must see the library here." Harry smiled engagingly at the pretty Philadelphian.

He hadn't shown *her* the library. Arwen didn't even know Brampton had one.

"I would really love that." Cali hid a yawn behind her hand. "Maybe tomorrow, so I can really appreciate it after some sleep? Or whenever you're able."

She followed Mark and a new batch of arrivals upstairs and for a moment the busy hall emptied, leaving Arwen and Harry alone.

"Are you ever going to speak to me again?" Harry asked.

"We've spoken."

"Don't be disingenuous."

"Why didn't you tell me who you are? It's not a little lie, like saying you've read *Moby Dick* or you'll call in the morning. I feel stupid and that is one of my least favorite emotions." She felt itchy in her skin and it made her surly.

Harry folded his arms and frowned. "I don't see why you're so annoyed. Forgive me if I'm pleased when people seem to like me for myself, not because I'm the future Lord Melbury, an event that is unlikely to occur for many years, what with my father being well under sixty and in rude health. Besides, the peerage is all rubbish now, completely outdated and of no use except for getting a table in snobbish restaurants. I doubt I will ever use the title."

"It's all very well to say that, but you've still got all this." Arwen stretched her arms out to encompass the house, the gardens, and all the other magnificence that was Brampton. "It's easy to dismiss what you were born with since no one can take it away from you."

He took her hand and held it tightly, almost, but not quite, to the point of pain. "You think so? Do you have any idea how difficult it is to hold onto a place like this? If I had any sense I'd have let my father sell it when he wanted to."

"Sell it?" Naively, perhaps, she hadn't thought much about the history and economics of Brampton. They had a big house and decided to turn it into a hotel. End of story. But of course it wasn't.

He spoke quietly, with an urgency unlike his usual relaxed, amused tones. "Three years ago, my parents decided they'd had enough of the place. It cost a fortune to maintain, even in a rundown state, and they wanted to move to Bali, where living is cheap and the weather is great. As a matter of form, since I'm their only child, they asked for my opinion. I was living in London and opened my mouth to say yes, of course, it was their house and their decision. But the words wouldn't come out. I realized I didn't want to give it up."

"I wouldn't either." Arwen stopped trying to pull her hand away, and he relaxed his grip. "It is gorgeous, though a bit on the large side."

"They thought I was mad and sometimes I think so too. I couldn't bear the thought of not having Brampton to come home to. So we came to an arrangement. My father handed the estate over to me and, as long as he lives seven years, I won't have to pay death duties on the value of the property. We sold the good pictures; the Rembrandt made enough after taxes to keep my parents forever, while some other paintings funded the conversion of the house. Between the hotel itself, shooting parties, and holiday rentals of cottages around the estate, we should be able to keep going."

"You were set to open this fall. Why did you agree to Duke's request to hold the wedding here? It seems like an awful lot of hassle."

"Come with me."

Off the hall, next to the Gold Saloon, there was a room Arwen hadn't seen before. Used to the high state of gloss that characterized the rest of the house, in the library she might have been in a different world. Twice as long as it was wide, it was lined with cases of deep brown wood that reached almost to the beautiful ceiling. Fancy plasterwork had been painted bright white, in contrast to the shabby state of the rest of the fixtures. Although the furniture—chairs and tables, Arwen guessed—was covered in dust cloths, the parquet floor was scratched with numerous loose sections. Odors of paint and dust hung about the room. The principal cause of the atmosphere of neglect was easily identified: the bookcases, covered over with giant sheets of clear plastic, were almost all empty.

The library was like a sleeping beauty, waiting to be reawakened to its former glory.

"What a beautiful room, and how sad," Arwen said.

"This is why I need Duke Austen," Harry said simply. "He offered me enough money to finish the restoration in here. It's my favorite room and a house isn't a house without a library."

"I agree. In my New York apartment, I give the name to a few shelves on either side of the fireplace." She stopped and smiled. "In terms of percentage of available space, mine might be bigger." She walked over to a couple of sections of shelves in the wall opposite the marble fireplace, the only ones occupied.

"Be careful," Harry said. "All the bookcases were removed from the wall so we could deal with dry rot in the wainscoting. They haven't been screwed back in securely."

Arwen stepped back and peered at the titles from a distance. Lots of novels and history and eastern philosophy, reflecting the interests displayed on Harry's nightstand. "Why so few books? Did you have to sell most of them?"

"It was a toss-up between a painting and the library, but in the end I couldn't part with rare editions that had been bought new by my ancestors."

"I can understand that. Books are personal. Knowing what people read brings them closer."

"My feelings exactly. The collection has been stored away, so when we ran out of money a year ago, it was too depressing having no books. I unpacked the books I had in my flat in London and stuck them in here. They're not properly arranged, but you are welcome to borrow anything you like."

"I'll be too busy with the wedding, I expect, but it's good to know I have options." He looked at her anxiously and she found that it was hard to stay really mad at a man in the middle of a library. "Thanks for showing me this, Harry. I understand now why you were so anxious for the wedding plan to go through."

"Does that mean I'm forgiven?"

She wanted to say yes; already she'd had to restrain herself from kissing him. Not a sexual kiss, but one on the cheek, between friends; a gesture of solidarity. But while her anger had subsided, her hurt had not. "You should have told me who you were. It wouldn't have affected my opinion of the hotel. And you especially should have told me who you were before we slept together."

He nodded. "No more lies, I promise. Can we revisit the issue after the wedding?"

"If everything between now and next Sunday goes perfectly, you may find me in a forgiving mood."

"That's something to look forward to. What would you like me to do?"

"Duke has his heart set on a hunt for his bachelor party. Most of these guys are from Silicon Valley, for God's sake. Can you prevent a bunch of geeks with guns from shooting each other? It's bad for business when half the wedding party is dead or in intensive care."

Harry gave the sleepy grin that never failed to make her insides quiver. "The gamekeeper who organizes the shooting at Brampton is thoroughly used to managing lunatics."

# CHAPTER
## SEVEN

O nly four more days until the wedding and Harry couldn't wait.

The strain of a weeklong event with almost one hundred residential guests was beginning to tell on him. He couldn't imagine how Arwen stood it. Her only outward sign of stress was a derangement of her sleek, shiny hair, but he knew she worried about everything. He had some excellent ideas about how to make her relax as soon as this damn thing was over. He'd enjoy them too.

"Good morning, Elf," he said, finding her staring at and baffled by the espresso machine in the family kitchen. "Let me do that. Did you hear that Nanny caught the Next Gordon Ramsey shagging one of the guests on a saddle horse in the stables?"

"Is Nanny okay?"

"She's pretty unflappable. I trust you're over your infatuation with the man. Faithless bastard."

"The guy is impossible. I wish the Original Gordon Ramsey had been available. Much less trouble. All in all things could be worse. Jane seems to have lost her mind, but that's normal for brides." She leaned in to breathe the freshly ground coffee while he enjoyed her proximity and her scent.

"She's not going to call it off, is she? I'm not sure I have a cancelation clause in my contract."

"It's her wedding dress. She has an incredibly beautiful designer wedding gown, but now she wants to check out a bridal shop in Melbury. Is it conceivable she'll find anything she likes there?"

"I have no idea, but I expect they can produce something suitably meringue-like. Do you have to go with her?"

"Thank God, no. She hasn't asked me and I only heard about it from Mark. Just an attack of the last-minute crazies, I expect."

He tightened the portafilter and slung an arm around her shoulders. "Don't you ever want a wedding dress for yourself?" That was a dangerous thing to ask, the kind of question he shied away from, not wishing to give rise to expectations. Antiquated institution or not, there was something about the peerage that put a gleam into the eyes of otherwise sensible women.

Not his Elf. She stepped away as though scalded. "While the coffee brews I'll run over to the hotel kitchen and make sure that lecher has breakfast running smoothly. Also make sure he hasn't put anything in the refrigerator reserved for the desserts being delivered from London. And that Sheila and he haven't gotten into a knife fight over the vegan dishes."

Babbling away, she backed out of the room. Harry whistled optimistically. Arwen was rattled and, if he wasn't mistaken, it had nothing to do with work.

TWO DAYS until the wedding and Arwen felt like she was running a marathon, overseeing the meals and entertainment for a solid week and dealing with one small crisis after another.

And then there was the tabloid photographer. This was particularly worrisome, given the heavy secrecy that had surrounded the wedding. As far as they could tell, there was only one. His phallic camera lens had been spotted peeking around a corner or sticking out from shrubbery. He'd been surprised several times, but the man was nimble on his feet.

He had to be driven off by Saturday because *People* magazine had an exclusive on the wedding itself in exchange for a hefty contribution to an animal rescue charity. No way was Arwen going to lose the chance of getting *her* wedding—all right, technically Duke and Jane's—in *People*, thanks to the squalid British tabloids.

On the whole, things had gone well and she worked well with Harry and Mark. Once the hotel was properly staffed it would be a fabulous location for any event. She was already thinking about how she could sell Brampton as a destination wedding site to American clients. Most importantly, the bridal couple was happy and the guests seemed to be enjoying themselves.

Meanwhile, she had a relatively easy day ahead of her. Harry had arranged to take all the men off, hopefully to kill birds and not each other. Jane and her maid of honor Roxanna were leading a bachelorette expedition off the premises. Arwen looked forward to a quiet morning at the gazebo, going over her lists, checking e-mail, and making calls to suppliers, then an afternoon overseeing the tent people and the florist.

First coffee and a soothing chat with Nanny in the giant kitchen. Since Harry was away she'd have to tackle the espresso machine herself. She'd watched him often enough. She found those big sure hands twisting the little metal containers of coffee into place very sexy.

"Arwen, honey." The last voice she would have expected greeted her at the kitchen door.

"Mom? What the f— … What are you doing here?" A familiar waft of patchouli hit her nose.

"Language, honey. You'll shock Nanny."

Nanny was taking the appearance of an eternal hippy from Pennsylvania with the same calm with which she'd witnessed the chef's sexual shenanigans. "Come in, Arwen. Molly and I are having a nice cup of green tea. Isn't it lovely that she's come to see you?"

Arwen and Molly hugged each other. "It's good to see you, Mom. You're looking great." She always did. Though Arwen often complained to her friends that her fifty-year-old mother hadn't changed her style since she was a teenager, the flowing floral skirts and gauzy tops suited her. She kept her skin in good shape by always wearing a hat outside on the farm and if her long curly blond hair contained any gray, it didn't show. Flamboyant beaded jewelry, collected around the world before she and Benjamin settled down, complemented her wardrobe.

"And you're looking tired, though I do like your hair like that. Makes you look less uptight."

"Thanks." She rolled her eyes. "Why are you here and where's Dad?"

"I've left him."

Tottering to the table, Arwen pulled out a chair and collapsed. "No." The one thing in her whole life she'd have bet on was her parents' devotion to one another. "Tell me what happened. No, first coffee."

"She's had a shock," Molly said to Nanny. "Give her some of that green tea."

"I need caffeine, preferably through an IV."

Molly handed her a mug of pale liquid. "Drink this. You need the antioxidants."

For all her new age airs, Molly didn't take disobedience well. It was easier to give in. "Explain," she said, taking a sip and wishing it was a latte. On top of everything else, she really didn't need green tea and parental drama.

"We were at a folk festival on the Isle of Man."

"I wondered what you were doing there."

"We took a trip to celebrate our thirtieth anniversary."

"Of what?"

"Don't be so ordinary, honey. Of the day we pledged our eternal love in the ashram in India. We've often told you about that."

"I didn't realize you did anything so 'ordinary' as observe an anniversary. So what happened to the pledge of eternal love?"

"Benjamin asked me to marry him."

"Mom, that's so sweet and romantic." Arwen had to get up and give her another hug. "Can I do the wedding? I promise it'll be just the way you want it."

Molly held her daughter convulsively. "We have never believed in the shackles of marriage. Without absolute freedom I cannot live with him."

"So don't marry. I think it would be lovely if you tied the knot, but it won't matter either way. Not after all these years."

"You don't understand," she cried, releasing Arwen and stretching her arms toward the ceiling. "Benjamin has betrayed everything I thought we held sacred. Nothing will ever be the same again."

Oh, for God's sake. She *really* didn't need this. "You always make such a big deal about things."

Nanny interrupted her sharply. "Don't speak to your mother like that, Arwen. Principles should be respected." The elderly woman made her feel six years old.

Arwen closed her eyes and rubbed her forehead. So much for a peaceful morning. She didn't think she could manage this crisis right now, or even take in the incredible fact that her parents had split up. "We must talk about this more, Mom," she said, "but I'm totally swamped at the moment. Where are you staying? Do you want to share my room here?"

"I reserved a room at The Bull's Head in the village."

"Once I'm done for the day here, I'll meet you and and we'll talk over dinner. Do you have enough money? Do you need my credit card?"

"Really, Arwen! Don't treat me like a child."

Arwen apologized and saw her mother out to her rental car. Her mom and dad must make up their quarrel; they had to. Meanwhile Arwen must get her day back on track, starting with a powerful infusion of caffeine.

THOUGH SHE DIDN'T HAVE time for her parents' nonmarital difficulties, the first thing she did when she reached the gazebo—temporarily free of Web-surfing, e-mailing, boozing, chatting guests—was to try, without success, to track down her father. She also left a message for her brother, who was doing his doctorate at Berkeley.

She could only hope Dad was on his way to find Molly. She just couldn't believe they would break up. All through her childhood they'd barely ever even argued. When she started kindergarten, she'd been mortified to discover that most kids' parents had the same last name and wedding pictures. Later she understood that it was a less rosy picture: divorce and stepparents were problems she didn't have to deal with. And even in conservative rural Pennsylvania a few women kept their own names after marriage.

It was ridiculous to care that her parents had never married, and most of the time Arwen didn't. They were always just there, at home with their organic crops, well-loved farm animals, and mutual adoration, expressed through inappropriate public displays of affection. And most of all, together.

Distracted as she was, she managed to get some work done then ruined her mood by doing a Web search. Jezebel.com had a feature on Jane's visit to the bridal shop, complete with pictures of her in a hideous wedding dress. Arwen's eyes popped out of her head: the byline was Roxanna Lane, Jane's maid of honor. At least no one could blame her, or Harry, for that one. Perhaps Jane had given permission for the picture.

At least Roxanna's piece gave no clue as to the location. Apparently they only had one photographer to worry about at Brampton. In fact the latest rumor reported by Perez Hilton was that Duke and Jane had emulated Madonna; the entire corps of paparazzi had besieged Skibo Castle, many miles away in Scotland.

On the way down from the gazebo, she thought she caught sight of a telephoto lens protruding from a rhododendron bush. She stuck out her tongue. Thankfully no one was going to pay for a photo of an obscure wedding planner with bad hair and an insane mother who wanted to get divorced without ever being married.

As the foot of the hill, emerging from the trees and shrubs on her way to the house, she met Harry. "Hello, darling, you're looking down in the dumps." His voice always seemed to improve her mood, however much she told herself it was strictly business between them.

"It's that photographer," she said, not wanting to talk about her family. "How are we going to keep him out? Could you drive him off with your gun?"

He was carrying a shotgun over his arm, to go with a very English country outfit of rust-colored corduroy pants, a green quilted vest, and tall black boots. Jane Sparks's historical romances tended to dwell on men in boots and she could see why. Hot.

"I could, but he'll just come back. I can't have him arrested unless he actually does some damage. I've talked to Duke about calling in a firm from London, but it's almost impossible to police such big grounds and we can't stop people from using the right-of-way foot-paths. Besides, a large security presence could have the effect of drawing more attention to the place."

"I don't trust those outfits," Arwen said. "I swear the paparazzi have spies in them. I have to ask this, Harry." She stopped, hating to voice her suspicions but she knew *she* had been super careful about confidentiality. She had a nondisclosure agreement in her contact with Duke Austen, and had demanded the same from all her vendors. "Could one of your staff have sold the story?"

"Anything is possible among so many," he said with a sigh. "Mark is making discreet inquiries and he's pretty good at rooting out the truth. But honestly I don't think so. We've had trouble here, before, with the tabloids harassing my parents and they aren't well liked. When they descend in force, they're like an invading army."

"The important thing is that no one but the official photographer gets pictures of the wedding itself. I'd like to get my hands on whoever tipped him off. I really don't need this aggravation on top of every-thing else."

"Sit for a minute," Harry said, carefully laying down his gun and patting a gothic-style wooden garden bench. "What you need is a neck rub and ten minutes of meditation. Empty your mind."

She didn't quite obey, but her brain abandoned parents and paparazzi in favor of the magic of Harry's hands. Leaning into his big body she felt her stress melt away, along with her resolve to keep him at a distance.

So he'd lied to her. Big deal. "Mm," she murmured.

"I've told you before, you work too hard. Once this bash is over, I recommend a few days' holiday at a luxury country house hotel. I happen to know the owner and I can get you a bargain rate."

That sounded great: a week in the Chinese bedroom in the family quarters, long walks in the park, no phone calls, meals in the kitchen with Nanny and Harry, evenings in the Gold Saloon …

However much she dreaded the mounds of work that awaited her in New York, she shouldn't abandon Valerie for much longer. "I need to get back to the city."

"You must find it very quiet and dull here."

"Are you kidding? I suppose it'll be quiet once everyone's left, but weddings themselves are always insanity." He smoothed out a stubborn knot in her shoulder. "Oh, that's good."

She stopped worrying about work and start imagining everyone gone except herself and Harry. Perhaps they could get together tonight, when the bachelor and bachelorette parties were out for their respective dinners.

Then she remembered her mother. She needed to talk sense into Molly. And into herself, too.

Harry was too good for a short vacation affair and there was no chance of anything else. Geography and background ensured that. Arwen wasn't in kindergarten now and her parents no longer embarrassed her—at least not with their marital status—but Harry belonged to a different world. He had parents who had been chased by paparazzi. Did that happen to all lords or were they celebrities? It was just one more reason why it was sensible for her to keep her distance before she started getting ideas about a long-term relationship. Harry might claim that being a lord meant nothing to him, but he would find himself an English woman who understood English ways. He was handy at fixing things and great at sex, but there was a whole lot more to life than those two admirable skills. Unfortunately.

"More?" His deep accents buzzed in her ear. She leaned back, sending the message *yes*. His fingers had unknotted all the tension in her neck and sent hot streaks through her veins. If only she could spend the whole day like this.

Then she thought about the exciting jobs that could come her way once the success of this wedding made the gossip rounds. It was her passport to the kind of party planning she'd always dreamed of. She mustn't forget what Luxe Events had at stake.

"No," she said. "I need to check on tomorrow's menus before the tent people show up."

"Stay a while."

"And you need to prevent mayhem on the hunting field."

"You're right. I need to get back to the shooting party," he said. "I suppose I should go. Do you think we could have a quiet dinner tonight, just the two of us?"

"I can't." Reluctantly Arwen stood up. "I'm joining the bachelorette party at the pub. I promised Jane."

A lie, but a necessary one. No way was she introducing her loony tunes mother to the future Lord Melbury.


WALKING a mile across country to the moor where the gamekeeper and his men had conveyed the shooting party, Harry reflected on the oddity of the tech billionaire's chosen stag party. He'd have expected something more conventional, like strippers jumping out of computer-shaped cakes. If that had been Duke's preference, he had no doubt Arwen would have laid it on without a blink.

She'd been wearing another of her chic little dresses and all he could think about was getting her out of it. Well, not quite all. He found her stimulating in a number of ways, but the undressing option was always at the back of his dirty male mind. He was the one who needed ten minutes of meditation. Having her pressed against him reduced his mind to porridge.

He was making progress. She'd pretty much forgiven him for being a lord-in-waiting and for his house's killer lack of Wi-Fi. By the end of the week he trusted that clothes would be removed. All very satisfactory.

Trouble was, he wanted more than that: to make her laugh and relax and stop worrying so much; to explore the vulnerability that peeped out from behind the tough (not hard-boiled!) exterior; to make her coffee in the kitchen every morning; to learn about her childhood on a farm and the mysterious parents she avoided talking about. They couldn't possibly be more bizarre than his and he wanted to tell her about them, too. With something like panic he realized she'd be leaving in four days and crossing the damnably wide Atlantic Ocean.

The thought of a quick shag followed by her return to America, then nothing more between them but an occasional e-mail, was depressing. But what did he have to offer her?

He'd listened to her and Mark chatting about places in New York he'd never heard of. A successful businesswoman with a glamorous life couldn't possibly want to take on a dull Englishman with a quixotic determination to save a white elephant of a house he couldn't really afford.

# CHAPTER
# EIGHT

The day before the wedding started badly. For the rehearsal dinner, at Jane's request, Arwen had ordered special cream dessert cakes from a London bakery. Apparently this outfit was the successor to Gunter's, a historic business that was big in Regency romance. The delivery had been made three days earlier and stowed in one of the giant refrigerators in the kitchen. That morning, it was discovered the thing wasn't working.

Since the Next Gordon Ramsey disclaimed all responsibility for a machine that didn't contain his creations, they had no way of knowing how long the cakes had been unchilled. Arwen wasn't about to risk giving a hotel full of guests food poisoning from bad cream. Compounding the problem, the Next G.R. steadfastly refused to turn around and provide desserts he hadn't been contracted for.

While venting her frustration to Harry, an unlikely savior appeared in the form of Duke's lawyer, Archer Quinn, who had made the acquaintance of a woman in a nearby cottage. Arwen didn't trouble to ask how a chef for one of the Boston area's best restaurants happened to be in the vicinity with a cooler full of desserts. She merely thanked God for the existence of Natalie Corcoran.

While she had signal, she called New York to check in with Valerie.

"Guess what," she said to Harry as they headed back to Brampton House from Natalie's house. "Val heard that our lunatic chef has lost his investors for a US expansion because he's impossible to work with. He's about to be the Ex-Next Gordon Ramsey and it couldn't happen to a nicer guy."

"Brilliant news. I take it you are no longer thinking of sleeping with the man."

"Puh-lease. He's the last man in the world I'd ever do."

"I'm encouraged. I just moved up the list a notch."

"Idiot. You're not an asshole."

"Thank you for the vote of approval."

"You're welcome."

They walked on for a few minutes, Arwen sneaking glances at him as they went. His habitual calm was wonderfully soothing and she realized that after spending much of the last month in England, she'd come to appreciate a measured approach to life. Take last night. The Bull's Head had been full of screaming wedding guests, so she'd taken her mother to The Pineapple of Perfection. It was a quiet night and Carol and Sheila had joined them and the four of them had a great chat over a bottle of wine.

Molly and Carol bonded over organic food while Arwen and Sheila talked movies. It was also one of the few times in her life that Arwen could remember spending time with her mom without her dad being present. Perhaps they just needed a vacation from each other.

Sheila occasionally got up to see to a straggler or two at another table and everyone was totally relaxed about it, so different from Arwen's life in New York where everyone wanted everything yesterday and it was her job to provide it. Her life didn't hold enough moments like this one, strolling through a gorgeous park in sunshine, with a good man at her side.

"Do you miss living in London?" she asked.

"Not at all. I had a job in a merchant bank and never knew how much I hated it until I left. Now I must try to make the hotel profitable. I could use an experienced wedding planner on the staff." He wore that hopeful, sheepish grin she found so appealing.

On impulse she tucked her arm into his. "Whatever our relationship is or will be, and at this point I have no idea, I'd like to say I've enjoyed working with you. You've been great the last few days." He looked a bit embarrassed, as though unaccustomed to freely expressed praise. "Are you blushing, Harry? You Englishmen are too adorable."

He recovered quickly enough. "Thanks, darling. Same to you. Together we are a well-oiled machine. Only one more day and I don't believe anything else can go wrong."

"Bite your tongue."

"Um, I think we talked about that phrase before."

THAT AFTERNOON, Arwen stood on the front steps of the mansion, making sure all was as it should be for the official group wedding pictures. A man with a very large camera sauntered around the corner, for all the world as though he had the right to be there. There was something familiar about him, although his face was concealed by the brim of a tweed cap. About to head up the drive, he turned and saw Arwen standing at the foot the front steps.

"Hello, bonnie lassie," he said with a cheeky grin. "I was hoping I'd run into you."

She knew him.

She'd been working on her laptop, sitting at the empty bar after lunch at the Next Gordon Ramsey's restaurant, waiting for His Highness to come out and discuss terms. This man—his name was Angus something—had taken the next stool and struck up a conversation. Charmed by his gingery good looks and mellifluous Scottish tones, she'd chatted for five or ten minutes. Although she had told him about her job when he asked, she was one hundred percent certain she hadn't mentioned Duke Austen or Brampton House. He must have got the truth out of the Next G.R. or his staff. She was going to kill that randy chef.

"Ms. Kilpatrick, is it not? I owe you for this gig."

Unless.

With horror Arwen recalled getting up from her seat to ask the maître d' how long his boss would be. Angus Whatsit could easily have taken a peek and one glance at her spreadsheet would tell him all he wanted to know.

*Crap, crap, crap.* It was her fault the paparazzo was here.

"I'm sure you remember our meeting. I feel we're friends and friends lend each other a hand. I'd be grateful if you'd give me a little insider tip about the time and location of the ceremony." He rolled the R in the last word with horrible emphasis. "If it's indoors I need a little time to find myself a good viewing spot when Duke and Jane tie the knot."

"No way." Arwen found her voice. "Since we're friends, I would appreciate it if you took your camera away and left the couple to their privacy."

"I'd like to oblige you, I truly would, but I have to feed my children." He handed her a card, which she accepted as though handling a scorpion. "Here's my number. I'm staying at The Bull's Head if you'd like to join me for a drink later tonight."

"Thanks, but I have too much to do."

"As long as you're employed as the wedding planner you do. I wonder if you'd keep your job if the happy couple knew how I found them." He shook his head mournfully. "I hope I won't have to tell, but the kiddies eat a lot. And then there are the school fees. I'll be getting along now, but I expect I'll hear from you later. I look forward to our chat."

Her stomach churned as she scowled at his cheery parting wave. With the nondisclosure agreement, Duke would be in his rights to fire her without paying a penny, and she wasn't sure even Jane would stick up for her this time. This was far worse than no Internet. She had screwed up. Big-time.

She jumped at the sound of the door opening behind her. "Do you know who that was?" Harry asked. He stood on the steps with his hands in the back pockets of his jeans, looking at the retreating figure of the Scotsman. "Snooper MacBracken, the most ruthless paparazzo in Europe. He's the one who caught Prince Harry peeing into a flower bed at a polo match and the Duchess of Cambridge scratching her bottom. Not to mention the famous shot of Silvio Berlusconi groping Gwyneth Paltrow."

"I had no idea you were such a tabloid fan," Arwen said, trying to pretend, just for a minute or two, that she didn't have a massive problem on her hands.

"They've given me and my parents grief on occasion. MacBracken's like a virus. He gets everywhere and there's no cure but to live with him. And he's not afraid to play dirty."

There was nothing for it but a full confession. "He's blackmailing me."

"Darling, what did you do? Don't tell me you've been having an affair with the former Prime Minister of Italy. Not a good idea. The man's an utter shit."

"This isn't funny, Harry. I have totally screwed up."

"It can't be that bad." He put his arm around her and gave her a squeeze. "Tell me all about it and we'll work something out."

"It's my fault he knows about the wedding here. I met him in London and he snuck a look at my laptop. Now he's going to tell Duke if I don't tell him everything he wants to know."

"Bastard. I told you he played dirty."

The man was a saint. "How can you be so nice when I was a heinous bitch about the Internet thing? Aren't you going to crow even a little bit?"

Pulling her into a full embrace, he rested his forehead against hers. "You didn't mean it, darling Elf. It's just your way to be a bit bitchy. It's one of the things I like about you."

She couldn't allow herself to relax into his blissful hold when she faced the worst crisis of her career. Neither did she have time to melt at having found a man who appreciated her for her worst traits. "Obviously I can't tell this Snooper guy what he wants to know, so I guess I'll have to face Duke and Jane. Even if they give me the boot, it's too late for them to move the wedding, so you and your library should be okay." She didn't want to have messed it up for Harry too.

"We can't have you getting the sack. I wouldn't know how to get through the next day or two without you. Let me think." She tried to pull away but not very hard. Instead her tension subsided by a degree at the confidence in his voice. "We're not going to tell the truth," he said, "not the whole truth, anyway. I have an idea. We can present it as a way of getting rid of Snooper without letting on how he got here in the first place. Let's find Mark. We'll need him to set this up."

AN HOUR LATER, summoned with the brief explanation that they needed to have an urgent discussion about anti-paparazzi measures, Jane and Duke joined them in the small sitting room.

"What's happened?" Jane said. "Surely we can get rid of one guy without too much trouble."

Duke raised an eyebrow at Harry and raised an invisible shotgun to his shoulder. "We'd better or *People* will call off the deal and the puppies and kittens will lose out. We're already on shaky ground with them."

"I've texted Roxanna to hurry back here. She's good at plotting."

Arwen exchanged a quick glance with Harry. They'd discussed the maid of honor's little feature on Jezebel and wondered if she could possibly be in cahoots with Snooper. Also, Harry had reminded her that Damien Knightly, Roxanna's boyfriend, had something of a media empire himself. But when she asked Jane about the Jezebel pictures, the bride had told her not to worry. It was some kind of joke that Arwen didn't have time to figure out.

"Let's get started," Harry said. "I can escort Snooper MacBracken off the estate a dozen times and he'll keep coming back since I can't actually have him put in prison. Worse comes to worst he'll call in his charming colleagues and we'll have a dozen of the bastards to deal with, not just one. However, old Snoops has a problem."

Arwen took up the narrative. "He tried to make me tell him where and when the ceremony will take place. We thought the best thing is to give him the information he wants."

"It's all right," Harry said quickly when Duke started swearing. "We'll set up a decoy wedding at the gazebo. I gather Jane has two wedding dresses. Arwen will wear one and I'll dress like Duke. With a veil and a hat respectively, we should be able to fool anyone at a distance."

Duke looked intrigued. "I'm guessing the fake bride will be

wearing that weird thing Roxanna showed in her article. I was praying you weren't really going to be married in that."

"No way," Jane said. "The real one is lovely and that's all you'll know until I walk up the aisle."

Consoling herself with the fact that her face would be covered when she wore the ugliest dress in creation, Arwen nodded. "We'll have a quick fake ceremony at the top of the hill so that Snooper will get his pictures. Then he'll be shown from the premises and hopefully be too busy selling his pictures of the false wedding to bother to come back."

"And when do we get married?" Jane asked.

"Immediately afterward. I already had a closed passage built from the house to the big marquee. The real guests—the fake wedding will be attended by the hotel staff—will get into place without anyone outside seeing them."


WHILE THE WEDDING party went off to change for the rehearsal and dinner in the State Rooms, Harry and Arwen planned setting up the gazebo—as he'd now become used to calling the Mausoleum—for the fake wedding.

Mark, predictably, was enchanted by the whole thing. "Bags I perform the ceremony for you two lovebirds. I have the very costume in mind. Now I'd better tell the staff to go home tonight and dig out their best clothes and Ascot hats. This could be the worst-dressed wedding in history, especially the bride." He nodded at the gigantic pouf of sequins and feathers that Arwen had fetched from the bridal suite. Much to her disgust, it fit her. "Now I must be off to find enough white tulle to drape the Mausoleum. And flowers in some really ghastly clashing colors."

Arwen sat on a sofa in the small sitting room, frowning at the endless lists on her laptop. Harry could feel her tension, yet she managed to keep going, no matter what the Fates bowled at her. When he'd accepted Duke's offer he'd been hopelessly naive about what was involved. The billionaire's wedding had been a baptism of fire and without the wedding planner it would have been a disaster. He hoped the bride and groom appreciated what she'd done for them.

She kept patting at her hair absentmindedly as though bothered by it. He remembered the shining bob she'd worn that first day, when he'd shouted at her in the car. Since the hairdryer incident her style had been looser, a little crazy, and he liked it that way. But he guessed that perfect hair was emblematic of the way she liked to keep everything under control and he couldn't help wondering why that was so. While respecting her organizational talents, his best moments with Arwen had been when she metaphorically took her hair down: the couple of times he'd been able to help her with a problem, or just given her a neck rub. And when they shagged. God, he wanted to do that again. And the other things, too. Now he was certain he wanted more than a temporary romance.

"So we're going to be married," he said. She looked up, as startled as he at the words that had popped out. "As the decoy bride and groom, I mean."

"I'm not happy about that. I'm more of a stage manager than an actor. I will worry about what's going on in the house without me to keep the guests quiet and inside."

"Sergeant Elf."

"Also," she said scowling, "I'll have to wear the most horrendously ugly dress ever made. Why did Jane and Roxanna have to pick out such a monster?"

"Perhaps they were drunk."

"I'm quite sure they were, but that's no excuse. I'd better call Snooper and set up a date." She put aside her computer and went to the telephone, a vintage dial phone that sat on a French writing desk along with a supply of Brampton House writing paper and envelopes. The first time she saw it, Arwen had teased him about needing a quill pen.

"Right," she said. "Eight o'clock, but not in the pub. I have all the information you need but no one, and I mean no one, must know we're meeting." She scribbled a note. "I'll find it. I look forward to seeing you, Mr. MacBracken. And if word gets out that I've met with you I'll cut your fucking balls off, you asshole." She slammed down the phone.

"I like the way you make dates," Harry said.

She wriggled her shoulders in disgust. "Just talking to him makes me feel dirty. How could I ever ...? Never mind. I'm looking forward to screwing him over royally."

"And I love it when you're vengeful." Harry patted the sofa. "Do you want a drink?"

"Better not. I need all my wits when I lie through my teeth. You know what I'd like to do? Watch something on TV. Pretend everything is normal."

For fifteen minutes it was. Climate change: right. No peace in the Middle East: right. England losing the test match: right. He could get used to observing the disasters of the world with Arwen beside him, problems so much worse than any that Duke's wedding had thrown at them. Well, perhaps not the cricket.

"Have you ever been to a cricket match?" he asked.

"I hate sports."

*Oh well, nobody's perfect.*

"Except rowing." She smiled at him so he felt goofy and didn't notice the new arrival until Arwen jumped up.

"What a gorgeous dress!" said a female American voice. "Is that what the bride is wearing?"

"Mom?" Arwen said. "What are you doing here? I was going to stop by the pub later tonight and see how you were."

"I promised Nanny my recipe for brownies."

Arwen hadn't said anything about her mother visiting and Harry had hardly seen Nanny in the past couple of days. Mrs. Kilpatrick had long curly blond hair, but he could see a resemblance to her daughter. They shared the same breathtaking prettiness.

"Not the special brownies, please! Nanny won't understand."

Harry grinned broadly. If she only knew what Nanny had put up with over the years of working for the Melburys. Mrs. Kilpatrick, if that was her name, looked like the kind of person who would get on well with his parents. "Will you introduce me to your mother, Arwen?"

"Harry, this is my mom, Molly Stanton. Mom, this is …"

"No need," she said. "You won't remember me, Hari, because I last saw you when you were three." To his amazement, she pronounced his name as only his parents did. "You're the image of your father and I'd recognize you anywhere."

Arwen collapsed into a chair. "You know Lord and Lady Melbury?"

"Of course I do. You've often heard Benjamin and me talk about our friends Lionel and Sonia from the ashram. And their little boy Harikrishna. How are they enjoying Bali?"

"Harikrishna?" she said faintly.

So his secret was out. "That's right," Harry said. "My legal name is Harikrishna Godfrey-Granville-Compton. The Honorable Harikrishna if we're being formal. H-A-R-I for short. I'm sorry."

"And I thought I was weird being named after an elf. No wonder you go by Harry Compton, and no wonder I couldn't find you on Google. I take everything back about you hiding your identity. I wouldn't blame you if you went into the Witness Protection Program." She laughed a little hysterically. "This is bizarre."

Molly held the wedding dress against her and admired herself in the Chinese Chippendale mirror over the console table. "Why is this down here, anyway? I seem to remember that it's bad luck for the bridegroom to see the dress before the ceremony."

"Mom," Arwen said, "I know it's counter to your principles, but on the other hand you'd get to wear that for an hour or two. How would you like to pretend to marry Harry tomorrow?"

WHEN ARWEN RETURNED from her tryst with Snooper MacBracken she bypassed the house, where she could hear the rehearsal celebration in full swing in the State Rooms. By now they should be dancing in the Gold Saloon, under the wedding fresco, and spilling out on the terrace to enjoy a gorgeous night. She ought to make sure everything was running smoothly. Instead, in an unprecedented dereliction of duty, she trusted Mark to deal with any unforeseen difficulties.

The world would continue to spin on its axis, and the wedding party would manage without her supervision for a few more hours. She was going up to the gazebo. In theory she was still at work, checking out the location for the fake wedding, but she hardly even fooled herself. She had another tryst tonight, arranged by text while she fed Snooper a pack of lies.

Dazzling Lighting Designers had done a brilliant job illuminating the pathways. The light seemed natural, mysterious, and wonderfully romantic, like wandering through a production of *A Midsummer Night's Dream*. The floodlit gazebo gave the illusion of floating above the park. Mark and one of the women from Extremely Costly Florals had swathed the columns surrounding the circular structure in white cloth and wound garlands of greenery and flowers around them.

As she climbed the hill, she saw Harry framed by the arched inner door to the building. Tomorrow he would be dressed in jeans and a T-shirt—Duke Austen's usual uniform and his too—for the fake wedding. Tonight he wore black tie and made her mouth water. With a slight adjustment—tall leather boots!—she could imagine him as one of the aristocratic heroes in Jane's novels. But he also meditated and was a "half-arsed" vegetarian and had parents who went to ashrams. And they were friends with her folks.

"Good evening, darling," he said as she reached the end of the climb.

"Hi, Harry. You look gorgeous."

"I was about to say the same thing." She shrugged. She hadn't bothered to put on a good dress to meet Snooper. She wished she'd stopped to change out of her slim red skirt and white silk blouse but she'd been anxious to get here. "How did it go with MacBracken?"

"Fine, I think. We won't know for sure if he swallowed my story until tomorrow. Let's not talk about him. I'm dying of curiosity to hear about Lionel and Sonia. You'll forgive the informality, but I've heard about them over the years without a single clue that they were English and titled. My parents are weird."

His smile made her heart flutter. "I've been dying to swap parental stories. First some champagne." Among the amenities provided for Internet seekers were a series of cushioned benches and small tables under the colonnade. On one of the latter was an ice bucket holding a bottle of his favorite Krug and a couple of glasses. "And a selection of Natalie's cakes. I had to fight the hordes for these, but I thought you'd be hungry after baiting the paparazzo."

Arwen moaned. He must have noticed during the tasting which were her favorites. "The dark chocolate and cherry cake. And the strawberry one. Did anyone ever tell you that you're a hero?"

Harry handed her a fork and a glass. "While you eat I'll tell you about life with the Noble Hippies, which is what the tabloids have called them as long as I can remember."

She shook her head, realizing that a simple online search of Lord Melbury would have revealed all. Being at Brampton had broken her of the habit of googling everyone and everything and she found she liked it. It made life more ... surprising. She washed down a mouthful of strawberry cream frosting with some golden bubbles.

"They were absurd, being hippies at least a decade too late. All very well in the Sixties but so un-Thatcherite. Despite everything, you can't help liking them, though as parents they were a mixed bag. When we weren't traveling—India was only the beginning—we lived at Brampton, letting the house fall down around us. I probably wouldn't have survived their weeklong descents into the world of magic mushrooms had it not been for Nanny. My grandmother insisted they hire her and she's the only reason I'm relatively sane. That and school and university, where I learned what normal life was like."

"No wonder you weren't worried about my mother's special brownies."

"Nanny's seen it all and nothing bothers her. Mummy and Daddy have given up mind-altering substances now, in favor of extreme diet fads. Although who knows what they are up to in Bali."

"What didn't you mention any of this?"

"I didn't want to frighten off a nice, normal American girl."

Champagne trickled down her throat while joy bubbled out of her. "The irony is killing me. All my life I wanted to be *normal*, but let me tell you about life on the farm."

He listened to the description of her parents' place, asking the occasional question and laughing at her recitation of the animals, from

Ferdinand the bull, through cows, goats, and chickens, all the way to Karma the cat and Dharma the dog.

"'It sounds delightful," he said.

"You know, it sort of is," she said in wonder. "My parents are kind people, to one other and to the world. I couldn't live there now, but I had a happy childhood, once I got over my embarrassment about their marital status and being so *different*." She wiped traces of chocolate icing off the plate with her finger and licked it. "Now if only my dad would show up and put an end to my mother's nonsense about leaving him. What does she think she'll do by herself? She'll be lost." She sighed deeply and slumped against the nearest warm vertical object, which happened to be Harry. "Your place is pretty neat too."

Some understatement.

"Sometimes it seems so beautiful I think I'm in a dream," he said. She knew just what he meant; together they looked down through the fairy-tale gardens to the great house, every tall window ablaze with light.

She wasn't trashed like the night in the Gold Saloon, just pleasantly buzzed. Maybe it was the single glass of champagne talking, but she no longer felt any reticence around Harry. "Do you know something? I was conceived at that ashram. When Mom found out she was pregnant, they came home and bought the farm as a healthy place to bring up kids."

"I've known you all your life, then." He drew her close and brushed his lips over her temple. "I knew there was a reason we never felt like strangers."

"We did too. Our first couple of meetings sucked."

"I was anxious about the wedding and the Internet. But I knew. The first time I saw you, when I had to back your car down the lane."

"What?" The way he looked at her was making her dizzy.

"That you might be the one."

Her breath hitched. "You are full of shit," she said half laughing. "You were trying to look up my skirt."

"Fine-looking legs and fated meetings are not mutually exclusive. In fact they complement each other very well."

She didn't believe him but … Her mind whirled. Could it possibly be this simple? "Perhaps you are too," she whispered. "The one."

He took the glass from her hand and placed it on the table. With equal care, deliberation even, he examined her face with his hands, tracing her eyebrows and nose, the rim of her mouth. Then he gave her a soft but lingering kiss. "You're incredibly pretty." He made simple praise sound like Shakespeare. Another kiss, and another. "I could fall in love with you."

Oh God, total mush. Every bone in her body turned to liquid and they melted into each other. She was on her back on the narrow bench with his weight pressing her down and they were kissing like they'd never stop. He tasted of champagne, chocolate, and strawberries and every other good thing in the world.

She heard the buttons of her blouse give way, felt his onyx dress studs cold against her breast, his hands hot on her thighs as he tugged at her skirt. She wrenched her legs apart to gather him in and hit something with her foot. The sound of broken glass on stone penetrated her lust-crazed brain.

"There goes the champagne," Harry said in a strained voice.

"That's a two-hundred-dollar bottle."

"Don't care. But we are in full view of any passing paparazzi or guests looking out of the window."

"Ew. I don't want that creepy Snooper watching us. He's probably already staking the place out for tomorrow."

"Let's go inside."

"The house?" she said stupidly. "It's awfully far."

"My darling Elf! Have you forgotten that the gazebo has been furnished with every comfort for the use of our Web-surfing guests?"

Of course it had. A cooler filled with beers, sodas, and bottled water. A selection of snacks. And a couple of comfy sofas. Big ones.

Her shoes had fallen off. "Careful, there's broken glass," he said and scooped her into his arms and carried her into the little building. There was a lot to be said for the muscle development of oarsmen.

· · ·

H<small>E'D NEVER CARRIED</small> a woman around, like Rhett Butler striding up the stairs in *Gone With The Wind*. She wasn't a large girl, but he was damn glad he didn't have to manage a staircase. And that the sofa was close by. They collapsed onto it, breathless and laughing before falling on each other again.

Thanks to Arwen, Harry was about to live out another of his adolescent fantasies: shagging in the Mausoleum. Gazebo was a perfectly good name for it; no one was actually buried there. It was merely a temple filled with life-size white marble statues, benevolent shadowy witnesses in a room lit only by the fairy lights strung up outside.

Better than the fantasy was the woman who would fulfill it. His chest was light with tenderness even as he responded to her on a baser level. No one had ever made him harder or happier. "I'm in charge this time," she said, ruthlessly disposing of his jacket and shirt. Studs and cufflinks pinged on the marble floor.

"I have a feeling you're always in charge."

"Turnabout is fair play." He watched hungrily as she wriggled out of her clothes and enjoyed her naked perfection while she stripped off his lower garments, fishing a condom out of his pocket. "You came prepared."

"Just like a boy scout."

"Day-um, yes," she said in what he took to be a kind of comic or regional American accent, making him laugh until she straddled his hips and the friction of her rubbing against his cock sent him out of his mind.

He was taken and ridden hard, her hands gripping his shoulders. Her hips twisted and, when she found the angle that pleased her, the clenching of her muscles drove him mad with pleasure. Their flesh grew hot in the chilly temple as their bodies clashed in desperate passion. His moans and her cries echoed off the stone walls. His eyes never left her face, beautiful in its intensity as she rode herself to climax. Then they rolled over onto their sides and he drove into her until he once more felt the shudders of her orgasm before he came.

They collapsed into a sweaty tangle of limbs and he held on to her as though he'd never let her go. Because he didn't intend to.

"Bloody marvelous," he said when capable of speech.

"Damn straight."

He had to kiss her, couldn't stop himself. He'd have liked to carry on all night, but he felt the chill on his damp skin. Groping on the floor he found his trousers and shirt. Not very elegant, but she needed something to keep her warm. He arranged the garments untidily over their shoulders and moved her against the back of the sofa to protect her from the night air.

"Thanks," she said, curling into him. They lay in a contented silence she was the first to break. "It's weird being surrounded by all these statues, even though they seem quite friendly. Who are they? Gods and goddesses?"

"Some of my ancestors: former Lords Melbury and their wives in classical dress."

"So we were doing it in front of a bunch of great-grandparents. What did they think?"

"Remember, I told you my family believes in love." No response. It was the second time he'd inched toward the word, said it even, but without declaring himself. He was mad about Arwen, but he wasn't sure she wouldn't bolt if he pressed her. He felt hopeful but not over-confident.

He adjusted his position so she fit against him like the last piece of a jigsaw puzzle and idly stroked her spine and the delicious curve of her arse.

*Keep it light.* For now.

"Will you follow in the family tradition?" Her palm ran over his right pec and shoulder, kneading the muscles. He'd better find a place for some serious rowing if he was to maintain an aspect of his physique that she seemed to enjoy. "You'd look cute in a toga."

"I'm not sure I want to be carved in stone, every blemish recorded for posterity. What about you?"

"When the Kilpatricks and the Stantons want family portraits, they use a camera."

"The Comptons have also discovered modern technology." He retrieved his phone from his trouser pocket, conveniently located near her left breast. "Let's get a picture."

"You have to be kidding! Like this?"

"I promise not to share it with anyone else. Come on. It'll be fun." Half grumbling she turned in his arms, and he held the phone over them. After a few tries he had a shadowy dual portrait that she agreed was acceptable. He e-mailed it to her, thinking it would be an amusing addition to a family photograph album, an (edited) story for their grandchildren.

# CHAPTER
# NINE

After Arwen kissed the "bridegroom" and sent Harry and Molly on their procession up the hill to the gazebo, she took out her phone and smiled goofily at the selfie Harry had taken last night. She couldn't stop looking at it.

He'd mentioned love twice. Did it mean something? Did she want it to mean something? She rather thought she did.

With half her mind she dealt with complaints: from Jane's mother, who didn't understand the reason for the decoy wedding and was sure she was missing something; from one of Duke's software developers who needed to go up to the gazebo and check e-mail *immediately;* and a particularly horny couple who had become notorious for doing it *everywhere,* and just wanted to be alone, *anywhere.*

While fending off their attempts to escape the house, she mooned about Harry and wished the wedding—both weddings—were over and done with so she could think about important matters.

Up on the hill, Harry and Molly said "I do" in front of Mark, dressed in an outfit he'd found in the attic: purple silk and breeches that once belonged to Harry's great-great-uncle the Bishop of Bath and Wells. A dozen estate employees armed with shotguns rounded up

Snooper MacBracken and a few other paparazzi, who had arrived just in time for the ceremony they couldn't possibly miss. They went quietly. As predicted, they were anxious to broadcast to the world that Duke Austen had been married in jeans and Jane Sparks wore feathers and sequins by an unknown designer. Later it was speculated, in the days before *People* magazine revealed the truth, that the bride's mother had insisted on having the gown made to her specifications.

Just as Duke, in the Savile Row suit he'd ordered for the wedding, and Jane, in Monique Lhuillier, were about to say their vows, Harry joined Arwen at the back of the great tent, lavishly decorated in Jane's wedding colors.

"Well," he whispered, his arm about her waist. "Are we home yet?"

"One more minute and we'll have done it. Don't jinx it now."

THE RECEPTION WAS in full roar. People were eating, drinking, talking, and dancing in another of the Super Luxurious Persian tents, furnished to resemble a Turkish harem. Six people had asked Arwen about doing weddings for them and two had expressed interest in Brampton House as the site. A number more promised to come back for vacations.

"We're both going to be busy," Arwen said to Harry as they took to the dance floor. "Awesome job, partner."

"I wish you were," he said, his English tones for once entirely serious. "My partner. It won't be the same running an event here without you."

She fixed her eyes on his neck, tanned against a crisp shirt of palest blue that brought out the color of his eyes. "I have a business in New York," she said, trying to think practical thoughts when his hands, loosely guiding her hips, sent her brain to the bedroom.

"From what you told me, Valerie seems to have it under control. How about opening an overseas branch of Luxe Events?"

"I suppose I could commute back and forth between New York and London." His palm moved around to her ass. "I can't concentrate when you're feeling me up like that."

"Great news." He did it some more. "You could have an office in the family wing here. We'll have excellent Internet, I promise. I cannot tell you how impressive the Wi-Fi is when it's working."

She looked up and his smile made her even more dizzy. "The size of your bandwidth tempts me."

"Is that all?"

No, that wasn't all. They danced on, to a song she didn't recognize, while she considered the madness of a trans-Atlantic life change because of a man she'd known for little more than a month. But cool logic was crowded out by the joy of Harry's presence and a lead weight in her chest at the thought of being without him. Sure, she could handle her stressful life without his calm support, but she didn't want to. Beneath his gaze, heated and a little bit anxious, she felt her heart become light as a feather.

Taking a deep breath and about to make the big commitment, her damned wedding planner's brain was distracted by the bride in her white dress. It struck her as odd, for Jane had changed into something slinkier for dancing. The couple whirling by were Molly, still in the hideous decoy gown in which she managed to look rather beautiful, and a man with a pony tail and a neat graying beard wearing a bolo tie: her father, Benjamin.

Thank God.

"Arwen!" Molly called. "Hari! Look who finally showed up."

The four of them stopped for introductions. "Do I take it you've forgiven Dad for having the nerve to want to marry you?"

"Better yet," she cried. "I've accepted him. If I'd known weddings were so much fun I'd have had one years ago."

"Congratulations!" Choking up a little, she hugged them both. Harry kissed Molly and slapped Benjamin on the back.

"I'm doing the wedding," Arwen said. "What do you want? Something in a field at home with all the animals wearing color-coordinated ribbons?"

"Oh no, honey. We thought we'd do it up properly and hold it at Brampton."

"Excellent idea," Harry said. "I'll give you the family rate. I expect Lionel and Sonia will want to come from Bali."

"Wow," Arwen said, when she and Harry were dancing again. "I didn't expect that."

"Our first booking. You definitely need that office." He drew her closer so she could feel his heartbeat against her chest.

Threading her fingers through his thick dark hair she drew his head down for a kiss. "That's not all I need," she said.

# ABOUT THE AUTHOR

Miranda Neville grew up in England, loving the books of Georgette Heyer and other Regency romances. She now lives in Vermont. Her historical romances published by Avon include the popular Burgundy Club series, about Regency book collectors, and The Wild Quartet. She contributed to the anthologies *At the Duke's Wedding* and *Christmas in the Duke's Arms*. *The Best Laid Planner*, which allowed her to use her lifelong knowledge of English roads, pubs, and kitchen appliances, is her first contemporary romance. She always has the most fun working with The Lady Authors.

**f**

# ALSO BY MIRANDA NEVILLE

### The Wild Quartet

The Second Seduction of a Lady (novella)

The Importance of Being Wicked

The Ruin of a Rogue

Lady Windermere's Lover

The Duke of Dark Desires

### The Burgundy Club

The Wild Marquis

The Dangerous Viscount

The Amorous Education of Celia Seaton

Confessions from an Arranged Marriage

### Other Novels

Never Resist Temptation

Secrets of a Soprano

### Novellas and Collections

Lords for All Seasons: A collection of Novellas

*P.S. I Love You* in At the Duke's Wedding

The Best Laid Planner in At the Summer Wedding

# WILL YOU BE MY WI-FI?
CAROLINE LINDEN

# CHAPTER
## ONE

*Duke Austen and Jane Sparks request the honor of your company at
their wedding on August 26th. Please join the happy couple for a week
of festivities and celebration …*

Archer Quinn turned over the expensive invitation. It was a
quarter-inch thick and gold-edged, but it didn't list a location. "That's weird," he muttered.

His secretary Denise looked up. "Something wrong, Mr. Quinn?"

"One of my clients is getting married." He looked around for the
envelope. "But I have no idea where." He tapped open the envelope
and let the enclosed cards fall into his hand. One was the RSVP card
with the dates of the event, which noted in small type that the
wedding was being held in England, but precise directions would be
disclosed only upon receipt of a guest's acceptance, for privacy
reasons. "I knew he was getting married, but I didn't expect to be
invited."

"Who is it?"

"Duke Austen."

Her eyebrows went up. "That will be quite an event. Are you going?"

Archer smiled halfheartedly. A week of festivities, the invitation said; he couldn't fathom taking off that much time just to attend a wedding, not even a client's wedding.

On the other hand, Duke Austen was no ordinary client. His company, Project-TK Industries, had gone public last year to the tune of nearly twenty billion. Austen was the It Guy of Silicon Valley at the moment, riding high on a wave of genius, ballsiness, and tabloid fascination. Archer had met him in a hotel bar a few months ago and spent the evening reminiscing about epic gaming sessions battling the Covenant as Master Chief in *Halo,* only to get a call two days later asking him to represent Project-TK. It was a lawyer's wet dream come true, particularly a freshly minted partner looking to make a splash at his new firm. Archer had talked through the engagement terms with Project-TK's company counsel, hung up the phone, and almost punched a hole in his office wall from elation. And when he told Jack Harper, the managing partner, Jack took him out for a drink. "I knew we made the right call hiring you away from San Francisco," his new boss had declared, beaming over his third glass of scotch. "Damned right!"

Still, a week in England didn't fit his current workload. "I don't think I can," he said, answering Denise's question. "Too much going on here." He was up to his eyeballs in work on a start-up called Brightball which, if all went well, would follow in Project-TK's very profitable footsteps. If all went badly because Archer vanished for a week ... he'd have plenty of time for vacation when Jack kicked his ass out.

"Of course. Still ..." Denise hesitated, then leaned forward. "It will be very romantic, I'm sure. He fell in love with a novelist and she wrote her books inspired by their love affair."

Archer gave her a wary, sideways glance. "What?" Romantic love affairs were not what came to mind when he thought about Austen. Obviously the man must have some moves, if he was getting married, but he was also rich, and in Archer's experience money made a lot of women blind to personality defects.

"Didn't you know?" Denise suddenly looked like an eager teenager who'd just discovered her favorite band was coming to town. "It was in all the papers. And the bride's novels are just lovely. Now you're invited to her wedding." There was definitely some envy in her voice.

"Right." Thank God; Denise's phone rang, and Archer escaped into his office. He forgot all about Austen's wedding until the next morning, when he sat down at his desk and beheld a brightly colored paperback in the middle of his blotter. *The Wicked Wallflower*, it read in curling letters, above the image of a woman in a long gown tearing the shirt off a man who lived at the gym, judging from his muscle definition. It took Archer a moment to puzzle out why such a book was on his desk. He took it to the secretarial bay.

"Um, Denise?" he began, leaning over the side of her station and holding it up in question.

She blushed, which was very atypical for her. Denise was usually unflappable. "Yes, it's mine. I know you haven't quite decided to go yet, but I thought just in case—"

"That's very"—What? he wondered. Unexpected? Strange? Somewhat disturbing?—"thoughtful, but I don't have much time to read …"

Her blush grew redder. Even the tips of her ears were pink. "Oh, well—I think it's a marvelous story and I bet you would enjoy it if you read it, but really I was hoping … if you did decide to go to the wedding … that you might ask her to sign it. The bride is the author and I would love to have it autographed."

Archer cleared his throat, hoping he wasn't blushing too. "Right. I just—right. Sorry." Now he was stuck. He imagined himself approaching the bride—a woman he had never met—and asking her to sign this book. Not for him, but for his secretary. Yeah, everyone would believe that. He caught another glimpse of the cover guy's sculpted abs, and resolved to work out more often. "If I go, I will definitely have her sign it for you."

The smile on her face made him feel guilty that he'd all but decided to decline. "That would be simply wonderful, Mr. Quinn."

"Call me Archer," he reminded her and went back to work.

But he still hadn't sent the RSVP two days later when his phone rang and Duke Austen himself was on the other end. After twenty minutes of rapid-fire questions about business, Austen suddenly asked, "Did you get the wedding invitation?"

"Yep." Archer reached for his bag and rummaged inside for the thick envelope. "Congratulations to you both. Where is it?"

"England. Jane wanted to have it in a real Regency mansion," said Austen, without a lick of concern for any inconvenience it might cause his guests to have the wedding three thousand miles from home. "We had to make a last-minute change after there was a fire at the original venue. We're keeping it low-key because I want privacy. We've got this whole place for the week—sorry, Jane calls it a sennight—so come whenever you want."

"Ah," began Archer, caught off guard. "I was checking my calendar—"

"It's not for a few weeks," said Duke as if that solved every problem. "Call my assistant and she'll book everything for you. I know you're a busy guy and Jane's got a whole system set up."

"Right," said Archer, digging out the RSVP card and trying to phrase his very polite, appreciative, but negative reply. "I'm not sure—"

"It'll be a good time. And we can discuss some new ideas without people breathing down my neck. Going public has some serious baggage."

Archer made a noise of quiet agreement. Public company governance was probably cramping Duke's freewheeling, agile business style, but that was the cost of taking other people's money.

"So I'll see you there," said his client almost absently. In the background was the furious clicking of a keyboard, as if he was already at work on his next killer app. "Good talking to you, Archer."

"And to you," said Archer as the dial tone echoed in his ear. He hung his head and pulled off the earpiece with one hand. His other hand still held the pen, poised over the "Is unable to attend" box of the RSVP card. The wedding was in less than a month, and now Duke expected him to be there. He went looking for Jack Harper.

"Of course you should go," was Jack's pronouncement.

"For a week? Brightball is getting desperate for funding." A start-up like Brightball needed venture capital to grow; they needed lawyers to make sure they didn't give away the store in exchange for that capital.

Jack waved it away. "And Project-TK will be a few million dollars in billing this year alone. You could find three more Brightballs at the wedding reception."

"So you're okay with it?"

"Go," exclaimed Jack. "I can handle Brightball; it's my client, after all. Go schmooze the hell out of Austen's friends."

And that was that. On the way back to his office, Archer walked by Denise's station. "I'm going to get your book signed for you," he told her.

She brightened. "Oh, thank you! And just think—you'll get to see the wedding of the year."

"Can't wait," he replied as he went back to work, and tried not to think about the wedding of the year.

THREE WEEKS and two days later, Archer remembered all his hesitations and then some. Too busy to leave? Check; he spent all six hours of the overnight flight working. Too remote an acquaintance to justify being there? Check; Denise had followed reports about the wedding in the major tabloids, and breathlessly related all the juicy gossip. People Archer had never heard of—and worse, people he *had* heard of—were rumored to be on the guest list. A-list movie stars, top tech gurus, big names in finance and politics, even a few minor royals ... He was sorry he'd agreed to go even before he had to pack. And that was all before he got off the train in the tiny town of Melbury, England, where a hired car was waiting to take him to the hotel ... which appeared to be in the middle of Sherwood Forest.

"Are we almost there?" he asked, not so much because he was anxious to arrive but because he was starting to hope the driver had made a mistake or a wrong turn. All he could see now were trees and hedges. Did utilities even run this far into the wilderness? Duke Austen had said he wanted privacy, but this was ridiculous.

"Yes, nearly," shouted the man back, grinding his gears as the car lurched to one side. The narrow road was one sharp, blind turn after another and Archer had long since taken hold of the strap above the door. "Just another mile."

Holy crap. Another mile of this. He leaned down to peer out the window. More trees. More hedges. Very rustic—and utterly unlike any place he would have guessed likely to host the wedding of a brand new tech billionaire. Why didn't the bride want a Caribbean wedding on the beach? Why couldn't her wedding planner have talked her into a private cruise in the Mediterranean, or a week in Fiji? If money was no object, why would any bride choose to have her big day in a place that made the moon look accessible?

Denise had told him all about the bride's novels, most of which he didn't remember. But he had retained two bits of information, both of which were assuming the aspect of bad omens: the bride wrote historical romance novels, set in stately old mansions, and she was rumored to be planning a wedding that would have made Jane Austen die of envy. He devoutly hoped this wasn't going to be a nineteenth-century wedding in more ways than one.

After another several minutes of being thrown from side to side along what passed for a road, the driver pointed. "There, you see it? Brampton House."

Archer exhaled quietly. It was indeed a sprawling mansion, right out of a PBS Masterpiece movie. The grounds looked nice, and one could only see a few construction vehicles off to the side. But his suspicious eyes noted the absence of utility wires, and when he dared a quick look at his phone, it showed a grimmer sight: zero bars of cellular service.

The driver pulled right up to the impressive flight of stone steps and leapt out to unload the luggage. Archer pressed a nice tip into his hand and took one of the man's cards. Who knew when he might need an escape vehicle?

The wide oak doors at the top of the stairs stood open. As the driver set the last of his luggage on the graveled drive, a man in an expensive suit came out to meet him. He had the broad cheekbones and impeccable grooming of a male model. "Welcome to Brampton House. I am Mark Delancey, the manager."

"Nice to meet you." Archer put out his hand automatically. "Archer Quinn."

The fellow shook his hand. "May I show you to your room? Mr. Harry Compton, who owns Brampton House, extends you a warm welcome on behalf of Mr. Austen and Miss Sparks." Behind his back two younger men, also clad in well-tailored suits, were collecting the luggage and carrying it inside. Unconsciously Archer straightened his shoulders and wondered if he'd be the scruffiest man at this wedding, even including the hotel staff.

He took the opportunity to scope out the house as he followed Mr. Delancey inside. Just as fancy on the inside as it was on the outside, with sleek marble floors and intricately carved woodwork around every doorway. The ceiling above put him in mind of a room in Buckingham Palace, which he'd seen on a tour a few years back. The stairs were wide and graceful, with a rich red runner up the middle and an ornate brass railing. They climbed two flights, then turned down a long corridor with doors on one side and tall narrow windows on the other.

"The property is still undergoing a bit of renovation," said the manager as he unlocked—with a real key, not a card key—a door almost at the corner. "A few rooms aren't quite ready, and Mr. Compton suggests you avoid them for your convenience. The library is the main one still in disarray, but if you find a door barred here or there, please don't be alarmed. The builders will do their utmost to keep noise and dust to a minimum so you can enjoy your stay with us."

"I'm sure it will be fine." Archer went into the room at the manager's silent invitation, and slung his laptop bag onto the desk chair. The room wasn't a typical hotel room, but only for the better. The windows were the same tall, narrow ones as in the corridor, and the room was flooded with light. The desk was wide and the bed looked comfortable. He walked to the window and looked out on rolling hills, stately oaks, and part of a garden. It was beautiful and peaceful and screamed of money. Even way out in the country, this much land—and a house this old and tastefully renovated—must cost a fortune.

The porters brought in his luggage and arranged it neatly and quickly on luggage stands, then left. Archer turned around to find the manager still waiting by the door. "Have many other wedding guests arrived?"

"Only a few, Mr. Quinn, but that will soon change. Mr. Austen has reserved the entire house for the wedding party, and we're expecting every room to be taken." He smiled again. The man looked like he could be on a magazine cover, or maybe on one of the bride's novel covers. "If you require anything at all, simply ask."

"I will. Thanks very much."

Mr. Delancey bowed his head and left. Archer exhaled and pulled out his phone, hoping its mute state was pure coincidence. Normally it buzzed with incoming messages or e-mail every minute or two, and it had been suspiciously silent since he left the train station. It was midafternoon now, which meant morning back at the firm's offices in Boston. He began every day with dozens of messages and e-mails, and only got more every hour, so he wasn't much surprised to see that the phone still had no signal. He dropped it on the bed and unpacked his bags, shaking his head as he hung his suits in the old-fashioned wardrobe in place of a closet.

The computer bag sat like an unexploded bomb on the desk. Archer considered ignoring it and stretching his legs with a walk through the garden, then reluctantly unzipped the bag and took out his laptop. Just a quick skim through messages, he told himself. As long as nothing was going horribly wrong with any clients, he would be justified in taking a day off. He'd left one of the firm's best associates, Elle Williams, in charge of most of his current matters while he was gone, but he still felt the need to check over her shoulder.

He found the Internet cable and the handsomely printed card with instructions for connecting, but when he plugged in, nothing came up. The indicator just blinked. He double-checked all the connections, undid them and reconnected, and still got nothing.

"Perfect place for an Internet billionaire's wedding," he said under

WILL YOU BE MY WI-FI?

his breath before snatching the key and heading off to find the manager.

He went back down the stairs and located the main desk, tastefully and discreetly tucked at the back of the wide airy hall. "I can't seem to get the Internet working in my room," he told the same suave gentleman who had shown him in.

"Ah yes." Mr. Delancey assumed a face one might wear at a state funeral. "I'm afraid we're having a technical problem with the cabling, sir."

Archer's bad feeling returned, worse than ever. "Have you tried rebooting the modem?"

"British Telecom will be arriving within a few days to repair it. I assure you we're working as hard as we can to restore service."

"Restore? You mean there's *no Internet?*" He'd been right: it was going to be a nineteenth-century wedding all the way.

"I'm afraid not, at the moment."

Archer just stood there. The concept of no Internet access left him speechless. Not at the moment? For how long, then—hours? Days? The whole week?

The manager was still talking. "I do apologize. Mr. Compton deeply regrets the inconvenience. If you require connectivity urgently, several shops and restaurants in town offer wireless, and of course one can purchase a mobile access plan—"

"I'd do that, but there seems to be a distinct lack of cell signal here."

The man's polished calm didn't waver in the face of Archer's dry tone. "Yes, unfortunately the house isn't in line with the nearest towers. We're down in a valley and I'm afraid there's not much I can do. However, there are spots on the grounds with better reception. If you don't mind a bit of a walk, the top of the hill directly behind the garden offers excellent reception. I've gone up there myself to test it."

Archer sighed. "The top of the hill?" It was one thing to contemplate taking a walk to see some of the famous English landscape, and another to face a hike up a hill in order to check his e-mail. He began to feel the sleepless flight and jet lag weighing on him.

"Yes, sir, it is a lovely walk." Mr. Delancey walked out from behind the counter and toward the back of the hall. Another pair of wide

115

wooden doors stood open there, framing a postcard-perfect vista of green hills and graveled paths into a lush garden. "Follow the path to the left—I find it offers the best reception, and there is a very handsome and comfortable gazebo if you care to sit and take in the view."

Archer summoned a grim smile. "Thanks."

Phone in hand, he headed out. Wedding of the year. Yeah, right.

# CHAPTER
## TWO

Natalie Corcoran stood in the open doorway of her borrowed cottage and watched yet another convoy of trucks roar and choke their way up the hill. That made eight today; yesterday it had been ten, one or two at a time, all straining and grinding their gears as they went up the road that led past the house. She caught a loud exclamation that could only be a curse word in some foreign language as the low-hanging branches scraped the top of one van. Saying a few bad words of her own, she snapped a photo of the traffic with her phone and texted it to her friend Pippa with the caption *Eighth one today!* She went inside and closed the door, not that it blocked the noise, and made a mental tally of all the lies her former college roommate and erstwhile friend had told her two months ago about this house.

First lie: that the cottage was quiet and isolated.

"It's in this little town in the country called Melbury," Pippa had said. "Actually not even in the town, it's at least a mile or two from it. You'll love it. Amaryllis goes there when she's on a creative binge and doesn't want to speak to anyone for weeks at a time." Amaryllis was Pippa's stepmother, moderately famous for her blown glass artwork and infamous in the British tabloids for her affairs with young footballers. Currently Amaryllis was in Albufeira, according to Pippa, soaking up sun and searching for inspiration.

"But I'm going to need access to a high quality market," Natalie had reminded her. "I'm writing a cookbook." Supposed to be, at any rate. Privately, she wasn't sure anyone would want a cookbook by her, but she had needed a face-saving reason for her sudden and abrupt absence from her family's restaurant. She could hardly tell her parents that she might kill her brother, or he might kill her, if she stayed; writing a cookbook had seemed like a brilliant excuse. Her mother, a chef, was delighted. Her father, a restaurateur recovering from a stroke, approved. And her brother Paul would just be happy she was out of his way so he could continue trying to ruin everything that made her parents' pride and joy special—or, as he called it, expanding their brand.

"There's a local market right in town," Pippa promised. "Just walk down and get as many organic eggs and as much fresh bacon as you need."

"Will it be filled with tourists?" Not that she had anything against tourists, but she was feeling a little antisocial and wanted peace. "Are there going to be people snapping pictures of the house from the road?"

Phillipa snorted. "No one ever finds that cottage. Melbury is perfectly ordinary, and it's not close to anything especially historical or scenic. Honestly, I thought I would die of boredom when I crashed with Amaryllis for a few weeks. It's the house that time forgot."

"Whoa. I need a real kitchen, Pip." Natalie had wondered if Pippa even knew what a real kitchen looked like. She'd certainly never needed to know; Pippa's father had made a fortune in banking before driving his Ferrari into a brick wall. In college, Pippa was infamous for almost burning down their apartment building by microwaving soup that was still in the can. Natalie would have bet good money she had never cooked anything in her life.

"Of course it's got a kitchen. Amaryllis thinks she can cook, so she put in everything state-of-the-art." There was a pause. "I'm sure it all works."

In fairness, Natalie had to admit Pippa had been right about the kitchen. Everything was absolutely up to date—although she was still puzzling out the idiosyncrasies of the massive AGA cooker—and it all worked splendidly. The icing on the cake was the walk-in wine cooler, which was mostly empty of wine at the moment and therefore a perfect giant refrigerator. Judging solely on the merits of the kitchen, Primrose Cottage was ideal.

But the second lie: no one would bother her.

"It's honestly in the middle of nowhere," Pippa had assured her. "There aren't even neighbors. The only house within two miles is an old manor house, and I think it's been condemned. No one lives there, the owners have moved to Bali. You can cook eighteen hours a day and never see a soul unless you go into town."

That had tipped her over the brink. Natalie was not by nature a remote or shy person, but the last year had left some serious scars on her psyche. A year ago, everything had been great. Her parents had still been in charge of the family restaurant, Cuisine du Jude, her mother in the kitchen and her father in the front of the house. Natalie loved Cuisine du Jude, or just the Jude, as they called it. She'd grown up there, folding napkins when she was a kid, manning the soda fountain and busing tables when she was a teenager, then helping out in the kitchen during college under her mother's expert instruction.

Judith Corcoran had been born to cook. There was no other explanation for her deft touch with flavors and textures, her eye for a beautifully arranged plate, her attention to the smallest influence on her diner's happiness. Tom, Natalie's dad, said he was the only struggling student who gained weight while putting himself through college on a shoestring budget, because his wife could make a four-star dinner out of a buck and a half's worth of ingredients. A few years after he finished his degree in business, he'd borrowed money from every family member with a hundred dollars to spare and opened a tiny, hole-in-the-wall restaurant. Judy cooked, Tom bused and managed. Soon they moved to a bigger spot, then to a nicer one with a patio on the river, and there they'd stayed, successful but more a local gem than anything, until three years ago when a renowned restaurant critic, in town for her son's college graduation, ate at the Jude. A month later her raving review appeared in the *New York Times,* calling the Jude "the most perfect date night restaurant in the world." The national morning TV shows called. Oprah visited. Judy Corcoran was invited on cooking shows left and right. And every table in the restaurant was booked up for eight months in advance.

Then it all went to pieces.

Tom had a stroke—thankfully not a debilitating one, but bad enough to shake everything up. The doctors decreed he should not work for at least six months; Judy declared she was taking a sabbatical to care for him and oversee his rehab. Natalie, who had been cooking alongside her mother since she was six, would take over the kitchen, and Paul, who had followed their father into the business side, would run the front of the house. That was fine with Natalie. The Jude had been her life, and she wanted to stay there forever, keeping up her parents' tradition. If only Paul hadn't gotten stars in his eyes from all the national press fawning over the Jude. All on his own, he decided that one location was not enough; they needed two or three or eight. And he'd gone and hired an architect to start planning these new locations.

The fight, when Natalie found out, was epic. Worse than when they were kids. Only this one hadn't ended with a spanking or being grounded. Their mother had intervened, white-faced and furious. "Stop it," she told them both. "You are too old for this. You owe your father better. Paul, there will be no expansion without your father's approval, and he's too weak to give it. If you ask him about it, I will disinherit you now," she said as he'd opened his mouth to argue. "Natalie, things cannot stay the same forever and ever." She'd looked between the two of them in the deeply disappointed way only a mother could manage. "You're not to speak to each other for two weeks. Cool down and act like rational adults."

"What about the Jude?" Natalie had protested. "We can't run the restaurant without speaking."

"Mick can mediate," said her mother, naming the Jude's sous chef.

Natalie tried, but within a week realized it wouldn't work. It turned out she and her brother were totally capable of communicating without speaking a word, and most of their exchanged glances could be translated as *you are such an idiot*. The day Paul had the nerve to have his architect out to the restaurant for lunch, Natalie lost it and dumped a bowl of soup on her brother. Paul called her crazy. Natalie called him a lying snake. Mick called their mother.

Writing a cookbook had been the only straw Natalie could grasp to save face. Banished from the Jude, she had to get away, as far away as possible, from her brother's subtle gloating. He wasn't getting his way just yet, but she'd blown her cred as the sane, sensible child and they both knew it. Thank God for Pippa, who had volunteered this cottage—a cooking paradise far enough removed from Massachusetts that she wouldn't be able to embarrass herself again. Even if Pippa had warned her it was next to a construction zone, she would have gone, but she'd gotten used to the relative quiet. The last week or so had made her feel like she was living in the middle of a highway.

Her phone buzzed. "Bloody hell," cried Pippa. Dance music throbbed behind her voice. "What the hell is going on?"

"Beats me, but it's big." She checked the clock. "Are you at a club at three in the afternoon?"

"But no one lives there! We used to traipse over the hill to have smokes when we were kids because it was deserted." A high-pitched laugh shrilled in the background. "Hang on, let me see if Amaryllis knows." The line went dead.

Natalie stayed where she was. After extensive trial and error and a great deal of cursing, she had mapped the irregular spots of cell coverage on the property. This spot right inside the kitchen door offered up to three bars, which was excellent by local standards. Near the window in the front bedroom upstairs one could usually get two bars, and the back bath sometimes got two. Pippa had warned her that she'd have to walk up the hill to get a steady three bars, or even four if the gods were feeling kind, but that was too much trouble. Natalie just left her phone in one of the more likely locations with the ringer turned up. Not that she wanted people to call her, as she was supposed to be a hermit these two months, but her mother would freak out if she didn't answer.

A few minutes later the phone went off again. "Oh my God. I swear I had no idea—Amaryllis says the Melburys decided to renovate the house and turn it into a hotel or some such." Pippa sounded mournful. "I am so sorry."

"Is it open?"

"I have no idea! Amaryllis said they have a website now. Hang on a mo."

Something butted Natalie's elbow. Oliver, the resident cat, pushed his round head under her arm, demanding a good pet. She scratched his ears, careful not to step out of the tiny bubble of cell reception.

"Sorry," said Pippa breathlessly. The noise behind her waned a bit. "Just ran into the coatroom. The house is called Brampton House. Google it, maybe you can find out what's going on. Although honestly, the last time I saw that house it looked like the roof would fall in, so I can't imagine how much work it needs."

That would explain the many vans and trucks struggling up the road. Natalie let her head fall back and stuck out her tongue at the ceiling. Just her luck. Oliver meowed again and jumped down. He padded to the door and began circling expectantly, so she went to let him out. She wasn't entirely sure Oliver belonged to Primrose Cottage, but there was a bag of cat food in the pantry. Because Paul was allergic, the Corcorans had never had a pet growing up, and Natalie found she rather liked it. Oliver was the perfect male: soft and furry, easy to feed, and he purred like a vibrator when someone scratched under his chin.

"So much for peace and quiet," she said to Pippa. "Well. The hotel is a good mile away or more. If it needs that much work, it can't be open yet, so I only have to suffer the traffic ..." She threw open the door and Oliver bounded out, only to draw up short and hiss. Natalie stared in furious disbelief. "You've got to be kidding me."

"What?" Pippa demanded. "What did you say?"

"Just tell me where the hose is," Natalie replied grimly. "There are two people—probably guests at the so-called hotel—having sex on your stepmother's patio."

# CHAPTER
# THREE

I t was a fifteen-minute walk to the gazebo, which did command a magnificent view as Mr. Delancey had promised. Unfortunately, the manager must have sent every other guest up the hill as well; three other people were already there when Archer reached it. A tall young man in a yellow hoodie was pacing in circles around the gazebo, talking computer code into his phone. A dark-haired girl was sprawled on one of the cushioned benches in the gazebo with her phone pressed to one ear, while an older woman was giving orders for dress alterations between hungry draws on a cigarette.

Archer walked upwind and pulled out his phone. To his relief it found signal and began downloading e-mail, though at a snail's pace. The programmer circled him—"You're killing the CPU by doing it that way ..."—and the older woman lit a new cigarette—"I don't want it down to my ruddy ankles, I'm not some crusty old dowager!"—while the girl began filing her nails—"I can't believe we have this whole place for a week! It's, like, really old and shit ..."

He hit two-dozen messages and walked a few steps away, trying not to overhear. Ten more messages, when there were probably two hundred waiting to download. He scrolled through, deleting most of the e-mail as banal or unimportant, but they were all from the previous night. One by one, ten more appeared on the screen. The programmer came around again, this time agitated and waving one hand—"I don't want it to call the server that often, it will crash the whole app!"—the older woman had moved on from the length of her dress to worse—"I want some beading. What do you think? Would beading around the neckline make me look jowly?"—and the younger woman fished out a beer from a cooler beneath her bench—"Check it out! I think I can see Windsor Castle from here! Do you want me to send you a picture?"

Archer eyed the signal indicator. Three bars, flickering up to four from time to time. He drifted a little farther down the far side of the hill. If Brampton House was in a valley, shielded from cell service by that hill, then there ought to be cell service many places on the other side of the hill, not just at the top. The signal held and he walked on, watching the messages slowly accumulate. The ground flattened out into a broad gentle slope of lawn. He was almost at the bottom of the hill, but he could still hear the older woman going on about her dress: "It has to match the shoes! Don't do the damn beading if it won't match the shoes!" He kept walking.

There was a line of trees, with a thin trail leading through and beyond it. Still scrolling through messages, Archer absently followed it. A muffled noise caught his attention, and then another. He looked up, and did a double take. Just behind the trees, a guy was lying on his back in the grass, with a girl grinding on top of him. She was clothed—barely—but her skirt hid any proof of actual intercourse. Whatever was going on under her skirt, both of them were obviously enjoying themselves a great deal. Archer averted his eyes and went the other way.

It was blessedly quiet out here and the air was crisp and fresh. For the first time he started to see why Jane Sparks had liked the place enough to drag her friends and family across an ocean. It was remote, sure, but that also meant privacy. Just last week Duke and Jane had struck a deal with a major magazine for exclusive wedding photos in exchange for a generous donation to Jane's favorite charity, and having it in the middle of nowhere would make it harder for the paparazzi to find them. Archer made a mental note to keep an eye out for anyone suspicious; it would certainly be easy for someone to sneak through the woods and angle a telephoto lens on Brampton House.

And then, out of nowhere, an alert popped onto his screen, asking if he wanted to join a Wi-Fi network. Archer stopped in his tracks. He tapped an app on his phone, and realized the Wi-Fi signal was nice and strong. It was also, unfortunately, password protected.

He deliberated. It was probably unneighborly to steal someone's Wi-Fi, but he had no idea where the neighbor actually was. It wasn't even his neighbor. He tried a few common passwords, none of which worked. Well, if he couldn't stealthily join the network, maybe he could talk his way in.

The track curved and wound through a meadow, where the grass was taller. A tall hedge ran along the side, and he realized it screened the road to Brampton House. So this was what lay on the other side of all those trees. Now that he wasn't risking life and limb along the twisting road, Archer could acknowledge that it was picturesque. Still very remote and primitive for a techie wedding, but beautiful.

Around a bend in the path he found the source of the Wi-Fi signal. A house of gray stone sat in the middle of a garden, with a small patio facing him. And—he actually stopped walking and took a deep breath —the most heavenly smell drifted from the open windows.

Led by his nose, he walked right up to the edge of the patio. It smelled of chocolate and coffee, and made him realize he hadn't eaten lunch, nor anything else today other than a wholly inadequate roll from an airport kiosk, washed down with a bottle of warm water. Oh God, what he wouldn't give for a good cup of coffee right now, and if it came with a slice of chocolate cake—

The door opened with a bang, and a woman stalked out toward him. A very attractive woman, with light brown curls bouncing around her head and a mesmerizing sway to her hips. Archer started to smile, but it fell off his face as she drew near. "Whoa!"

"This is private property," she said acidly in an unmistakably American accent.

"I'm sorry, I didn't know." He took a step backward and kept his eyes on the large meat cleaver she was pointing at him. "There's no sign marking the boundary of the hotel grounds."

She seemed to bristle. "You're staying at the hotel?"

"Yes," he said warily. Her tone indicated that was not a mark in his favor.

"What the hell is going on up there?" She waved her free hand at the road. "A dozen trucks a day go up and down that road."

"Just a wedding." He kept his voice calm and unthreatening. She was holding the cleaver like she knew how to use it.

"A wedding. It's not even supposed to be open!" She shook her head, and curls spilled over her face. She swiped them back, and shaded her eyes to peer up the hill. Unthinkingly Archer gave her another quick once-over. A long white apron hid most of her, but her fitted shirt showed off a nice pair of breasts. On her feet she wore clogs, but her legs to the knee were bare. Cleaver aside, she was damn fine.

"Could you please tell everyone else at the hotel that this house, and this garden, are not part of the hotel grounds? If I find one more jackass out here—"

"I don't recommend you cleaver them, even if they trespass," he said when she pursed her lips in disgruntlement.

"What?" She stared up at him. He'd thought her eyes were brown, but now he saw they were more hazel, with gold and green sparks and only brown around the edges.

"The ..." He motioned with one hand, still upraised in the universal gesture of surrender. "The meat cleaver. I don't think English law would pardon the use of a cleaver even on a very rude trespasser."

"Oh." She looked at it, and her face eased. All the hard lines of fury disappeared, and the look she gave him was almost sheepish. "Sorry about that. I was chopping up a chicken for pot pie when I saw you."

"And here I thought I smelled chocolate and coffee," he said. "It must be the English countryside."

She laughed—just for a moment, but enough to make his breath catch. When she smiled, she was gorgeous. "No, it's coffee and chocolate now. Chicken later, if Oliver doesn't eat it." Her eyes grew round. "Oh my God, if that cat eats my chicken—"

"That cat?" By a lucky stroke, he'd caught sight of a big gray cat napping in the sun at the edge of the patio. When the woman whirled around to see where he pointed, then exhaled in relief, Archer felt an irrational burst of relief himself. Oliver was a cat, not a guy. He wanted her to stay and keep talking to him. Preferably without the cleaver raised in his direction.

"Yes, *that* cat. He likes to help himself ..." Her voice tapered off and she stood a little straighter. The smile disappeared from her face. "I'm sorry it looked like I was going to chop off your head. People from the hotel have been wandering down here and making themselves at home."

"There's no cell service there. The manager is telling everyone to go to the top of the hill, and it's gotten a bit crowded. I was just in search of peace and quiet." He showed her his phone as if it would prove his innocent intentions.

Her lips quirked. "And the couple having sex on the lounger awhile ago? I didn't see any phones, but maybe they'd left them in their clothes."

"You're kidding." She gave him a dour look, and he choked back a laugh. Apparently the horny couple had retreated to the woods only after being chased off the patio. "Okay, I have no reply to that. But I swear I was just trying to check my e-mail." He decided to take a gamble. "In fact, I noticed you're broadcasting a nice, strong Wi-Fi signal. Is there any chance you'd be willing to let me borrow your network ...?"

"No." She turned and headed back toward the house.

Archer scrambled after her, shoving his phone into his pocket. "The entire hotel has no Internet service; technical issues with the cables or something. I brought a lot of work with me that I just have to get done. There's a woman on top of the hill right now, shouting into her phone about beads on her dress, and whether they'll make her look jowly or not."

"Too bad," she said without turning her head. "Not my problem."

"Of course not, but I'm not asking to impose on you. I can work out of sight. I'll pay your Internet bill for the month," he added in desperation.

She had reached the door of the house. This close to the windows, the scent of coffee and chocolate was intoxicating, and overwhelming.

He felt like a junkie, shaking and salivating at the prospect of a fix. And his phone was still laboring to download messages at the slow, slow speed of British rural data networks. But the woman stopped on the step, barring the door, and crossed her arms in an unmistakable refusal. "No. I don't know you, I don't know who you are, but the answer is no. First it's just you, then half the hotel guests will be here. I do not need anyone hanging out around the patio, for Wi-Fi or after-noon sex or anything else."

"Uh." He blinked, distracted by the way she said "afternoon sex" with a tart lilt that made him wonder how opposed she really was to the idea. He was lightheaded from hunger and the tantalizing smell of chocolate, but mentioning afternoon sex was really unfair on her part. Now he had to think about it. And the way she folded her arms plumped up her breasts even more. "Right. But I swear to God I won't tell a soul where I'm getting Internet access. I don't know ninety-nine percent of them anyway."

Her brows went up in disbelief. "Really? Then why are you here?" She went inside and closed the door.

Archer jumped to the open window. "For work," he called in.

"Go away," she called back.

"Please?" he tried once more.

She gave him a glare, and slammed the cleaver down through a piece of chicken. "No!"

Archer put up his hands again and backed off. "Got it. Sorry to bother you. Good luck with the chicken."

But the smell of chocolate, and the image of her well-shaped ass striding away from him, stayed in his mind during the long walk back to Brampton House.

# CHAPTER
# FOUR

N atalie was tinkering with the controls on the large AGA stove when there was a knock on the cottage's front door.

She considered not answering it. It was probably another wedding guest, out roaming the countryside. She shook her head, remembering the tall, good-looking American guy who'd invaded the garden yesterday—in search of Wi-Fi, of all things. Amaryllis must have the most happening patio in England, what with random people having sex on the lounger and hot guys wanting to check their e-mail there. For a moment the thought crossed her mind that if anyone had to get naked on the patio, she really would have preferred it to be the Wi-Fi guy.

She wrinkled her nose, reminding herself that she didn't really want to see anyone naked on the patio. She didn't want to see anyone, unless it was someone who could explain the quirks of the oven. She'd thought she had it solved, until she burned two trays of chocolate cookies yesterday. But when the knock sounded again at the door, she dropped the manual and went to see who it was.

A large bunch of flowers greeted her when she opened the door. "Hello again," said the hot guy from yesterday.

"Hi." She leaned against the doorframe and resisted the urge to smile back at him. He had a really attractive dimple in one cheek when he grinned.

He made a show of looking at her hands. "Not armed today?"

"Not at the moment."

"That's a relief. I brought peace offerings." He handed her the flowers and a bag she recognized from the lone gourmet food boutique in town. "For disturbing your peace yesterday."

Intrigued, Natalie took the bag. Her brows went up as she peeked inside and saw a variety of expensive ingredients. "Tahitian vanilla and Belgian chocolate?"

"I could smell that chocolate thing you were baking yesterday in my dreams." He half-closed his eyes and an expression of rapture drifted over his face. "I think I'd kill for a plate of it."

"Here I thought you wanted my Wi-Fi password," she said lightly.

"Oh, I'd like that as well." He paused. "Do I have to choose only one?"

She folded her arms and shrugged. "You haven't got either right now."

He grinned, showing off the dimple again. "I sure don't. Archer Quinn, overworked lawyer, ignorant trespasser, and helpless chocolate lover." He put out his hand.

With only a slight hesitation she put her hand in his. "Natalie."

His grin deepened. "Very nice to meet you, Natalie."

"Likewise." At least, she thought so. He did look like a nice guy— or rather, he looked like a pretty hot guy who was acting very disarming and charming. She wondered what he really was.

"Obviously I began badly yesterday, and I came first to apologize." He cleared his throat. "It was not my intent to trespass on your property and I unreservedly apologize for any alarm it may have caused you. Furthermore, I should have introduced myself and laid to rest any fears you might have had that I was an axe murderer prowling the neighborhood."

"That's why I took my cleaver," she pointed out.

"I did notice," he agreed with a hint of a smile. "Would you have used it, if I had been an axe murderer?"

"Of course," she said in the same serious tone. "I can disembowel a whole turkey in four minutes. I doubt a man takes much longer, once you whack off the head."

He blinked. "You disemboweled a turkey? Good Lord, what did he do to you?"

Natalie snorted with laughter before she could stop herself. "Nothing. I just wanted to eat him."

He blinked again, and then his eyes warmed. "Really."

She ignored the speculative tone. "Yep. Stuffed his guts with cornbread, sage, and sausage, roasted him for three hours, and served him up on a platter. He was delicious."

Archer Quinn inhaled a ragged breath. "You've got to stop talking about food that way. Between the memory of the chocolate yesterday and the idea of a roasted turkey, I almost passed out here on your steps."

"Haven't they got good food up the hotel? I've seen enough catering vans headed up there to feed an army."

"It's hotel food," he said, as if that explained everything. "You can't smell it baking. My mother used to make this chocolate pudding cake … It was my favorite thing in the world."

"Chocolate pudding cake, huh."

"With vanilla ice cream on top." He winked. "The way to this man's heart."

For some reason her cheeks felt hot. "I was asking in a purely professional capacity. I'm working on a cookbook."

"Really?" He perked up. "If you need any samples tasted, I'd be glad to help out."

Natalie shook her head. "First you want free Internet, now free food. Thank you for the flowers, Mr. Quinn, but I have to get back to work—"

"So do I," he said hastily. "But I need reliable Internet to do it."

She pursed her lips, unwillingly charmed by the flowers and Tahitian vanilla. "What do you do again?"

"I'm a lawyer." He pulled out his wallet and handed her a business card. *Archer Quinn, Partner, Harper Millman LLP*, it read, with an address in Boston.

She frowned. The lawyer Paul had hired as part of his expansion plans had been an arrogant prick, with a full head of white hair and a flashy Rolex. He'd treated her as if she were a child throwing a temper tantrum when she didn't agree with Paul's ideas. "I don't like lawyers."

"No, no, no," he said quickly as she straightened, preparing to close the door. "I'm a very harmless sort of lawyer. I just write boring business memos."

She paused, one hand on the door. "I really need peace and quiet."

"And I will not bother you," he promised. "You won't hear one peep from me."

Natalie deliberated. He had good gift sense. He appreciated the smell of baking. These two things had an outsized effect on her judgment. Also, he was very kind to the eyes, as her mother would say, and she was hardly immune to that. "You can't come in the house."

"I don't need to," he replied at once. "The signal on the patio is excellent."

She frowned again. "How do you know that?"

"Phone app." His teasing grin reappeared. "How about a trial of a few days?"

That dimple was dangerous. Natalie poked around in the gift bag to avoid meeting his brilliant gaze. Belgian chocolate, threads of saffron, imported balsamic vinegar, even a bottle of wine. She lifted it an inch to read the label and barely suppressed a start of surprise. He must have spent well over a hundred bucks on all this. "I suppose a day or two couldn't hurt."

"Great." He sounded relieved. "Thank you."

"Why do you need to work so desperately? Aren't you here for a big fancy wedding with all sorts of events?"

He laughed a little sadly. "If only. The groom is my client; he invited me because ... I'm not quite sure. But the work can't wait, so I'll have to miss whatever wedding festivities are planned."

Natalie fiddled with the bottle of wine. "Boring business memos, huh."

"Lots of them," he said glumly.

She gave in to the pull. He would stay out on the patio, and if she snuck a peek from time to time, it wouldn't hurt anyone. It might even do her good to exchange a word with someone other than Oliver from time to time. "All right. Whenever you want, the patio is yours."

His face eased into a more honest smile. The dimple was back, and crinkles appeared around his dark blue eyes. God, he was good-looking. "How about now?"


ARCHER HAD LEFT his laptop case out of sight. Just bringing it with him seemed to taunt fate, but thankfully Natalie was agreeably softened up by his apology gift. He'd gone all out on that, because an extensive ramble of the Brampton House grounds hadn't turned up any other source of Internet. He supposed he could go sit in one of the cafés in town, as Mr. Delancey kept suggesting, but he much preferred a quieter place to work. The patio behind her house began to look idyllic, especially after he ran into the hotel owner, Harry Compton, who confirmed—reluctantly—that the Internet at Brampton House was well and truly screwed until British Telecom deigned to come repair it. The Wi-Fi signal at the stone house became his only hope.

And blessedly his gamble had paid off. He scooted the patio table a little more into the shade of the brick wall that ran down one side of the garden, and opened his computer. It had taken over an hour for his e-mail to finish downloading yesterday. Even slow Wi-Fi would be an improvement, and there was a chance she'd bake something delicious again to perfume the air.

"Here." She came out the kitchen door with a scrap of paper in one hand. "You'll need the password."

*Primrose123,* he typed in, quietly elated when his laptop connected and the Wi-Fi indicator blinked to full strength. "Thanks. Why primrose?"

She stopped in a patch of sun and blinked. Her hair looked reddish gold in the sunlight. "This house is called Primrose Cottage. It used to be part of the Brampton House estate, I think, like an old-fashioned mother-in-law quarters."

He grinned. "That explains why it's separated from the main house by a hill."

She snorted with laughter. "I didn't hear that! My mom would make an excellent mother-in-law."

"So would mine," he returned, "but I understand why it's on the other side of the hill."

She shook her head and went inside, closing the door. Still grinning, Archer got to work.

He hadn't been wrong. Working on the patio was idyllic. There was a cool breeze, but plenty of sun warming the air. It was quiet, with only the rustling of the plants and an occasional noise of pots clanking or water running from inside the kitchen. The Internet wasn't blazing fast, but it was quick enough that he could remotely connect to his desktop in Boston. And then there was the smell. She was baking blueberry pie, he guessed; not as good as chocolate cake, but still mouthwatering aromas.

After a while the kitchen door opened. Deep in a dense paragraph about corporate director elections, Archer didn't look up until she stopped beside his table.

"I have a favor to ask," she said. In her hands was a tray with five small plates, each one containing a mound of blue-violet blueberries and crust, and a tall glass of water.

"Does it involve eating anything on that tray?" His stomach growled at the thought. Archer glanced at his watch and saw with a start that it was past two o'clock. And he hadn't brought lunch.

"It involves tasting everything on this tray, and giving me an honest evaluation of the samples. You did offer."

He closed his laptop and pushed it to the far end of the table without taking his eyes off the tray. "A gentleman keeps his word. Bring it on."

She set down the tray and placed one plate in front of him. A wavering number "1" was drizzled in chocolate sauce on the far edge of the plate. "Let's start with this."

Gingerly Archer scooped a bite onto the fork and tasted it. For a moment he let it sit on his tongue, then he began to chew, until his eyes drifted closed in bliss. The berries were tiny and tender and bursting with juice. "It's good," he managed to say, spearing another bite.

"In what way?" Natalie drew a small notebook from her apron pocket and made a note. "Is it too sweet? Too chewy?"

He chewed more carefully this time, thinking. "No, not too sweet. There's something else in it ..." Another bite, this time with more biscuit-like crust. "Something sharp. Not my favorite, but still edible."

"Ginger." She wrote some more. "Next sample."

He took the plate drizzled with a "2" and dug in. "This has more than blueberries," he said in surprise.

"Blackberries," she muttered. "Good, or not?"

Archer ate some more. Each plate held only a few bites, so he tried to concentrate on each one. "Not as good as just blueberries."

He tasted his way through two more plates, washing each one down with a good drink of water. Once the initial Pavlovian reaction to the sight of food—dessert, no less—had ebbed, he found himself watching his hostess. Now her hair was tied back with a red kerchief around her head, and there was a tiny gold heart on a chain around her neck. Her apron was covered with dark blue blotches of blueberry juice, and she must have an itch on one leg; from time to time she would lift one foot and rub the toe down the back of her other ankle. It was oddly sexy.

"Last one." She set the fifth and final plate in front of him.

"Just as I was getting good at this," he joked, reaching for the fork. "At least, I hope. Am I getting good at this? Is it helpful?"

She nodded. "Definitely! I've baked all these a hundred times. It's good to have someone else's opinion to make sure I'm not just reinforcing my own inclinations."

"What kind of cookbook are you working on?"

"My family owns a restaurant. I'm writing a cookbook based on my mother's recipes from the kitchen there."

"It must be sold out every night, if this is what the food tastes like."

Her mouth twisted in a bitter way. "Something like that. What do you think of number five?"

Obediently he took a bite. What was wrong with the restaurant? God knew he wanted to eat there now, if only for the desserts. "It's got ..." He concentrated on the plate in front of him. "It's got lemon in it."

"Very good." A faint smile crossed her face as she wrote on her notebook. "Anything else?"

"Yes." He took another bite. "This is the best one, by the way. Is it cinnamon?"

"And cloves. Why is it the best?"

Archer scraped up another bite. "I have no idea, but it's unbelievable. Would it be rude if I licked the plate?"

She laughed and put the notebook back in her apron pocket. "Not rude, but a little gross. You just ate half a blueberry cobbler."

"And loved every bite of it." He regarded the empty plates with some sadness. "What were you testing, with these five?"

"Variations on flavorings. I have a base recipe, but wanted to add subtle changes to allow for different tastes. One has more exotic flavors like ginger and five spices, one has nutmeg and lemon, one has cinnamon and cloves …" She stopped and looked sheepish. "Do you cook?"

"No, but I am a very appreciative diner." He grinned, and she laughed. "My mother is an excellent cook."

"Chocolate pudding cake," she said.

"Angels in heaven don't know what they're missing in my mother's chocolate pudding cake."

Natalie smiled. "I'd love to have that recipe."

"Well, I'd like to taste your version of it. I mean that literally," he said when Natalie kept on smiling. She was gorgeous when she smiled. "I'll get the recipe, and we'll see if you can make it as well as she can."

Her smile faded a bit. "I doubt it." A chill seemed to blow across the patio. "You don't have to get it on my account."

Archer could have smacked his own forehead. What had he said? Didn't women love a man who adored his mother's cooking? Or did that make him look like a mama's boy who would forever find other women lacking? "No trouble," he said lightly. "She'll think I'm wasting away on bad takeout and overnight me a frozen cake. So even if you never bake it, I still win."

She busied herself with the dishes. "Suit yourself. Thanks again for your help."

"No prob—whoa!" The big gray cat had jumped into his lap. "Hey there, cat."

Natalie set down the tray with a clink. "Oliver! Come here!"

Archer scratched the cat's head as it began purring and kneading his shirt collar. "He's fine. Just really big."

"He's enormous," said Natalie with a sigh. "I only feed him one scoop of kitty food a day."

"I bet this garden is free of mice and voles, though."

"Ew." She looked askance at the cat. "I let him sleep on my bed."

*Lucky cat*, thought Archer. "He's an outdoorsman, used to hunting for his dinner." The cat certainly still had claws, which were digging into his chest now. He put Oliver down, giving him a few rough strokes down the back as the cat's purr grew louder.

"He's not mine," she said, as if that explained her revulsion at the cat's predatory tendencies. "He just belongs to the house, which is also not mine."

That was interesting. He could tell from her voice she was American, but apparently she was also just visiting. He found himself far too interested in Natalie the baker. "So where's the restaurant?" he asked, trying to get back to a happier topic that might make her smile again.

It didn't work. If anything, her expression grew harder. "In Wellesley, outside Boston."

He perked up, choosing to ignore her frosty answer. Not only was she American, she came from his new home state. "Hey, I just moved to Boston! Which direction is Wellesley from the city?"

"West." She picked up the tray. "Thanks for tasting."

"You're welcome," he said to her retreating back. She didn't look at him again, and the door closed behind her with a bang. Archer looked at Oliver, now rolling on his back in a spot of sun. "You could have warned me." He leaned down and gave the cat a quick rub on the belly. "Any other subjects I should avoid? No? Maybe? Thanks for the advice." Oliver just purred, flexing his feet in the air. Archer sighed, cast one more glance at the firmly closed kitchen door, and went back to corporate director elections.

# CHAPTER
# FIVE

For the next two days, Archer Quinn appeared on her patio. Natalie knew he was there early, because she checked every morning when she came downstairs. He liked the mornings, she thought; he arrived before nine every day with a travel mug of coffee. True to his word he kept out of her way and never knocked on the door. He spent a fair amount of time talking on his phone. The kitchen became unbearably hot with the giant AGA on, so she had to keep the windows open, and that meant she listened to his voice in the background. Even without making out most of his words, she came to like the sound of his voice. More tenor than bass, but with a little rasp to it. After a while she could distinguish between callers. Most of them sounded like business colleagues, from the random bits of conversation she overheard, but there was someone called Elle who made him laugh. Natalie found herself wondering who it was, and in a moment of weakness she looked up the firm on his business card. Elle Williams was another lawyer there. Natalie wondered if he was dating her, or wanted to date her, then she called herself an idiot and walked away from the computer. It was none of her business.

There was one significant benefit to his presence. At least twice, other wedding guests wandered into her garden, and before she could go set them straight, Archer did it for her. Apparently there was still no Internet to be had at the hotel, and more than one guest had followed the same path to her Wi-Fi signal. Without ever giving away that he had the password, Archer pointed them in the direction of town and described the best spots for cell phone reception. Natalie wondered if he also told them the crazy woman in Primrose Cottage was liable to come after them with a meat cleaver, but if he did, she never overheard it.

She could see why he made a good lawyer, though. He was friendly without being smarmy, never rude, and had a logical argument for everything. Everyone seemed to part from him on good terms. Even his phone calls were cordial and good-humored, which didn't fit with her view of lawyers.

Not that it was any of her business.

She was whipping egg whites when her phone rang. She pushed the heavy stand mixer away from the counter edge and reached for her phone. "Oh, hi, Mom."

"Hi, sweetie. How are you?"

"Whipping up some meringue today. The weather is perfect for it."

"That's my girl," said Judy Corcoran with approval. "What are you making?"

Natalie turned back to the mixer and caught a glimpse of Archer. There was a thin frown of concentration between his brows as he typed away. The sun fell across his shoulders, making them look very broad, and shone on the top of his head, picking out the bit of wave in his sandy hair. With some effort, she pulled her eyes away.

"Natalie?"

"Um, cake," she blurted. "I've been doing desserts for over a week now. The pies are done, as are the cobblers and the ice creams. I have four kinds of cake on my list, then a few more cookies, and I'll be done with dessert."

"Sounds like a good pace." Her mother's voice softened. "And how *are* you?"

She stopped the mixer and checked the egg whites. Almost ready. She turned it back on. "Just fine, Mom. How is Dad?"

"He's doing very well. The physical therapist has him writing letters now, so he wrote a long list of instructions for Paul."

She knew her mother had done it on purpose, but the mention of her brother was a bridge too far. "That's great. I remember the little notes Dad used to put in my school lunches. I miss those notes."

"And how about your brother?"

"I don't miss him as much," she replied evenly. "Can we talk about something else?"

Her mother's sigh was sad. "When are you going to be ready to talk to Paul?"

*Never.* She debated ending the call and blaming it on the meringue. "Not now."

"He was wrong, Nat, but so were you," her mother admonished. "I know you just want what's best for the Jude—"

"But we can't agree on what that is, Mom. He wants to make us a franchise and open eight more locations. He wants to take on millions in debt and put our name on restaurants all the way across the country. I just don't think that's a good idea. It will ruin everything I love about the Jude."

"Not everything, I hope," said her mother tartly. "I'll still be there, as will your dad. What do *you* want to do?"

Natalie hit the switch on the mixer and stared out the window. It was a gorgeous view, one she'd become accustomed to, and one she would miss when she finally had to return to the States. It was even better with Archer sitting off to one side, now leaning back in his chair and holding his phone to his ear. "I don't know, Mom," she said softly, right at the same moment Archer said, "Hey, Elle, is this a good time?"

His voice carried across the stone patio, through the open window. "Is someone there?" asked Judy.

Natalie cringed. "Yeah. Well, no, not really. It's just someone borrowing the Internet connection."

"Someone?"

She heard the veiled curiosity in her mother's question. "There's a fancy hotel nearby, apparently, and they're hosting a big wedding. Their Internet went out and one guy walked over and persuaded me to let him use the Wi-Fi here."

"I hope he's a nice guy."

It occurred to her that here was the perfect distraction from Paul. "Seems very nice, so far."

"Really?" Judy was losing her noncommittal tone, edged out by interest. "Good-looking?"

She watched Archer stretch one arm over his head and grin at something Elle said. Colleagues, or more? *Not her business.* "Yes," she murmured absently to her mother.

"And he's in your house? Every day?"

Natalie snapped out of her momentary trance. "Not *in* the house, he sits on the patio and works on his laptop. I'm working, too, remember?"

"The way to a man's heart is through his stomach," said her mother. "Take him something to eat."

"Mom! I am not trying to—to—"

"What?" asked her unrepentant mother. "You don't have to shag him—isn't that what they call it over there? It sounds so British. But it's how I got your father, and I just think—"

"Oh, Mom, my meringue is ready," Natalie exclaimed, snapping the mixer on full speed and leaning down so the whir of the motor filled the line. "Gotta go, give Dad a kiss for me, bye!" She ended the call and almost threw the phone across the counter.

Ugh. Was her mother having some kind of midlife crisis? Natalie had friends whose mothers were almost rabid about seeing them married with a few kids. Her mom had never been that way ... although she had always been the most open parent about discussing sex, which had mortified Natalie and Paul to no end. She'd once offered to buy condoms for any of their friends, which was just too much to contemplate. Natalie admitted her mother's openness was wonderful when she actually wanted to talk about something delicate, but other times ... ugh.

And if her mother could see Archer ... She dared another glance at the patio. He was still on the phone, now using a headset. He moved his hands as he talked, almost like he was sculpting his words in the air. Her gaze lingered on his hands for a moment, on those long expressive fingers. Mom would approve. Mom *did* approve, without even seeing him.

"Idiot," she told herself, and went back to her meringue.

NOW THAT HE was keeping his head above water with work, Archer began to enjoy being in England. There were events for the wedding guests every day, but he mostly skipped them in favor of walking down to Primrose Cottage. It was quite pleasant working on Natalie's patio. Every day some new delicious smell would drift out her windows, although she didn't ask him to taste anything else. Archer spent a shameful amount of time trying to guess what she was making every day. He fantasized about peach cobbler, chocolate cookies, and strawberry pie—and increasingly about Natalie herself. Just the sight of her through the kitchen window stoked his interest.

Even when he didn't strictly need to work, he walked down to the cottage. There was always something he could do for some client, after all. True to his promise, Jack was handling the work for Brightball, although Archer had stepped in to answer a few questions. Bill, the founder, was excitable, and Archer could tell he was absorbed in something that had him keyed up. Hopefully it was some innovative invention. Distracted by the aromas from the kitchen, as well as the glimpses of Natalie herself, Archer didn't pay it too much mind. Brightball was Jack's client, after all.

But he did need to focus on his top client when they met. Duke Austen had been only a fleeting presence as far as Archer knew; he must be occupied with wedding preparations and rehearsals and whatever else went into planning the wedding of the year. So much for talking about new ventures or any other business. The wedding planner, a dark-haired intense woman named Arwen Kilpatrick, seemed to be everywhere at once with a schedule in her hand, often with the hotel owner Mr. Compton at her side. Archer hoped she was giving him hell about the lack of Internet and reliable cell service.

Still, Archer thought he'd better go to the cocktail hour, even though he knew very few of the other guests. Contrary to Denise's tabloid scouting, there were no movie stars or royals at the event, but

Jack Harper's prediction that he could find some new clients was well-founded. Archer spent a half hour chatting with Piers Prescott, Duke's college roommate. Prescott came from old money, but had the spirit of philanthropy one didn't often find in the private equity sector. Unfortunately he also had a good memory for names.

"Quinn, from San Francisco," said Piers thoughtfully. "Any relation to Ted Quinn, the venture capitalist?"

Archer was used to that question. In San Francisco, he'd heard it all the time. Quinntillion, his father's venture capital firm, was based there, and it was legendary in financial circles. Archer never used his full name, but any time someone discovered he was really Theodore Archer Quinn II, they would exclaim, "You must be Ted Quinn's son!" He'd moved to Boston partly to get away from it.

He took a breath and nodded. "He's my father."

"Well." Piers looked mildly impressed. "Quite a history."

He doubted the man meant Ted's personal history, the one that mattered to Archer. "He's a legend," he said evenly, not adding his personal qualifier: *and a legendary jerk.*

"I think my family firm did some business with him." Piers gave him a rueful glance. "If I recall, it was a bit bruising."

Archer raised his glass in mock salute. "That's the Quinn way. Sorry; I don't have anything to do with Quinntillion."

"No, I'm sure I would have remembered if Ted's son had been part of his firm," muttered Piers with a curiously grim expression.

Archer shook his head. "I went the other way. Computer science, then law. Which all worked out brilliantly when I crossed paths with Duke." He grinned. "We both rocked Master Chief."

Piers frowned, then groaned. "Don't say *Halo*. Duke wore out our Xbox on that game. I can still hear the Gregorian chant soundtrack, and it makes me break out in hives."

"Yep," said Archer proudly. "I won the campus tournament."

Piers eyed him. "How ... impressive."

He laughed. "My crowning achievement!"

"What's that?" Duke had come up beside them. "Stealing my lawyer, Piers?"

"Another *Halo* warrior? Hardly."

Duke grinned. "Whatever. Hey, Archer, come meet Jane."

Piers moved off as Duke led him through the scattered guests to a pretty blond woman. Archer had seen her before, but he'd never actually met the future Mrs. Austen. She was friendly and pleasant, thanking him for coming to the wedding as if she really meant it, and it triggered something in Archer's memory.

"I wonder if I could ask a favor," he said to her. "My secretary Denise is a big fan of your books, and she sent one of them with me in the hopes you would sign it."

Jane's mouth opened in surprise, then she beamed. "Of course! Which book?"

"Er." Archer cleared his throat. *"The Wicked Wallflower."*

An evil grin spread across Duke's face. "Oh, that's a good one. My favorite, in fact. That's the one where a man finds himself engaged without having to propose."

Jane gave him a look. "I would be thrilled to sign your book," she told Archer.

"It's for my secretary," Archer said again.

"Have you read the others?" Duke was enjoying this. "You don't want to miss any. *Wallflower Gone Wild* ... whoa. I had to take a cold shower."

"Duke!" said Jane in exasperation.

"My secretary says you're her favorite author." Archer decided to ignore his client for a minute.

"She should be." Duke gave his future wife a scorching look. "Those books are badass."

Jane widened her eyes at him, but her smile ruined any reproof she might have meant. "You just made my night, Archer! Do you have the book?"

"Up in my room."

"Shall we go up? I don't want to forget and the next few days will be frantic."

They all walked up to his room. Archer pretended not to notice the whispered conversation between Duke and Jane, but he did catch a few heated glances between them. Duke had his arm around her waist and must have been whispering something dirty in her ear, from the way Jane was blushing.

While Jane sat down to autograph Denise's book, Duke prowled the room, glancing out each window. "Where do you run off to every day?"

"To get some work done. I can leave the office, but it won't leave me."

"Right." Duke squinted into the sunset lighting up the west-facing windows. "Someone told me you found an Internet connection."

"Maybe."

His host's electric blue eyes flashed at him. "Where? I had to separate two programmers from each other's throats yesterday. They can't survive offline."

Archer shook his head with an air of regret. "I was sworn to secrecy. If I told you, I'd have to kill you."

Duke snorted. "Fine. Jane will be disappointed; she thought you were sneaking out to meet women, since you didn't bring a date."

For some completely unaccountable reason Archer found his throat needed clearing. Twice. "No. Just me and my laptop." Hidden away in Natalie's garden paradise, living for the little plates of sweets she brought out. He had a sudden memory of her rubbing one foot along the back of her other ankle, scribbling in her little notebook the whole while, and felt an unhealthy flush of heat suffuse his body.

"Your laptop makes you blush like a girl?" Duke grinned wickedly. "Don't forget I'm marrying a romance novelist. I know the signs, dude. I hope the woman you, ah, *aren't* sneaking out to see is a babe."

Archer was spared having to reply when Jane crossed the room to them. "Here you go." She handed Archer the book. "Tell your secretary I'm going to send her a copy of my next book before it comes out."

"She'll love that."

"Shall we go back down?" Duke draped his arm around Jane's shoulders. "Or not? I can't let one of my programmers get laid more often than I do at my own wedding."

"Oh my God, don't mention Rupert!" Jane groaned.

"How can I not?" returned Duke. "Is there a single person at this wedding who hasn't seen him and his girlfriend getting busy somewhere?"

Archer remembered the couple dry-humping out beyond the gazebo. "Are they the couple who can't keep their hands off each other?"

"I think they're sweet," said Jane sternly. "Just … indiscreet."

"Exhibitionists," muttered Duke to Archer.

"Well, maybe a little," agreed the bride, her face pink.

"So are we going back down?" Duke asked. Jane rolled her eyes at her fiancé, but went with him. At the door, Duke paused, glanced back at Archer, and hissed, "Ask her to the wedding."

"Who?" Archer tried to pretend he had no idea what Duke meant.

The groom smirked. "You know who."

The door closed behind them and Archer was left to contemplate it in silence. Ask Natalie to the wedding? He liked the idea, except that he didn't know her very well and had obviously said something wrong the last time they spoke. He wouldn't mind seeing her in a slinky dress, nor watching her walk around in high heels. He also wouldn't mind getting her out of the dress and heels, but he warned himself not to go there. And there had to be better place to take a woman than a wedding, where everyone would be drunk and prone to saying stupid things like, "When are you two getting married?" That was too much stress for any first date.

On the other hand … He was only in England for a few more days. Even though she was also from the Boston area, she might not be going back any time soon. Archer hesitated, then admitted to himself he would like to see much, much more of Natalie.

# CHAPTER
## SIX

He walked down to the cottage the next morning and set up his laptop on the patio table as usual, but when he opened his e-mail, it failed to download. The internet indicator just blinked, indicating it wasn't finding a signal. Archer tried a few things, but still came up empty. The Wi-Fi was down.

Tentatively, he knocked on the garden door. After a minute the window opened and Natalie stuck out her head. "What?"

There was a streak of something dark on her cheekbone. Probably chocolate. The idea of licking it off popped into his brain, sudden and intense. He cleared his throat to get rid of the thought. "Uh, the, uh, the Wi-Fi seems to be out."

"Is it?" Something beeped behind her. "Shit!" She disappeared from the window.

Archer deliberated. He needed that Wi-Fi. He had also, unfortunately, sworn to stay out of her way, and it seemed clear there was a bit of chaos going on in the kitchen. While he stood there, she reappeared in the window. "Sorry about that, but I don't have time to fix it. Maybe tonight." Another timer started beeping, and with a roll of her eyes she vanished again.

A whole day without access to his e-mail? Thanks to the last few days he wasn't behind, but he wasn't ahead, either; "out of the country" didn't translate into "unavailable for work" at Harper Millman. There was always the gazebo, he thought grimly. He could work with half the wedding party up there shouting into their phones, right?

He knocked again, then turned the knob and cautiously opened the door. As expected, it looked a bit out of control. No less than four pots steamed and bubbled atop the stove, and Natalie was stirring one, peering ferociously into the depths. "Maybe I could fix the Wi-Fi," he offered.

A timer beeped and she smacked one hand down on it, silencing it without a glance. "It's not my computer. It's kind of old and takes a good bit of cursing to get working."

"I'm pretty good with that type of machine."

Still stirring, she glanced at him. Her face was flushed pink and her hair was curling up over the scarf tied around her head. "They teach that in law school?"

"I was a computer science major before law school." He gave a hopeful grin. "I swear I won't break it."

She hesitated, and another timer went off. "Oh, fine, go ahead and try." She threw open the oven door and bent down to look inside. "Perfect," she breathed in apparent delight, lifting out a pan.

Archer unthinking agreed, blatantly staring at her ass, which was exquisitely displayed in a pair of faded jeans. "Absolutely."

Natalie looked up, stray curls falling around her face. "What?"

He coughed, averting his eyes. "In there, you said?" He pointed at random.

"Yeah." Her attention switched back to the pan in her hands. "These are just right. Where's my pen?"

He left her making notes on whatever she'd baked, which smelled damned good, and went in search of the modem. She was right—it was an old machine, but it was also one he knew rather well. Back in college, he and his roommate had taken apart PCs like this for fun. Their room had looked like a factory exploded, but on the bright side, they built the most epic gaming system Harvard had ever seen.

The PC was set on an ornate desk that looked like something the Queen of France might have used. He followed the wires until he located the modem and other hardware, crammed into a large drawer in a squirrel's nest of cables and office supplies. What a mess. Whoever lived here had spent some good money on a very tasteful renovation of a really old house, then set up a computer system from the Dark Ages. Shaking his head, he pulled the drawer open and started unplugging things.

NATALIE BAKED six perfect trays of madeleines before wondering what Archer was up to. A quick look at the clock revealed it was past one, which meant he'd been working on the computer … a really long time. He usually walked down the hill before nine. By now she was used to seeing him sitting out on the patio as she worked, and twice she'd caught herself glancing out the window before remembering why he wasn't there.

She made a few more notes on her madeleines and tossed her pen on the counter. Maybe it had been just a bit stupid to invite him to go fix the Wi-Fi. Who only knew what was on Amaryllis's creaky old computer, and now she'd just gone and let a complete stranger poke around it. The guy didn't seem dangerous or hacker-ish, but she had no basis for that. She pulled the scarf from her head and went into the office. "How's it going?" Then she looked around. "Oh my God, what did you do?"

"Don't worry," he said absently, his fingers flying across the keyboard. He had put two thick books on the Art Deco movement beneath the monitor to raise it up, and there was a jumble of cables and wires and electronic boxes in the middle of the floor. The drawer where everything usually went was open—and empty.

Natalie blanched. Pippa had told her not to mess with anything, that it was all a little touchy but should work as long as she didn't move things around. "This isn't my computer! I have to leave every-thing the way I found it …"

He turned. "It's a miracle it worked at all the way it was. The modem cable was pinched in the drawer, and half this stuff doesn't work but was still plugged in. And when I started looking at the machine—"

"Whoa, why were you looking at the machine?" Shit; did Amaryllis have personal financial files on there? Nude photos? Given the hot young footballers she dated, it was a strong possibility. Natalie's heart lurched. Pippa would kill her. "Usually just unplugging the modem thing and plugging it back in works."

"Really?" He cast a skeptical eye on the discarded electronics. "That's a shock. No, I went to look at the software—nothing else," he added as if he could tell she was having an invasion-of-privacy freak-out. "The machine is all but crippled with malware. It's got a well-known virus that was slowing it down to glacial speed. Didn't you notice?"

Nope. "Well, I knew it was really old," she muttered in her own defense. "Old computers are always slow."

He grinned. "This one was beyond slow. It would drive me insane, so I started cleaning it up, and ..." He checked his watch. "Time got away from me. Is it really after one?"

"Mmm-hmm." She nudged the tangle of stuff on the floor with one toe. "Please tell me you're going to put all this back together."

"Not on your life. Some of it's so old, there's no software to support it. I'll be glad to box it up for the owner, but he doesn't need any of it."

"She." Natalie gave the pile another worried look, then pushed the issue from her mind. She certainly wasn't going to go poking through, trying to figure out what everything was and how it might connect. A big note of apology to Amaryllis would have to suffice. "So is it working again?"

He turned back to the screen, where various status bars were inching forward. "Should be soon. It will be much faster once this is done."

"Well, that would be nice." Slowly she came across the room. "How does a computer science major end up a lawyer?"

"Change of heart, I guess."

She glanced sideways at him. There was more to it than that, from his carefully light tone. "Is that your connection to the wedding going on up there? It's some big technology guy getting married, right?"

His mouth quirked as if at some private joke. "Maybe. But I'm here strictly for business reasons." He turned the chair around and gave her a rueful smile, the one that made him look young and almost bashful. "Would I be down here mooching off your Wi-Fi every day otherwise?"

"How would I know?" She opened her eyes wide. "Maybe you're a workaholic who doesn't even know how to have fun."

For a fraction of a second his eyes dropped. Not bashfully, but openly—though quickly—checking her out. "I hope that's not true."

Natalie opened her mouth, and nothing came out. Archer was a successful guy—smart, hardworking, funny, decent, and way too good-looking to be a real lawyer. It had been a long time since someone so obviously *right* checked her out. "So, no date for the wedding?" His eyebrows went up, and she hastily added, "I assume if you had a date, you'd be spending more time with her. Or him, as the case may be, because sometimes it is, you know, and that's fine."

His smile had started in the middle of her speech and grew as she rambled on. "If I had a date, she would no doubt be furious at me for working," he said, laying particular stress on the female pronoun. "But I haven't got a girlfriend, here or at home."

Thankfully something on the computer beeped, and he turned around again. Natalie took advantage of the moment to let her head drop back. *Smooth, girl,* she told herself. Not that she was hitting on him. She was just nosy. But she was also unreasonably pleased that he wasn't in a relationship. The more appealing he got, the more she'd thought he would be. Guys this *right* did not freely walk the earth.

"Here you are," Archer said, writing something on a sticky note and pressing it down on the desk blotter. "The password was too easy and obvious; at least three other people have been freeloading on your system, and one of them seems to like porn."

"What?"

"Unless it's your thing," he said without missing a beat. "I'm not judging."

"I am not downloading porn!" Natalie wondered who the heck it was. Maybe Charles, the old duffer who came to work on the lawn and gardens every other week. She'd thought he was just reading a book, sitting on that bench beside the front door during his break. Hmm.

"Like I said, no judgment." Archer stood up and stretched his shoulders. He looked at the modem and router, now happily blinking little green lights. "Damn, I miss this," he said, almost to himself.

"Fixing computers from the dinosaur age?"

He flexed his fingers, snagging her gaze. He had really nice hands, she noticed again. "*Doing* something. Yeah, it's old, but when it was new, that was a top-of-the-line machine. I used to take those apart in college. My roommate and I were complete geeks; we booby-trapped the bathroom door down the hall with a little flashing light, and we wired a statue near our dorm with a speaker so we could spook tourists. I spent more time trying to write an AI essay generator than I spent writing actual essays, and nearly flunked an English class because of it. Still … It was fun."

"Why'd you give it up?" she asked softly.

The fondness of things remembered faded from his face. "Life changes."

That was the truth. Natalie wondered what had changed in his life to make him give up hacking his way around computers—maybe money? If he could afford to spend his college years taking apart "top-of-the-line machines," he must have had money—then. But now he spent his days hunched over a laptop looking beleaguered when he should have been on vacation, enjoying the wedding events.

"Right." She cleared her throat, suddenly wishing she wasn't wearing her worn-out jeans and a plain T-shirt. She shoved her hair from her forehead and cringed as her finger touched something gooey on her cheek. Not that she was hitting on Archer, or even interested in hitting on him. She turned back toward the kitchen, furtively swiping the gooey stuff from her face. "You want some lunch?"

Somehow Archer felt that being offered food again was a victory. He followed her into the kitchen, where she began pulling out plates. "I have roast chicken and coleslaw," she said. "Nothing very gourmet."

"Sounds great." He propped one shoulder against the doorway and watched as she fetched an armload of containers from the refrigerator. The dark smear on her cheek was wider and lighter now, as if she'd tried to wipe it away. "What are you baking today?"

She glanced up and flashed him a quick smile. "Madeleines. I also had a brain wave about ice cream overnight, even though I already did the ice creams, so I started a few custards as well."

"You're making ice cream?"

"Uh-huh. Did you think it was produced in a chemical factory somewhere?"

"No, I just didn't know anyone could make it at home," he said. "It comes from the store in a box, like pasta."

She snorted and carved some slices off a fat loaf of crusty bread. "You can make pasta at home."

He whistled in quiet astonishment. "Maybe *you* can."

Natalie laughed, opening another container. "I am just as amazed that you could fix that old computer, so we're even. Rosemary mayo?"

Dumbly he nodded. Not only did it sound good, he was beginning to get a whiff of it. And there was something very sensual about the way she handled food. Her head tilted to the side as she swirled a dollop of mayonnaise onto the bread, then laid some tomato slices and lettuce on top of it. The blade of her knife glinted as she ran it through a whole chicken breast, the skin dark chestnut and speckled with herbs or spices or something. One by one she layered the sliced chicken on the bread before bringing the knife down through the sandwich, cutting it into halves. He had a strong feeling she'd made everything from scratch, and when he asked, she confirmed it.

"Of course. I'm writing a cookbook, remember."

"With recipes for mayonnaise and bread?"

She laughed again. "No, although they're both easy to make. I want my cookbook to be the sort of thing people turn to every night, not only for basics like a quick roasted chicken, but for dinner parties and special occasion meals. I start with easy, basic recipes, then add on layers of extras or different flavor variations. Most people don't have time to make mayonnaise, although ..." She gave him a secretive little smile that made his stomach tighten. "I did include one recipe for how to flavor mayonnaise from the jar. A few chopped herbs and a squirt of lemon juice make a huge impact." She scooped out some coleslaw onto both plates, set a sandwich half on each, and handed him one. "Let's eat."

Archer was only too happy to obey.

"So when does the cookbook come out?" he asked as they ate on the patio. He'd pushed his laptop aside and now Oliver the cat lay on top of it. Archer barely glanced at it, fully diverted by the succulent sandwich in his hands and the fascinating woman across from him.

She took her time answering. "I don't know. I have to finish writing it."

He nodded. "Is the publisher getting impatient for it?" One of his clients had written a book on a computer language once, and Archer had helped him find a literary attorney for the book contract.

Natalie played with her coleslaw, chewing very slowly. Too late, Archer recognized the signs of someone who didn't want to answer. "That's not really my business. Never mind."

"No, it's okay." She took a deep breath. "I don't have a publisher yet. Writing a cookbook was … Well, it was an excuse to get out of Wellesley. My brother and I had a big fight about our family restaurant and I needed to get away."

He just listened.

"This house belongs to my college roommate's stepmother," she went on. "When I told Pippa I needed a hideout, she offered it."

He glanced at the house. One never knew what real estate was worth, but someone had spent a lot of money renovating this house. "Pretty nice hideout, if you ask me."

She smiled, a little pensive. "Very nice." She seemed to rouse herself from whatever had dampened her mood. "So you just moved to Boston?"

"From San Francisco. But I went to college in the Boston area and liked it. Still do."

"You moved back for work?"

He winked. "An offer I couldn't refuse."

"Something that combines computers and law," she guessed. "I have a guess whose wedding it is up there. The shop in town only sells trashy newspapers and they are full of rumors about Internet millionaires."

Archer pushed back his plate and heaved a happy, sated, sigh. "I don't do the computers anymore, just the law. But being able to speak the language helps with my clients, who include"—he tapped one temple—"many very successful Internet entrepreneurs."

"Oh?" She raised one eyebrow teasingly. "So it's no one famous getting married?"

He made a stern face. "I can't really discuss it. Client confidentiality, you know."

One side of her mouth curled upward, giving her a sly, sexy look. "Got it." She folded her arms and rested her elbows on the table. "Why not computers? You said you miss it."

It was his turn to take a moment before answering. "I loved it," he finally said, slowly. "I got my degree in computer science and did a couple of years as a programmer. I wasn't brilliant," he added, "just generally competent and brash as heck." Duke Austen had hacked the *New York Times* front page as a middle-schooler before channeling his intellect into more socially acceptable—and profitable—directions. Archer had been a very competent mid-level programmer, who would have written search engine algorithms forever if he'd stayed.

She ran her finger along the edge of her plate, picking up a bit of mayo. She stuck out her tongue and delicately licked it off her fingertip. Archer stared, feeling the stirrings of a very different sort of hunger. Every time he saw Natalie, he liked her more and more. Damn Duke and his suggestion of asking her to be his date to the wedding.

"Why law?" It seemed her voice had grown throaty and seductive with that lick of mayo.

He hesitated. "Because of my father."

"Oh." She tilted her head to one side, obviously picking up on his discomfort. "My mother runs the kitchen in our restaurant. I'm following in her footsteps, too."

Archer gave a sharp laugh. "My father's not a lawyer. He told my mother he was divorcing her three weeks after she was diagnosed with breast cancer. She's so tenderhearted, she told him to go—her cancer was pretty advanced and I think she didn't expect to survive. But I could have killed him. He'd been banging his assistant for some time, but to leave Mum at that moment ..." He shook his head. "I had a friend whose mother did divorce law, and she turned out to be a real shark. Thanks to her, my mother ended up with a good settlement and guaranteed lifetime health insurance. I was impressed. I wasn't really hitting it out of the park as a programmer, so I decided to go into law." He shrugged. "Divorce law didn't do it for me, but corporate law did, and not many attorneys really know their way around tech clients. So that's my specialty."

Her face had grown soft and compassionate during his story. "How's your mother doing now?"

"Quite well. She got an experimental drug in a clinical trial and it beat back the tumor. She gardens, she paints, she bakes ..." He forced a grin. "If living with my father for twenty years didn't kill her, cancer seemed unlikely to."

"Ah. Still haven't forgiven him?" She sounded understanding.

His jaw clenched. "No." Not forgiven, nor spoken to in years, and Archer was very happy to keep it that way. Ted Quinn was a heartless bastard. He'd been an absent father and an indifferent husband, and Archer didn't care if they never saw each other again.

For a few moments all was quiet. Natalie drew circles in the remnants of her coleslaw with her fork. "I still haven't forgiven my brother, either. He's actually the reason I left. I take it your father is in San Francisco?" Surprised, he nodded once. "My brother followed my father into the restaurant administrative side. I cooked, Paul learned accounting. But Paul wants to turn the restaurant into a chain, with locations around the country, and I just ..." She huffed in controlled temper. "I think he's wrong. It will ruin what's special about us."

"Which is?" He leaned forward. The sun was on her hair, giving her a halo of red-gold curls. That smear of chocolate was still on her cheek, and he couldn't stop staring at it.

"It's called Cuisine du Jude, after my mother Judy. We made the big time with a review in the *New York Times* restaurant section, calling it the most perfect date night ..."

"Date night restaurant in America," he finished with her. "I've heard of it! Wow."

"Ever been there?" she asked.

"Nope. Couldn't get a table." He shook his head in amazement. "The managing partner at my firm, Jack Harper, takes his wife there every anniversary. I overheard his secretary making next year's booking before I left—for March."

"Oh, good." She beamed in pleasure. "I love being part of someone's anniversary tradition!"

Archer's lungs seized up. Oh hell; she was something when she smiled. It lit up her face and made her eyes sparkle.

"Well." Natalie pushed her chair back. "I'd better get back to custards, and you've spent all morning fixing that old computer. Thanks for doing that, by the way."

"My pleasure," he said, still mesmerized.

She picked up the plates and went back into the kitchen. Archer seized the glasses and followed. Inside, she was scraping the plates over the sink, and moved aside as he put the glasses on the drainboard. "Thanks," she said again, looking up at him with a smile.

Archer stared at her. Slowly her smile faded, and the same awareness he felt prickling beneath his skin seemed to affect her. "What?" she said in that throaty voice. "Have I got something on my face?"

"You do, actually." He raised one hand and ran his thumb over the dark smear. Her breathing hitched, but she didn't move. Even more slowly, he repeated the motion. "I think it's dried chocolate," he murmured.

A wash of faint pink came into her cheeks. "Probably. I was making chocolate custard earlier ..."

His mouth crooked up. Of course. "My favorite."

"I thought chocolate cake was your favorite," she breathed, not making any motion to retreat as he angled his head closer to hers.

"Chocolate is my favorite." He brushed his lips against hers. "And this." He kissed her, lightly, his fingertips barely touching the bottom of her chin. Hesitantly her lips moved against his, and then her fingers wrapped around a fold of his shirt and pulled. Archer didn't waste a moment; his fingers slid around the nape of her neck and he drew her against him with his other arm.

He'd thought she smelled good; she tasted even better. Her mouth opened under his and she tasted of rosemary and, faintly, of chocolate, and he thought he'd never get enough. Her fingers flexed, gripping his shirt even tighter, and she rose up on her toes, kissing him back. Her tongue met his, hot and bold, and Archer felt the ground give way beneath his feet. He could kiss this woman forever.

She gave an audible gasp when he broke the kiss so he could taste more of her skin. "I don't even know you." Her voice was that husky whisper that drove him wild.

"I know." Nor did he know her, but he meant to remedy that. His lips brushed the chocolate smear on her cheek and he had a sudden image of licking chocolate off every part of her.

"This is really fast."

"I know," he said again, nipping her earlobe between his teeth. Fast and hot and more intense than anything he'd ever felt in his life.

A fine shudder went through her. "But it feels so damn good … Are you sure you don't have a girlfriend?"

"Completely unattached." He kissed her jaw. "You?"

She gave a faint shake of her head, which exposed her neck better to his kisses. "No one."

"Do you want me to stop?"

For a moment she was motionless, then another very tiny shake of her head. "No."

He smiled, his mouth against hers again. "Good." He held her tighter, and reveled in the feel of her body moving against his. It was shocking how badly he wanted her—he'd gone from intending a one-time kiss, exploratory and romantic, to crowding her against the door and fending off the driving urge to slip his hand up her shirt and hike her legs around his waist and …

Something buzzed. Archer ignored it, but Natalie jumped. "Archer," she said in a shaky voice. "Your phone is ringing."

"It does that a lot." Reluctantly, he let go of her. It felt like molten lava flowed beneath his skin, slow and thick and scorching. Natalie's face was flushed and her eyes were bright, but she turned her head and stared at the far wall of the kitchen. He took a step back to keep from kissing her again, and pulled the phone from his pocket. It was Duke Austen, and he silently cursed his VIP client's shitty timing as he answered the call. "Hey, Duke."

"Bad news," said Austen grimly. "Some tabloid dick seems to have gotten wind of the locale, which is going to screw up the magazine deal. Jane is really upset."

Archer said a few more curses inside his head. If a tabloid published wedding photos first, the magazine deal was off—along with any hope the couple had of having a private wedding. Brampton House would be crawling with paparazzi within a few hours if word got out, no matter how many security firms were hired to keep them away. "Are you sure? Has he published?"

"I don't know." Duke's voice seethed with anger. "What can we do?"

He sighed. This wasn't his area of expertise, but Duke was his client. He gave Natalie an apologetic glance and stepped away. She gave a jerky nod and began making a clatter with dishes in the sink. Archer lowered his voice. "Let me make some calls. I'll get back to you."

"Where are you?" demanded Duke.

"On my way back to the hotel. Give me twenty minutes." He ended the call. Natalie was still washing dishes, scrubbing energetically. "I have to go," he said quietly.

She nodded, her curls bouncing. "Okay."

He stepped up behind her and laid his hands on her hips. A muscle tensed in her waist, but she didn't look at him. "I don't want to."

"Well." She inhaled deeply as he pressed his lips to the back of her neck. "Can't always do what you want to …"

Wasn't that the truth. He wanted to stay right here, exploring the velvety skin at her nape, breathing the intoxicating tropical smell of her skin, kissing his way along the slope of her collarbone. He wanted to throw gasoline on the sparks that smoldered between them and walk into the blaze. For a lingering moment he ignored the call of duty; he refused to think about how many calls he'd have to make to solve Duke's problem.

Natalie took a long, shuddering breath and twisted around in his arms. Her hands landed flat on his chest. "Archer—"

"Don't tell me it's too fast unless you want it to stop now," he whispered, tucking her against him once more. "Do you?"

Her gaze dropped. "Not at the moment …"

"Good. Neither do I." He kissed her again, hard and hungrily. "I'll see you tomorrow."

Looking dazed, she nodded. He bent his head and licked the chocolate off her cheek. "My favorite," he breathed again, right next to her ear. She gave a soft moan, and he made himself let go of her and walk away without looking back.

# CHAPTER
## SEVEN

Natalie scrubbed at the dishes until they would have passed muster at the White House. Her skin felt electrified, and she did not want to think about how close she'd come to having sex with a man she'd only met four days ago, up against the kitchen pantry door.

She swiped at the chocolate on her face again. *You don't have to shag him*, echoed her mother's voice in her head. *Yeah, but what if I want to?* she silently retorted. Her mother had probably said that only because Natalie was definitely not the type who would. Even in college she'd never gotten serious with a guy within the first month. Now she was so turned on by one kiss from Archer, if he'd made any move to take things further she would have dragged him into the other room and started tearing off her clothes.

"Okay," she said aloud, horrified by the breathless tenor of her voice. "Okay. You're a little deprived." Although she hadn't felt so bothered by that yesterday. "It's just hot when a guy comes on to you like that." So hot, her knees were still shaking. "Get over it, Nat."

Her phone shrilled loudly then, and she nearly dropped the glass she was washing for the fourth time. Her heart leapt into her throat.

Archer? But no—he didn't even have her phone number, and when she seized the phone, it was Pippa's ID on the screen. Taking a deep breath and telling herself it was relief and not disappointment, she answered. "Hi."

"Are you still terribly oppressed by the traffic?" said her friend in greeting. "I've been feeling just awful for telling you it would be quiet."

"Oh ... I'm surviving."

"Are you sure? Because I'm willing to trade you, my flat in Hammersmith for the cottage. The kitchen's not as big, but I'm a rotten friend for sending you into a construction zone when you only asked for peace and quiet. I can drive out tonight and help you move."

"No, don't," she mumbled. Archer was only here for a wedding, which meant he'd be gone in a week or so. That already sounded short.

There was silence on the phone, almost palpably curious. "Are they done, then? I thought you were ready to detonate the road to put an end to it."

"I got used to it, I guess ..."

"Natalie," said Pippa carefully, "are you okay? You sound stoned."

She let her head fall back. "I'm not stoned." She paused. "I have a serious case of lust for one of the guys attending the wedding at Brampton House," she said in a rush, almost hearing Pippa's mouth drop open. "I just kissed him. And made out with him."

There was a long silence, then Pippa said in her most proper, bossy voice, "Put the real Natalie back on the line, please."

"I know! Totally not like me! But I did, and Pip"—she lowered her voice to a whisper even though only Oliver the cat would hear her—"I would have done more."

"Oh my God, was he not into you?" demanded Pippa. "Boot his ass out the door."

"No, his phone rang." She looked out the window, but Archer was long gone. Oliver sprawled on the table where he usually worked. "I think it was work. He works a lot."

"Details," commanded Pippa.

Natalie obliged. Not that she knew much about him, as was blindingly clear from the brevity of her explanation. "He said he'd see me tomorrow," she finished. "What do you think: should I have sex with him or not?"

Her friend snorted with laughter. "You're absolutely gagging for it! I say sex. Lord knows I never saw anyone worth shagging in Melbury; hot men are like the Loch Ness monster around there."

"Not this week. I've seen people who must be wedding guests. More than one has been hot."

Pippa swore. "You would find the one week in eternity when there are attractive men in town. I lived there for *two years*, Nat, and saw nary a one."

"You only spent summers here."

"Two endless summers without so much as a buff delivery man. Carpe diem."

Natalie rubbed her toes down the back of her leg. "You don't think he's just looking to hook up because that's what people do at weddings?"

"Natalie," said Pippa with great patience, "who cares? You want to shag him; if he wants to shag you, where is the problem?"

"You are the worst conscience a girl could ever have," she told her friend.

Pippa laughed. "I'm the evil genie on your shoulder, not your conscience! Look him up online to satisfy your nerves, then put on that red dress you have and wear nothing underneath."

"I didn't even bring that dress!"

"Then wear any old skirt. If he wants you, he won't notice anyway."

"Good-bye, Pip." She hung up and put down the phone. Pippa was wilder than she was—although the very fact that Natalie was considering sleeping with Archer, after only one kiss and zero dates, hardly left her feeling more virtuous. Still …

She went into the other room, averting her eyes from the pile of discarded electronics on the floor. She opened the browser and typed in Archer's name in the search bar. And she learned … He was a lawyer. The first several pages of results were all legal related, although they did load much faster than usual, as he'd promised. She clicked the images tab, and the screen filled with his face, giving her another little jolt of attraction. They were mostly professional photos, but one caught her eye and she clicked it. It was Archer, several years younger, with an older man who had to be his father. The resemblance was unmistakable. *Ted Quinn of Quintillion Capital and Archer Quinn of Scarsdale Phillips LLP,* was the caption; it had been taken at a charity event in San Francisco. Natalie's gaze lingered on Archer's face. He was smiling, but it was almost grim and forced. His father's smile, on the other hand, was straight out of a mouthwash commercial. Archer said he hadn't forgiven his dad even years after the divorce. In fact, it sounded like he still hated his father. That sounded ... implacable. Rigid, even.

With a shake of her head, she went back to her original search. She was only contemplating a brief fling. It didn't really matter what his family relations were like because she would probably never meet them. She only cared that he wasn't a crazy person, now that he knew about her family restaurant and could find her again, and the Internet was hardly likely to tell her much about that. The only thing to do was put some form of restraint on her hormones and try to get to know the guy. She closed the browser and went back to the kitchen, even though she had very little interest in custards or madeleines anymore.

DUKE'S PROBLEM did not turn out to be easily fixed. A handful of photos, allegedly of Jane in her wedding dress, had ended up online, and the magazine was threatening to jettison the charity deal. Duke was in a fury, although he had to back down a bit when Archer discovered the maid of honor had posted the photos—and that her date was the publisher of several tabloid newspapers.

"You invited Damien Knightly, owner of *The London Weekly?*" he asked incredulously. "Duke—no offense—but what were you thinking? Did you make him sign a nondisclosure agreement?"

Duke scowled. "No. But I know he's behind these photos. Roxanna wouldn't do this to Jane on her own."

Archer exhaled and paced around the room. "I wish you'd

mentioned this earlier." He raised his hand in appeasement as his client scowled harder. "How bad are the pictures?"

"Fugly as hell," said Duke. "Can I shoot the guy? We're going hunting tomorrow."

"Please don't." Archer winced.

"Whatever. Maybe I can get Compton to shoot him; it's his property. But Knightly's not the only problem; there's a sleazy freelance photographer also lurking about. Jane was in tears over the deal falling apart, and I admit it's been kind of nice not having my every action on TMZ." He made a face. "I thought the attention would go away, now that I'm settling down."

Archer gave him a look. "Seems like not. I'll call Tom and have him get in touch with the magazine people, expressing your outrage over the suggestion that you've violated the deal and reaffirming your commitment to it. Can I say the photos are probably frauds?"

"Whatever it takes," said Duke moodily. "I just don't want someone watching us from behind every tree."

"I understand." He already had his phone in hand to look up the number for Tom Kincaid, the entertainment attorney at his firm who'd done the magazine deal. Archer didn't know much about that area of law, but Duke was his client and it was his responsibility to see that it was fixed.

"Thanks, dude."

Archer went back to his room. This wasn't a call he could place from the top of the hill, where anyone might overhear what was confidential and potentially very costly. And if he walked back to Natalie's garden, he wasn't sure he'd be able to keep his full attention on the question at hand. She'd looked unbelievably sexy when he left, her face flushed and her hair rumpled and her eyes dilated with desire. If Duke hadn't called him, Archer wasn't sure they wouldn't have ended up naked. He felt like he was being swept away by an avalanche; the first step had seemed small and fairly innocent, but now he was almost in free fall. He couldn't wait to see her again. He was dying to kiss her again. He reached for the landline to call Tom, hoping his colleague would find a quick solution.

But there wasn't one, and he ended up on a conference call with

Tom and the magazine lawyers. Archer foresaw his evening slipping away. He looked longingly out the window toward Natalie's cottage. It was hidden from sight, but if he closed his eyes he could still picture her leaning against the pantry door, head back, throat exposed all the way down to the so-tempting valley between her breasts. Damn it. He was almost ready to make the charity payment himself, just to be done with this so he could go back to Primrose Cottage.

Duke knocked on his door at one point, in search of an update, and Archer could only give a tentative thumbs-up. He'd boldly claimed the dress photos were fake, and while the magazine lawyers weren't completely convinced, it had given them pause. After some haggling, Tom got them to agree that they wouldn't exercise the termination clause until after the wedding, when they would have their own unquestionably authentic photos to compare to these blurry shots. Duke readily agreed to hire more security to prevent any more lapses, and vowed to remind all guests that they were not to post photos online.

Finally the magazine lawyers said they would confer and get back to them. Tom promised to stay on it, and Archer hung up the phone in relief. Duke slapped his shoulder in gratitude, and invited him to come have a drink with him and Jane. Curious to know why Jane hadn't kicked out her maid of honor, Archer went, but Jane only thanked him effusively before being swept away by a tall redhead, who turned out to be that maid of honor, Roxanna Lane. So she was the one who'd brought the tabloids right into the wedding party and nearly ruined the magazine deal? Archer watched her for a few minutes, until a guy in an expensive suit came and put his arm around her waist. That must be Damien Knightly. Duke had said Jane was in tears over the possible breached deal, but she was chatting amiably enough with Roxanna and Knightly now.

Well. Let Duke sort that out. Archer had more important things to think about now, like the next time he could see Natalie. Fast, she'd called it. He knew that, but didn't want to change anything. At the moment he was completely willing to let himself be swept away by the avalanche. But he also didn't want to end up a broken, bruised mess when it stopped, which meant he had to back up a step. Slow things down, just a tiny bit, without sacrificing any of the heat between them.

He needed a plan. And the way to a chef's heart … had to include chocolate.

# CHAPTER
# EIGHT

atalie had barely come downstairs the next morning when Archer tapped on the kitchen door. She pushed it open, unable to stop the smile that spread across her face as he presented her with a small posy of flowers.

"Good morning," he said.

"Thank you." She held them to her nose before plopping them into the sink. "That's a nice way to start the day."

"I can think of one better."

Her toes curled in her slippers. Without hesitation she raised her face, inviting him to kiss her. He did so at once, his hand molding around the back of her neck to pull her to him. Just as Natalie began to list toward him, forgetting every bit of her overnight resolution to be more circumspect and get to know him, he lifted his head. Saving her from herself, she thought.

"And I brought breakfast." He held up a paper bag. "Stole it from the kitchen. The chef up at the hotel is a real prick, but he can cook."

She pushed the door closed. "How nice it will be to eat something other than my own cooking!"

"I thought as much." He pointed at a cabinet with a questioning look, and she nodded; plates were in there, along with coffee cups. She started the coffee as he took some pastries out of the paper bag. "I also thought it was fair, after you fed me yesterday, that I feed you. My first thought was dinner, but then someone at my office scheduled me on a call for dinnertime." He made a noise of disgust. "So I thought of lunch … until the concierge informed me there are only two decent places to eat locally: the village pub and a vegan restaurant called The Pineapple of Perfection."

Natalie began to laugh at the aggrieved expression on his face.

"I grew up in San Francisco," he argued. "I have nothing against vegan food, and sometimes it's quite good. Sometimes … It's seaweed." He shuddered. "And that left breakfast."

"Breakfast is my favorite meal of the day," she told him, still laughing. "Thank you."

"Really?" His eyes heated and skimmed down her body. "It might be mine too."

"Because of coffee?" She rested her elbows on the counter and cocked her head, feeling sexy and flirty. She wore her cutoff denim skirt, the one that ended well above her knees, and a long-sleeve shirt that was tight and stretchy with a deep V in front. It was not cooking attire. But as Archer's gaze slid right down to her breasts, it felt like the giant AGA had been on for hours.

"Coffee," he murmured distractedly, "and other things."

"Such as?" God, Pippa would cheer if she could hear how throaty Natalie's voice had gone. Even to her own ears she sounded like a phone sex operator.

He lifted his gaze back to her face. "Such as doing something right. Not rushing it."

"Were you rushing it yesterday?"

He shook his head slowly, his eyes fixed on her. "But I don't want to risk anything."

Her cheeks warmed. "You're doing fine so far."

One corner of his mouth curled upward. "Thought so."

Thankfully the coffee machine beeped, and she busied herself with it. Was there *anything* wrong with him? Most guys she dated were happy to let her cook for them, including serving. Archer moved around the kitchen as she fixed the coffee, finding napkins and even a vase for the flowers. By the time she had the cappuccino prepared, he had set the table, complete with bouquet, and stood waiting to pull out her chair. It felt so comfortable, so *right*, she almost didn't know what to say.

"Chivalry," she joked lamely, letting him seat her. His fingers ran over her shoulders and lingered at her nape for just a moment, but it was enough to send a thrill down her spine.

He took the seat next to hers. "My mother told me it would make an impression."

"She gives good advice." Natalie studied the selection of pastries. "But then, making an excellent chocolate pudding cake is already a sterling recommendation."

"I quite agree. And speaking of that—" He fished a folded paper from his shirt pocket. "I got it. My gift to you, as no cookbook should be without chocolate pudding cake."

She unfolded it and read the printout of a scanned, handwritten recipe. His mother had elegant handwriting, and she made very careful and exact notes about how to melt the chocolate and how to tell when the cake was done. Natalie was impressed. "It looks delicious."

"You can tell from reading the recipe?" He bit into a large frosted bun.

Natalie selected a sticky roll covered with finely chopped nuts. "Somewhat." She took a bite and closed her eyes. It *was* good. "Just like I bet you can tell from reading a contract if something's a good deal."

His eyes had riveted on her mouth as she ate. "Yeah," he murmured. "Usually."

She ran her tongue over her lower lip, turned on by the way he watched her do it. "I hope your mom didn't mind you giving it away."

"Not at all." His lazy grin reappeared. "Better that than I try to make it myself."

"It doesn't look that complicated."

"Maybe not," he replied, "but it needs to be done just right. When it is …" He put his fingers to his lips. "Heaven." He carried the kiss to her hand, lying on the table. "When it's not …" He shrugged, swirling his fingers over her hand. "Crap."

"Now I don't know if I can ever make it," she said unevenly, mesmerized as his fingers moved up her wrist to play with the sleeve of her shirt. "The pressure ..."

"Mmm, you'll rise to the occasion," he whispered. "Lick your lip."

"Why?"

"You've got something sticky on your upper lip, and if you don't lick it off, I will."

She stared at him. Then she reached out, dragged her finger through the frosting on his half-consumed bun, and smeared it on her lip.

Archer let out his breath. "I was hoping you'd do that," he said before pushing his chair back and hauling her into his lap. Natalie's short skirt rode up around her hips as she straddled his thighs and he cupped both hands around her head for a scorching kiss. She slid her arms around his neck and stomped any lingering voice of hesitation into silence. It wasn't too fast if she wanted him as desperately as he wanted her. It didn't matter that she hadn't known him since nursery school, not when everything was just so right with him.

"Damn." He pulled back, breathing hard. "I keep losing my train of thought around you. You said two things yesterday. One, that this was going very fast, and two, that you don't know me." He paused to brush his lips against hers again, then looked her right in the eyes. "I don't feel inclined to change the first, but I can change the second." He settled her more comfortably on his lap. Something inside her quaked as his hard-on pressed against her thigh, but aside from a brief catch in his breathing, Archer didn't acknowledge it.

"Let's see ... My birthday is August fourteenth. I tend to get a little crazy about San Francisco Giants baseball, but not other sports. My real first name is Theodore." She raised her brows and grinned, and he gave her a stern look. "Don't you dare use it. It's my dad's name. My mother is named Patricia and she lives in Sonoma wine country. It's beautiful out there, you'll love it."

Natalie ignored the way her heart jolted at the veiled suggestion she might ever visit his mother. "Is that where you grew up?"

He shook his head. "San Francisco. My father's firm is there and we lived in the city."

She ran her finger down his collar. "What is venture capital?"

Very subtly, he tensed. "Investment money."

"And that's what your dad does?"

His eyes grew dark and for a moment she thought she'd crossed a line. "Yes."

Natalie bit her lip but forged on. "You said you hadn't forgiven him, but it sounds like the divorce was a while ago. I only had the blowout with my brother a few weeks ago and I don't think I could endure being angry at him for years. It just struck me as ... well, as odd that you haven't spoken to your dad in forever."

For a minute he didn't answer. "My dad's a hard man, Natalie. I don't hate him, but I don't really like him, either. I don't care that he divorced Mum; he was a rotten husband anyway. But he made her feel like shit when he did it, and you know what? He's very good at that. He's a manipulator and a snake oil salesman who always covers his own ass and is more than willing to throw other people under the bus. On the other hand ..." He ran one hand up her bare thigh. "I think you and your brother are on the same team, when the going gets tough, and that you actually like him. My dad is only on his team, and he's only likable when he wants something from you."

She nodded. That was fair; not every parent was admirable and worthy of respect. And Archer was right about her and Paul, despite the feud between them now. She was still angry at her brother, but not as much as when she'd left. "I have another nosy question," she said, changing the subject. "Why haven't you got a girlfriend?"

He leaned back, his eyes glittering at her. "I work a lot."

"So you haven't got time for anyone?"

"No, I haven't got time to meet anyone." His gaze dipped to the V of her shirt. "Usually." Without thinking she subtly arched her back, and his breath caught again. "And when I hadn't met anyone, there was no reason to blow off work ... It's a vicious cycle."

"You should try working in a restaurant," she said lightly. "I'm free between two and four, then again after midnight."

"So if I ask you out for coffee at three, you'll be available?"

"Are you asking?" she asked coyly, batting her eyelashes and trying not to blush while she hoped he said *yes*.

"Just checking." His hands had relocated to her hips, just above where her skirt was bunched up. "Anything else you'd like to know?"

She could ask anything, she realized; he was telling her without asking similar questions in return. He was also enormously aroused, yet hadn't made a move, even though the thought had crossed her mind—more than once—that if she took off her underwear, they could have sex right here and now on this chair. But he wanted to get to know her. He'd brought her food and flowers, which counted as a proper date. Pippa had said it didn't matter if he only wanted a wedding hookup, but if it turned out he wanted more ... something like a real relationship ...

"So you don't have to work today?" she asked, feeling reckless and a bit wild.

His smile was edged with promise. "Today I am blowing off work. Today we're going to have fun."

ARCHER RETURNED to Brampton House in a buoyant mood.

After breakfast, he and Natalie had walked into the village. They bought sandwiches and a bottle of wine at the tiny gourmet shop and ate a picnic lunch on the grass in a nearby park. He told her about the wedding, including the grouse-hunting bachelor party he had skipped that morning, and she told him about her family's restaurant, like the time a diner wanted to propose and put the engagement ring in the frosting atop his girlfriend's cake, but didn't pop the question before she ate it, ring and all. Natalie had decided to get a cat, based on her time with Oliver, and Archer regaled her with stories of his mother's various cats until she laughed so hard she cried. She teased him about his love of dessert by describing the cakes she'd baked recently, which were all stored in Primrose Cottage's walk-in wine cooler. He was entranced. When his phone buzzed with a reminder of his business call, he was astonished to realize they had talked all day. He walked her home and said good-bye with a kiss so hot, he very nearly forgot that he had to leave.

He jogged up the stairs to his room, finally beginning to wonder what Jack wanted to talk about. His boss had e-mailed the previous night to set it up and had only said it was in regard to funding for Brightball. Archer had almost stopped thinking about that client entirely, between Duke's tabloid trouble and Natalie. But if Brightball finally had some funding, Jack would probably want him to revise the financing documents. For once Archer planned to defer it. He could work on the plane home, but until then he was going to keep having fun.

After the warm day outside, his hotel room felt lonely and dark. There was no smell of chocolate baking, and he couldn't see Primrose Cottage. He even missed Oliver the cat jumping up and trying to lie on his keyboard. With no Wi-Fi, he could only review the notes and documents he'd already downloaded to his laptop, catch up on his billing, and wait for Jack.

The call was almost a half hour late. Sunk in thought, watching clouds drift across the twilight sky as he wondered if Natalie would still be awake after this call ended, Archer jumped when the phone on his desk rang, the muted trill loud in the quiet room.

"Archer," boomed Jack's voice over the line. "Hope we aren't keeping you from the bachelor party or anything."

"I wouldn't skip that for you," he said. Just for Natalie.

The other man laughed. "That's right, you're on vacation."

Archer cast a jaundiced eye at the billing worksheet open on his laptop. He'd logged over thirty-five hours since setting foot on English soil. Some vacation—aside from Natalie's cooking, anyway. "If you say so. Is Bill there?"

"Hi Archer," piped up Bill, his voice vibrating with suppressed eagerness. "Big day, huh?"

"No, the wedding is this weekend." But somehow he knew Bill wasn't asking about the wedding.

Bill just laughed.

"The good news is that we've got a funding offer," said Jack. "A fantastic one. We've been working out details with the investors this week. I'll let them introduce themselves, but I set up this call to hammer out the main terms. Hold on a moment and I'll get them on the line."

Archer raised his eyebrows, doodling a string of dollar signs and a large question mark on his notebook. Who was this investor? Bright-ball had enormous potential, but so far had fallen short on convincing the venture funds to chip in more than a pittance.

"Hey there, I'm Rick Garner," said a new voice. The name rang a bell, but Archer couldn't put his finger on it. "Glad to join you all; I'm looking forward to working with everyone. I'll be the point person on Brightball."

"Good morning," said a voice with a faint German accent. "Dietrich Metzer here."

Well, shit. The bell rang crystal clear this time, even before Rick Garner added, "And our principal will be sitting in on the call today."

"Good morning, gentlemen. Hello, Archer," came a rich, genial voice. It was a movie star voice, the kind of voice hired to record commercials for expensive luxury cars. It was a compelling voice, one that could persuade you to pay ten percent above your absolute price ceiling and still make you feel like you got a bargain. It was a voice that could tell a woman with third-stage breast cancer that she was being divorced, and make her think everything was her fault.

Archer flung his pencil at the wall, not caring that it left a black dot on the wallpaper. "Hello, Dad."

"Nice of you to join us, Mr. Quinn," said Jack.

"Quinntillion is investing twenty-seven million in the company," piped up Bill, sounding far too pleased with himself.

Archer smiled grimly. So this was what had got Bill so excited. Too bad he had no idea what he'd gotten himself into. "When did this come about?"

"All in the last week. Jack led the negotiations." Bill paused. "I thought he would let you know."

"Archer's overseas at the moment," said Jack quickly. "What with the time difference and all, I just hadn't found time to bring him up to speed."

"No sweat. Well, as you can imagine we've got quite a bit of stuff to talk about ..." And Bill plunged into the terms of the new investment. Archer let Jack do most of the talking, just as he intended to let Jack do most of the work. This was obviously Jack's doing; if he'd wanted Archer's input, he would have asked for it days ago, before Bill became enamored of the idea of Quinntillion money. Ted Quinn was reputed to have the golden touch, after all, and when he invested, he invested big. That didn't mean he didn't get something for his money, though; Ted always demanded what he valued most, which was control. No doubt Bill had barely thought past all the ways he could use Quintillion's money. The full extent of the devil's bargain he'd made wouldn't dawn on him until much later, when he found himself eased out the door of the company that was his entire life.

When the call finally ended, Archer hung up, counted to ten, and dialed Jack's number. "It must be my birthday," he said in false delight. "You forgot to jump up and shout, 'Surprise!'"

Jack's sigh echoed across the Atlantic. "I wasn't keeping it from you. You've just been hard to reach, and I wanted to tell you myself."

"On the phone with our client listening? Your presentation skills need work."

"You've been gone almost a week," retorted Jack.

"That doesn't mean I haven't been working, and I don't just mean socializing with our firm's other clients, as you strongly encouraged me to do." They both knew Project-TK meant far more to their bottom line than Brightball, at least for the moment.

"To be honest, Archer, I didn't think I would be the one to get Quinntillion involved in a deal with any of our clients."

Archer stretched out his legs. He'd put his feet up on the bed a while ago, about the time he decided he was done working—for the rest of his trip. "And if you'd asked me, I would have advised you against it."

"Why the hell would you do that? Helping clients connect with venture capitalists is a part of our service."

"Yes, isn't it?" He laughed, a little mockingly. "Except I know how Quinntillion operates. You'll see what I mean when you get their term sheet." During the call, Ted's attorney, Dietrich Metzer—who looked and sounded like a nerdy Swiss banker but who was in reality a rapacious, soulless vampire—had said almost nothing. Archer knew that was pure deception. He'd worked at Quinntillion when he was a teenager, and had seen in person how coldly Metzer would cut someone out of their life's work if it led to a bigger payout for Quin-ntillion.

"They're going to elevate Brightball from marginal start-up to the leading innovator in optical technology."

"Yeah, and in the process they're going to eat away at Bill's control." Some inventors were good with that. They started a company, got it running, sold out, and took their payout to start something newer and more exciting. But Bill lived and breathed Brightball. Archer didn't think he'd want to cede control to Quinntillion or anyone else.

This time Jack's sigh was exasperated. "But that's why we have you, Archer, to look out for Bill's rights. He needs the money, you know how to protect him from Quinntillion's more outrageous demands, everyone will be happy. Why are you acting like I pissed in your coffee?"

He put back his head and stared out the window. Natalie's house lay directly on the other side of that hill. *I don't like lawyers,* echoed her voice in his mind. At the moment, he didn't like lawyers, either, beginning with Jack Harper.

"Jack, did you bring me on just to get business with Quinntillion?"

His boss chuckled. "It didn't hurt, being Ted Quinn's son."

All right; fair enough. He'd suspected as much, although no one at Harper Millman had ever brought up his father. But saying it out in the open had a strangely freeing effect on Archer's thoughts. The vague discontent he'd felt for the last few months suddenly crystalized, and what he wanted became clear.

"You should have done more diligence." Archer sat up and flipped his notebook closed. "If you had, you would have known that this was the first time in six years I've spoken to my father, about business or anything else." If Jack had asked, Archer would also have told him that he'd never try to steer a client toward a deal with Quinntillion, and that he'd regard any such deal as if it had been made by a hostile firm. Not that it mattered now. "I assume you've already talked to Bill about this conflict, and he's still willing to have me working on this?"

"Absolutely!"

"Then do me one favor from here on: no more bullshit surprises, okay?"

"Fine."

"I also want to form my own tech practice within the firm," Archer went on. "Duke Austen has some big ideas in the works. I want to take Elle Williams and create a dedicated team to bring them out. Some of these ideas will generate work for years to come, and I need more than spotty time from an ever-changing variety of associates."

"A tech practice?" Jack sounded doubtful. "I'd have to run it by the other partners ..."

"Do that," said Archer, his gaze moving to the hill outside his window. Natalie was probably getting ready for bed by now. Coming to England had been an awesome idea, even if it led to him working with his father. "But if he doesn't approve, I'll be leaving the firm. And Duke Austen will come with me."

"Whoa," exclaimed Jack. "That's blackmail!"

*That's the Quinn way,* Archer thought. "Not really. Just bald facts. Let me know when I get back to Boston."

"I'm sure we can work out a plan that will suit everyone," Jack began, but Archer was done.

"I have to go, Jack. Good talking to you." He hung up the phone and checked his watch. It was too late to go back to Primrose Cottage, so he went to the unofficial hotel bar, the back patio. Piers Prescott walked by, headed to the pool with a towel over his shoulder.

"Making up for missing the drunken shooting party this morning?" Piers nodded at Archer's glass of scotch.

He took a swallow. "Nope. Celebrating telling off my boss."

Piers's eyebrows shot up. "Why?"

"For manipulating me into working with my father."

"Manipulating?" Piers frowned. "What the hell?"

Archer drank some more scotch, feeling better and better. "You know my father; he's all his reputation cracks him up to be. I haven't spoken to him in years. But tonight, my boss admitted he hired me partly to get business from dear old Ted, which he's just done—and I have to work on the deal. So I told him to go fuck himself."

"Literally?" There was surprise, but also a tinge of envy in the other man's voice.

"More figuratively." Archer imagined Jack Harper's face during their conversation. "But he got my meaning."

Piers Prescott stared at him with a very odd expression.

Archer grinned. "If you're wondering, it feels fantastic."

"Right," murmured Piers.

"Archer!" He turned to see Duke striding across the patio. "More trouble with the magazine deal."

Of course there was. Archer didn't even care this time. He felt like nailing someone's hide to the wall, and a sleazy tabloid hack was as good a choice as any. He thunked his glass down on the bar. "Then let's go crucify the bastard."

# CHAPTER
# NINE

Archer slept late the next morning. After dealing with more outrage from the magazine lawyers—this time over photos of the groom and groomsmen aiming rifles at a cowering paparazzo—he'd had another scotch. When he woke, the sky was dark gray and thunder rumbled in the distance. Normally he would have opened his laptop and spent the morning working; half the wedding party had come home drunk from the bachelor and bachelorette parties the previous night, and the hotel was fairly quiet. But today he pulled on his sneakers and went for a run, finally feeling like a weight had lifted off him. And as he ran, he made a list.

First, he had been working too hard. It hadn't been a lie when he told Natalie he had no time to meet anyone. Now, however, he had greater motivation than ever to delegate more work, especially work related to Brightball's new investor.

Second, he did want to have his own specialty practice. It was good to be in a firm, with guys like Tom available when his clients needed something extra, but Archer wanted more independence. Having a client like Duke Austen gave him leverage, and he was ready to use it.

And third, he was going to use his greater autonomy and increased delegation to find more free time. Because he had met someone now, and he was ready to blow off work for her. The avalanche had tumbled him head over heels until he had no idea which way was up anymore. The only thing he knew was that he wanted to know everything about her, every little thing that made her laugh or frown or roll her eyes. He wanted to perfect the art of making her cheeks flush pink and her voice go throaty and he wanted to make her come in his arms. He had two more days here, and he meant to spend both of them with her.

That last line of thought quickened his steps until he was almost flying up the gravel path. He took the stairs two at a time, pausing only for a group of women heading down. The bride was in the center of them, glowing with delight. The wedding was tomorrow, he realized, and when Jane caught his eye he gave her a big grin. *Thank you a hundred thousand times for inviting me,* he silently told her. He headed to his room, took a quick shower, and changed. Then he grabbed his key without a second glance at his laptop or phone. Time to see what delicious something he would get to lick off Natalie's skin today.

He went out the back of the house, only to almost run into the wedding planner and hotel owner, who seemed to be having an argument.

"It's completely blown," Arwen Kilpatrick was saying furiously. "Dead. Who knows how long it's been out, and now everything is spoiled because *of course* it would be hot these last few days—"

"But it was only one of four," Harry Compton countered. "It can't be that bad, darling."

"Harry, we have *no dessert!* Not even a bride cake!"

Archer, already starting to detour around them, slowed. No dessert? That sounded intrinsically bad, but her voice was frantic, almost shrill with despair. He tried to think what was planned for today that could have caused a lack of dessert to be a major problem ...

Oh, right. The formal rehearsal dinner. He hesitated a moment, then turned around.

"Excuse me," he said to the arguing couple.

The hotelier immediately stepped in front of Arwen. "How can I help you?"

"I might be able to help you," he said, watching the wedding planner. "It sounds like there was an equipment malfunction in the kitchen."

"Everything is under control," Compton tried to say but Arwen was having none of that.

"One of our refrigerators died, Mr. Quinn." She drew herself up and managed a smile that was remarkably poised. "But don't worry, I still have almost seven hours to find dessert for nearly a hundred people. I've had worse problems."

"And I have a suggestion." Archer thought of Natalie's wine cooler, filled with barely tasted cakes and pies. "Your neighbor is a chef, writing a cookbook. I know she's been baking desserts for at least a week now. I've tasted some of them and everything is otherworldly."

Arwen's smile slipped a bit. "I'm sure they are, but my desserts came from a top bakery in London."

"She's the deputy chef at Cuisine du Jude, in Wellesley, Massachusetts." Archer was betting a celebrity wedding planner from New York City would have heard of it. If Jack Harper had trouble getting reservations there, it was exclusive and excellent.

And sure enough, Arwen's eyes went wide. "Oh my God," she breathed, turning to Harry Compton. "The most perfect date night restaurant in America! This might work."

Compton looked disconcerted. "A chef? No, the only neighbor is Amaryllis Sonnier, the artist. She's not even here; she spends every summer in Portugal."

"And she's lent her house to Natalie, who has a walk-in wine cooler filled with cakes."

"Cuisine du Jude is exquisite," Arwen babbled. "I ate there last summer to check it out for a client. *Exquisite*. If she can cook half as well as Judith Corcoran ..."

"Natalie is her daughter." Archer grinned.

Arwen looked at Compton, who shrugged. "I have to give it a shot," she said. "Mr. Quinn, I take it you'll introduce me?"

"I was on my way over there now."

"If this works, I will kiss you," declared Arwen, falling in step beside him. Archer just saw the scowl that crossed Compton's face before he, too, set off through the garden toward Primrose Cottage with them.

NATALIE NOTICED when Archer didn't come down to her cottage the next morning. She told herself it was because of the rain, but then the clouds blew away and still the patio was empty, save for Oliver stretched out on the table where Archer usually worked. Natalie tried not to scowl at the cat. It wasn't his fault Archer hadn't come.

She hoped it wasn't her fault.

The day they'd spent together had been ... well, pretty nearly perfect. He was funny. He was considerate. He was thoughtful. He bought really good wine for a picnic on the grass. His kisses made her feel like a goddess, and his hands made her think pornographic thoughts. The attraction between them might be roaring along at a breakneck pace, but as Archer said yesterday, she didn't feel like stopping it.

But then where was he?

No. She refused to make herself crazy wondering why he wasn't there. He was a grown man and had things to do. Just because he'd kissed her senseless ... several times ... didn't mean anything. It was pure coincidence that he hadn't shown up after they made out like horny teenagers and then had a daylong date. No, she was a mature, independent woman who would not torture herself trying to understand the mind of any man. She spread out her notes on cookies, trying to decide where to start, and told herself to concentrate on her own work.

It didn't happen. Today, for the first time, she didn't feel like baking. Not even her go-to classic chocolate chip recipe was enticing, nor her scribbled suggestions about oats and nuts and dried fruits. She flicked through the pages, unable to decide, then took out the hand-written recipe for chocolate pudding cake. It did sound good, and Archer had dared her to make it ...

In a huff, she went out onto the patio and dropped into the chair, pushing her legs out straight in front of her. She tipped her head back, letting the sun warm her face. Oliver got to his feet and stretched, then walked across the table and climbed into her lap, purring hard. Natalie ran one hand down his back, smiling up at the sky. At least one male still wanted to get on top of her.

"Maybe I ought to take today off, too," she said to the cat. "I could walk back to town and look in the shops." Such few shops as were in town. "Do you need any kitty toys, Oliver?" His big paws, darker than the rest of him, flexed against her knee. "I don't even know what toys cats like."

"Jingle bells," said Archer from somewhere behind her. "And feathers. At least that's what my mother's cat likes."

Natalie started, and Oliver jumped off her lap with an offended meow. "Oh, hi," she said stupidly, feeling her face turn red. She got up, brushing the cat fur from her skirt.

"Good morning." His eyes warmed as he smiled. She could only smile back like an idiot as his gaze flicked up and down, hot and brazen. "I have a question to ask—actually a tremendous favor—but before I ask, I want you to know it's totally fine if you say no."

"Uh-oh." She tried to laugh even as her heart stuttered ridiculously. "That sounds ominous."

"No, it's just …" He hesitated. "I know you're not a fan of the wedding chaos, but the bride and groom are actually really decent people. There's been a malfunction in the kitchen with one of the refrigerators …"

The smile slid off her face. "Okay," she said tonelessly when Archer paused again.

He ran one hand over his head, ruffling his hair and raising the wave. "One of the refrigerators died, all the desserts for tonight's rehearsal dinner went bad, and the wedding planner—also a nice person—is in a bind. I know you have a bunch of cakes in the cooler, and I thought maybe you would be willing to help her out."

So he hadn't come down today because he'd been busy chatting with the wedding planner. And he hadn't said one word about yesterday, or asked how she was, or made any sign there was anything at all between them. He wanted her to bail out the same wedding party that had clogged the road, ruined her peace and quiet, and led to random people getting naked on her patio. How did a woman respond to that?

Archer obviously realized he'd gone wrong. "Shit. You'd never know I talk to people for a living. Well—will you just meet her for a minute? I swear to God if you don't want to do it, you don't have to, and I'll send her back up to the hotel."

Natalie lifted one shoulder. "Fine."

He gave her a reassuring smile and loped back out of the garden. He'd obviously brought the wedding planner with him—taking things a bit for granted, she thought sourly. But when he came back a moment later, there were two people with him, a woman with thick bangs cut in her shiny dark hair and a tall man with sharply angular features that managed to be handsome despite being so pronounced.

"Thank you," declared the woman fervently before anyone else could speak. She rushed forward, hand outstretched. "Arwen Kilpatrick. I'm thrilled to meet you—your mother is a visionary and a genius. What she does at Cuisine du Jude is simply amazing."

This made Natalie smile. She shook the woman's hand. "She is. I'm Natalie Corcoran."

The tall man also put out his hand. "Harry Compton," he said in crisp English tones. "I own Brampton House."

She shook his hand, too, although with less enthusiasm. He was responsible for all the traffic on the road, after all. "Hi."

"I hope Archer explained what happened. One of my refrigerators died sometime overnight and everything spoiled—ten cakes from one of the best bakeries in London. The buttercream is in puddles." Arwen took a deep breath. "If you could help in any way, I would be prostrate with gratitude. Money is no object, either. I am desperate, and Archer said he thought he'd died and gone to heaven when he tasted your baking." A glimmer of a smile crossed her face. "I expect Judith Corcoran's daughter must have milk and honey in her veins."

Natalie's reserve was thawing. "Not quite." She glanced at Archer, who looked guarded but hopeful. She remembered it was his client getting married; saving the day would be as much a win for him as it would be for Arwen. "Before you write a blank check, why don't you taste? I do have a bunch of cakes in the cooler, but they may not be what you want."

"*Cake* is what I want," said Arwen. Mr. Compton choked on a laugh.

"I made these this week, but they've all been sampled," Natalie warned as she led the way to the cooler. She hit the switch for the lights and pulled out a tray of chocolate cakes, all missing one thin wedge. "I couldn't bear to throw them out yet. What's your pleasure —chocolate?"

"They all look divine."

No baker could fail to respond to the look of greedy joy on Arwen's face. Natalie turned to Archer. "Would you mind getting some plates and forks?"

They tasted milk chocolate, dark chocolate, and chocolate with cherry filling. Natalie went deeper into the cooler and got out the vanilla cakes, some with coconut, some with strawberries, and one with marbled chocolate and cream cheese frosting. These were almost frozen, but came to freshness in a few minutes when cut into half-inch slices.

"Oh my God, I can die happy right now," moaned Arwen, taking another tiny bite.

"I still have lemon cake and two strawberry tortes," Natalie offered.

Arwen shook her head and put down her plate. "I don't need to taste any more. I want the lot; will you sell them to me?"

"All right." She thought the woman would hug her. "And please give a credit to Cuisine du Jude, and maybe mention there's a forthcoming cookbook with all these recipes."

Arwen laughed. "Done! You have saved my skin. I'll send a van down to pick them all up at five o'clock; is that okay? If the Next Gordon Ramsey squawks about giving me a refrigerator then, I will kill him with my bare hands."

"Which one will be the bride's cake, darling?" Harry Compton had mostly focused on tasting, but now he reached out—to Natalie's surprise—and smoothed away a stray bit of frosting from Arwen's mouth.

The wedding planner seemed to tilt in his direction as his thumb lingered on her lip, then caught herself. She sighed. "I can't worry about that. We'll just have to do without." She caught Natalie's raised eyebrows. "I had a special cake for the bride and groom's table, covered with fondant and real flowers. It's in the waste bin now."

"I could make one of those," Natalie heard herself say. "It would be tight on time, but I could probably do it …"

Arwen stared at her, perfectly still. "I would give you my firstborn baby if you could replace that cake."

"No thank you," said Natalie wryly. "I might need some help, though …"

"At your service." Archer winked at her. It was the first time he'd spoken since she brought out the coconut cake. "If you think I'll do."

Slowly, she smiled. "Let's give it a try."

Arwen and Mr. Compton left, promising to send the van and anything she needed from the caterer's supplies up at the hotel. Archer waved good-bye from the kitchen door, then closed it.

Natalie smiled, tucking up her hair. "Ready to be my slave?"

He caught her around the waist and kissed her, hot and intense and dizzying. "Yes," he said in a rough voice. "But first we have to bake a cake."

She toyed with a button on his shirt. "I missed you this morning." It just popped out before she could tell her brain not to admit it.

"I missed you too. Stupid fucking work kept me up last night." He backed her up against the pantry door and kissed her again. Her knees went weak and she clung to his neck, reveling in the weight of his body pressing hers hard against the wood. His hands ran down her waist, over her hips, and back up. She felt high as a kite, feverishly hot and giddy with excitement. He missed her. "You taste like coconut," he breathed, flattening his hand on the small of her back. "I love coconut."

"Better than chocolate?" She tugged his head back so she could run her tongue down his neck. He growled and leaned more heavily against her. Natalie shifted, moving her hips against his magnificent erection. How they were going to bake a cake now was beyond her.

"Whatever you taste like is my favorite." His mouth returned to hers, his tongue plunging deep, and Natalie forgot about cakes of any flavor.

"Okay." When he finally lifted his head and pressed his forehead to hers, his heart thundered against her palm, spread on his chest to hold his shirt. "Okay. How long does it take to make a cake?"

"A while …" Almost against her will, she started to tick through the steps in her mind. "Four to five hours, I think."

He exhaled. "Then this will have to wait." His hand, cupped around her butt, squeezed, and he slowly let her go. "Ready to bake?"

She was ready to tear off her clothes and throw caution to the wind, along with her panties. Hell, they probably wouldn't be the first people to have sex on these counters. But she had promised Arwen she would make the damn cake, and Archer had said only *wait*, meaning they were going to pick back up where they left off, so she let him back away and reached for her apron. "If we must."

For someone who claimed not to cook, Archer was at home in the kitchen. He rolled up his sleeves and followed her every direction. Thankfully Natalie had thrown a pair of square pans into the many boxes of baking supplies she'd shipped from home, so she set him to lining those with parchment and buttering everything. She swept aside all the cookie notes and busied herself with butter, sugar, and eggs as she mentally planned the cake. She still had fresh strawberries in the refrigerator, and a half-gallon of thick English cream to make a filling between the layers. There was no fondant in the kitchen, but she could make a rich buttercream frosting and slick it as smooth as glass. A quick piping of a lacy pattern with tinted frosting would finish the cake, and if Arwen had clean fresh flowers at Brampton House, she could add a few at the last moment.

Natalie had spent many hours baking with her mother, where naturally she fell into the junior role. Now that she was shoulder to shoulder with Archer, though, she realized how much she'd changed in the six weeks she'd spent in England. It felt right to be in charge, to direct every step of the creation—*her* creation, not a copy of her mother's work. Judy didn't even do wedding cakes, but Natalie was making one up on the fly. And it was fun.

When Archer dropped an egg on the floor and swore, she only laughed. When she caught him licking the empty bowl while she spread batter into the waiting pans, she flicked flour at him. When he lobbed a dollop of batter back at her and it landed on her cheek, she protested until he pinned her against the dishwasher and licked it off with soft, gentle kisses. She'd barely set the timer for the cakes before he lifted her to sit on the counter and went back to kissing her. Natalie closed her eyes to the messy kitchen and curled her legs around his waist to hold him closer.

"When are you going home?" he whispered some time later, nuzzling her ear.

"Hmm?" She had her hand inside his unbuttoned shirt, mesmerized by the feel of his skin, so hot and firm against her fingers.

"Home." He nipped her earlobe. "To Boston."

Home to Boston. To her parents. To the Jude. To her brother, and the feud still simmering between them. Her fingers slowed to a stop.

"I'm leaving on Sunday," Archer went on. "But I want to see you again—soon, and often. How much more cookbook do you have to write?"

Only quick breads and biscuits, she realized. She'd gone through meats and seafood, vegetables, salads, pasta, and now dessert. Amaryllis would be coming home in a month, putting an end to her stay anyway. Soon she'd have to pack up her pans, and her pride, and go back to face her family. "I don't know when I'm going home," she murmured.

Archer pulled back, finally picking up her mood change. He took her face in his hands and studied her. "Why not?"

"I guess I'm not looking forward to it."

He just waited. Natalie sighed, letting her head tilt into his hand, so warm and strong and comforting. She'd liked his hands from the start. "I left because I lost my temper and poured soup on my brother, in front of a restaurant full of people. I haven't been there since, because … Well, because I acted like a crazy bitch and I know it."

"Do you want to go back?"

She blinked. "I do! Of course I do!" Although … Did she? Now she was used to being in charge of the kitchen. If her dad was recovering, her mother would come back to Cuisine du Jude, and as much as Natalie loved cooking with her mother … "I think I do."

Archer was quiet for a minute. Inanely, Natalie felt grateful; the men in her family were used to filling any silence, overriding any uncertainty, always ready with their advice whether welcome or not. "You know," he finally said, "if you wanted to open your own place, I know some investors ..."

"My own place!" She scoffed. "What would I do with my own place?" Besides desserts and breads. She may have bragged about being able to disembowel a whole turkey, but her favorite thing was baking, from crackers and scones to cookies and—as of today— wedding cake.

Archer lifted one shoulder. "If you go into wedding cakes, Arwen would probably throw a ton of business your way. She offered you her firstborn child, after all."

Natalie laughed, and then she thought about it. A bakery? Without effort, plans started sprouting in her mind. It would get her away from Paul, yet offer the brand expansion he wanted. She would have her own kitchen, make her own menu, try her own experiments, but with ties to the Jude. And it would work well with her cookbook, provided she could find a publisher. Those were *her* recipes, no longer her mother's. The cookbook had begun as a face-saving project, but had gradually become something she really cared about. The fact that it was now associated with meeting Archer only made it better.

"You could think about it." Archer gave her a slight smile. "I may be useless in the kitchen, but I do know how to form a company."

She wound her arms around his neck. "You are definitely not useless in the kitchen."

While the cakes cooled, she set him to cutting the strawberries into thin slices so she could make the whipped cream filling, flavored with framboise and vanilla. Archer leaned his head over the mixer and inhaled deeply, sighing in pleasure. "This has been the best damn vacation of all time."

She laughed. "And you spent most of it working on the patio!"

He fed her a heart-shaped strawberry slice. "That should tell you how awesome the other parts have been, to outweigh thirty-five hours of work."

The afternoon sped by. As she split the cakes and filled them, they talked about what would be involved in setting up a Cuisine du Jude bakery, legally. Archer told her it could be structured so that she was the head of the bakery division and somewhat independent of Paul. Thinking of herself as head of a business made Natalie shake her head, but now the idea had grown roots. As she spread the buttercream over the cake, stacking the layers and smoothing away loose crumbs, the bakery took shape in her mind.

The van arrived while she was piping the last few swirls of pale violet icing, and she felt a thrill of pride as the caterers boxed up her work and carried it away almost reverently. Archer caught her behind the kitchen door as the caterers loaded the van. "I'd better go back and shower," he said. There was flour in his hair and he had buttercream all over his shirt. "I'm coming back later."

Natalie slid her hands around his waist. "I thought I'd go oversee the dessert course. Just in the kitchen. Maybe you can walk me home."

"You bet," he growled, and kissed her hard before following the caterers.

A loopy grin stuck to her face, she watched him go, waving once as he leaned out the window and blew her a kiss. The van pulled away, and she went back into the house to clean up, both herself and her kitchen.

But she stood over the batter-spotted counter and reached for her phone instead. She tapped on her brother's contact, and their last round of texts came up on the screen.

*I don't think you can replicate what Mom & Dad do in LA or Chicago,* she'd said.

*Not trying to replicate, Nat. Build and grow,* Paul had replied.

*How can you build a brand without doing more of the same?* she'd asked.

*More of similar, not the same,* was his answer.

Two days after that exchange she'd poured soup on him.

It would be lunchtime in Boston. Paul was probably at the restaurant. She could picture him walking through the dining room making sure everything was set, opening umbrellas on the dining patio if the weather was nice, helping restock the bar or even clean up a mess in the kitchen. He was there as much as she was, because he loved the Jude as much as she did—in slightly different ways, but no less dearly. She took a deep breath and typed out a new text.

*What would you think of a Jude bakery location?*

For a moment her finger hovered over the Send button, then she resolutely tapped it. It was the first thing she'd said to her brother in two months. Maybe she should have spoken to her parents first. Maybe she should have slept on it. Maybe—

The phone buzzed in her hand. *Possibility. Where?*

*Boston area,* she typed back. *Run by me.*

She almost held her breath, waiting to see what he would say to that last bit. Their mother had ceded most business control to their father, but Natalie wasn't willing to do the same with her brother. If she started a bakery, it would have to be her shop, not run at Paul's, or even Dad's, direction.

*Only baked goods or serving lunch as well?*

She let out a shaky breath. The peace offering had been accepted. *Lunch possible if the Jude will supply meats/soups/etc.*

The next reply came almost at once. *That could work. Discuss when you get back?*

Natalie grinned as she typed *Sure.* Then she quickly texted her mother about the exchange, feeling as if she'd just shed a huge weight. The fight had cast a dark cloud over her whole family. Her parents would be so happy to put an end to it, they'd probably be waiting at the airport with balloons.

She glanced out the window, at the green hill sloping up beyond the garden, hiding Brampton House from her sight. She had her first event tonight—under her own name, not just Cuisine du Jude's—and Archer was going to walk her home. She ran upstairs to shower and change.

# CHAPTER
## TEN

The cocktail hour was well underway when Archer reached the reception. He took a beer and wandered about, restless without Natalie. She was coming up to the house, she'd said; was she here already? It would be rude to leave the party, but he had nothing to say to anyone else.

The dinner was a smashing success, as far as he could tell. When the guests sat down in the Gold Saloon, at each place was a small, hand-lettered card announcing that the dessert tonight had been provided by Natalie Corcoran of Cuisine du Jude of Wellesley, Massachusetts. From the murmur of amazement that went around the tables, Archer guessed the restaurant's fame had spread far and wide. He wished Natalie could hear it, then decided he could just tell her about it later. Knowing what was coming made the rest of the meal—excellent otherwise—seem endless. He managed to get through it by chatting with a few programmers at his table, including the amorous Rupert and his girlfriend. They took some good-natured teasing about their romantic activities, which didn't seem to bother either of them in the slightest.

When dessert was finally served, the guests grew a bit quieter. Mr. Delancey opened the doors, and a parade of catering staff wheeled in elegant dessert trolleys. Each held a gleaming tower of fine china plates bearing slices of cake, arranged to showcase the variety of options. And at the end of the train came Natalie, pushing a trolley with the special bridal cake they had made together, now adorned with deep purple roses. Even in a plain black skirt and white shirt, like all the other servers, she was gorgeous. Archer found himself grinning like an idiot as she went past all the other tables to the head one, where Jane and Duke sat with their immediate family. If the expression on Jane's face didn't convince Natalie that she could make it as a bakery owner, nothing would.

The other carts circulated along the tables, offering each diner a choice of cake slices. "Which would you like, sir?" the waiter asked Archer.

"Doesn't matter," he said without taking his eyes off Natalie. "They're all fantastic."

He caught up to her after dinner, as the guests began to filter out. Music started up somewhere for dancing, so he swept her into his arms and spun her around.

"That went better than I thought it would," she said, beaming.

"People were fainting away in ecstasy as they ate." He kissed her. "Do you want to dance or shall we go?"

She smiled and went up on her toes, pressing against him. "Let's go," she whispered.

Archer grabbed her hand and headed for the door, stopping only to snag a bottle of champagne at the bar. Duke Austen, walking by with Jane plastered to his side, saw them. His eyes flicked toward Natalie, then back to Archer, and he smirked. Archer just raised the bottle in salute and kept going, through the garden, up the hill, toward the stone house with the quaint name, the best Wi-Fi of all time, and plenty of privacy to make love to Natalie all night long.

"Thank you," she said as they walked.

"It was all you. And a success like that deserves a toast." Archer popped the cork and offered her the foaming bottle.

Natalie laughed as she tilted it to her mouth. "True, but I meant for your idea earlier. About the bakery."

"That was all your idea too." He took a drink himself. "But one I selfishly applaud. I'll be first in line when you open."

She kicked off her shoes and scooped them up. "You know, it never occurred to me until you said that. My brother wants to open other restaurants, and I was so focused on preventing that, I never tried to find a compromise that would suit us both. I texted him today and I think he likes the idea too."

"The art of a good deal. Everyone gets something they want." He offered her the bottle again.

"I should probably find a lawyer, huh?"

Archer made a face. "Lawyers suck. You hate them."

"Really?" She tugged him to a stop. "I'm revising that opinion."

He caught her against him. "Don't do that. Just ... Make an exception."

Her arms went around his neck. "Yeah," she whispered. "You're definitely the exception."

"Natalie." He inhaled deeply as she kissed his throat. "We need to walk faster."

"Why?" She nipped his skin and he shuddered. He was already so hard, he wasn't sure he *could* walk faster, but ...

"Because otherwise I'm going to throw you to the ground right here and now. So unless you want grass stains on your skirt ..."

With a peal of laughter she broke away. She took another gulp from the champagne and danced backward out of his reach. The path to Primrose Cottage had never seemed longer as they strode through the damp grass, passing the bottle back and forth. They reached the familiar patio, lit by the glow of the kitchen lights.

Natalie turned to walk backward again, her gaze riveted on him as she unbuttoned her white shirt. His eyes burned as she ripped it off, exposing her lacy pink bra. He barely managed to leave the empty champagne bottle on the table where he'd spent so many hours working before he grabbed her around the waist, lifting her up the steps to the door. With some laughing and a few whispered curses, she fumbled the key out of her skirt pocket and he let them in, almost stepping on Oliver as they crashed into the kitchen and up against the pantry door.

"We seem to have a thing for this door," she gasped as his hands covered her breasts.

"It's the best damn door in the world," he growled.

She tugged on his tie. "Prove it."

Shaking with lust, he ran a hand up her leg. Her skin was bare, all the way up. She wasn't wearing underwear. "Shit," he said hoarsely. "Thank God I didn't know that earlier ..." She started to laugh, but he ran one fingertip between her legs, probing into the soft, wet folds, then sliding inside her. That made the laugh clog in her throat until she stopped breathing entirely.

He groped in his pocket while she made short work of his belt and zipper. She took the condom from him and he let her; his entire being was focused on the gentle but firm touch of her hands on his cock as she rolled it on. Her skirt was already around her waist and he almost came on the spot as he pushed hard inside her.

Oh *God*. There—this—that was what she'd been craving. Natalie bit down on her lip to keep from moaning out loud, then remembered there was no one within a mile to hear her. "Again," she panted, clinging to his shoulders. Archer laughed even as he cupped his hands beneath her butt so she could hook her legs around his hips. Then he began to move.

She pushed and writhed, seeking the perfect friction between them. His mouth moved ravenously over her, teasing the skin beneath her ear, sucking at the curve of her throat. The champagne and the thrill of the wedding guests' reaction to her cakes had already sent her flying high; now she thought she would literally burst. The door behind her back rattled every time Archer surged into her, sharp and hard and fast enough to make her toes curl and her breath degenerate into ragged gasps as her orgasm built like a tidal wave inside her. Oh God—she wasn't ready—or maybe she was—

"Yes," she cried as he drew it from her, long and sinuous and crackling with electricity. "Oh my *God*, yes." She was out of her head, punch-drunk on the high of good sex. He changed his angle, driving hard and deep, and wrung another aftershock of climax from her as his own hit. He leaned his full weight into her and exhaled a long, low groan, and she tightened her grip on him. Partly because she didn't want to fall, but mostly because she didn't want to let him go.

Ever.

Archer moved against her. "How do you feel about the door now?" he murmured against her throat.

"I love it. I have to get one for my apartment at home."

His shoulders shook in a silent laugh. He raised his head and kissed her, softly and sweetly. "I want to stay the night."

She nodded. There was nothing else to say.

He let her down onto her feet and eased away. Gratefully, Natalie leaned on the counter as he put himself back together. Her legs were shaking and her heart was hammering. She hadn't even known it could be that good. "Oh," she said dazedly, catching sight of the pan she'd left on top of the AGA. "I forgot. I made you something."

Archer peeled off his jacket. "Did you?"

She raised a corner of the tinfoil covering the pan. "You said you wanted to see if I could make it as well as your mom …"

He went still in the midst of pulling loose his tie. "Is that—?" His voice was hushed and incredulous.

She nodded, reaching for a spoon. "Chocolate pudding cake." She scooped out a bite and held it up.

"Good Lord in heaven." His eyes rolled upward as he ate. "You made this for me?"

"Who else?" Natalie grinned. "I had just enough time between when you left and when I had to go to Brampton House …"

Archer spooned up a second bite and fed it to her. "Now do you see?" he murmured.

Her eyes widened as the light chocolate cake turned silky on her tongue. "Mmm."

"Exactly," he breathed, a moment before he kissed her. His fingers stole up her back and snapped the clasp on her bra. She pulled it off as he shed his shirt and finally they were skin to skin. "Natalie," he whispered, nibbling her ear. "I think I'm in love."

She blushed. "Because of the cake?"

His mouth quirked. "The cake only made me say it out loud. But you should know this isn't just a hookup for me."

She touched his chin. There was a tiny cleft there she had never noticed before. "Not for me, either."

"If you want rid of me, you'd better say so now."

For a few heartbeats her thoughts raced. "And if I don't?" she asked slowly.

"I'm going to take you upstairs and shag you six ways to Sunday," he said in a surprisingly good—and terribly sexy—British accent.

"Well," she said softly, winding her arms around his neck. "I like your terms. We have a deal, Mr. Quinn."

NATALIE AWOKE to find herself alone in bed, although Archer's presence was all around. His shirt still hung from the top of the door, and his tie was on the bedside table. When she rolled over, she could smell him on the pillow next to hers. For a moment she just wallowed in it, feeling blissed out and mellow. He had indeed shagged her six ways to Sunday: on the bed, in the shower, and once from behind, when she woke up spooned against him while his marvelous hands wandered purposefully over her until she was begging for more. At the memory, she smiled a sleepy, satisfied smile and wondered where he was. His clothes were still here, so he must be as well.

A distant rattle made her eyes fly open, and a muffled curse made her sit up. That came from the kitchen. What on earth …? She got out of bed and pulled on her robe, tying it around her waist.

Sure enough, Archer was in the kitchen. The table was set for two, and he was standing in front of the open refrigerator. A large number of pans were on the AGA and in the sink, and she realized he'd been making breakfast.

"Good morning," she said, her voice scratchy—probably from screaming her head off in ecstasy all night.

He whipped around. Clad only in his suit pants with a dishtowel draped over his shoulder, his hair rumpled and a scruff of whiskers darkening his jaw, he was the sexiest sight she'd ever seen. Something inside her lurched as he smiled his lazy, sly grin. "Good morning."

"You look busy." She motioned to the dishes, the table, the stove.

He looked around at the mess. "I hope I get points for effort. My actual cooking … Probably not." He grimaced at the sink, and she leaned over to see two ruined eggs and a handful of blackened toasts.

Helplessly she laughed. "Major points for effort."

"Good. At least I didn't ruin the strawberries." He came around the table and kissed her, first lightly, then wrapping his arms around her and deepening the kiss. "Good morning."

"It is, isn't it?" She could have purred like Oliver as his hands went down her back.

"Today is the wedding," he murmured. "I have to go." She made a soft noise of agreement as his hands found the hem of her short silky robe and eased it upward. "Come with me," he said then.

Her eyes popped open in surprise. "I don't know anyone in that wedding!"

"You know me." He tipped up her chin and kissed her again, the long, hypnotic kiss that messed with her brain. "Jane and Duke would be happy to have you, and Arwen would probably rearrange every table to get you in, after the way you saved her rehearsal dinner."

"So," she said breathlessly, trying to regain her ability to think. "So. You want me to come with you, like a date?" It felt weird to ask that; usually she went on several official dates with a guy before she slept with him. Not that anything had gone "as usual" with Archer, and so far it was turning out far better than usual.

"No," he said slowly. "I think I'd rather you come with me like a girlfriend."

She jumped. "We've barely known each other a week! We haven't gone out on a regular date …"

He grinned, dipping his head to the side in that endearing way he had. "The wedding will be the first. And tonight will be the second. Then there will be a lot more once we get home."

"And we've already had sex," she went on nonsensically.

"Which will also happen again." His eyes darkened as he tugged at the sash of her robe. She couldn't even blush as he pushed it open and ran his hands over her bare skin, making her melt inside. "Right here on the kitchen counter, just as soon as you agree to come to the wedding with me."

"That's unhygienic," she whispered as he backed her up against the counter.

"Hot," he retorted. He scooped up a bit of whipped cream from a nearby bowl and swirled it around her exposed nipple.

Natalie moaned helplessly as the cold cream hit her skin. "Archer …"

"Say yes." He bent his head and licked at the cream. "Just to the wedding date for now."

She couldn't move. She was barely keeping her balance. As if he knew, he ran his fingers through the whipped cream and then dragged them down her body, from the notch of her collarbone, down between her breasts, over her belly, right between her legs. "But—but— You asked me to be your girlfriend. You even said the L word."

"I did." With shocking ease, he boosted her to sit on the counter. He tugged the robe off her shoulders and then pushed her knees wide, his face dark and taut with hunger as he looked her over. Natalie stared back in fascination. He yanked over a chair and knelt on it to start licking away the trail of cream he'd painted on her. And as his mouth leisurely moved lower, Natalie gave herself over to his persuasion.

"So, are you thinking about it?" He glanced up as he eased her back.

"What?" Her wits were scattered by the heat of his mouth on her flesh and by the anticipation of what was coming. No one had gone down on her in years and she was taken off guard by how badly she wanted it now—from him.

"The date part." He ran his fingertips lightly up her inner thigh, and she flinched so hard she almost fell over. "And the girlfriend part."

"Exclusive girlfriend?" she asked, not shocked by how ragged and husky her voice was. It was a miracle she could form words at all.

"The one and only."

"I … I'm thinking …" she said faintly.

His eyes glittered. "Good." His hands spread wide on her thighs and he lowered his head.

She had a hazy thought that if this was some sort of boyfriend audition, he was acing it. His lips were soft, his tongue firm. He held her in place as she rocked and twisted, blown away by the sharp pleasure of his mouth. He seemed to know exactly what to do, backing off just when it grew too intense, alternately gentling or dominating. She forced open her eyes to look in wonder on this man who had learned her so well so fast, and met his scorching gaze head-on. He was watching her, reading her ... Then he pushed two long fingers inside her and broke her, his mouth pulling on her clit as she came, harder than she'd ever come in her life.

"Still thinking?" he rasped several minutes later, sounding as though he'd just run the marathon.

Dumbly, she shook her head.

"I heard you scream *yes* at least three times."

She smiled, uncaring that she was sprawled on the kitchen counter with traces of whipped cream on her skin. She would never forget this kitchen. "Did I?"

"You did." He pressed a lingering kiss to the inside of her thigh. "Was that your answer?"

With some effort she pushed herself upright. He grinned, looking rumpled and devastatingly sexy. She'd been right about him from the start—guys this *right* didn't walk into a girl's life every day. "Yes—times three."

# ABOUT THE AUTHOR

Caroline Linden was born a reader, not a writer. She earned a math degree from Harvard University and wrote computer software before turning to writing fiction. Since then the Boston Red Sox have won the World Series four times, which is not related but still worth mentioning. Her books have won the NEC Reader's Choice Award, the Daphne du Maurier Award, the NJRW Golden Leaf Award, and RWA's RITA Award, and have been translated into seventeen languages. She lives in New England.

Visit www.CarolineLinden.com to join her newsletter, and get an exclusive free story just for members.

# ALSO BY CAROLINE LINDEN

# THE DAY IT RAINED BOOKS

## BOOKS

KATHARINE ASHE

# CHAPTER
## ONE

*The City of Brotherly Love*

Except for the sexy stranger, the park was empty when Cali Blake pulled the library's shiny new bookmobile up to the curb and jumped out. Commanding his usual bench near the south entrance, he wore the same blue chamois shirt over a T-shirt and the hat that covered half his face. As always, he was reading the paper.

Today's choice: the *Wall Street Journal*. He must be feeling serious. Cali liked it better when he read the *Philadelphia Star*. Then she let herself imagine crazy stories, like how a librarian found a government bond worth millions inside a book that'd never been checked out.

Other than the hat guy, Cali had the park to herself.

Green Park wasn't green or even much of a park. It was a square of concrete with a ten-foot chain link fence on one side, a single tree, and a handful of benches cemented to the ground. The only signs of life were the man on the bench and pigeons picking at trash. But it wasn't quite nine yet. Cali's regulars would arrive soon.

She waved at the hat guy. Apparently seeing her through both his newspaper and hat brim, he nodded.

She flipped the lever to open the van's rear door and lower the step, then shut off the engine and walked to the back of the small white bus with *BOOKMOBILE* painted across the side.

Books were stacked all around the sides and to the ceiling. A shelf ran down the center of the van, packed spine to spine too. She'd restocked this morning, adding a few more Spanish and Korean kids' books, some of the thrillers Roy liked, and a few new cookbooks for Maggie and fashion magazines for Masala. She restocked every day now. Despite the naysayers, the bookmobile was thriving. When the Philadelphia big-money Prescott Foundation rejected the grant proposal that she'd spent months helping the library's grant writer prepare, she'd almost given up hope. Then the library got an anonymous donation from someone who'd read her interview in the *City Paper*.

She pulled out her director's chair and set it on the sidewalk dappled with cigarette butts and syringes.

"Open for business," she hummed to herself. The air was fresh after yesterday's rain. The cityscape on one side didn't impress—battered apartment buildings with broken windows—but rose spectacularly on the other, with skyscrapers designed by Stern and Jahn. Behind it all a bright blue sky proclaimed summertime.

The hat guy turned a page.

His legs were long and stretched out in front of him, knees apart, his feet planted firmly on the cement, owning that corner of the park without effort. He wore the usual faded Levis and half-laced work boots too. A hint of dark hair peeked out under the hat above his collar.

Cali silently wished for a heat wave so he'd take off the button-down. The way he moved, like he had every muscle in his body in perfect control, gave her a hunch he'd have great arms. She liked great arms. A lot.

He had big hands, too, strong-looking with prominent veins, proof that he worked out, probably at one of those garage gyms the petty dealers used, where you could trade a fifth of Jack or a gram of crack for a month's membership.

When she was waiting for bookmobile patrons, like now, sometimes she stared at his hands holding the paper like some guys held a football. Like he'd been born with a newspaper in his hands. Not a smartphone. *The actual printed word.* At those moments, with her pulse a little quick, she prayed he wasn't a drug dealer. Having a secret semi-crush on a drug dealer whose face she'd never seen was so completely wrong in so many ways.

It didn't matter, though. She wasn't looking for a guy who spent his days sitting around doing nothing. She'd already had a guy like that in her life. It ended badly.

"Miss Cali Blake, where you been all my life?" called a crackly voice from down the sidewalk.

"Right here waiting for you, Roy." She gave the stooped, retired trash collector a big smile. A woman in a flowing skirt with gold loop earrings walked on his arm like she was strutting a catwalk. "Good morning, Masala," Cali said. "I brought you a present." She snatched up *From Helen of Troy to Madame Pompadour: Women's Hair in History.* "Orange today. Nice."

"It's called Tangerine Dream." Masala patted her weave and gave Cali's straight hair tied back in a ponytail the weekly once-over. "Cali girl, you let me do something with that nothing you got there, and you'll get yourself a man in no time."

"Thanks, but no thanks. My boss would freak if I walked in with Technicolor hair." Not that any library patrons ever saw her. Until she'd started taking out the bookmobile, she'd been stuck in the basement stacks mostly. They'd given her this gig because they'd assumed it would flop. Best to keep the failure on a lower rung of the staff ladder.

It hadn't failed. With the anonymous donation, the mobile unit was set for a trial period of a year, but it'd taken off in only two months. Already Cali was in love with the project and the people she met on her stops. They couldn't believe she was bringing books right to their doorsteps—for free. Every day she felt like Santa Claus. And she got to spend time in neighborhoods where the families actually knew each other and the businesses had been around for decades.

"For you, sir." She handed Roy the newest hardcover Dean Koontz.

Maggie appeared across the street, her short, crisp strides reminiscent of days when modest women wore narrow skirts to their ankles.

"This one's for you, Miss Maggie." Cali proffered her *15-Minute Recipes*. "No more frozen dinners."

Maggie's wrinkled face was all smiles. "Cali, you're a ray of sunshine in this old neighborhood."

"What'd you bring Junior to read?" Roy gestured toward the hat guy.

"He's got his paper." She lowered her voice. "I've been meaning to ask: why do you call him Junior?"

"Boy's got the same name as his father," Roy said. "What else do you want me to call him?"

"Oh. Huh. I wonder what his father thinks of him spending every day in this park reading the paper." Her father would've thought it was peachy, as long as he had a bottle of Hennessy on a bench waiting for him. Later, he'd settled for cough syrup.

But as far as she could tell, the hat guy wasn't a drunk. His clothes were a little worn but clean, and he didn't move like a drunk. He moved really... *sexy*.

Masala gave a rippling chortle. "Oh, Cali girl. Junior don't come around here every day. Only Friday mornings, when you're here."

Cali's stomach did a little flip. "Really?"

"I think he likes our California," Maggie said to Roy and Masala.

"So this is either a coincidence," Cali said, still in a whisper, "or I should call the cops."

Roy waved his hand. "Junior wouldn't hurt a fly. Men that read, like we do, only got the most honorable of intentions."

Cali laughed. "Honorable, huh?"

"Why don't you go on over there and say hello?" Maggie said.

"Because I'm not looking for a man." Even if she were, she didn't have time to date. "Now I'm going to stop whispering about somebody like he's not within earshot, okay?"

Masala gave her a saucy look, fuchsia lips pursing. Roy shook his head. They all settled on their regular benches, which were divided into individual seats with iron bars so people couldn't sleep on them.

"What's going on with you this week, Cali girl?" Masala asked, tucking the book about hair into her enormous spangled purse.

"I got invited to a wedding. A really big society shindig."

"You gonna take me as your date, sweetheart?" Roy said.

"I would, dear. But I'm not going. It's in England. It's going to be a grand party at a huge old mansion with lots of fabulously rich and famous people. The groom is paying for everybody to stay there for a week. He's a billionaire."

"*Billion?*"

"I kid you not. It's a real fairy-tale wedding. I'd love to go. The bride, Jane, is my old college friend who works at the New York Public library. She's also a best-selling novelist now. Maggie, I gave you Jane's book last month. You loved it."

"That book about the girl who pretended she was engaged to a duke? I did!"

"Why aren't you going, girl?" Masala demanded.

"I can't afford it. Home care visits for Zoe would be insanely expensive. And of course the plane ticket would cost a mint. It's just way too much." Paying the rent was way too much too. And buying groceries. And the insurance deductible for her sister's therapy and meds. And pretty much breathing.

Maggie sighed. Masala frowned.

"But the real problem," Cali said with a mock-sober nod, "is that I don't have a dress."

"You don't have a dress, girl? Now that's a fib. I seen you in a dress right here."

"I mean I don't have a dress that's appropriate for a party like that. Those women will be wearing stuff that costs hundreds of dollars, maybe thousands, with jewelry and shoes to match."

Roy whistled low.

"I bet you have the shoes," Maggie said.

Cali grinned. "You bet right." Thank God for the discount shoe warehouse.

"Buys 'em and never wears 'em. Women are crazy, I say."

"A girl's gotta have her fun," Masala said with a pat on Cali's hand. "You keep on buying those shoes, and someday we'll find someplace nice for you to wear them. Maybe sooner than you think."

A group of kids burst out of the daycare across the street, followed by two women.

*"Hola,* Señorita California!" a little one yelled. The rest joined in like a chorus.

*"Hola,* guys." Cali met them at the van and started collecting books they'd brought to return. After that they searched for new treasures on the shelves. She stayed busy till eleven, then packed up. Her friends had gone—Masala to her salon, and Maggie and Roy to bingo at the church. She gave the hat guy a wave and climbed into the van.

Her next two stops went well, too, and she returned to the library with a lighter van and a much lighter heart. Almost light enough to forget about how she couldn't go to the most exciting party she'd ever be invited to in her life.

She texted her sister *Home soon,* and went into the staff room to grab her purse. When her boss stepped into the open doorway, she knew it from the heavy scent of Axe For Men.

"I'm thinking about changing the van's Friday route," Dick said, flipping through papers in his hands.

He was only doing this to hurt her because she'd enjoyed her day.

"You can't," she said, initialing her mileage in the bookmobile's logbook. "The donor specified the routes."

Dick laughed. "Do you really think that the anonymous donor of the bookmobile cares where we drive the thing?"

"Since he specified the routes, I think he must. Or she." She turned her back on him, pulled her purse out of her locker, and managed to avoid slicing her palm on the broken zipper.

Dick was still standing in the doorway. Now the papers were stuffed in his pocket and he jingled car keys in his palm.

"Going out tonight, Cali?"

"Every night, Dick."

"You're so hot in those jeans, Cali."

"You can get fired for saying that to me, Dick." She'd once spoken about his inappropriate comments to the director of the library, Cara Schaeffer. Cara had taken Cali's complaint very seriously. But Dick had stellar ratings from all his female employees except Cali. Cara documented the complaint, then privately told Cali she should try to get hard proof of the harassment. Overwhelmed with complications in Zoe's medical needs at the time, Cali couldn't fight both battles at once, and she'd let it drop. Anyway, Dick's father was a state representative, with all sorts of political connections. She'd never win.

"Don't be so sensitive. You know it's all in fun," Dick said. He knew she couldn't afford to lose this job or hire a lawyer. He gave her a smile just patronizing enough to prickle under her skin. "Got a date tonight?"

"I sure do." She always did when he asked.

He twirled his keys around his forefinger, the Mercedes logo prominent on the fob. "Does he pick you up in a CLS63 Benz?"

She pulled her purse tight over her shoulder and faced him. "He picks me up in a limo, actually."

His eyes slithered down her body. "Do you do him in the limo, Cali? With the driver watching? I bet you like it when the driver watches."

She walked toward him. "Move, please."

Some nights he didn't step aside right away. Some nights he made her ask nicely.

He didn't make her ask this time and she went into the corridor.

"After you bring the van back tomorrow," he said behind her, "I want you to start the claimed-returned list. It needs to be finished by Monday night."

"Fine." Drudge work. Depending on the collection, it would take hours. She'd have to ask her neighbor, Mrs. Fletcher, to grocery shop for her and Zoe again. Third time this month so far. But Dick always made her pay for rejecting him. This time she was getting off easy.

LATER, while helping her sister wash her hair, she invented stories about the sexy hat guy to distract herself from worries and amuse Zoe.

"Maybe he's a spy hired by Dick to take incriminating vids to send to the anonymous donor so I'll get fired."

"Or he's a really lazy drug dealer," Zoe said, rubbing her spiky locks with a towel. Four years younger than Cali, she was infinitely hipper.

"Or maybe beneath the hat he has three eyes and an alien brow ridge, and he's just hanging around in the park to study humans before the big invasion." She shook two pills from a bottle and dropped them onto Zoe's palm.

"You should tell him go to the mall instead." Zoe swallowed the pills with water from a plastic Iron Man cup. Zoe had a thing for Tony Stark. "More people there."

Cali smiled.

"But I like the other scenario best." Zoe ran the three fingers on her left hand through her damp hair. "The one where he's the anonymous patron of the mobile library just checking up on his investment. Wouldn't that be great? If it'd been him all along?"

"Sure. Other than the alien explanation, it's the most likely."

"He's hot, right?"

"I've no idea. I've never seen his face."

"But you said he's got a hot body."

"I think so." The Levis and loose button-down didn't reveal much. But his shoulders were broad. And once, when he'd gotten a phone call, stood up, and loped out of the park, the chamois shirt had caught in his belt. She'd liked the way his jeans hugged his hips. A lot. Too much. "He's got a great butt." Tight. *Hot*.

"Nobody says butt anymore, Cal. Do you ever read those magazines you check out of the library?"

"I get them for the ads." She paged through Cartier watches, Manolo Blahnik shoes, and DKNY lingerie. And fantasized. "Ass. He's got a great ass. Are you happy?"

A sleepy smile creased the scars around Zoe's lips. The meds were kicking in. "When's Jane's wedding, again?"

"In four weeks."

"You have to go. Cut loose for a change." Zoe's eyelids drooped. "You've got a week of paid vacation you'll lose if you don't use it."

She'd been saving it for emergencies. The more Zoe healed, though, the less she thought she'd need it. But it was always best to be careful.

"Cutting loose isn't my style, Zoe."

"You're going to England, Cali. You're going to meet a hot, rich guy, have a crazy whirlwind romance, and he's going to fall in love with you," her sister said dreamily. "Then we'll get to live in a mansion like we would've if Dad hadn't turned into such a fuckup."

Cali brushed a lock of hair off her sister's brow, fingers scraping over the hard skin where the burns had penetrated to the bone. "Night, goofball," she whispered.

THE NEXT DAY, after Cali brought the bookmobile back to the library, she sent a quick text to Zoe, *Have a good time watching junk TV w Mrs. F.* Then she got to work on the claimed-returned list. An hour into the project, Dick showed up and tried to crowd her up against a shelf. She slammed the heel of her palm into the side of his face, slipped out while he was cursing, and ran to the bus stop, shaking with fear and rage all the way home.

The minute she got inside the apartment, the bad night got worse. Zoe's eyes were glassy.

"It hurts, California."

Cali knelt beside the wheelchair, wrapped her arms around her sister's shoulders, and tucked her face against Zoe's leathery cheek.

"I know. I'm sorry. I'm so sorry." But inside she was weeping the same words she always wept on nights like this: *Damn that drunken bastard to hell.*

After she got Zoe to sleep, she sat beside the bed holding her hand for a while, dozing. She couldn't turn in yet. Too many things to do first. Bills to pay that Medicaid wouldn't cover. Dishes that'd been stacking up for days. Laundry. She would put in the clothes first. If she was lucky, the guys from 3G wouldn't be smoking joints in the laundry room and everything she owned wouldn't smell like pot for the next week.

Slipping her hand out of Zoe's, she shut off the light and gathered up the dirty clothes and towels from the floor. Throwing them all in the plastic laundry basket, she grabbed last month's *Vanity Fair* to read while the machine filled up, and opened the apartment door. Her foot slipped on paper on the threshold. It was a thick envelope. Across the front in neat, bold type was *CALIFORNIA BLAKE*.

It couldn't be an eviction notice. She'd paid the rent. Last month. But their landlord knew she'd get it to him as soon as she got paid, and he was always cool about it.

She stuck the envelope in her back pocket and went downstairs. Smoke hovered around the open door of the laundry room and she almost reversed direction. But she had exactly one clean pair of panties left.

Trying not to breathe, she said "Hey" to the guys from 3G, opened a washer, and dumped in the clothes. Then she put her quarters in the slot and measured the soap. Waiting for the basin to fill, she pulled the envelope out of her back pocket and opened it.

And stared.

She shook her head, but the contents remained the same. One round-trip ticket to London Heathrow Airport in her name for the week of Jane's wedding. One contract for a week of nursing care from the five-star home care company Cali wished she could afford, with her name at the top, and *PAID* marked after the hefty total at the bottom. And one $800 gift certificate to Joan Shepp, an upscale women's designer boutique.

The washer clicked into cycle and started to gyrate against her hipbones. Numbly, she poured the soap in a careful ring and shut the lid.

Then she looked through the documents again.

This could not be real.

She didn't believe in fairy godmothers. She didn't believe in miracles. And she sure as heck didn't believe that a little secondhand marijuana smoke inhalation could turn an eviction notice into a dream come true. Which meant that Maggie, Masala, and Roy had pooled their money for this. She'd no idea where they could've scrounged up this kind of cash. Probably from under their mattresses.

She couldn't accept it, of course. Monday she'd make a detour to Green Park from her usual route and return it to them after thanking them profusely. She'd only ever seen them at the park on Fridays, but aside from her sister, they were the best friends she had. God bless the anonymous donor of the bookmobile, or she never would've known them. And God bless her friends for this gift.

Later, despite Dick's harassment earlier and Zoe's pain, despite the empty checkbook and the brown mark on her last white blouse from the sucky dryer, she went to sleep smiling.

. . .

"You're not telling me the truth."

"Cali girl, are you calling me a liar?"

"*Masala.*" She didn't have time for this. She'd already gotten a late start after spending fifteen minutes on the phone with the home care service, begging for the name of the person who'd purchased the contract—unsuccessfully. Now she had to get the van back on its route or she wouldn't have enough time at her first stop. She looked desperately around Masala's hair salon, but everyone just looked back like she was crazy. She thrust the envelope at Masala. "Please. You've got to take it back."

Masala folded arms draped in filmy hot pink polyester. "I can't take nothing back that I didn't give."

"Then give it back to Roy. Or Maggie. I can't accept it."

"Why not? If somebody wants to be fool enough to give you that kinda money, you're an even bigger fool not to accept it."

"But—"

"Let the good deed be worth something, Cali girl." Masala's voice gentled. "If you give it back, whoever it was that gave it to you is gonna be disappointed."

Masala unfolded her arms and circled one around Cali's shoulders. She squeezed tight.

"Do something crazy for once, girl. Go to that fairy-tale wedding. And when you come back, you gonna tell us all about how you met Prince Charming and had the time of your life."

# CHAPTER
# TWO

"Yes, both plants in Indiana will be closed. The plant outside of Columbus too." Piers clutched the phone against his ear and listened to the voice on the other end. Below him, the city reclined in glittering array, the Schuylkill River snaked in a silvery-green ribbon to the north, and the sky was a hazy late-summer blue. Cars, cabs, and buses passed by fifty-seven floors below. Across the river, a train pulled out of 30th Street Station and, farther south, a helicopter lifted off the pad at the University of Pennsylvania Hospital.

On the other side of three layers of tempered, laminated, floor-to-ceiling glass, Piers heard none of it.

"The total?" He turned from the view and looked at the spreadsheet on the screen atop his mahogany desk. "Eleven hundred and forty-six employees terminated. They'll receive the usual compensation package. We got this one ripe for plucking. Now that we've stopped the bleeding, we'll make a huge profit." He paused, gathered his courage, then dove in. "But, actually, I've been thinking about the plant in Gary, and I don't think we need to—"

The voice came at him again. He listened. He always listened.

When Jacob Taylor Vaughan Prescott, the most powerful man in Philadelphia, spoke, everyone from the parking valet at the Union League to the governor in Harrisburg listened.

"Right." Piers sucked in breath through his nostrils. "Will do." But the call had already gone dead. He pressed the *End* button anyway, as if it could wash away the nausea he felt climbing up his throat. "Will do, Grandfather," he mumbled.

Meager compensation packages for men and women who'd been working in those plants for years. Some of them for generations. Pathetic. *Immoral.* But business was business. They were already deep into the post-acquisition strategy, and the plants had to go. To Mexico. Or China. Or Bangladesh. Anywhere they'd cost less to operate.

Acquisitions like this one were the worst part of his job. Countless people suffered while Prescott Global raked in the money.

Dragging his fingers through his hair, Piers turned again toward the window.

"Mr. Prescott?" His secretary's voice came over the intercom.

"Yes, Mrs. Crowley?"

"The board meeting has been moved to tomorrow at noon."

"Saturday? I can't do it."

"Your grandfather rescheduled it. Would you like me to tell him you won't be able to attend?"

He'd tied his tie too tight when he'd returned to the office at lunchtime. It was choking him. "No. Not yet."

"Yes, Mr. Prescott. Your mother is on line one."

He moved to the sleek bronze and ebony phone on his desk. "How long has she been waiting?"

"Twenty minutes."

He picked up the phone. "Why didn't you call my cell?"

"It's lovely to hear your voice, too, darling."

A chuckle loosened his chest.

A lawn mower's buzz came over the line. His mother must be in her garden at the house in St. Davids. Since his father's death a year ago, she spent most of her time there instead of down at the shore—to be closer to him and Amy, he suspected.

"What's up, Mom?"

"Come to dinner tonight."

He raked his hand through his hair again and squeezed his eyes shut. "I can't. I've got a stack of—"

"Come to dinner tonight, Piers."

His hand halted. "Why? Is something wrong?" Not Amy. His little sister never got into trouble. He waited for his mother to say his brother's name.

"Nothing's wrong. But you need a break, and I've just picked the most delicious baby corn. I'll make you a steak."

"I don't eat steak anymore, Mom." Not with his stress level. One Prescott man dead of heart failure before fifty-five was enough.

"You don't eat anything anymore. Come have steak and corn. I'll make iced green tea. The antioxidants will counter the effects of the steak."

He smiled. "All right, but is early okay? I've got a load of work to do before I catch a plane tonight." He'd said it. Aloud. But three hours ago he'd already known he would go. Weeks ago, actually—the minute California Blake had told Roy and the others she'd received an invitation to his college roommate's wedding.

Piers didn't believe in mystical signs. But this coincidence was too good to ignore. And this morning at the park she'd confirmed it. She was going to Jane and Duke's wedding.

"Off to New York?" his mother asked.

"Not this time." The tension gripping his chest: *gone*. "Thanks, Mom. Looking forward to seeing you later." He hung up and pressed the intercom button. "Mrs. Crowley?"

"Sir?"

"Please tell my grandfather and the directors that I won't be attending tomorrow's meeting. And place all my calls on hold for a week."

A moment's silence.

"For a *week*?" Her unflappable monotone broke.

"I'm taking a vacation." He looked out at the city, to the north.

He was going to England.

# CHAPTER
# THREE

*London Heathrow Airport*

The passport control officer looked squarely at Cali. "Purpose of your visit to the UK?"

She looked squarely back. "Pleasure."

He pressed a stamp onto the little blue page and handed her the passport. "Enjoy your holiday, Miss Blake."

"I know you need a vacation, Cal," Zoe had insisted for four straight weeks. "And you obviously need some action. For God's sake, you're lusting after a drug dealer whose face you've never seen. Go meet a hot, rich guy and have hot-rich-guy-wedding-party sex. Have an impulsive fling for once."

But Cali didn't do impulsive flings. And she definitely didn't do hot, rich guys. She did Ted in Reference, once, two years ago. For a guy with encyclopedic knowledge, he'd known nothing about sex. She'd also done Chu in Accounting. Twice. Excruciatingly dull. She'd given him a second try just to see if he'd had an off night. He hadn't. Still, those guys had been like her. Struggling to make it. Just moderately cute. *Safe.*

"Wedding party sex isn't safe," she'd said, hoping Zoe wouldn't question her resistance if she played the STD card. "Guys who hook up like that with women are bound to have all kinds of diseases."

To that, Zoe had said, "Screw safe. No, actually, buy a box of condoms and screw a hot, rich guy. Then tell me all about it when you get home. A girl's got to live vicariously. Now go catch that bus or you'll miss your flight."

She'd boarded the plane with her stomach in knots. As the flight attendant announced phones had to go on Airplane Mode, Zoe had texted: *Wedding party hookup or don't come home.* Cali laughed. By the time the plane touched down in London, the knots had turned into tingles.

Now she hefted Mrs. Fletcher's 1990s floral suitcase from the baggage claim turnstile. The wheels squeaked as she walked toward the exit for public transportation. Men in dark suits were holding placards with names on them. One read *BLAKE*.

Cali's smiled broadened. It was totally a sign—a sign that she'd been right to do this. When she'd left the apartment, Zoe and the nurse were already dishing about their favorite soaps, and Mrs. Fletcher promised to do the grocery shopping midweek. And both of them plus Masala and Maggie had been thrilled with the presents she'd bought with the remainder of the gift certificate to Joan Shepp after she'd picked out the cheapest dress in the boutique.

Yes. All would be well at home. And she desperately needed a vacation. She hadn't had one since she was a teenager. Now she'd have a whole week to do nothing except read, relax and enjoy Jane's company. Silently she thanked her secret patrons, trying not to feel guilty that Masala's shop needed a new marquee, Roy still hadn't bought the walker he wanted, and Maggie's shoes were worn out. She had to believe Masala: if she didn't allow herself to enjoy this trip, she would disappoint them.

And now that she was on the other side of an ocean from her reality —worries and bills—a wedding party fling with one of Duke's techy friends didn't sound bad. With a lift in her stride she walked past the sign that was more than a sign. It was a welcoming beacon.

"Miss Blake?"

She kept walking.

"Miss California Blake?"

She turned. The man holding the *BLAKE* sign was looking at her.

"Yes?"

He came forward. "Good day, miss. I'm George. May I take your bag?"

"How do you know my name is Blake?"

"I was given a description of you, miss."

"A description? Who—? Oh, Jane Sparks must have arranged for you to pick me up."

"Very good, miss." He tugged the suitcase handle out of her grasp. "Right-o. Shall we be off?"

"Where are we going?"

"To Brampton House, miss."

"All the way to Brampton House?"

"Yes, miss. The car is fully stocked with refreshments and the windows can be darkened if you care to sleep en route."

She didn't have international cell phone coverage. She couldn't call Jane and check this out. But if this guy was some sort of con man, he was really convincing. Jane was providing her bridesmaid's dress; she might have sent her the tickets, after all. Cali hadn't asked. If Jane wanted the gift to be anonymous, she'd respect that. After the way her father had treated her mother for years, respect was big in Cali's book.

She followed the driver out of the building to a long, shiny black car on the curb. A Rolls-Royce. She stared at the hood ornament: a woman leaning forward with her arms stretched back, cloth billowing out that looked like wings. The Spirit of Ecstasy.

Her heart fluttered weirdly. *Another sign?*

Sitting back gingerly on the sleek black leather, she accepted a glass of champagne from George and didn't mention that it was eight o'clock in the morning. Maybe English people drank champagne at eight o'clock. Maybe really rich people just drank champagne whenever they wanted.

After only a few sips, her eyes were fogging as she stared at the fields flying by out the window.

She awoke to the car slowing and turning onto a long drive

bordered by giant overhanging trees. The house was magnificent, like the sorts of houses on PBS miniseries about the English aristocracy, all stately elegance and ponderous grace. And this would be her fantasy-land for *an entire week.*

Retying her ponytail, she dabbed on the coconut lip gloss she'd grabbed in a rush of nerves at the drugstore checkout counter yesterday. She'd gone there for one item only: a package of ultra-pleasure condoms. She didn't know when she'd have another chance at this, and she wasn't about to show up unprepared.

The car rolled to a stop and Jane came running out of the house. Dressed in a sweater set and pencil skirt, her hair perfectly styled with pearl stud earrings peeking out, she looked exactly like when they'd been at state college together.

"Cali!" She kissed her on both cheeks like a fashionable New Yorker, then hugged her tight like a small-town girl. "How was your flight?"

"Great. Jane, thanks so much for—" She stopped herself. "Well, for all of this. I'm so happy to be here."

"How's Zoe?"

"Really good." A lot more often, now.

"I'm so glad to hear that."

Two men came from the front door and down the steps. Cali recognized Jane's fiancé right away. Duke Austen, tech genius and start-up wizard, was in the news all the time. He was really good-looking, in a T-shirt-wearing, tech-genius kind of way.

"Cali, this is Duke," Jane said. "Duke, meet my library buddy at State. We worked in the stacks together."

Cali had never shaken the hand of a billionaire, but Duke just smiled with genuine warmth and shook her hand like a normal person.

"Thanks for coming, Cali."

"And, California Blake," Jane said, turning to the other man, "this is Piers Prescott, Duke's roommate from Stanford. Piers lives in Philadelphia, too, so you should have a lot in common."

A shock of nausea at the name turned abruptly to proper confusion.

Meltingly gorgeous blue eyes. Vibrant like Superman's. But warm.

She'd often seen the crown prince of Prescott Global in Philadelphia newspapers. Only a few months earlier, he'd been in the Lifestyle section of the *Inquirer* after he'd shown up at a benefit for the Philadelphia Orchestra with a woman who was not his longtime girlfriend. The *Star* fed off the breakup for weeks. Even the *City Paper* mentioned it.

The pictures hadn't done him justice. Tall, with broad shoulders and tousled hair the color of black walnuts, he wore his perfectly tailored slacks and sleek button-down like they'd been made for his athletic body. Under the shirt collar, a thin gold chain descended beneath a winter white T-shirt.

He extended his hand. Around his wrist sparkled a black and gold Marvin C 1850.

"Hello, California Blake," he said in a voice that made her hot where no man's voice alone had ever made her hot. "It's a pleasure to meet you."

Every feeling in her rebelled against shaking the hand of a member of the family whose foundation had brutally rejected the bookmobile grant proposal. But she couldn't refuse in front of Jane and Duke. She put her hand in his, then tried to pull away quickly, but he held fast. Strong. Confident.

She forced out, "Hi."

Teeth white as the sails of a million-dollar catamaran flashed between his lips. His smile seemed genuine, pleased, like he'd nothing better to do than smile at her. Finally, he released her.

When Jane started talking to her again, he didn't stop looking. He was staring. At her. But that wasn't possible. Firstly, she was sure her hair looked like the end of Ron Weasley's broomstick. Secondly, she was A Nobody and Piers Prescott was definitely A Somebody. Thirdly, she knew what a sleepless night sitting up followed by a nap in a car did to her face. And fourthly, *he was so hot*. Cut jaw. Gorgeous eyes. Incredible body encased in thousands of dollars' worth of casual wear. Confident stance. Easy stride.

As a bellman carried her suitcase into the house and they all followed, Piers Prescott was right behind her, so close he could read the label on her Target-brand jeans if he wanted to look at her butt —*ass*. She resisted craning her neck around to check.

Inside, the house was all marble and dark woods and gilt and spectacular wealth tempered by fantastic elegance. Fantasyland.

"Wow," she whispered.

"This is Mark," Jane said. A handsome man with wickedly stylish clothes and carefully windblown hair approached. "He's the manager here. Mark, this is Cali Blake, one of my bridesmaids. Take good care of her."

"Welcome to Brampton, Miss Blake," he said with a delicious English accent. "I'll show you to your room."

"We'll have drinks on the pool deck at six, Cali, and dinner after that," Jane said as Cali followed Mark up a broad, grand staircase. The bellman with her suitcase trailed along, because apparently a grown woman couldn't carry her own bag or find her room without two other people to assist her. But she wasn't about to embarrass Jane by acting like she'd never been in a five-star hotel before. She had, after all. A lifetime ago.

"Sounds great." She glanced at Piers Prescott. Looking like the cover of *GQ*, he was still watching her. It was too bad he was a Philadelphia Prescott. If he'd been anybody else, his smile alone would've put him at the top of her wedding party hookup wish list. But beggars couldn't be choosers. Duke was sure to have some other friends who were cute without also being the enemy.

SHE WAS EVEN PRETTIER CLOSE up than Piers had expected. As he watched her perfect ass while she walked up the stairs, he knew he was the biggest jerk on the planet.

He shouldn't have done it. At the park, when she'd told Roy and the others how she couldn't attend Jane's wedding, she'd tried to mask her disappointment. But he'd seen how much it hurt her not to be able to afford going. He'd wanted to make that hurt go away, to give her a real vacation. After all she did for others with little compensation, she deserved it.

That didn't mean that the moment he'd left the park that morning, he should've called his secretary and told her what to purchase and exactly where to have it delivered. But he never ignored an inspired idea. He made it happen, and he never screwed up. His instinct had made his family's company millions of dollars.

"Jane!" the wedding planner called from the hall.

"Looks like I'm needed." Jane pecked Duke on the cheek and headed off.

Duke said, "Pool?"

"Sure." During the two years they'd been roommates at Stanford, they'd spent as much time playing pool as studying. In those years, Piers had been rebelling against his grandfather's iron code of discipline. The choice of Stanford instead of Yale or Harvard had in itself infuriated his grandfather.

It'd been his last hurrah. Until now.

"Duke, have you ever given money to a woman you don't know?"

Duke slanted him a scowl as they entered the billiards room. "Haven't ever needed to."

"Not that kind of transaction. I donated the funds for a nonprofit project that Jane's friend California is involved in."

"She's a librarian, right?" He racked the balls.

"Yeah." Piers chose a cue stick. "It's an urban outreach project."

"Good for you, man."

He leaned over the table to break. "It seemed like a good investment." *Right.* Throwing money away on lazy good-for-nothings, his grandfather would say. Piers focused on the cue ball and imagined his grandfather's face on it. He snapped his stick. Two stripes sank into corner holes.

He'd funded the bookmobile project solely for the satisfaction of doing something his grandfather would hate. That California was doing spectacularly with it, far beyond what the grant proposal promised, was just a bonus. Friends of his along the van's routes told him the same thing he witnessed at Green Park: the bookmobile was hugely popular. But it wasn't the books that kept people coming back. *She* did. Vibrant, sincere, smart, with a smile that lit up her face like a beauty queen's, she drew people to her. They loved her.

Piers wanted a piece of that. He wanted a piece of her. The way his life had been going, he needed something genuinely good in it.

"She didn't look like she knew you," Duke said.

"She doesn't know I donated the money. No one does. I had a provision written into the grant specifying that if anyone publicly connects my name to the project, the funding will be withdrawn." He'd needed to rattle his shackles, but for himself only. He'd no intention of airing his family's disagreements in public.

"So you can't tell her?" Duke asked.

"It's a legally binding provision."

"Trapped yourself into secrecy. But I don't suppose you ever thought you'd meet her."

He hadn't only thought it. He'd engineered it. "Right," he mumbled. His sister Amy once had a stalker problem in college. That guy had bad intentions. Piers's intentions were all good. But by making it possible for California to come to this wedding without telling her, he'd slipped into a dangerous gray area.

He clipped the cue ball. It glanced off the five and rolled to a stop.

He couldn't tell her about paying for her trip without first telling her about the donation. If he told her either, there was every chance she'd think he was an asshole.

According to Caroline, of course, he was. She'd told him so every time she tried to get him to propose. Then she'd arranged an in-your-face hookup with an oil mogul who'd thought it would be fun to steal something from a Prescott. Caroline had hoped it would nudge him into jealously proposing. Instead, he told her it was over. The next day the oil guy gave her an enormous engagement ring that she splashed all over the Internet. Piers was fine with that. If the world thought she'd dumped him, the world was welcome to the misinformation.

Duke lined up his cue stick. "Don't worry about it. She'll probably be happy to find out it was you."

Piers gripped his cue and tried not to think of the man who'd inspired his subterfuge. His grandfather's secretary was already trying to find him. He'd never disappeared like this. It was like breaking out of prison.

But he never would've come here if California hadn't.

He set his cue stick on the edge of the table and angled it to hit lucky seven. He would spend some time with her this week. Then he'd risk it. Whatever the consequences, the idea of telling the whole truth for once felt too good.

# CHAPTER
# FOUR

*Brampton House*

Cali slept straight through to Sunday morning. With a stomach rumbling for food, she cracked her eyes open to the daylight, looked out the window across rolling English fields dotted with sheep, and smiled so widely her face hurt.

The light on her room phone was blinking. "Order room service whenever you like," Jane said on the message. "It's supposed to thunderstorm later today, but until then we'll be at the pool if you want to hang out. The info sheet on your desk will give you the schedule of the week. Mostly, just have fun!"

Cali perused the schedule while she waited for breakfast to arrive. The estate was vast, with pathways and little country roads all around it. If the storms held off, she'd put on her running shoes and go exploring later. But first she had to explore the house.

She took a quick shower while waiting for breakfast to arrive, and was finishing up a heavenly Belgian waffle when the hotel manager knocked.

"Good morning, Miss Blake. I hope your first night at Brampton was comfortable."

"I slept wonderfully, thanks. But call me Cali, please."

"Jane told me you are a sister bibliophile." He extended a slim booklet to her. "Lord Melbury's library is under renovation currently and it's a tragic mess. But I thought you'd be interested in this."

Cali flipped through the catalogue. "Wow. This is an amazing collection. Is it all accessible?"

"Only a fraction of the collection is available at this time. But feel free to borrow any book you see. If you decide to poke around, though, you'll want to wear something that doesn't mind dust."

"Great." Nothing she owned minded dust. Discount off-the-rack was like that. "Thanks a bunch."

"Jane is at the pool now. Take the stairs at the rear of the house to the garden level and you'll find the path easily."

He left and she changed into her bathing suit. A little swim to clear her sleep-groggy head would do her good.

When she got to the pool, she wasn't so sure any head-clearing would happen.

Piers Prescott wearing a swimsuit was not simply good-looking. He was a god. Tan. Cut. Muscular everywhere it counted and lean everywhere else. He stood at the other side of the pool talking to a couple of guys. He turned his head, looked straight at her, and smiled.

"Cali, you're finally awake!" Jane called from a lounge chair. "Come meet Roxanna."

She dragged her attention away from the god-man and went to the bride. Jane introduced her former roommate. Roxanna was a striking redhead with a sexy, über-hip aura and a sardonic grin.

"We've been ogling the pool boy," she said. "Very hot."

"Really?" She glanced around, but no one was as interesting as Hot Philadelphia Big Money. And he was staring at her. Again.

"Looks like you don't need a pool boy, though," Roxanna said slyly.

Cali snatched her gaze away. "What?"

"Piers Prescott is checking you out. No wonder. You look amazing in that suit, though you should wear a bikini. You'd kill in a bikini."

"Thanks... I think?"

Jane laughed. "That's just Roxanna, Cali. Don't mind her."

"He's definitely interested," Roxanna said. "And he's single now. He used to date Indie rockers. That's how he got on the radar."

"The radar?"

"Roxanna works for Jezebel.com," Jane explained.

"He never dated anybody for long until he started seeing Caroline Colby," Roxanna said. "Everybody was shocked when they broke up after four years."

"Really?" She tried to sound casual. Cool. Unimpressed with gossip.

"Caroline Colby is as blue-blooded as they come. Perfect for a Prescott," Roxanna said. "Everybody figured they'd get married, but she got engaged to someone else right away. So he's available. And he's still staring at you. You should get on that."

Cali blinked. "Get on what?"

Roxanna grinned. "Jump him. You should jump him."

"Roxanna, you're making Cali blush."

"I'm not blushing." Rather, burning up. But Roxanna had already turned away and didn't hear her. "Hey, Jane, Mark told me about the library here." Desperate attempt to change the subject. "Have you seen it?" It was one thing to joke with Zoe about having a wedding party hookup, another thing altogether to actually plan one. Especially with a Prescott.

"I haven't had time yet." Jane sipped her cocktail and peered at her as if she knew exactly what Cali was thinking. Back in the day, they'd constantly scoped out cute boys in the library. *Boys*. Not gorgeous multimillionaire *men*. Rather, gorgeous multimillionaire *man* who was walking toward her now.

Cali stood up abruptly. "I think I'll take a look at it now."

She fled. Wishing she had international phone coverage so she could text Zoe to say she absolutely, positively was not interested in hooking up with Piers Prescott, she changed into the oldest of the clothes she'd brought and went in search of the library.

It was amazing. A large room lined with wooden bookcases, it boasted a carved ladder stair on a rail, a white marble fireplace that picked up the fresh white paint of decorative plasterwork everywhere, and a collection of furniture under sheets. As Mark had warned, it definitely needed the renovations underway; the parquet floor was a mess of scratches and warped boards, and it smelled like mold and rot. Clear plastic sheets protected the shelves, but only a few contained books.

She moved toward them. The one book she really wanted to see wouldn't be here now: an original 1813 three-volume edition of Jane Austen's *Pride and Prejudice*. It must be in safe storage somewhere. Still, she pressed her nose and palms to the sheer wall that separated her from the meager remnants of Lord Melbury's collection.

A tearing sound.

A loud, cracking creak.

The plastic gave way under her hands.

Everything fell. Plastic. Volumes. Pouring down like rain. Cali jumped aside and slammed into the ladder. Something hit her shoulder. Books clattered on her head, knocking her over.

Hands clamped around her shoulders and dragged her from the deluge, slamming her face against a hard chest.

The bookcase thundered to the floor behind her.

Everything went silent. All she knew for an instant were her thudding heartbeats, the soft cotton of a T-shirt under her cheek, and the scent of delicious cologne.

The hands released her. She stepped back and looked into Piers Prescott's handsome face.

*His* chest. *His* cologne.

Air compressed in her lungs. "Oh my God! The books!"

She twisted around.

*Carnage.*

Books everywhere. Smashed beneath the fallen bookcase. Spilling out to either side. Opened. Pages torn and folded. Bindings bent.

Her hands covered her mouth. "*Oh.*" No breaths. "Oh no. No no *no.*" Horror. All horror. All the time. Like one of those hole-in-the-wall theaters that only played *The Texas Chainsaw Massacre* and *Halloween I–V.*

"Are you all right?" she heard behind her.

She swung around to the bearer of the cologne that was too perfect and dreamy for this horrible moment.

"How are you?" He reached out as if to touch her shoulder, then retracted his hand.

She rubbed her head where a big book had connected. "Fine. Mostly. Thank you for grabbing me." She twisted back to the books. "But… Oh my God."

"They said thunderstorms today, but it looks like it's raining books inside."

A little ripple of pleasure went right up her spine. He had *the sexiest voice*. Low and confident. And he'd read her mind.

She wrenched her attention away from the disaster to look over her shoulder. "I think I broke the bookcase." Oh, *God*.

"You didn't. Look. It wasn't attached to the wall. A light breeze could have toppled it."

"Are you sure?" Her voice sounded airy. His hand running along the edge of the wall was long-fingered, strong, just as handsome as the rest of him.

"Pretty sure." He moved around the pile of books, plastic, shelves, and scattered plaster to the next case. He grasped the side and it wobbled. "This isn't attached either."

"Maybe they disconnected them for the renovation."

"I suspect." He returned to her and stood looking down at her. "Still fine?"

"Yes." Except that she couldn't really breathe. Now it was from both the disaster *and* him. She knew he was a corporate shark, that he ate struggling companies for breakfast, and that behind that carelessly tousled hair was a brain that had been summa cum laude at both Stanford and Wharton. But he was just *so handsome*. She'd never hung out with guys this handsome.

But he wasn't any guy, and it wasn't just his features. It was the warmth in his very blue eyes and the set of his mouth, like he might be about to smile, but could get really serious really quickly too. It made his classical good looks vibrate with grab-him-and-kiss-him sex appeal.

She wanted to. Now.

Grab him.

And kiss him.

She was *out of her mind*.

"What were you doing in here?" he said, never taking his eyes off her.

"Looking." Single words seemed to be all she could manage.

"Looking at?"

"Library. Um… Books?"

"Oh, books. Yeah, I've heard of those." He smiled. Her insides did a sharp little clench of pleasure.

*No.*

Not *this* feeling. Not now, with a pile of destruction at her feet *that she'd caused*. Not *this man*.

"I'm guessing you're not a big reader," she said.

"I read the paper."

"Online news."

The corner of his very fine mouth crept up. "Pretty dismissive there, huh?"

She wouldn't be so dismissive if she had a computer at home, and if she hadn't spent every evening for a month on the library's public computers helping the grant writer do research for the application that his family's charitable foundation then viciously rejected.

"No. I just prefer books," she said. "They're…" Dust from the crash still floated in the air, in her nostrils, settling on her lips. "They're tactile."

"You like to touch what you see?" He seemed suddenly closer. Or maybe it was just because his voice had dropped a few notes. But he couldn't be flirting. Guys like Piers Prescott didn't flirt with her. Guys like Piers Prescott didn't know she existed.

"I like to touch what I read, yes. And smell." *He* smelled incredible, the way a woman dreamed a man would smell but never actually experienced. "It's the reason I work in a library. Books have scent."

"I'd forgotten that."

"You forgot?"

He was still looking right into her eyes. "I don't have time to read books."

"I guess you wouldn't." He was too busy dismantling mom-and-pop companies and selling the parts to the highest bidder. "I'm sure you have other priorities," she said with herculean restraint.

"Other priorities. Right." Finally he looked away, glancing at the pile of tumbled books. "Any recommendations?"

"In here? You just said you don't have time to read books."

He looked back down at her and this time only his eyes seemed to smile. It simply took her breath away. Breaths. Gone. Just like that.

"I'm on vacation this week," he said.

"You're not working at all?" This she found unbelievable. "For a whole week?"

"Yeah." With a relaxed, sexy shrug, he leaned his hand against the wall, effectively trapping her between him and the mound of catastrophe. "This week I'm all about playing." His gaze slowly slid down her body.

This was *not happening*. It couldn't be.

"Jane Austen," she blurted out.

His brow creased beneath the softest, silkiest lock of hair to ever dip toward a man's eyes.

"Jane Austen?" he repeated.

"The book I'd most like to see from Lord Melbury's collection. The reason I came in here and enacted this horrible scene." Her voice wasn't quite shaking, but nearly. Because of the books. But also because of him. Which was stupid. The ruined books were much more important. He was just a guy. Albeit, a Prescott: patron of all things Influential and Important.

The Prescott Foundation hadn't funded the bookmobile, but it had given a huge sum to the library for a special exhibition on Great White Dead Men that was opening in a month. Actually titled *America's Heroes,* the exhibition featured pieces related to a select group of historical figures, all men of power and wealth, like John Hancock's personal diary and Henry Ford's earliest designs. Several were loaned from the Prescott family's private collection. Missing from the exhibition were other heroes who'd made huge marks on American history, like Rosa Parks or Dorothy Day or Martin Luther King Jr. Just men like Piers Prescott's grandfather, head of Prescott Global, except the men in the exhibit were already dead.

But it didn't seem to matter to her body that the man before her was the heir to Bad Guys Inc. Her pulse tripped along swiftly. And she found herself dying to respond to the grab-him-and-kiss-him urge. To forget about being careful, responsible, frugal, and uptight. For once she wanted to go a little bit wild.

"LORD MELBURY'S collection includes an original edition of *Pride and Prejudice*," she said. "Ever heard of it?"

She looked adorable, dusty and defiant at once as she challenged him to admit his ignorance. Piers didn't mind it. He'd nothing to prove to this woman—this woman who hadn't yet given him one of the sparkling smiles she gave him in the park every Friday morning.

She didn't reserve those smiles for Philly, though. She'd smiled brilliantly at her friends down at the pool. But she was resisting his flirting.

That intrigued him. Women didn't resist him. Men didn't in business or anything else. He always got what he wanted, except in one matter, and he was complicit in that: his brother's escape from Prescott Global. That ten years later he was still sitting at his brother's destined desk in the family's skyscraper was the reason he'd first seen this woman.

"I haven't read it. Should I?"

She twisted up lips the color of every hot fantasy he'd ever had and gave him a clear-eyed assessment.

"It probably wouldn't hurt." She ducked under his arm. He pivoted, following her progress to the other side of the bookshelf lying facedown on the pile of books. "It's not here, of course. I'd kill myself if I'd damaged it."

She crouched and started straightening the books. For a moment he let himself admire the snug pull of her jeans around her curves. Then he crossed his arms loosely and leaned his shoulder against the wall.

"You'd kill yourself over a book?" She'd nearly done so six months ago, the day he'd first seen her in Green Park, doling out books from a backpack to kids while a pair of dealers eyed her from across the street.

"A very precious book." She brushed a wisp of dark hair from her face. She always wore it up, hiding the length. He wanted to see it down and flowing around her bare shoulders.

"But really, all books are precious," she said, focused on the volumes in her hands. They looked relatively new to him, but she seemed truly anguished. "I suppose your family owns so many expensive things, like cars and vacation houses, that mere books seem insignificant in comparison."

"Not exactly."

"I feel terrible about this," she said quietly.

Something else shone in her eyes now. Worry. Serious worry. The destruction meant more to her than the damage to the books.

*Money.* She thought she'd have to pay for this.

That couldn't happen. He wanted to protect her now, the same way he'd wanted to protect her the first time he'd ever seen her.

"If anybody asks, we'll say I did it." He gestured to the pile.

"What? No." She stood up, frowning. "That's not right. It's a lie."

Like pretending he'd just met her yesterday. "But it could easily be the truth. Put me in a library and I'm like a bull in a china shop."

Her brown eyes that made him want to do things to her—*X-rated things*—swept him up and down again. Assessing.

"I don't believe it," she said. "I don't believe you're ever careless about anything."

But he'd been careless with her. From the start. *He should tell her.* What was the worst that could happen? She'd tell someone else, the news would get around, and the funds would revert into his bank account. Rather, they'd get tied up in legal knots for months.

Her attention shifted to the doorway and her smile hit him full force in the gut.

"You found her, Piers. Great," Duke's fiancé said blithely and looked at the pile on the floor. "What a mess. Mark said it's still being renovated. I'm glad the rest of the house isn't like this."

"I knocked over a bookcase," he said.

California was staring at him, her honest, expressive eyes very wide, her lips parted.

"Listen," he said quickly, "I'm going to find someone to clean this up. Careful with those other shelves, California. They're loose."

He'd never run from a woman. In his life. Not even his sister when she'd regularly asked him to take her dateless friends to parties. He'd done it. He'd do anything for Amy. And for his brother. Hell, for a decade his life had been about helping out J.T.

Now he ran. At close proximity, California Blake was smarter, sweeter, and a hell of a lot sexier than he'd anticipated. And honest. Her emotions showed so clearly in her eyes. When he told her the truth, he wouldn't have to guess if she thought he was slime. He would know it. So, according to the provisions of the library grant and his own reliable instinct, he simply wouldn't tell her.

"CALI DOESN'T TRUST MEN," Jane said as she sat down beside Duke, a glass of wine in her hand. She crossed her legs.

Duke turned his head to look at her. "Where's this coming from?"

Jane speared Piers with a stare. He and Duke had been having a drink. Relaxing for a moment, the kind of relaxation he hadn't had time for since college.

"Piers is hitting on Cali," Jane said.

Duke nodded at him. "Nice choice, bro."

Jane shoved her elbow in her fiancé's ribs. "Don't play around with her, Piers. She's not like the shallow socialites you're used to. She's a genuinely good person, and she's had a really rough time of it since high school."

"What happened in high school?" He succeeded at sounding casual. Over the past decade he'd perfected sounding casual when he felt everything but.

"Her father was a corporate lawyer. Lots of money. Trips to Vail and Paris and wherever the superrich crowd went. He was a partier. He'd married a waitress at Hooters and it was a wretched mistake. He left her three or four times. Then, when Cali and I were at Penn State, her mom died in iffy circumstances."

"Suicide?" Duke said.

"Prescription pills. By then, Cali's dad had been drinking a lot and screwing up. After Cali's mom OD'd, he lost it entirely. Everything went: his job, the big house, investments, cars, savings. Her sister was

241

still in high school and Cali had to drop out of State so she could carry all three of them. Then, a few years ago, he burned down their house."

Piers swiveled his martini. "Was he drunk?"

"Passed out. There was a lit cigar, but drugs too. He went to jail."

Duke whistled low.

"Cali was studying when the fire started," Jane said. "She was taking night classes from community college so she could finish her degree and get promoted from library page to associate. She dragged her father from the house. Her sister was asleep upstairs. The firemen rescued Zoe, but she was really badly burned."

Piers hadn't known. He could have found out. He'd never wanted to. He eavesdropped on her every Friday morning, but she knew that; she lowered her voice when she didn't want him to hear. Anything else he learned about her, he'd wanted to hear from her directly.

"The house wasn't insured for fire. So Cali finished her degree in record time and has been working her tail off at the library ever since. It's been hard for her and Zoe in the past few years," Jane said. "She doesn't need you messing around with her head, Piers. And she definitely doesn't need more lying jerks like her father."

"That's harsh, Jane," Duke said, but he took her hand.

"I'm sorry," Jane said. "I didn't mean it that way. Just don't play around with her, Piers. Okay?"

He didn't want to play. He wanted to know her. To actually know her. But he'd already made that undoable. Yeah. Great idea, trying to take away her hurt. Great plan to make her wishes come true.

# CHAPTER
## FIVE

*The Park at Brampton*

T he morning began with a spectacular thunderstorm that broke directly over the house and woke Cali from dreams of Piers Prescott touching her.

The night before at the casual barbeque dinner, he'd been more gorgeous than a greedy corporate ogre should be allowed. He'd only come near her once, when she'd stood at the bar alone. He asked if she'd gotten hold of the Austen novel yet. She told him Mark, the hotel manager, had let her see it and she'd been in heaven. Piers smiled at her and looked right into her eyes the way he had in the library. Then several of the other women guests swarmed all over him. He hadn't approached her again. But a few times she'd found him watching her.

It was unnerving. And incredibly arousing.

She'd never before dreamed of making out with a man. It took her a few minutes of staring up at the canopy above her five-star mattress to shrug the sensations from her body and switch on her rational brain. But her blood still felt zingy. She needed to get outside. The estate covered acres and acres. She would take a run. And on her run she would reconsider Zoe's and Roxanna's advice.

He was gorgeous. He was only thirty-ish and already a millionaire. He was so completely out of her league he would never be interested in her if she weren't here. Guys like Piers Prescott only cared about money, power, and good looks.

But her imagination was now a train hurtling out of control. She thought about touching his chest. She thought about the way he'd touched her in the dream. Then she thought about him on top of her, between her thighs, pressing her into that five-star mattress.

A run. She needed a long run. Immediately.

And probably a fling. Zoe was right: she was wound up so tightly from stress that she was fantasizing about a guy she'd barely met. A golden opportunity to release tension, to kick loose for the first time in years, was in this house now. And he could probably use some rebound sex after the split with his longtime girlfriend.

*No.* Bad idea. She wanted nothing to do with the Prescott family, not even a casual fling. Best to steer clear of him. She would find one of Duke's other friends who seemed nice and interesting *and moral.* Then she could release tension without sacrificing any self-respect.

She dressed in running shorts and a Lycra tank, and stretched for her run. Then she went looking for a man. A specific man.

She found Lord Melbury's son, Harry Compton, in his residence, knocking dirt from work boots in a long hallway inside the side door to the house. It seemed a very plebeian activity for the heir to a lord of the realm. But she supposed nobles put their boots on one foot at a time too—and took them off, muddy.

Sick in her stomach, she apologized for the accident in the library. Pleasantly reserved in the way only Englishmen could be, he was a complete gentleman. He assured her that few of the books were damaged and all were easily replaceable. The bookcase hadn't suffered any harm either. He seemed more worried that she'd been injured. She assured him she'd only gotten what she deserved for being so careless. Then she offered to pay for the damaged books, which he politely refused.

With a much lighter heart, she set off across the estate.

And promptly got lost.

She hadn't run in the countryside in ages, and Brampton wasn't exactly laid out on a grid. Thunderclouds rumbled ominously. A droplet of rain splashed on her face. She'd no idea how far she was from the house.

In the distance, a white temple structure rose amidst gorgeous trees and glorious shrubs on the top of a hill. She remembered having seen it from the house. Thunder boomed. As she ran toward the gazebo, the sky split open. Buckets. Cats and dogs. Noah's Ark-worthy. Lungs burning, she sprinted.

Splashing up the steps of the gazebo and ducking inside, she came face-to-face with the man of her dream.

*Of course.* Sweaty and flushed, dripping rain from the tip of her nose, her hair plastered to her head, and gulping breaths, she had to bump into Mr. *GQ* in the middle of nowhere. He sat on a marble bench against the inside wall, his slacks dry and his pristine white linen shirt undone to the third button. He had an iPad mini propped on one knee, and he wore a pair of leather Ferragamos worth more than her monthly rent.

He looked up. And did a double take.

"Hey."

She swiped water from her dripping chin. "Hi." The pouring rain almost drowned her out.

He set down the tablet, stood, and came forward, his gaze dipping to her legs. "Thunderstorm running? Is this a new Olympic sport?"

"Yup. I'm a favorite to medal next year." She told herself it didn't matter that she was a mess. She didn't need to impress him. The bookmobile had funding for at least a year. She didn't need to go begging to any Prescott now.

*Not for money.*

She couldn't help thinking about her dream and where he'd touched her. If the storm hadn't woken her, she might have started begging in that scenario.

"It should be over soon." He sounded smooth. Assured. Relaxed. While her insides were like a carnival. She kind of hated him for it. But she already hated the Prescotts anyway.

"So, I think it would be best if I set something straight right away," she said.

"Good idea."

She blinked. "It is?"

"Yeah."

"But you don't know what I'm going to say."

"If you think it's important, I'd like to hear it." He sounded completely earnest.

This wasn't how she'd thought things would go with him. She hadn't planned on saying this at all. But she had him trapped, penned in by sheets of rain. He had to listen. It would entirely ruin her golden opportunity, but the words bubbling up in her now were much more important than a fling.

She shifted from one foot to the other and her shoes squelched. "I helped prepare a proposal that the library submitted to your family's foundation for a mobile library unit that drives through underprivileged neighborhoods, lending books. The foundation rejected our proposal."

"It receives many proposals," he said guardedly. It was the first she'd seen him less than entirely confident. It gave her a moment's pause.

"I know it can't fund everything," she admitted, but she had to say this. "It wasn't the rejection itself that I objected to, but the tone of it."

"The tone?"

"It was scathing and insulting. It suggested that the project was naively conceived and a waste of money, and that if the people it intended to serve really wanted to improve themselves, they would finish high school and get jobs instead of lazing around expecting taxpayers to entertain them with free books. It intimated that the people who live in those neighborhoods are all drug addicts and illiterate, so what good would it to do to offer them books except give them something to sell in exchange for their next hit? I've never read anything so ignorant and condescending in my life."

"I can understand that."

"Powerful, rich people just don't get it that people struggling to make ends meet want to read good books too. But they can't afford them. Or they can't afford bus fare to get to the closest branch library. And they can't afford overdue fines when they have to work overtime to pay the heating bill or send their kids to school with lunch, so they can't make it back to the library to return a book on time. Or they're too old to get around and they can't get books easily. Or they're teachers and they don't have the money to buy new books or to take their students on field trips to the library, but they still want to give the kids the world. The bookmobile is for those people."

"It's clearly a valid program, California."

"It *is*. But people like your family, who sit in their elite ivory towers and dictate how the world turns, don't think of anybody's happiness except their own. You're all about gala balls to celebrate your latest billion-dollar deals and dismantling companies to ship them overseas. You have no idea how the so-called little people struggle to get by every day. You can't see beyond your upturned noses. And to call the Prescott Foundation a charitable institution is ludicrous when it only gives money to high cultural events like art gallery shows and symphony performances intended for people with three-BMW garages and vacation houses in France. It's awful and wrong and you should be ashamed of yourselves."

"I know."

The air rushed out of her lungs. She pushed a sodden lock of hair back from her forehead. "You do?"

"Yeah. I agree with you."

She couldn't wrap her head around it. "Are you saying this just so I'll shut up?"

"No. I actually agree with you. My grandfather is a prize bastard with a sense of entitlement longer than his yacht, and he wants to control everyone and everything around him. I don't like the way the company or the foundation do business any more than you do."

"But..." She shook her head. "I didn't expect you to say this."

"Clearly." He smiled slightly. The rain had let up but a gust of misty wind swept through the gazebo and brushed his collar wide open, exposing a portion of perfectly toned chest. Goosebumps skittered all over Cali's skin. She clamped her arms across her breasts.

"You must be cold," he said, putting a hand to his shirt buttons. "I didn't bring a jacket out here, but—"

"*No.*" She stepped back. "No, I'm fine." If he took off his shirt and gave it to her she would die. Or attack him. "I'm cooling down pretty fast. I should finish my run now." She glanced at the iPad. "What are you doing out here? Don't tell me… You're secretly plotting to over-throw your grandfather, but he found out and bugged the house, so you had to come here to communicate with your guerilla army of spies?"

His warm eyes glimmered. "There's no Wi-Fi or cell service at the house. Someone discovered a signal here and I came to give it a try." He glanced around. "I'm surprised there aren't twenty other people here now."

"I thought you said you were all about playing this week."

"I said that because you looked beautiful and I was flirting with you. Which you resisted valiantly. Now I understand at least one reason for that."

His directness was as sexy as the rest of him. He stepped forward, the wind pressing the linen against his arms and chest.

"Listen, Califor—"

"Why did you come looking for me in the library? Jane said you did."

"I wanted to get you alone."

Nerves zipped right up the center of her body. "We're alone now."

"We are." His voice sounded low. "And I'm suddenly thinking I'm not prepared for this."

"But I think I am." Taking two quick steps forward and balancing on her squishy toes, she pressed a kiss on the sexiest lips she'd ever seen. Sexiest she'd ever *felt*. Soft and angling instantly to meet hers. The scent of him. The flavor. So good. *Too good.*

She started to pull back.

He wrapped his hand around the base of her skull and took over.

He kissed her like he'd had this in mind from the start and knew she would be okay with it.

*She was.* She so was.

Urging her lips apart, tilting her face up, he fit their mouths together perfectly. Slow, deep, and bone-meltingly good, he kissed her like he planned to kiss her all day. And he tasted like a god. And smelled like heaven. His hand on her neck and the expensive scent of his skin—so *incredibly good*. Her whole body woke up, hot and trembling and delicious. He slipped the tip of his tongue along the inside seam of her upper lip, then came inside her, stroking her tongue and making her ache where she hadn't in ages—except in her dream last night.

But this was no dream. This was his fingers sinking into her wet hair and his tongue in her mouth and his lips making her want to taste even more of him. Her shirt felt far too tight and the impulse to press her breasts against his chest felt totally natural. The impulse to press her entire body to him felt even stronger.

She broke away and gulped in air.

His gorgeous blue eyes seemed unfocused. Like he was floored too.

*Wrong*. This wasn't how wedding party hookups were supposed to happen. When she was all done up in a sexy dress, she was supposed to get tipsy and have irresponsible sex in a coat closet. Not perfect kisses in the middle of the day, wearing soaked running gear.

But he was looking at her like she was sexy *now*. And like he wouldn't need a coat closet.

*No.*

Not this man.

Not *her*.

What did she know about wedding party flings anyway? She preferred to get to know a man before she slept with him. That this man didn't feel like a stranger was an illusion caused by his unexpected reaction to her harangue and by his good looks. And his scent. And his flavor. And the way he kissed her as if he knew just how she wanted to be kissed.

*Impossible.*

"What am I doing?" she heard herself utter.

He nodded. "Kissing me."

"This doesn't happen in reality."

"It just did."

"Not to me," she insisted.

"I repeat."

She backed up and tripped down a step.

"California." He reached for her, but she turned and jerked into the rain.

"I've got to go... Now... Bye."

She bolted. She'd only ever run from Dick. Now she ran from Piers Prescott for the opposite reason. But both came down to fear.


SHE TASTED AMAZING. Like honey and salt and heat. And she kissed like she wanted sex. Like she wanted sex with *him*.

That had not been his purpose in buying her the plane ticket. Not *entirely*. Now she'd gotten spooked, just as Jane had warned. Possibly because she didn't know what he wanted from her.

He didn't know either. A few weeks ago, he'd wanted nothing more than to give her the vacation she deserved. And to meet her.

And to tell her. He'd wanted to tell her how he'd funded the bookmobile, but tell her in some place that she couldn't run away from as soon as she knew. He hadn't realized it until now. He'd wanted to trap her into liking him, to launch a hostile takeover that looked appealing on the surface, so he'd be sure to win.

Now she'd run away. And he still hadn't told her.

He walked down the hill to the house through the wet grass, passing another poor soul on his way to get cell service at the gazebo. Archer Quinn, Duke's lawyer, was a good guy even if his father, venture capitalist Ted Quinn, reminded Piers too much of his own grandfather.

"Hey, Piers," he said as they passed. "You might want to be on guard for paparazzi. They're eager to get photos of the wedding, but I'm sure they'll snap pics of anyone they can sell."

"Typical. Thanks for mentioning it."

"I suspect you're missing as much work this week as I am. Prescott Global never sleeps, hm?"

"Unfortunately not. Heading up there for the signal?" He gestured to the hill's apex.

Archer glanced at the gazebo. "Up there. Yes. Right. See you, Piers."

Piers started toward the house again. *Damn paparazzi.* Not ideal if they got wind that he was attending this party. He'd counted on a little more time to remain off his grandfather's radar.

Fortunately his grandfather didn't read online gossip news. The business gossip blogs had covered every detail of Piers's relationships with women. He and Caroline had occasionally fed the bloggers information, to keep them satisfied and because Caroline liked to be in the spotlight. She liked full disclosure.

Full disclosure wasn't necessary with California Blake. She was getting what she wanted: the bookmobile plus an all-expenses-paid vacation, and she seemed happy about it. If she wanted sex, he'd give her that too. Since seeing her tight little curved body in that wet shirt and shorts, he looked forward to it.

He told himself she didn't need to know what went on behind the curtain, that his methods weren't wrong.

And he knew he was telling himself the same story his grandfather had been telling him for years.

# CHAPTER
## SIX

*The Town of Melbury*

O n Tuesday morning, Jane told Cali that Roxanna needed pictures of the wedding dress for her boyfriend, publishing mogul Damien Knightly, who wanted to scoop his competitors on the wedding of the year. But Jane and Duke had promised exclusive photos to *People*, with the proceeds going to an animal rescue foundation. So Jane came up with the idea of staging a fake bridal gown shopping excursion, and Roxanna would release pictures of that instead.

Cali gladly went along to Oldwart's Bridal Shoppe in the village, eager to be far from anywhere she might accidentally bump into The Best Kisser in the World.

As they watched Jane pirouette around the shop in a series of tacky polyester gowns, she and Roxanna laughed till their sides hurt. One dress was so covered in feathers, Jane looked like a chicken—albeit a pretty chicken.

But it was bittersweet fun. Unless she won the lottery, she'd never be able to afford even a cheap gown like these. She loved Jane. That her old friend might have paid for her trip made her love her even more.

But she had nothing in common with the rest of the people at this party. She wasn't a computer genius or a publishing mogul or an ace lawyer or a popular journalist or a best-selling novelist or a successful wedding planner throwing the party of the year.

And she was so far from the society debutantes and hip Indie rockers that Piers Prescott dated, it made her laugh.

Thinking about his kiss made her hot all over, but she just couldn't get near him again. One-night stands weren't for her, and anything more had Wrong Side of the Tracks Tragedy written all over it. Because it wouldn't turn into *Pride and Prejudice*, where she ended up with the rich stud. Instead, it would be *Pretty in Pink*, with the original ending they'd shown test audiences before they switched it, where she ended up with the poor goofy boy, not the rich gorgeous boy. Except in her scenario, there wasn't even a poor goofy boy waiting for her at home, just medical bills and gross Dick.

They left the shop and crossed the street to a quaint little pharmacy, and Roxanna went inside to buy something.

Cali turned to Jane. "You are a truly beautiful bride."

"Even in polyester?"

"In anything. But I've got to know: Did you pay for my trip here?"

"No. Didn't you?"

She shook her head. "Someone sent me the ticket."

"You don't know who?"

"It had to be my friends at a park I visit every week. We've gotten pretty close and they knew how much I wanted to come."

"That's the sweetest thing I've ever heard."

Roxanna came out of the store and gave her a quick once-over. "Cali, did you bring anything sexier? All I've seen you wear are those loose slacks and boxy shirts."

"I don't own anything sexier. But I have a nice dress for the rehearsal dinner."

"This party is a week long. You shouldn't be hiding what you've got until the end, especially when Piers Prescott is interested."

Her dumpy wardrobe hadn't stopped him from kissing her in the pouring rain. And he'd said she was beautiful. *Beautiful.*

"Thanks, but I don't think—"

"It's not about thinking. It's about doing, and doing it now so you don't waste a minute of fun." Roxanna gave her a saucy grin. "I brought lots of extra clothes. I know just what'll look fantastic on you."

Cali bit her lip.

"Trust her," Jane said. "What's the worst that can happen if you let loose for once?"

Roxanna dressed Cali like Zoe used to dress Barbie dolls, trying her in every outfit imaginable before fixing on one: white camisole, silky shirt that didn't close at the front, and Cali's own hip-riding jeans. Roxanna threaded the belt loops with a filmy scarf and left it hanging to either side of the fly.

Cali fingered the imported silk. "Why untied?"

"Quick access."

A zing went right through Cali's quick-access area. She attempted breathing. "We're not going to have to go through this every day, are we?"

"Ingrate." Roxanna stepped back to assess her work. "You look hot. Aren't you even going to check yourself out in the mirror?"

"I trust you." She couldn't bring herself to look. It was too weird. Too much something she'd never do. She felt like an alien in her own skin. An alien terrified of going downstairs now. Earlier, when they'd returned to the house, she'd seen Piers across the foyer and felt like giggling. She *never* giggled.

But she'd never been much of a hider either.

"Thanks, Roxanna. This is really great."

"I'll have a porter deliver those to your room." She pointed to a pile of clothes on the bed. "Wear them. Piers will go crazy."

When Cali went down to cocktails later, the room was already full of guests, except Piers. Cali had time to take a few sips of wine, to check out the antiques and paintings and brocaded draperies, and to feel her nerves loosen before he appeared. He stood in the doorway talking to Duke's lawyer, Archer. They were both handsome men. And at least one of them tasted like heaven.

"How do you like the hors d'oeuvres, California?"

The wedding planner, Arwen, stood beside her.

"Hors d'oeuvres?" Was that what the kiss in the gazebo had been? An appetizer? Should she consider it a foretaste of what she could have? Was she an idiot for shutting down that possibility when she wanted it so much that she'd let Roxanna dress her up like a paper doll?

"One of the new ovens wasn't properly calibrated. It burned the hors d'oeuvres." Arwen pinched her lips. "But please don't tell Jane. We fixed it in a jiffy."

"The hors d'oeuvres were..." She glanced at Piers. "Absolutely delicious." He was looking at her. "I want more."

"Excellent," Arwen said with satisfaction.

Piers didn't approach her. But he didn't stop watching her. Cali chatted with other guests and tried to relax. She failed. Eventually she ended up in a group of Duke's friends who were talking about the huge success of his new start-up. Nearby, Roxanna caught her eye, then looked meaningfully to Cali's side.

Cali turned her head. Piers stood beside her.

"Hey." His voice was warm and low. Then he lifted his drink to his mouth and said something to the others about the TSE versus NASDAQ. He wore a gold signet ring and his hands had the pronounced veins of a man in excellent physical condition. She knew this already. She'd seen him in a swimsuit. In the library, she'd had her face pressed against his chest. Still, seeing his hand at such close range after it'd been on the back of her neck to hold her mouth to his, she got shaky inside.

*No.* This was just wrong. She was a grown woman, not a dizzy teenager. And he was a corporate monster, no matter what he'd said in the rain. Actions spoke louder than words. Cliché, but true. She didn't need a fling with him. She needed a nice, relaxing vacation and to watch her friend walk happily ever after down the aisle.

Piers turned his head to her, smiled, and Cali nearly dropped her drink.

She fled.

She couldn't go outside. It was raining, and as much fun as she'd

255

had in the rain yesterday, she couldn't chance that again. She glanced back. Piers was moving away from the group. Toward her.

Scuttling down the hallway she went through the first door she saw, and found herself in the biggest half bath she'd ever seen. Also, the most gorgeous, with a marble countertop, bronze fixtures, Italian tile, and a Hollywood salon style mirror. She fell back against the counter and covered her face with her hands.

How had she come to this place where she was simultaneously lusting after a man and running away from him? She wasn't this person. She was insanely busy and constantly stressed. But she wasn't a ditz.

The door opened and Piers came in and shut it behind him.

She sprang up. "What are you doing?"

"Cornering you."

"What if I'd been…" She gestured toward the commode.

"The door wasn't locked. You were trying to escape me."

"I might not have been."

He lifted a brow.

"I'm a lousy liar," she admitted.

"Hey," he said, leaning back against the wall. "I don't want to pressure you."

"Really?" She crossed her arms. "You followed me into a bathroom."

"You ran away into a bathroom. After running away from the gazebo."

"Who follows a woman into a bathroom? Haven't you ever heard of privacy?"

He offered her a skeptical look. "Do you think this personal space thing might be coming a little late?"

The edge of the marble counter cut into her butt. "Would you have believed it before the gazebo?"

His smile was slow and assured. "What do you think?"

She thought that from the moment he'd walked down the steps of Brampton onto the drive, she'd been doomed to spend the week lusting after him.

"Look, there's something going on here," he said. "I just want you to know that I'm available."

"Available?"

"For whatever you want."

He couldn't be saying what she thought he was saying. Not so directly. But guys like him probably did everything this way. No one would tell them not to, and they probably always got whatever they wanted.

Which was exactly what he was offering to her now.

"Whatever I want?" she repeated.

"Anything. You call the shots."

"Anything?" Apparently she could not find original words.

His smile went from tempting to devastating. He meant the kind of anything she'd been fantasizing about last night.

She couldn't speak. This was her chance. A wedding party fling. A brief hookup. Simple, uncomplicated fun. *Release.*

She sucked in courage. "I do have something in mind." Straight from her dream.

"Do you?"

"I'd like you to feel me up over my jeans." *She'd said it.* "Now."

His Adam's apple shifted under smooth, tan skin. His surprise was incredibly sexy. "That's it?"

Her courage plummeted. "Yes. Why? Isn't that enough for you?"

He came three steps forward, right into her space the same way she'd stepped right into his at the gazebo.

"I get to touch you," he said. "How couldn't that be enough for me?"

Why did he always say the right thing? Did he have a stockpile of lines to get women in bed?

*Don't think about it, Cali. Just enjoy.*

He smelled like heaven. It was his outrageously expensive cologne, she knew. But it was also him. His scent. She recognized it already and it made her knees weak.

"Are you going to do it?" She sounded breathy. Like the ditz she wasn't.

"Yeah. I'm going to do it." He didn't sound breathy. He sounded really certain.

Then his hands were sliding around her hips, strong and as certain as his voice. She gripped the counter to either side of her as his fingertips strafed her bare skin above the low-cut waist of her jeans, flicking under her camisole. It felt good—his skin against hers. It felt amazing. She liked his hands on her hips. She liked it how he held her gaze, as if he wanted to see how she enjoyed his hands on her.

"I have one condition," he said in a low voice.

"You didn't say anything about conditions." His hands were curving around her butt, the way he might try out the steering wheel of a Ferrari for the first time. A Ferrari he knew he'd own soon.

"You'll like this condition." He cupped her butt on both sides, his hands encompassing her.

*She liked it already.* "What is it?"

"I want you to turn around."

"Turn—?" Her throat caught. There was a mirror behind her. The lights around it were some kind of softly brilliant bulbs, and they were all blazing now.

He wanted her to see him touch her.

She'd never made out with a man in bright light. Something about it seemed wrong. Embarrassing. But she'd never made out with a man as gorgeous as Piers Prescott either. She could just look at him and forget everything else.

When she shifted around and her thighs came up against the edge of the sink, she didn't look at him, though. She was too floored by her own reflection. Cheeks flushed, lips soft, hair tumbling over bare shoulders where the silky shirt had slipped away, jeans riding her hips and nipples poking through the thin white camisole, she looked like a sex kitten.

"I hope you're seeing what I'm seeing," he said. "Because what I'm seeing has been making me crazy all night."

"Do it," she whispered, her gaze glued to his hands bracketing her hips.

His right hand slipped along the waistline of her jeans, the thumb toying with the silver button before his fingers traveled down the fly.

His touch was so light she barely felt it. But she could see it, his tan skin against the faded jeans. His slow, uneven breaths brushed her ear. It made her wild inside.

He dipped south, between her legs. Not lightly.

She couldn't hold in the feelings. *"Ohh."* He stroked over her crotch and she moaned again. Her thighs parted. She moved into his touch, her eyelids drooping but her eyes on his hand moving on her, making her hot, making her throb so fast it shocked her. Through the denim he found her clit. He massaged it. Her knees buckled.

"Good?" he asked, his voice rough.

"Yes," she whispered, astounded that she was allowing this with a total stranger. That she'd asked for it. That she wanted it to go on and on. "Incredibly good."

He braced her, holding her against his hips with one strong hand, the other flipping open the button of her jeans and unzipping the fly. She felt him hard against her butt and it made her even hotter. *She'd made him hard.*

"If you want me to stop," he said, trailing his fingertips along the edge of her panties. "You're going to have to tell me."

"I don't want you to stop." She didn't recognize her own voice. "Yet."

His fingers slipped under the lacy cotton and he knew exactly where to go and exactly what to touch. She shuddered into it. He stroked and her joints were like water. A man she barely knew had his hand inside her jeans and her brain screamed a single word: *more.*

"California Blake," he murmured into her ear. "I find you unbelievably sexy. And I want my tongue"—he met her gaze in the mirror and stroked a fingertip over her clitoris—"here."

She gasped upon the jolt of pleasure. Then she closed her eyes before she could beg him to put his tongue there. But it didn't stop the rush of tightening pleasure, or the knowledge that his hand was in her pants and she'd still have to see him tomorrow. She didn't care now. It'd been ages since she'd felt anything like this—*never like this*—and she was so close, her breaths fast and hips rocking into his hand. He ran his other palm up her waist and covered her breast, passing his thumb over the nipple, and her body reacted with a delicious shudder, her eyes flying open.

It was even better watching, feeling his hands on her and seeing the heat in his eyes as his hand caressing inside her panties made her desperate. She arched her back, grinding against his hard-on, and her orgasm surged.

A knock came at the door. "Anybody in there?"

"Damn it, I didn't—" Suddenly his hands were gone. Then he was at the door, flipping the bolt just as the handle jiggled. "—lock it." He swung his gaze back to her. "Just a minute," he said more loudly.

A minute? Another five seconds would've done it.

"Hey, man, I gotta whiz and the other johns are too far away," came from the other side of the door. One of Duke's tech boys. "Make it fast, will you?"

"Try the bushes out back," Piers said, the edge of his mouth curving up as he held her gaze.

"It's raining," the guy complained.

Cali sucked in breaths and shook her head. The moment was over, the pleasure scattering in embarrassment and guilt. *What had she been thinking?* Having tawdry fun—or any fun of this kind at all—wasn't for her. This was just a sign that proved it. Her shaking hands fumbled on her zipper. "It's over," she whispered.

Piers came to her, grabbed her hip with one hand and dragged her to him, and cut off her protest with his mouth. He kissed her powerfully and possessively, like he had at the gazebo, so real and raw that his hand slipping beneath her panties now seemed perfectly natural—his fingers stroking, urging, exactly what was supposed to happen.

His words came against her lips. "Let me get inside you."

She clutched his hard biceps. "Yes."

He pushed up into her. It had to be two fingers. She was stretched deliciously, dying as he thrust.

"*Oh, yes.*"

He was *doing it.* And she was *letting him.* Pleasure spiraled, intense, desperate. Higher. Tighter.

She climaxed in a sudden, jolting shudder. For a moment she

couldn't breathe; everything was suspended—thought, action, sense—his arm around her holding her up. She gasped for air.

He said so close to her lips she could feel the words, "Now it's over." His hands fell away from her and he stepped back. With an utterly confident grin, he unlocked the door and went out, closing it behind him. She heard him say something to the waiting guy, then his footsteps receding.

She zipped her jeans, turned on the faucet, and splashed her face with cold water. She was hot all over, inside and out. And thoroughly, completely *relaxed*. Relaxed like she hadn't been in memory.

Head ducked, she opened the door, said "Um, hi," to the tech boy, and practically ran to her room.

# CHAPTER
## SEVEN

*Brampton House & Environs*

*He's looking for you everywhere.*

*I don't give a rat's ass.*

After a pause, Piers's secretary texted back, *Pardon me, Mr. Prescott?*

He typed, *I'm sorry, Mrs. Crowley. Put my grandfather off as well as you can. I'll be home Sunday. Thank you.*

Piers jammed his phone into his pocket and descended the hill from the gazebo toward the house. He was far too edgy.

After midnight the night before he'd spent two hours at a makeshift basketball hoop nailed to the side of the old stable, teaching Harry Compton how to shoot. When Mark appeared and revealed he'd been a walk-on during his Princeton days, Piers challenged him to a pickup game. Anything to burn off the state that California had put him in with her sighs and moans and thorough willingness to be fucked in a public restroom.

It hadn't worked. Afterward he'd nearly gone to her room. But he couldn't. If he wanted even half a chance with her, he needed to show her he had something on his mind other than sex.

Because he did. The sparkling smile, the devotion to her sister, the charitable work, the brain, the nervousness around him as if she weren't used to men, and the sweet little body all pointed to one certainty: sex wouldn't be enough. Sex would be great. He'd bank on that. But it was only part of what he wanted from California Blake.

So today he would do things differently. Today he would hold himself in check and speak with her like he respected her and wanted to know more than what she had in her pants. Then, when he'd shown her he was good for more than a quick orgasm, he would tell her about his interference in her life. He hoped she would understand that he'd intended it for the best, and that he could trust in her discretion about the donation.

When he reached the house, he went straight to her room. Scraping an oddly unsteady hand through his hair, he knocked.

"Just a sec!" She opened the door. Her eyes popped wide. "I thought you were room service."

"Depending on what you're hungry for, I could be."

Her cheeks turned brilliant red.

*Damn.* Fail right out of the gate. But her hair was rumpled, and she clearly wasn't wearing a bra beneath the thin T-shirt, and her very short sweat shorts revealed her very lithe legs.

This was going to be tougher than he'd thought.

"I'm sorry," he said. "That wasn't well done of me."

She crossed her arms over her breasts. "I'm not sure why you think so. I should really be the one apologizing."

"I don't understand."

"Well." She shifted from one bare foot to the other. "One of us did the other a favor last night, and the one who did it wasn't me."

Aha. Right.

"That's not how I operate, California."

Her dark eyes retreated. "Operate?"

He really was an idiot. New concept. Felt not good. "Poor word choice. I mean that I don't consider sex in terms of an equal barter economy."

"More of a free trade system?" She offered a tentatively playful smile. He felt it in his chest.

He'd never before felt a woman's smile in his chest. Never.

"Something like that."

"Do…" She swiped her hair back from her brow, a nervous habit he'd noticed she had. It made him want to thread his fingers through that drape of hair and kiss her until her nervousness dissipated. He wanted to taste her again and make her sigh.

"Do you want to come in?" she said uncertainly.

"No. I want you to come out." *Success.* He could, in fact, control himself. "There's a public stable a few miles away and I'd like to take you horseback riding."

She blinked. "Horseback riding?"

"Do you ride?"

"In all my spare time when I'm not skiing in the Swiss Alps or sunning on the Riviera? Yes. Definitely, I ride."

He withheld his smile. "The weather is clear and I'd like to spend some time with you away from the others. Will you come with me?"

She stared at his chest, then into his eyes. "I don't have boots. I'll have to see if Roxanna or Jane brought a pair in my size."

Now he did smile, in relief and because she'd done the hair-swiping thing again, which momentarily revealed the tight peak of her breast that he'd touched the night before.

Now he was salivating over a clothed breast. Thirty years old, but he felt like a teenager with this woman.

He backed away from the door. "I'll meet you downstairs." He would be the perfect gentleman, keeping his suggestive comments and his hands to himself. He would succeed in his goal of getting to know her and letting her get to know him.

Twenty minutes later when she appeared in the foyer wearing tight jeans and a T-shirt that revealed every contour of her body, Piers knew he was doomed to tragic failure.

. . .

THIS HAD to be another dream, because it bore no resemblance to real life.

Cali knew how to ride. It'd just been years since she'd done so. When their house in Gladwyne went, along with the cars and savings, every expensive lesson she'd taken as a child had gone too. She missed riding. Like reading, it could be a peaceful, solitary activity.

Today she felt anything but peaceful. Even a jaunt along quaint country paths and fields dotted with sheep and strewn with picturesque cottages couldn't calm her nerves. It all seemed straight from a movie set, not least the man cantering along beside her.

He slowed his horse to a walk and she reined in.

"You ride well," he said, his eyes skimming her body appreciatively. Roxanna had insisted on the tight jeans. "I'm thinking you're the spy with secret talents after all."

"That's me, California Blake, licensed to kill. And to do other things too."

He ignored her suggestive tone. Or he simply didn't notice it. She was a pathetic novice at this hookup thing.

"How did you come to be named California?"

"My parents were catastrophically wrong for each other. To try to fix the relationship, they had me. Yes, people really do have babies to try to save their marriages. Desperate people. They said I was supposed to be their gold rush."

"Were you?" He didn't respond to her forced humor. She liked that.

"Only fool's gold." She dismounted and watched him come down easily from the saddle, the way he seemed to do everything—with nonchalant confidence. "I guess I don't have to ask who you're named for, Piers Vaughan Prescott the third."

He motioned for her to go before him toward the stable. "Not 'the third,'" he said behind her. "I was named only after my father."

She gave over her horse to a stable hand. Piers followed her into the sunshine. He gestured toward a path that wended away from the parking lot. "Walk off the cramped muscles?"

"You assume I have cramped muscles from that?"

"No. But I do. I spend my days at a desk or in a car, not on a horse."

He smiled beautifully and she was momentarily speechless. In a sort of daze, she went toward the path.

"I've never read about your father in the papers," she finally managed. "Does he try to stay out of the limelight?"

"He passed away last year."

"Oh, I'm so sorry."

"Thank you. But the business press was never interested in him anyway. He wasn't involved with the company."

"He wasn't?"

"No. He escaped. Got out early. Joined the circus."

"He did not."

"No." He grinned. "He fixed boats down at the shore."

"Fixed them, or had a fleet of them that he raced?"

"Fixed them. He was a mechanic. A rebel. He did what he wanted despite my grandfather. And he was happy."

"But not you?"

For a moment he walked beside her without speaking. "Someone has to prepare to run Prescott Global," he finally said. "My grandfather isn't young."

"Well, you've made a fortune at not being a rebel, so that ought to comfort your cold, ruthless heart."

He gave her a sidelong glance. "Gearing up to harangue me for elitism again?"

"I'm considering it. And rampant greed."

His smile was simple and genuine. His teeth were perfect. She'd had some costly orthodonture in her youth. But Piers's smile came straight from a movie set. Just like this incredibly elegant stable. And Brampton. And everything about this week.

"I feel like I'm in a nineteenth-century novel where the girl of exceedingly modest means gets immersed in the wealth and luxury of highfliers," she said.

"*Vanity Fair?*"

She'd never met a man who'd actually read *Vanity Fair*. "You saw the movie?"

"I might not have the opportunity to read novels now, but at one time I did."

At that time he'd chosen to read not Stephen King or James Patterson, but nineteenth-century literature? It wasn't fair for one man to be so comprehensively sexy.

"Understood," she said. "But I was thinking more like *Pride and Prejudice*," she admitted.

"She marries the rich guy at the end of that one, doesn't she?"

"Yes."

Twitters of birds in the nearby copse and a sheep's bleat were the only sounds to break the charged silence.

"Fan of happily-ever-afters, like your friend Jane?" he finally said.

She considered giving him a pithy comeback. She decided on honesty. "It's the reason I read. In books, everything can turn out well in the end."

"But not in real life?"

Not in her real life. "Real life is messy." This was the perfect moment to ask. "Why did your girlfriend break up with you?"

"Someone told her I'd once gotten so angry at work that I threw a chair through a fifty-seventh-floor window."

"Really?"

"That was one of the reasons."

"She was clearly a lightweight."

He chuckled. "You wouldn't have broken up with me for that?"

"I wouldn't have been dating you in the first place."

He gave her a direct, skeptical appraisal. He knew the effect he had on her. She'd made it clear at the gazebo and in the bathroom.

She shook her head. "Nope."

His smile disappeared. "Why not?"

She thrust out her hand. "Hi, Mr. Piers Vaughan Prescott, Junior. I'm Cali Blake, lowly library associate, food stamp hoarder, coupon cutter, and sale hunter whose apartment heat works every other day during December and every third day in January. Nice to meet you."

He didn't take her hand. "You like to say things that you think will shock me. They don't."

"Because you're far too sophisticated for that?"

"Because I think you're cute."

She ducked her head. "Being poor isn't cute, Prescott."

"I didn't mean—"

"It's okay. I'm just really out of place at this party. Obviously."

"You're still doing it."

"Doing what?"

"Saying things to put me off." He looked displeased. Not pissed off or irritated or any of the ways men tended to react when a woman said something they didn't like, like they didn't understand why she couldn't stop being a pain in the butt. Instead, it seemed almost as if he were disappointed. Which made no sense.

She swallowed awkwardly. "I really shouldn't be saying anything at all."

"Why not?"

"Well, I'm guessing we didn't come out here to talk."

The light in his eyes seemed to change. "What if I told you I only want to talk?"

"I'd know you were lying."

"Lying. Right." He took her shoulders in his hands and bent his head to cover her mouth with his.

She didn't think. She just kissed him. And she let him kiss her. She let him thread his fingers through her hair and pull her to him, and she let him into her mouth and tangled her tongue with his until heat came between her legs.

Finally she let herself touch him. Lifting her hands, she placed them on his waist. Hard muscle. She fanned her palms up and over his chest. She thought she heard his breathing hitch, but knew she hadn't. Not this man, who could have any woman's hands on him.

But he'd brought her out here today. Today he wanted her hands.

And she wanted his. More urgently with every meeting of their lips. When he cupped her breast, she didn't object. She moved into it, sliding her hand over his butt and finding firm muscle beneath his jeans. He came deeper into her mouth and she lifted onto her toes to get closer. He banded an arm around her and pulled her flush up against him.

"Oh, wow," she whispered. He was all hard. Everywhere. Entirely. At the pressure of his erection against her abdomen, her insides bucked. *"Oh."*

He stroked across her nipple and she moaned again and wanted to be naked and underneath him. Now.

Too quickly. Too soon.

She ran her hands over his shoulders and into his hair. Soft. Silky. She twined her fingers in it. His scent made her crazy. It made her want to stay in his arms forever, just kissing him. She didn't want to push him away or shock him or hold him off. She wanted to know him. In every way. Every inch of his body and other things, like his birthday and his favorite color and his ideal day. He kissed her like he wanted that too. He kissed her like *this* was his ideal day.

"This is going too fast," she said beneath his lips.

"This is supposed to go fast." He took her mouth again and his fingers caressed perfectly.

He was right. *Wedding party hookup.* She made herself silently repeat the words. She repeated *rebound sex,* too, to remind herself why he was with her now. "Okay."

His hand slipped beneath her shirt. Stroking up her waist, skin on skin. Surrounding her breast. Over her bra, his thumb circled the nipple. "I've wanted to touch you since the moment I first saw you."

A car horn honked. "Cali! Piers?"

They broke apart.

She blinked. It was still daytime and they were still on the path past the stable, screened by some trees, for which she was now immensely grateful.

From the parking lot she heard Jane's cousin Cassidy say, "Piers's Alpha Romeo is here. They've got to be here."

Cali looked up at Piers.

Gaze fixed on hers, he said huskily, "This isn't finished."

"Okay." She straightened her shirt and walked toward the parking lot.

Cassidy was standing beside a car full of people. "Hey, guys! I'm so glad I found you, Cali. Yesterday you said you really wanted to go on the tour at Edmonton Vineyards. It's in a half hour. I was looking for you at the hotel and Mark told me you'd come here. Do you still want to come?"

"Oh." Cali moved toward her, brushing back from her hot face hair that'd come loose from her ponytail. "I'm not really dressed for it."

"You're perfect," Piers said softly.

Her heartbeat tripped.

"Guys," Jane's other cousin, Kimberly, said from the car. "I'm not feeling great." She looked completely green. "Too much champagne and sun at the pool, I guess. I think I should go back."

"If we take you back to Brampton," one of the techies in the car said, "we'll miss the winery tour."

Piers halted a few yards short of the others and touched Cali's elbow. "I can take her back to Brampton," he said quietly, "but my car only seats two."

She looked into the most gorgeously warm blue eyes ever. "That's really nice of you."

He gave her a smile—a private smile, she thought. Then he helped Kimberly into his car.

"He's already seen that vineyard anyway," one of the others said as they drove away. "His family used to vacation in Tuscany with the people who own it."

Cassidy turned to Cali with a friendly smile. "How was horseback riding?"

"Great," Cali said, crossing her arms over her stomach and staring out the window at the postcard scenery. "It was great."

# CHAPTER
# EIGHT

*The Carriage House*

As the sun angled low, Cali dressed in one of Roxanna's sexy outfits, shook off her discomfort, and went to find Piers. She desperately needed to unwind and he knew how to unwind her. If she let herself think about this beyond the opportunity for physical release, she would drive herself insane. So she wouldn't. He would like it and she would get what she needed. Everybody would be satisfied.

But he'd disappeared. He couldn't be found in the house, the gardens, at the pool where people were drinking cocktails while swimming, or in the drawing room where some of the others were playing charades. Unlike the American version, English charades seemed to involve making up little plays and using as many dirty words as possible.

Cali grinned as she watched from the sidelines. But she wasn't in the mood for games. Not this sort of game, anyway.

Maybe he'd left for the evening. There was no reason he would've told her that he was leaving Brampton, only her fantasies that had swiftly expanded to include him in everything she did this week.

"You look like a little lost lamb, Miss Blake," Mark said as she wandered into the foyer.

"Please call me Cali. I'm not like the others here. You don't have to treat me like royalty."

He came out from behind the marble desk. "But you are royalty, darling. Everybody who stays at Brampton gets the royal treatment."

"Not tonight, apparently," she mumbled, feeling strangely abandoned, and angry at herself for feeling that.

"I know what you need," Mark said.

"A stiff drink?"

"A stiff something else entirely."

Oh, good lord. Even the hotel manager could tell she needed to get laid.

"And I think I know someone who can help you with that." He pointed at the open front door through which a luscious summer breeze wafted, and toward which a luscious man walked from the direction of the parking lot. "Go get him," Mark said and nudged her forward.

Piers wore a dark blue shirt of some fabric that looked entirely neat yet entirely casual, khakis that had to have been tailored in Paris or Milan, and keyhole aviator sunglasses with blue lenses a shade lighter than his eyes. When he saw her, he smiled.

"I was just coming to find you," he said, halting very close to her, as if they were together. As if he didn't mind everyone seeing that they were together.

"Here I am," she said on a little puff of breath.

He removed his glasses. Dolce & Gabbana. Easily three hundred dollars. Probably his throwaway pair.

"You look amazing," he said.

"Thank you." Guilt prickled at her over her own charade. "They're not my clothes. I can't afford two-hundred-dollar skirts or fifty-dollar camisoles."

"I don't know what a camisole is, but if it's any of the pieces of clothing on your body right now, I approve."

Raucous laughter came through the house's windows, followed by a drunken female shriek of delight. Charades was clearly revving up.

"Sounds like they're having fun," he said with a glance toward the window. "Were you planning to join them?"

She couldn't stop staring at his jaw. His mouth. His perfect cheekbones. His hair that curled up just a bit at the edge of his collar. "Not particularly."

He brushed his fingertips along her forearm. "Want to get out of here?"

"Yes." She tried to steady her nerves. "But I'd feel bad going far."

"Hm. I've an idea." He took her hand and drew her toward Brampton's old stable block. The carriage house portion had been converted into a garage, like in the movie *Sabrina*, the Audrey Hepburn and Humphrey Bogart version. Piers's hand held hers, strong and secure, and her heart did weird patters. Did wedding hookups hold hands?

He opened the door, switched on a light, and released her. He gestured toward the cars: the Rolls-Royce limo, a silver Porsche, Damien Knightly's dark green Aston Martin, Piers's red Alpha Romeo, and Harry Compton's muddy Landrover.

"Take your pick."

"Take my pick? Are we going somewhere after all?"

"No." He looked down at her with unmistakable intention in his eyes.

"Um… How about the limo?" She moved toward the Rolls-Royce, trying not to stumble on her rubber band legs. "I came from the airport in this, but I slept most of the way so I didn't really get to enjoy it."

When she'd ridden in it with Jane and Roxanna to the bridal shop, she'd thought about how Piers probably had a limo at his beck and call back in Philly. She trailed her fingertips along the shiny black hood and over the Spirit of Ecstasy ornament. It felt wild. Decadent. Just the way a backseat tryst with a hot man should feel.

"I bet you ride in cars like this all the time," she said.

"Not usually. Limos this size have bars." He opened the car door. "Shall we?"

"There's a fully stocked bar up at the house."

"True. There are a hundred people up there too."

"You like to drink alone?"

"I'd like to drink with you alone." He didn't mean drink. He meant he'd like to finish what they'd started after the horseback ride. The depth of his voice and the set of his beautiful mouth said it.

She wanted to finish it too. All she had to do was to keep her emotional fantasies in check and she could have a night she desperately needed.

He took her hand again, this time to help her climb into the limo, then he got in after her and closed the door. Confronted by the reality of what was about to happen, she didn't know where to put her hands or any other part of her. She perched on the edge of the seat as he opened a camouflaged refrigerator.

"Aha," he said, pulling out a full-sized bottle of champagne. "Very nice." He reached for two cut crystal champagne flutes, uncorked the bottle smoothly, and poured. "It's even chilled."

"Did you plan this?"

He offered her a glass. "I might have."

Cali's throat had never been drier. She sipped. "This is delicious."

He sat comfortably back into the black leather and set down his glass. He didn't intend to drink, and he wasn't even bothering to pretend.

Her body felt electric, tingling, and fully awake. And *insanely nervous*. She gestured with her glass. "How much do you suppose this costs?"

"About two hundred and fifty dollars."

"That doesn't seem so bad for a case."

"A bottle."

Champagne shot down the wrong way. She gasped. He leaned forward and put his hand on her knee.

"Are you okay?"

"Yes." She coughed. "Just choking on a ten-dollar sip there."

"Good." His hand, big and warm, traveled up her thigh. "Because I'd like to get this meeting started, stat." His thumb halted just shy of the apex of her thighs, his grasp confident.

"I didn't know about the meeting." She stared at his hand, so close to where it had been two nights ago when he'd given her the quickest holiday she'd ever had. "Someone forgot to send me the memo. Should I have prepared?"

"No preparation necessary." He took the glass from her and set it aside. "Just active participation." His palm came around the back of her neck and drew her forward.

His mouth was hot and he tasted good. Like expensive champagne. And lust. And something else. *Enjoyment*. He was enjoying her. Enjoying giving her pleasure. It came so clearly through his touch, his fingers curving around her shoulder, and his kiss, slow and lavish, as though he wasn't in any hurry, as though his first intention wasn't to get something from her but to please her.

She wrapped her arms around his shoulders and let him pull her onto his lap. They kissed like that, his hand unmoving at the top of her thigh and his other in her hair, their mouths increasingly hungry. She wanted to get closer, struggled to. But she couldn't in this position.

She straddled him. He stroked hair back from her forehead, drew her down to him, and kissed her briefly, firmly, then backed off to meet her gaze. Then he kissed her again, longer. Then he kissed her and didn't stop. Her hands went to the buttons of his shirt, unfastening them, and his hands were on her thighs, curving toward her bottom. She ran a palm across his chest, loving the sensation of his taut skin and muscle, and cupped her other palm over his fly.

"California." His voice was ragged. "You're—"

She caught his words with her mouth and bore down on his erection, drunk on the caress of his tongue inside her and rocking against him. He grabbed her hips, jerking her to him, and the heat flared so hard a moan tore from her throat. She wore the merest scrap of a G-string. An unzipped fly, a condom, and she could have what she wanted immediately. What she needed. In a car. In a garage. Where anybody could enter at any time.

"We shouldn't do this," she gasped as she ground into him.

"We really should," he said at her collarbone, his tongue lapping at her skin, his teeth nipping.

*Rebound girl*. She was a rebound girl for him. Anybody who saw them now would think that. And he was her wedding party sex. But no one would believe that's all she wanted from him. *She* didn't believe it.

"Here," she clarified. "We shouldn't do this here. Someone might come." She grappled at excuses—to slow it down and make it last longer, or to end it before she lost herself entirely. "They might see us."

"Tinted glass," he said against her neck, his mouth making her crazy, desperate to press even harder to him. "Anyway, let them see. Give them inspiration."

She did *not* want to think of Dick telling her she liked it when the limo driver watched. She opened her eyes and the hottest man alive filled her vision.

"Okay." Her voice was shaky. "It's just this once, anyway. Just one night. Right?"

His hands scooped her camisole to her breasts. She lifted her arms and he pulled it over her head. His gaze upon her was fevered and she shivered. But he didn't move to touch her.

"What?" she whispered.

His chest rose hard. "Didn't have you figured for black lace."

"JC Penney six-ninety-nine demi-cup special."

"Thank you, JC Penney," he whispered like a prayer.

She laughed, but then his hands were cupping her breasts, the pads of his thumbs crossing the lace and teasing her nipples, and her laughter turned into a sigh, then a gasp. He swept his thumbs under the lace. His skin brushed against her nipples, beneath the sheer cups, stroking.

She pushed his shirt off his shoulders. Her fingers circled a bicep, but didn't get very far around it. He was all lean muscle, all rippling, smooth, mobile, hot, perfect male beauty from shoulder to wrist. She leaned forward and licked his bicep. He tasted like sea-salt chocolate. She bit the muscle lightly.

His hands caught her around the ribs. "Cal—California," he stuttered hoarsely.

"Is this okay?"

"More than okay."

"I love nice arms, and yours are…" She kissed his skin. He smelled so good. *So* good. "Very nice."

She felt a rumble of laughter and his hands moved on her, stroking down her sides, then up, his thumbs brushing the undersides of her breasts. "I officially retract all the complaints I've ever made about tennis and squash." But something about his voice sounded strange.

She lifted her head. His eyes blazed. He surrounded her face with his hands, sank his fingers into her hair, and pulled her mouth to his. He kissed her deeply, thoroughly, as if he could only have her like this. The tips of her breasts grazed his chest. She pressed into his erection and felt the rise of her orgasm, and wanted it. Wanted him.

In a limo.

Where anybody could see them. Where anybody might now be watching.

She broke away. "I can't do this. Not here."

He gripped her waist. "All right." His heartbeats sped beneath her palm. "Why not?"

She climbed off his lap, grabbed her shirt, and dragged it over her breasts. "There's someone at work. Dick."

He straightened. "A man you're involved with?" His voice was rigid.

Her eyes flew to him. "No. A creep who refuses to understand that I'm not interested."

He scraped his hand slowly through his hair. "Okay," he said.

"A few weeks ago he said something inappropriate about me in a limo."

"Harassment?"

"He said he thought I'd like being watched by the driver while having sex with another man. He's disgusting."

Piers was silent a moment. "Do you want me to break his legs?"

She couldn't help smiling. "Would you?"

"Happy to. I've got the muscles for it, after all." He flexed his biceps.

She laughed. He was trying to dispel her unease, but his protectiveness felt nice. Unfamiliar. *Fantastic.* "Or you could just have him fired." She grinned. "But secretly, so he doesn't know it's because of me."

His face went perfectly still.

"What?"

He buttoned his shirt and reached for the door handle. "Let's get out of here."

She climbed out after him. It was the first time he hadn't waited for her to precede him through any door.

"Piers, I didn't mean that. I know your family doesn't control everything in Philadelphia." Just most everything. "I'm sorry."

He looked down at her. "I'm the one who should be saying I'm sorry, California. I really want this, but I've gone about it all wrong."

"This?"

"You." He didn't touch her. "Listen, I've got to take care of something tonight."

Oh, no. *Oh*. Shame. Embarrassment. *Hurt*. Maybe he thought she was playing too hard to get, or she wasn't worth the wait till they made it up to the house and a bed. Or he wanted to keep their fling private. Gazebo. Stables. Carriage house. All far from the party. Whatever the case, this delay wasn't working for him.

"Can I see you tomorrow?" he said.

"We're staying at the same hotel. We're attending the same party." Hurt made her tongue sharp. "You'll see me tomorrow whether you want to or not."

He frowned. "I do want to. And you know that I'm asking if tomorrow we can take up where we left off here."

"Do I know that?"

"Yeah. You do. Don't for a minute imagine I'm letting you go this easily."

She had nothing to say to that. Her emotions were completely jumbled. But her emotions weren't even supposed to be involved in this.

"May I walk you back to the house?" he said quietly, as if he understood.

"No. I think I'll stay here for a bit." She rested an unsteady hand on the Aston Martin and attempted a jaunty smile. "Soak up a little ambiance. Maybe swipe one of these hood ornaments for the bookmobile. The kids would love it."

He touched her beneath the chin, tilted her face up, and kissed her softly. He separated their lips, but remained close and seemed to breathe deeply. Like he was breathing her in.

"Okay," he said. "I'm going." He held her for a moment longer. "Now." He released her and left without looking back.

She sprawled back against the hood of the sports car and tried very hard to think and feel nothing at all.


WALKING BACK UP to the house fifteen minutes later, Cali met Jane and Duke strolling from the direction of the garden.

"What are you doing out here alone?" Jane asked, looking around as if she expected to see someone else.

"I was looking at the cars in the carriage house. I loved the limo, Jane. Thanks for sending it to the airport for me."

Jane tilted her head. "I didn't. Did you, Duke?"

"Nope."

"Another gift from your friends?"

"Must be." But she hadn't told Maggie, Roy, and Masala exactly where she was going. She hadn't even known it till right before she boarded the plane. To deter paparazzi, Jane and Duke had kept the wedding's location a secret till the last second. But the limo driver, George, had already known she was going to Brampton. Maybe Zoe had hired the limo. Or Zoe and Mrs. Fletcher combined. After they'd robbed a bank.

She went into the house and joined in the game of charades for a while. But her head was muddled, and glancing around at all the fashionable, successful women, she couldn't stop thinking that Piers would not come looking for her tomorrow, no matter what he'd said. That he was finished with this hookup or else he wouldn't have ended it prematurely. And that it was for the best.

Saying good night to everybody, she went to the library. There were no lamps. By the hallway light, she searched through piles of books that someone had neatly stacked beside the bookcase, which had been refitted to the wall. A recent, leather-bound edition of *Pride and Prejudice* was near the bottom of a stack. What were the odds?

She carried it back to her room, removed the sexy costume she'd worn to entice a man who was completely wrong for her, and curled up in bed with Elizabeth and Darcy.

. . .

Piers palmed the phone in his room, went to a chair by the window, and typed in his grandfather's number. He stared at it.

Then he deleted it and dialed another number.

Miraculously, J.T. answered. "What's up, bro?"

"I want to quit," he said aloud for the first time in his life.

"Big surprise." Calm. Relaxed. Like J.T. always was these days. From the background, an owl's throaty call came clear across the line. In Montana, where his younger brother had been when they'd last talked, it wasn't yet dusk.

"Are you at Mom's?"

"Blue Ridge. Where are you that you've had this predictable revelation?"

"England. The revelation didn't come just now." Only the urgent need to act on it.

"So why call me tonight, Suit?"

J.T. had called him Suit since he went to Wharton. Until then, since they'd been boys, he'd called him Scope, for stethoscope.

"Dad regretted leaving the company." Piers stared into the darkness of the English countryside. "Every time the family got together for holidays and he saw Grandfather, it was in his eyes. He wanted to be a good son, and he wanted to give Mom more than he could on his income. And us."

"She had everything she needed. So did we."

Sounds from the terrace floated up to the open window, laughter and music.

"Do you ever regret it? Leaving?"

J.T. laughed, a deep, comfortable sound. "You made it so I never had to. My hero."

Piers could imagine his younger brother now, kicked back before a campfire, jaw scruffy for the first time in years, a cold beer in his hand. J.T. had quit the Secret Service two months earlier and wasn't showing signs of looking for work at present.

"Seriously, though," he said.

"I regret it every day," J.T. said. "For about five seconds. Then I remember how much I hated it and the feeling goes away. Don't waste your life hating it, Piers. I know you've got a real conscience. You always did. Listen to it for once."

"Do you ever listen to your conscience? Or does the roar of your Harley drown it out?"

"It's an Isuzu."

"Right." Piers's grin faded quickly. "There's a woman."

"A woman?"

"Yeah. She's pretty special." Extraordinarily special. Real and honest and sweet-tasting and sexier than any woman he'd known.

His brother laughed.

His shoulders prickled. "What?"

"You're an idiot, Suit. Why do you think Dad left the company?"

Piers thought of his parents together on the boat, or in their little house in Ocean City, or working in his mother's garden in St. Davids. They'd spent every day together until the day his father died.

"Right," Piers said into the phone. "Thanks."

"You're welcome." Another moment of silence. "Piers?"

"Yeah?"

"Thank you, man. I don't think I've ever said it to you before. But… thanks."

"Night, J.T." He set down the phone. As soon as he was stateside on Sunday, he would see his grandfather. It was time.

# CHAPTER
# NINE

*The Park, Pub, Stable, Pool & Garden*

Apparently, in order to hunt grouse in England, one had to rise before the stock exchange opened. In Japan.

"They'll accidentally kill each other unless someone who knows what he's doing is around," Duke said to him as the New Yorkers gathered in the misty dawn by a truck swathed in green. Someone had distributed monogrammed flasks to everyone and the guys quaffed liberally while the gamekeeper handed out rifles. "Or they'll kill themselves," Duke added in a mumble.

Piers stretched his neck muscles. "I've never hunted grouse." He'd spent the night at his desk putting his current projects in order, composing a series of memos to his secretary, and updating spread-sheets. If he planned to resign from the company when he returned home, he'd leave strong. No unfinished projects.

Now he wanted sleep. But some fool had planned this as Duke's bachelor party.

"At least you've hunted," Duke said. "I think Knightly has too," he grumbled, casting Damien Knightly a dark glance. "And Harry, of course. Anyway, it's more than I can say for these guys. Come on. Let's go pretend to shoot our dinner."

Few birds were shot. Much alcohol was consumed. Piers stayed sober. He'd rarely wanted a bed so much—except at the moment when California had said she wouldn't make love to him in the limousine.

If he were at home and he'd worked all night, he'd drink a pot of coffee and return to his desk. But he had an appointment with a library associate later, and he needed sleep now. This time when he got her alone, he wouldn't let her go until she knew everything.

CALI WIGGLED her sparkly manicured fingertips like a movie star. A movie star who'd been dumped by *a man she wasn't even dating*. A movie star who'd only wanted a little wild wedding party fun and instead got a "We're closed, come back tomorrow" sign shoved in her face.

She swiveled her foggy gaze around the pub. It was the Cutest. Pub. Ever. All wood and quaint and Englishy. Everybody was here. Everybody except Philadelphia Big Money. Of all the men who'd gone hunting for Duke's bachelor party, and even the men who hadn't, Piers was the only one *not* now in the pub flirting with Jane's fashionable, successful, New York City friends with whom she'd toured a gorgeous estate and drunk tea all day. Then Prosecco. Then tequila. Lots of tequila.

But she should be happy he wasn't flirting with Jane's friends now. Right? Because he should be flirting with *her*. He should be feeling her up over her bra and telling her he hadn't figured her for black lace.

Abruptly she was reminded of the reason for the three empty shot glasses in front of her nose. How could he say things like that and then just... just... *abandon* her? For almost—she counted on her fingers —*nine, ten*—she had to recount some of her fingers—*seventeen hours* she'd seen neither hide nor hair of him.

Hide nor hair. She'd never really thought about that expression. Piers Prescott's hide was very nice. Smooth and firm. Nibbleable. Arms like Apollo. Or Ares, the god of war. Or, really, any god. They all had good arms because, well, *gods*.

His hair was run-your-fingers-through-it dreamy. *He* was run-your-fingers-through-*him* dreamy.

Nibbleable wasn't a word, maybe. But he was nibbleable. Nibbleable nibbleable nibbleable. *All over.*

The room spun. She closed her eyes. This was getting her nowhere. If she were her mother, she would find him and throw herself at his feet and beg him to want her. If she were *her,* on the other hand, which she was, she would find him and give him a piece of her mind for leading her on without coming through. She had expected wedding party sex from him, and by golly he should have delivered.

With firm decision, she pushed herself away from the bar and slid off the backless stool attached to the floor.

"Whoa, Nellie." Someone caught her and set her on her feet. She blinked to bring him into focus.

"Thanks, Duke. Nice Duke." Good Duke who was very hot and successful and yet did not string a girl along and then disappear for *seventeen hours.*

A piece of her mind. She'd give it to him. *Stat,* as he'd said.

"Do you know where your friend Piers is?"

Duke put a hand on her shoulder to steady her. "My friend Piers is back at the house. He was up all night working. Then we left early with the guys. I think he's sleeping now."

"Working?" she said. "Hm?"

"Can I find someone to drive you back, Cali? Jane's looking like she needs my attention right now, or I'd—"

"No, thank you! I don't need a man to take me anywhere—like walking me up to the house so he can go *work*—like I believe *that*—or anywhere else."

She wended her way through dancing, laughing, happy fashionable people to the door and out into the village. The waning sun made her blink for a sec. Then she set her unsteady feet on the path to the big house.

PIERS AWOKE after several hours of astonishingly satisfying sleep. *The sleep of the just,* he wanted to believe. At least *the about-to-be just.*

Informed by Mark that everyone was at the pub and stone drunk, he went to the stable in search of the basketball. He'd no desire to drink and every desire to be as clearheaded as possible when California returned from Jane's bachelorette party.

Basketball located, he was walking to the door when California appeared in the square of pale light there. In jeans that hugged her hips and a sheer shirt, she looked good.

Really good.

Enough to eat.

"Hey." He couldn't manage more.

"Mark said you were here. What are you doing?" Something about her voice was off. She blinked with emphasis and swayed ever so slightly. Drunk.

"I was looking for this." He gestured with the basketball, then dropped it and walked toward her. "But I was only passing the time until you returned."

She set her hands on her hips in a fierce stance. "What did you have me figured for?"

"Figured for?"

"You said you didn't have me figured for black lace. If not that, then what did you have me figured for?"

Unpredictable, women.

"Nothing," he said.

"Nothing? You fantasized about me *naked*?"

"By nothing I mean I haven't really fantasized about you that way." *Much.*

Her eyes opened like a wounded doe's and her lush lower lip seemed suspended. "You haven't fantasized about me?"

"Of course I have."

"But you just said—"

"I fantasized about *talking* to you, California. I fantasized about getting close enough to discover the color of your eyes. I fantasized about learning the scent of your skin. And I fantasized about being alone with you and having your lips under mine. So you see, I already had plenty to occupy my imagination without pondering your underwear preferences."

She was staring wide-eyed and he'd said far too much. He opened his mouth to tell her—*finally, to tell her*—and she took the step that closed the space between them, pushed him back against the stable wall, and pulled his head down to press her mouth to his.

She climbed up him like he was a tree. He caught her up with his hands under her ass, tasting tequila on her lips, feeling her thighs clamp around his hips, and hearing the pop of his shirt buttons as she tore them open. Then her hands were on his chest and her sweet tequila tongue was in his mouth.

He got hard fast. There was no way he was going to make love to her in this condition. But he wouldn't pass up a few minutes of her hands all over him. One hand on the back of his neck, the other on his chest, she gyrated against him and moaned against his lips. Her hand descended and grasped his cock with perfect certainty. Sucking in breath, he let her work him.

*Holy hell.* A few minutes was going to be too much.

*"Wait."* She clambered off him, pushed him away, and held her palms out in a stop gesture. She stumbled back several paces. "I don't want to do this drunk."

He made his brain function. "I don't want you to do this drunk either."

"I'll be back later."

"Okay."

"Don't go anywhere."

"I won't move."

An intoxicated giggle bubbled from her. "Well, you can *move*. Just don't *go*. Away from the estate. You know. Far."

"If you'll be back here sober to make love to me, California, trust me, I'm not going anywhere."

She bit her lip, gave him an adorably sexy-shy smile, and left. Piers leaned back against the wall and groaned.


The digital alarm clock flickered a muted blue 12:04 a.m. when Cali awoke to darkness. Mouth sticky, head heavy, and stomach roiling, she stumbled into the bathroom, drank two glasses of water, swallowed three Ibuprofen pills, and fell onto the bed again.

She hadn't gotten more than mildly tipsy in years. She'd only gotten truly drunk a few times in her teens, before her father started drinking enough for the whole family. Today she'd drunk for the worst of reasons: because a man had disappointed her. She pressed her face into her palms and wanted to scream. Becoming both her mother and father in the same day was a lifetime low.

Heaving herself off the bed, she stepped into the shower and let hot water run over her, washing away the dumbass woman she'd become for a few hours. Toweling off her hair, she pulled out one of Roxanna's flippy little miniskirts and a sexy tank top. She chose her bra and panties carefully, tucked several condoms into the skirt's back pocket, slid her feet into a pair of sequined flip-flops, and went to keep her scheduled wedding-party-sex appointment.

He didn't answer her knock at his room. Some of the others were still partying downstairs, but she didn't find him there either. She didn't have to search for him for long, though.

Only underwater lights illuminated the pool, and a single towel lay on a chair. He was doing laps, his gorgeous arms cutting the water in classic Piers fashion—easy, confident, strong. She got a little light-headed watching.

Mid-lap, he noticed her. He stood up, submerged to his hips. The water glistened on his shoulders, chest, and the tight ripples of his abs.

"I wasn't that drunk," she said. "I remember everything I said."

"I hope so."

"You didn't stay in the stable." She let herself grin, but her lips were wobbly.

"It's been seven hours. I couldn't be still. Adrenaline, you know." He was teasing. But serious. She understood. "You're sober now?" he said.

"As a judge."

"Want to come in here?"

"Do condoms work underwater?"

His chest rose and fell roughly. "Pretty sure they do."

"Let's not take any chances."

KATHARINE ASHE

"All right." He walked up the steps and over to her. He didn't pause to towel off. Taking her face between his hands, he bent his head and kissed her. Cool lips got hot in seconds. Then he was delving, their tongues tangling, their breaths coming hard and fast. The muscles of his arms beneath her hands contracted and he dragged her to him. Water soaked through her skirt. She didn't care. She pressed against him and felt his erection. Hard already. *Wild heat.* No more delays. She had to be skin-to-skin with him. This had to happen *now.*

She pulled off her tank top. A sound of pure masculine pleasure came from his chest. His hands caught her beneath the arms and he flattened her against his bare torso. Her belly came in contact with the hard rock of his abdomen, and she spread her thighs to feel his arousal against hers.

"If we start this here," he growled, "it's going to happen here."

"Bedroom?"

"Boathouse is closer." He grabbed her hand and pulled her along the dark pool deck.

On the path to the lake, her flip-flop caught in the pebbles and she tripped. He grabbed her up in his arms again and they were all over each other in an instant. Mouths frantic. Skin hot. His hands on her waist, then cupping her breasts. Unsnapping the front clasp of her bra. Her hands on his butt.

His palms surrounded her breasts, thumbs passing over the nipples, making her whimper.

"Jesus, Cali," he said huskily over her lips. "This feels so right."

She knew it. Everything about him felt right. His hands on her. His mouth and scent and every word he said.

*No.* Not his words. Words lied. This was just about his body. And lust. Sex. A fling. No emotions. No perfect words that made her heart flutter.

He gripped her waist tight. "Wait, listen, I've got to tell you—"

"Don't talk." Her hand dove down his swimsuit. "Just do me," she said, stroking. "Now."

He scooped her into his arms, but she wanted more than kissing now. She whipped a condom out of her pocket, tore it open, and pressed him back against a tree as she slipped her panties off. The sight of him ready for her made her damp. And hot. She encased him in the condom, wrapped her arms around his shoulders, and let him lift her onto his cock. He fit himself inside her, thick and hard, making her gasp and gulp air.

"You okay?" His voice wasn't steady.

"*So* okay." She moved on him and laughed in exultation. *This*. This pleasure. This intensity. This completely, irresponsibly wild act of rebellion from her careful, cautious life. She needed *this*. He held her butt and pulled her snugly onto him and she clung to his shoulders. But he was so big and in this position she couldn't feel him where she needed it the most. She pressed to him in frustration. Closer. *Closer*. Not close enough.

"Oh, *ohh*. I can't— I— Take me down."

"Take you—"

"To the ground. *Please*."

He took her to the ground in the grass beside the path. All around were night sounds, and him between her thighs and inside her, and crazy, unbelievable pleasure. He thrust into her fast and hard, just like she wanted it, their mouths ravenous and hands urging. It didn't take her long. She came in a frantic frenzy of pleasure. He drove into her and groaned deeply.

"California Blake." He dipped his head beside hers. "Where have you been all my life?"

# CHAPTER
## TEN

*Heaven*

She had prickers in her butt. Rather, in her *ass*. Whatever the terminology, this would not be easy to explain at the Free Clinic.

She winced as Piers helped her to stand.

"What's wrong?" he said. "I didn't hurt you. Did I?"

"Nope. Not in the least. The opposite." She tried not to cringe. "It's embarrassing. But I think I'd better go back to my room and take care of it."

His hand tightened around hers. "What is it? Tell me."

"I think I got some... well... prickers... in my... um..."

He was obviously trying not to smile.

She glowered "Don't you dare laugh."

"I won't. I'm really sorry." He drew her into his arms. "However sorry I am, though, I'm not letting you go so quickly just because of this."

"*Just* because of this? It stings like crazy."

"Did I mention that I'm a doctor?"

"A doctor?"

"Mm hm." He kissed her temple, then beside her mouth.

She tilted her face up to let him. "You are not."

"Sure am. Got my MD right before the MBA. Figured it'd make me more marketable."

"You're a Prescott. That's all you need to be marketable."

"Okay, I'm not a doctor." He kissed her below her ear in the place that made her unsteady inside, and hot, despite her stinging butt and the remnants of orgasm lingering in her.

"Would you believe I was pre-med in college?" he asked.

She shook her head. "You weren't."

"For three years. I wanted to be a doctor. Every summer during high school and college I volunteered at my uncle's free clinic."

Her throat was abruptly thick. "Your uncle has a free clinic?"

"In North Philly. Always in the red. Family scandal. Nobody mentions it." His hands on her back felt like a dream. "Now let me doctor your battle wounds," he said low and seductively. "Then we'll come up with some ways to entertain you that won't disturb the—ah—area."

"Entertain me?"

"And me." He grinned, a gorgeous smile of pure sexy fun. It should make her laugh, not sweep the air from her lungs. She forced herself to chuckle. In response, he kissed her on the mouth, a long and increasingly lush kiss, his hands holding her tightly, as if he actually enjoyed simply kissing her. He was the perfect hookup guy. The perfect wedding party fling.

"Let's go to your room," she whispered.

"Right this way, ma'am."

He took her hand and led her into the house through a back entrance. They ended up in an unlit stairwell in the part of the building that was still under renovation. As she ascended the first step, he touched the small of her back.

"Take care," he said, his palm secure on her.

She stalled. "What are you doing?"

"Nothing. Supporting you."

"S—Supporting…?" Air wouldn't come.

"California?"

She couldn't see his face very well. She reached out and found him in the dark.

His chest. Her fingertips. Only that contact. But she felt it everywhere. Beneath her ribs.

"Wow," she whispered. "Wow."

His chest expanded roughly beneath her fingertips.

He pushed her back to the wall and covered her mouth with his. She put her hands in his hair, then all over him. In less than two minutes, a condom wrapper was open, her thighs were wide, and he was brushing aside her flippy skirt. He picked her up and pushed inside her.

"*Ohh.*" She closed her eyes on the darkness. He filled her entirely. *Perfect.*

"California," he said gutturally, and shoved her up against the wall with the force of his thrust.

"Again," she moaned. "Please, again."

He gave it to her again, and again, rough and fast, his hands gripping her hips, forcing her onto him. Sweat slicked the insides of her thighs. She slid, rode him, and came hard in a shower of sensation. He strained into her, and she felt him jerk inside her.

Loosing one hand from her hip, he grabbed the back of her head and kissed her hungrily, like he wanted her. Still. *After* orgasm. She wrapped her legs around his waist. Their kiss devoured.

Eventually she had to gasp for air. He pressed their brows together.

"Best"— she panted—"wedding party sex"— smiling deliriously— "ever."

His breaths seemed to catch. In the close silence of the stairwell, she heard him swallow hard. "Right." The word sounded short.

With great care he drew out of her and set her feet on the floor.

Oh, no. What kind of jerk was she?

"Um. What I mean is…" She smoothed her skirt over her thighs. "I've never done this before. Wedding party hookup sex, that is. This is a first for me."

"Is it?" His voice was very low. He hadn't moved away. She wished she could see his eyes.

"Yes." She tried to keep her tone casual. "Have you?"

"No." In the dark he touched her cheek with unerring accuracy, as though he knew exactly where her face was. He kissed her mouth. Softly. On her swollen, sensitive lips, the gentleness was breathtaking. "Only with you," he said and kissed her again tenderly.

She told herself she didn't need to believe him. She just needed him for the weekend.

Praying he couldn't feel her hands trembling, she flattened her palms on his chest. "What do we do now? Next?"

"Whatever we want." His lips brushed hers, softly again, as if he were trying to seduce her. "How's your ass?"

"My ass?"

"The prickers?"

"I—I forgot about them."

"You forgot about them." She practically heard him grin.

She slapped a palm over her mouth. "I can't believe I just admitted that. Your ego—"

"Is feeling mighty fine at this moment."

"Do you still want to play doctor?" She could feel her cheeks flaming.

"If you're the patient, most definitely."

This time they made it to his room. He opened the door and touched her elbow to guide her inside. The moment when he hadn't done so—last night in the limo—bothered her more than ever. He seemed too confident to be the jealous type, and she'd made it clear she thought Dick was a creep. But Piers had been so distracted—*upset?* —that his habitual gentlemanliness had disappeared.

He switched on a light. Decorated with historical elegance like hers, his room however was a suite: luxurious, with a king-sized bed, a separate sitting area, and a gorgeous antique desk upon which sat only a sleek laptop. No clothes littered the floor. No coats hung on the backs of chairs. No half-finished bottles of water dotted the dresser, only the room key he'd just placed there.

"Wow. You're so... neat," she mumbled.

From behind, he slipped his arms around her waist and bent to kiss her neck. "I travel all the time," he said against her shoulder. "I hate hotel rooms."

She turned her head and he lifted his.

"You travel all the time but you hate hotel rooms? What kind of life is that?"

"Not much of one." He curved his hand around the lower part of her butt. The skirt bunched in his fingers. "Take this off and lie down on your stomach." He released her and went into the bathroom. "I think there's a first-aid kit here."

Abruptly nervous again, she did as ordered. She shouldn't be nervous, but she now discovered that furtive, explosive sex in public places was a lot easier to handle than a bedroom scenario. "Find anything?"

"No antiseptic." He came back into the room, halted, and looked directly at her bare behind with such stark appreciation that she couldn't help smiling.

"So...?" she said.

He seemed to shake himself from a stupor and opened a cabinet. "How about vodka?"

"I've had more than enough to drink already today."

"I mean for the prickers."

"You're going to bathe my wounds in *vodka*?"

"They do it in Russia."

"Is that true?"

"I don't know. Probably. I've never been wounded in Russia. I said it to impress you with my worldly experience." He palmed two tiny bottles. "Chopin or Grey Goose?"

"What's the difference?"

"One was a composer. The other is a bird."

"Chopin."

He sat on the bed beside her, and she watched the fluid flex of muscles in his chest as he passed his fingertips over her lower back.

"Nothing here now but red marks," he said, dousing a cotton ball and dabbing it lightly over her lower back where her skirt had ruched up while he'd been driving into her on the ground. The alcohol was cool on her heated flesh, and only stung a little. "Would you like me to call the desk for some Benedryl?"

"It's not that uncomfortable now. Does it look bad?"

"Not too bad." His touch was incredibly gentle.

"You're an excellent medic. Thank you, Doctor." She smiled against her shoulder.

"You are so beautiful." She could hear the restraint in his voice.

"Even with a rash from prickers?"

"Even so." His hands bracketed her thighs near the top.

"What are you doing?"

"Entertaining you. As promised." His fingers dipped to strafe her clitoris. She sucked in air. "And me," he said and caressed again. She watched him, her body tightening as he stroked. He circled her entrance and her eyelids fluttered closed as she tilted her hips up, feeling him. Wanting him moving in her again.

"Let's do it again," she whispered, astounded at herself. She'd never been this forward about sex. Apparently throwing caution to the wind meant abandoning it entirely. "Now."

"I could mount you like this," he said. "From behind. It would be easier on the area." His voice smiled.

She'd never done it like that. There was something dominating about it that'd always made her squeamish. But her world was spinning from his caresses. "Do you want to?"

"I want to be with you any way you'll allow it."

"Yes." She pushed into his touch. "Yes. Do it."

"What happened to 'Do *me*'?"

"Me. It. Just *do*. Please. Now."

"Your wish…"

He did it. He did *her*.

He reached for a condom. Then, pressing her knees apart and drawing up her hips, he penetrated her in one, steady, agonizingly slow thrust. They groaned together.

He stroked into her again, and again, caressing with his fingers, trapping her between his hand and his cock. She heard herself panting and backed against him hard. But he drew out, controlling the pace, never giving her everything, taking her slowly from needing him to craving him.

"Wow," slipped through her parted lips. "You're good at this."

"I was thinking the same of you." His voice was low, strained. "I've got to have you." He gripped her hips in both hands and dragged her onto him and finally let her have his entire cock. She shuddered uncontrollably. She couldn't believe it, but she was coming. Already. With nothing but him inside her and the rhythm of their thrusts. He went deep. Incredibly deep. Touching her core. She clutched him. Tightening. *Tighter*. Imploding. Pleasure everywhere. She cried out.

He withdrew from her. But she hadn't felt him finish.

She turned onto her back. Taking her up in his arms like a rag doll, he dragged her onto his lap. He entered her again and tangled his hands in her hair, and his gaze claimed her features one by one. Gripping his shoulders, she sank onto him. He kissed her.

They did it like that for a long time. She didn't know how long, but she'd never had a man inside her for more than the few minutes it took them both to come, and sometimes only him. Piers didn't seem to be in any rush. He stroked her hair back from her face and kissed her mouth and neck and moved in her in a long, slow, sensuous rhythm, as if the pleasure for him wasn't in orgasm but in being joined with her like this. When finally she climaxed again, he was watching her face.

"California, you are incredible. I can't get enough of you."

She clung to him and let the shudders ripple through her and told herself that they were only words and that words couldn't hurt her.

"Did you?" she said softly beside him.

Piers's veins hummed with energy. He couldn't sleep. No rest for the wicked. Especially not for the wicked whose years of wickedness were swiftly coming to an end.

But he'd thought he was alone in wakefulness.

Hands tucked under her cheek, she had curled up on her side beneath the sheet, disguising the beauty of her body. The lids drooped over her dark eyes. But wariness lurked in them.

"Did I what?"

"Did you really throw the chair through the fifty-seventh-floor window?"

This was it. Truth time. And when he told her, there was every chance she'd bolt.

"No. I left the building and told the driver to take me anywhere in the city that my grandfather had never been. Turned out he'd never been to a lot of places." His smile arose from deep in his chest. "That was a good day."

She stared at his mouth. "Tell me why you went to work for your grandfather."

He looked up at the ceiling. "When my brother was fifteen, he ran away from home. He was an unusual kid, genius intelligence and always acting out against our grandfather. Still, Grandfather was already grooming him to become his successor, enticing him with gifts and driving in the guilt one toy, one bike, one expensive electronic gadget at a time." The anger he'd felt on behalf of his little brother back then stirred again in him. "But J.T. wasn't wired that way. When he disappeared, my mother flipped out. My father was still recovering from his first heart attack, so I left Stanford in the middle of the semester and drove to every place I could imagine my brother would be. It took me weeks to find him. He was in a very bad way. On the edge of doing serious harm—to someone. So I promised him I'd take over his destined place in the family's business if he promised to never disappear again. We made a deal: if he always told me and our parents where he was, we wouldn't tell Grandfather."

"You saved his life."

Piers ran a hand over his face. "I don't know. Maybe. He's still unpredictable." He chuckled. "But he's okay now."

"When did he get okay?"

"He joined the Marines when he was nineteen. When his tour ended, he went into the Secret Service. And three years ago he saw our grandfather for the first time in years. It went fine."

"So." Her voice was soft. "After that, why did you keep working at Prescott Global?"

He turned his face to her. In the dim lamplight that shadowed her eyes, with her hair falling over her shoulder, she took every word he knew and made them mean nothing.

"Maybe you like it," she said, "or you wouldn't have stayed for so long."

"I like winning."

"You could win at something that's good for other people. People who aren't rich stockholders, that is."

"You make it sound simple."

"It is. You have no idea how fortunate you are, Piers. You have money, education, and influence. Unless you turn into a lying drunk like my father did, I don't see how anything stands in your way of doing what you want."

"I've been thinking that lately, actually." She had inspired it. But he had to end the worst lie right now. "How did you get so smart?" he murmured instead.

"I read." She shrugged a naked shoulder and he wanted to bite it. Then the rest of her. He wanted to win *her*.

"While you're working?" he asked, because otherwise he'd say, "I funded your project and bought you the ticket to England," and he would not win her. This independent, wary woman would not like having been played as his party favor. That's how she would see it, no matter how he apologized. His gut ached.

"It's one of the perks of the job." She gave him a sparkling smile. "The bookmobile is much more work for the same pay. And the hours are insane. I'm doing a lot of overtime."

"I give you back your question: why do you do it?"

"A few years ago our house burned down and we lost everything. Other than my sister's beautiful face, the only things I missed were my books. There are people out there who can't afford an e-reader or a trip to Barnes and Noble or even Wal-Mart. Those people deserve to be able to escape their troubles for a few hours in stories, just like the rest of us."

"This is the first time I've escaped in years."

"If you read books you could escape every day."

He smiled. "*Pride and Prejudice?*"

A tingly dance started up in Cali's stomach. He paid attention to her when she spoke. Men didn't often pay attention, not even when they wanted to have sex with her, and never after sex.

"Do you know why women love *Pride and Prejudice*?" she said. "Because it's the fantasy of having it all, no matter how humble or poor, being smart and showing the rich guy that he's got something to learn." She lifted her hand and let her fingertips travel up his corded forearm to the impressive biceps. She traced the muscle's arc. "There are a lot of guys like you that need to learn a few things. Humility. And compassion for people who are different from you. I think that's why I applied to your family's foundation. It's definitely why I did an interview in the *City Paper*. I wanted to tell my friends' story, so the rich guys could learn."

He took her hand in his and turned onto his side to face her. "They did."

"Who?"

"I read the interview."

Her heart did a little flip. "You read it?"

"You told it straight, without sentimentality, but with wisdom and understanding. It was amazing."

"Amazing?"

"Yeah." Piers's gaze was shifting back and forth between her eyes, as if looking for something. It seemed like he was about to say more, but that maybe he wasn't sure about it. Cali's heart beat too fast. She wanted to hear what he would say. She wanted to wrap her arms around him and ask him to hold her so close that no air would fit between them. She wanted this night to last longer than the weekend. Much longer. And she wanted it far too much.

*Wedding party hookup.*

*Rebound sex.*

She made her voice casual. "Were you and Caroline Colby ever engaged?"

He didn't answer for a moment. "No."

"Not after four years?"

He lifted a single brow. "You follow the gossip news?"

"Know thine enemy," she said with a shrug.

"I was never your enemy, California." His thumb stroked across her palm, sending shimmers of sleepy desire through her.

"Four years is a long time. Why didn't you get engaged?"

"It was casual between us. Business. And social."

She didn't know how that was possible for four years. Or four weeks. Or four days. The problem she always had, the problem she'd inherited from her mother, was that when she gave her heart even a little, she couldn't help giving it all—like to her father who'd left them repeatedly. After every abandonment, then every return and heartfelt apology, Cali had forgiven him and kept loving him. Until the doctors removed Zoe's bandages. At that moment, she swore she would never let herself love him again.

Suddenly the room seemed airless, her lungs suffocated. Cold panic thrummed in her limbs.

She slid out of bed, fumbled with her panties and skirt, and pulled them on.

"Are you leaving?" Piers's voice sounded strange. She couldn't look at him. She tugged her tank top over her head and stuffed her bra into the waistband of her skirt, then jammed her toes into the flip-flops.

"Tomorrow's a big day. Rehearsal dinner and all. I've got to get at least an hour or two of sleep." She whipped her hair into a ponytail. She had to look at him. She couldn't just use him for fantastic sex and leave without even meeting his eye. She *could*. But she'd have to see him again this weekend. Then maybe she would see him someday down the road, like at Jane and Duke's tenth wedding anniversary bash or something.

Who was she kidding? After this week she would never see Piers Prescott again unless it was in the news.

She stuck her hands in the skirt's back pockets, oh-so-cool, her back screaming from the tank top scraping over the rash. She turned to him.

He was propped on an elbow, his dark hair falling over his brow, the snowy white sheet strewn across the delicious T-bone of his hips. His very blue eyes were very intense.

"Is this because of what I said about Caroline?"

"No," she lied. "It's like I said, tomorrow's going to be a big day."

"You can sleep here. I won't make a move on you." The glimmer returned to his eyes. "At least not until daylight. Scout's honor."

"I'm a light sleeper. I'd better go to my room." She retreated from the bed. "Thanks. I had a good time. A great time, actually," she said, the words a little rushed.

"So did I." He sounded dead serious, but he gave her a hint of a smile.

As she walked the hallways to her room the panic still lapped at her and she still couldn't breathe.

# CHAPTER
## ELEVEN

*On the Lawn*

A man hid in the bushes. A man with a telephoto lens camera pointed through a first-floor window.

Cali's running shoes were silent on the thick grass as she slunk up behind him, swiping the sweat from her face. She'd slept late and gone out right away. Thanks to Piers, her body was completely relaxed. Now a run would put her head back in the right place. And after a few weeks without seeing or touching him, or breathing in his scent, or hearing his mocha latte voice, she would be completely fine again.

The paparazzo angled the camera tighter into the six-inch crack at the bottom of the window. Something was going on in the room, obviously. Or not. Paparazzi weren't picky.

She tiptoed up behind him, preparing a rant about invasion of privacy. Jane's voice came through the crack.

"*You* funded Cali's bookmobile?"

A man responded. She couldn't hear the words. But she knew the voice—the sexy, confident voice that had murmured romantic things in her ear before, during, and after he'd made her buck like a wild horse.

"Oh, my God, Piers!" Jane exclaimed. "This is a fantastic coincidence. Why didn't you tell her?"

"The donation carries a legal stipulation." He must have come closer to the window. Cali could hear his words. "If my name becomes associated with the project, the funds will be withdrawn."

"Cali wouldn't tell anyone. She's the most honest person I know."

"Which is why I haven't told her. If she were asked who funded it, she wouldn't be able to deny knowing."

Her foot cracked a stick nestled in the grass. The paparazzo swung around. He looked at her face.

"Whoa, lass," he said, his Scottish accent pronounced. "You're not looking at me with those dagger eyes, now, are you? Because I haven't done a thing. Yet."

"Get out of here." Low. Dark. Like a demon murderess.

"Will do." He scurried away.

*Nausea.* Pins prickling across every inch of her skin.

Piers had been lying to her all week. She understood his justification. Her father had always had airtight justifications too. She'd believed them every single time. Until the last.

She couldn't think. Her thoughts tripped over one another. Why would he privately fund the bookmobile? He didn't even read books. Unless he'd been lying about that too. Guys like him—*like her father*—said anything to elicit a response, to charm, to get what they wanted.

Oh, God. Why was she so comprehensively a fool? Again and again?

She ran to the front door and through the house to her room. She hung out the Do Not Disturb sign.

Fifteen minutes later, when Piers knocked and spoke through the door, she didn't answer. A few minutes later, the phone rang and then the message light blinked.

An hour after that, he returned. "California, are you there?"

She buried her face in Elizabeth and Darcy's story and tried to pretend that she had never met Piers Vaughan Prescott Jr.

.  .  .

"Cali knows." Jane took a glass of wine from a passing waiter and shook her head. Across the lawn, the band had started playing. Jane and Duke's guests trickled out of the house for cocktails on the lawn before the rehearsal ceremony. The bride sipped her wine. "She doesn't want to talk to you."

"Did you tell her, Jane? Is it public knowledge now?"

"No. She said she heard it through the window accidentally. But it doesn't matter how she found out. You should have told her."

At Jane's side, Duke shrugged. Beside him, Damien Knightly offered Piers a sympathetic lift of his brows.

"Best to err on the side of too much information, I'm discovering," Damien said.

Piers turned his eyes to the terrace again and his heart did a peculiar stuttering beat. California walked out of the house. She'd thrown off the tight, leggy style she'd adopted here and now wore a nondescript dress like the clothing he was used to seeing her in at Green Park. He started toward her. She saw him and changed direction.

He went after her. He'd screwed things up, with his life and with this woman. But his grandfather had taught him one useful thing, at least.

Never back down from a challenge.


She couldn't escape him. She'd hidden in her room all day, but she couldn't miss Jane's wedding rehearsal. There had to be something between throwing herself at him and giving him the cold shoulder. He'd given the library a huge sum of money that had propelled her dream into reality. She was grateful. She would address this with dignity, self-respect, and professional courtesy.

In the late afternoon sunlight he looked like a movie star in a dark linen designer suit, with his signet ring and priceless watch and the slim gold chain disappearing beneath his collar—a chain she had discovered carried a Saint Christopher medal, patron saint of travelers.

He'd said he hated hotels. Another lie.

"California."

She halted. "I know you're the anonymous donor of the bookmobile."

His face looked grave. "Is that why you wouldn't see me today?"

"Did you know who I was before I arrived here?"

"I did."

"How? Did you come to the library to spy on me?"

"Not the library. Every Friday morning in Green Park."

Oh. No. *The sexy hat guy.* How hadn't she realized it? But the watch, the signet ring, the designer clothes and the huge aristocratic mansion that now framed him all explained it. Out of place. Out of reality. The two worlds—hers and his—had nothing to do with each other. Without having seen his face in the park, she couldn't have possibly realized he was that man.

"Why didn't you tell me?" she managed to say. "As soon as we met?"

"What would I have said? 'Hey, babe, have sex with me because I gave money to your pet project. No strings attached, honest.'"

"Why not? You should have."

"You would have believed that?"

"Yes. I think. Maybe." She squeezed her eyes shut. "No. Probably not. I'm not comfortable with the professional line that crosses."

He ran a hand through his hair and looked away briefly, then back at her squarely. "You'll be even more uncomfortable when you've heard the rest."

"The rest? There's more?" But abruptly, she knew. "*No.* Did you buy my ticket to come here? The nurse for my sister? The dress? The limo?" She couldn't catch her breath. "You overheard me telling Roy and the others about it that day, didn't you?"

He held her gaze and said nothing.

Her throat clenched up. "Oh my God."

"Don't even try to blame me for this," he said, his voice low. "You happily used it, even not knowing who'd sent it."

"I thought my friends pooled their money!"

"If you didn't want to use it, you didn't have to."

She backed away. "Are you one of those sick stalker guys who's got way too much free time and money on his hands and makes women like me into psycho projects?"

"No. I don't have any free time. I am a vice president of an international corporation. I sleep four hours a night and spend exactly two waking hours a week not working, and you know exactly where I am during those two hours."

She felt hot all over, feverish. "You obviously spend time working out."

"Squash meetings. Running meetings. Biking meetings. Tennis meetings. Last week I spent two hours rowing up the Schuylkill negotiating the hostile takeover of a machine company. Guys in my line of work like to show off. Half of our meetings happen while we're playing sports. And even if I were a psycho stalker, do you really think I'd admit it?"

"That's comforting."

"I'm a good guy, California. Don't make this into something it's not."

"What about work this week? You're here now."

"Until I heard you mention it at the park, I'd only planned on coming for tomorrow."

He'd taken a week off work just to meet her, when he could've met her any Friday in the park? She couldn't believe it. This wasn't real.

"Why do you come to Green Park?"

He looked away, then down at the ground. She'd never seen him do that; look at the ground like he didn't know what to say. A weird chill shimmied through her.

"If you expect me to believe you're not a stalker," she said, "you're going to have to give me a good reason that you spend your only free time in a rundown park."

He gestured vaguely with his hand. "Chair. Window. Fifty-seventh floor."

"You started going to that park every Friday *then*?"

"Not quite. But I went there sometimes, when I needed to get away from work, and other places in the city too. Then in February I saw you at Green Park giving books to some teenagers cutting school. A couple of dealers were standing on the corner and you didn't seem to have a clue you could be in danger. I hung around to make sure you drove away okay."

He'd come to protect her?

"And the bookmobile?" she said through stretched vocal cords.

"When I read your interview in the *City Paper* and learned that the foundation rejected the grant proposal, I financed it privately." His eyes fixed hard in hers. "I did it because I knew my grandfather hated the very idea of it."

"You knew he'd hate it if he found out."

"No. He won't ever find out. I did it because I had to do something for myself, something I really believe in, or I'd actually throw the chair out that window."

"If your grandfather despised a project to build a roller park in front of the Liberty Bell, would you have financed that?"

He frowned. "No."

"I don't understand why you didn't tell me. I wouldn't have told anyone you were the donor."

He ran his hand through his hair, retousling the tousle. He looked incredibly uncomfortable, but still incredibly good. It was so unfair.

"I wanted you to come here," he finally said.

"You know," she said, her words shaky, "I'm poor. I don't know anyone famous, important, or rich except Jane and now Duke. And I don't wear designer clothes or drink two-hundred-dollar bottles of champagne—or any champagne at all. But I'm a person, and you can't go around using your money to make people move around like pawns on a chessboard."

"Sure I can," he said. "I do it every day."

*Gut punch.*

"Wow. Okay." Gulping back the shock, she turned and walked away.

"California," he called after her. He caught up. "California, please stop."

She halted but couldn't look at him.

"That's my life," he said. "That's been my life for years. But not with you. I didn't—I don't think of you in those terms."

"Of course you do. You thought you could throw money at me and you'd get what you wanted. It's the Prescott family MO. You don't even know that's what you did, do you?"

"Maybe at first it was like that, I'll admit. But not later. I just didn't want you to think you owed me anything." The sun shone in his warm eyes and on his gorgeous face and his hair was perfectly imperfect and everything about him screamed *Not for you, Cali!* "You came to the park every week and I liked what I saw," he said. "I wanted more of it."

"So you took me out of the place that makes me *me* to do that? I can't deny that I wanted to come on this trip and have some fun. But I'm a little smarter than you think I am, Piers. I don't fall for guys like you."

"Guys like me?"

"You didn't like what you saw in the park. You liked what you thought I could be if I was with you in a fancy house and wearing a fancy dress, schmoozing with people like you. Well, you've had that. I hope you enjoyed it. I'll leave the dress on the nightstand before I go so you can loan it to your next fixer-upper girl." She swung around, but his voice stopped her.

"I have enjoyed my time with you. Until about ten minutes ago, it was the best time I've ever had."

The words sounded like a line, but his voice didn't. It sounded deep and real, the way he'd sounded when she'd been in his arms last night. But he was a hugely successful businessman. Guys like him were experts at selling people lines.

"I don't know what to think."

"California." Her name on his lips was so completely sexy, forceful, but still a little tender. "I wanted to be with you. I still do."

"This isn't *real*." Real wasn't horseback rides across sprawling estates or limousines or black-tie dinners or a gorgeous guy telling her she was incredible. Real was her sister's scars. Real was her father's prison cell. "I realize I should jump at the chance to see more of a guy like you, but—"

"What is this *guys like me*? How about just *me*? How about seeing more of not a member of a category of men you mistrust, but the specific man that is me?"

"You don't understand." He'd never met her father when he'd worn thousand-dollar suits. He'd never seen her mother pop six pills at a time because even dressed up in jewels and designer clothes, she was still a waitress inside and never felt like *enough*. "You can't understand."

"I understand that you're a hypocrite," Piers said flatly. "You want me to see you as a person, but you're not willing to give me the same courtesy. All right. You can't see guys like me. I get it. I… get it." He took a breath that visibly lifted his chest. "Okay. It's been fun. Thanks. Thank you. See you around." He stared at her for another few seconds. Then he turned toward the house and walked away from her. His shoulders were broad, his stride athletic, confident, and so unbearably sexy she felt actual pain in her stomach.

He'd thought she was beautiful when she was wearing shapeless clothes and covered in dust. He could talk about English literature in the middle of the night, after sex, without rolling his eyes or falling asleep. And he'd given her the best vacation of her life without attaching any strings to it.

"Piers, wait."

He halted and his rigid shoulders seemed to ease. He looked around at her.

"I'm sorry," was all she could manage.

"Are you?"

"About being a hypocrite. You're right. I'm not being fair." She was so nervous her words shook. "This…"

He walked to her. "This?"

"This has been the best time I've ever had too."

His mouth relaxed. He surrounded her waist with his hands and bent to touch his lips to her cheek. "It's about to get even better."

This couldn't be happening to her. *Rebound sex,* she silently repeated. *Wedding hookup.* Anything but this surge of real feelings inside.

"Wear the dress tonight?" he asked as he cupped her elbow to guide her toward the big party tent where everybody was gathering for the rehearsal ceremony. "Then you can leave it on the floor of my room instead of the bed table."

She tried to ignore the pleasure of his touch, so unconscious for him, she thought, at once gentlemanly and possessive. It turned her insides out. Every time he touched her, it made her forget everything except how good he felt.

She disengaged from his hand. "What if I don't want to have sex with you again? What if I think you'll say anything to get it?"

"But you do want to have sex with me again. And you can never be sure I won't say anything to get it." He looked at her squarely. "You know everything now, California. It's time to decide to trust me or not. It's up to you."

"If I said I'd rather not have sex with you this weekend, what would you think?"

"I'd think you were testing me."

Not *him*. She needed clarity now. This was about testing herself.

"If I promised I wasn't," she said.

"I would have to respect that. I wouldn't like it. But I would respect it. And I'd know I was to blame for it anyway."

Throat thick, she nodded.

He smiled, and this time it was a tentative smile. Uncertain. "Will you still wear the dress?"

"Are you sure? It's very sexy."

His smile broadened. "I deserve the torture."

# CHAPTER
# TWELVE

*State Rooms & Bedroom*

The right shoulder strap of her slinky little black dress kept slipping down. Every time it slipped, Piers's gaze went there. It made her feel sexy. Desired. Wanted.

Probably the same way her mother felt when she'd met the man she married.

But her mom hadn't been forewarned. Cali was. She could keep her feelings safe for a few more hours.

Except for those brief, feverish glances at her shoulder, her unofficial date for the rehearsal dinner party was ideal. He brought her drinks when her hand was empty, but didn't press them on her; clearly he wasn't interested in getting her drunk. He made interesting conversation with everybody they talked to, always relaxed but attentive. And he stayed with her, not leaving her side. When at times she moved away from him, after a bit she would look for him and find him talking with whomever. But he always knew when she looked at him, and he would come to her again.

When the dancing started, Ideal Date turned into Fantasy Date. First, he didn't assume she would dance with him; he asked politely.

Second, he danced like he'd been taking ballroom dancing lessons since he was five. Third, he held her in all the right places to help her look like she'd been dancing since she was five, too, and close enough that she could smell him and get crazy from it, but not so close that he could cop a feel unnoticed.

He had to know he was a woman's dream date. Still, when the party was winding down and he walked her to her room, he looked as uncertain as she'd ever seen him.

Without touching her he said, "Would I be crossing the respect line if I asked for a kiss good night?"

She felt like she was fifteen and on her first date again. "No."

A slight smile. "May I kiss you good night, California?"

"Yes."

His lips brushed hers, and then briefly covered them. Too briefly. He backed away. "Good night." His voice was husky.

She reached out and grabbed the lapel of his coat. He took her into his arms and for the first time in her life Cali had an old-fashioned, necking-at-the-door good night kiss.

It wasn't enough. Not nearly.

How dangerous could it be to indulge one last time? She knew the score now. He knew she knew it. They were both adults. She ran her hands under his jacket, over his ripped pecs.

"I don't want you to go," she said.

"Then don't make me go."

She tugged him into her room.

He stopped upon the threshold. "Is this because you trust me now?"

"This is because the weekend isn't over yet."

His gaze looked so intense, but not pleased.

She shrugged and the strap of her dress slipped off her shoulder. "Can you be okay with that?"

"Yeah," he said. "For now."


WITHOUT SPEAKING, he laid her back on the bed fully clothed and kissed her throat, her neck, and the valley between her breasts where the dress was cut out in a diamond shape, until she asked him to remove it and kiss everywhere else too. He ran his hands along her body from the hem of the dress to the tips of her fingers as the silk slipped off, and she lifted her hips then her back to allow it. Then she kicked off her panties over her black silk heels.

"These are impressive," he said, studying a stiletto and trailing his fingertips along her calf, ignoring her otherwise entirely naked body. He was playing with her. Cali wondered if he wanted to make her beg him to touch her, since she'd said she didn't want to sleep with him.

"They're dangerous," she whispered, watching his face.

"For a thunderstorm runner they would be," he said with a smile. "Do you ever worry about twisting your ankle and falling?"

"I worry about falling. Always."

His hand slipped beneath her knee. "Why do you chance it?"

"There are three things I love. My sister, because she is the strongest person I know. Books, because"—she sucked in breath as his fingers traced the inside of her thigh—"because they never abandon you. And insanely high-heeled shoes, because the cautious daughter of a careless man needs at least one place to rebel."

He removed her shoes and placed them beside the bed. Then he bent to her mouth and kissed her until she wrapped her arms around his neck.

"I lied," she whispered.

His mouth hovered over hers. "You lied?"

"That's not all I love."

A moment's pause. "What else?"

"The people I've met on the bookmobile routes. I love them. They make all the bad go away." She trailed her fingertips along his jaw. "And I love Jane, and now Duke by association. And mocha lattes." This man tasted even better. "And being picked up at an airport in a limousine, even if I'm not having sex with anyone in front of the sweet old driver." She smiled against his lips.

His hand curved over her hip. "I'm sure he appreciated your discretion."

"I have no discretion right now."

"You don't need it with me."

"I need it with you most of all," she confessed, foolishly. Then she swore off words for the remainder of the night.

When he unfastened his belt, she helped him. When she caressed him, he kissed her as if his hunger for her was constant and could be satisfied only in deep kisses that left her shaking and raw. When she invited him into her, he touched her until she couldn't bear to be empty for another moment, then he filled her.

"You have a beautiful heart, California," he said into the profound silence of their locked bodies. "I don't suppose you would consider giving it to me?"

"What?" she whispered.

"Cali, I'm falling hard."

She gripped his arms. "Falling?"

"Fallen." He moved in her like he was savoring her, the powerful, steady rhythm of his body making hers reach for him. But this was wrong. It wasn't supposed to happen this way. She was supposed to be able to walk away on Sunday with a day-after smile and a memory of a fantastic fling that would cheer her up when life got especially hard. Sex in a garden—yes. Sex in a stairwell—heck yes. Not beautiful, overwhelming sex in a bed, with him saying unbelievable things. If he did this, it would ruin the fantasy. It would make everything false.

"Don't say that." Her voice scraped.

He brushed his lips across hers. "It's the truth."

"You don't know me. I don't know you. We just met." Like her parents, married after two weeks, madly in love and a tragic mistake.

"We met months ago. We've spent every day together."

"No."

He surrounded her face with his hands. "Every street corner, every park, every building, every shop you've driven to. They're my favorite places in the city. The people, my closest friends. You know me."

She knew his scenery. That was all. She knew only what he wanted her to know.

Aloud, she didn't argue it. She let him give her body what it needed, and she gave him pleasure in return. When it was over and he held her, she remained awake, gorging herself on his scent and heat.

As soon as his breathing deepened, she disentangled her limbs, moved to the far edge of the bed, and turned her face away.

When she awoke to sunlight he was gone and she exhaled a sigh of relief.

She descended to discover the house abuzz with happy wedding day festivities, but no Piers anywhere. She appreciated having the time to settle more securely back into her own head, and sanity. But she wondered where he was. Probably at the gazebo, online, arranging other people's lives like a chess master, and making them think it was what they wanted.

Jane and Duke said their vows and kissed lovingly, and everyone erupted in cheers and applause. It was beautiful and romantic and perfect and Cali's heart swelled with happiness for her friend.

Piers still hadn't appeared, which didn't surprise her. He'd gone, obviously. She confirmed it with Mark.

"He had a business emergency in the States. The call for him came outrageously early." Mark smiled. "But I assumed you knew. I tracked him down in your room."

She'd slept through it. He'd let her.


ON SUNDAY MORNING Cali ran around the estate's perimeter and, once again, ended at the gazebo. One of Duke's tech girls was there with a laptop. Cali borrowed it to check e-mail.

Work messages cluttered her inbox, including one with the subject heading "Back to Work" that Dick had sent yesterday morning.


*Cali,*

*Now that the bookmobile project is dead, I'll look forward to seeing you again in the main branch, Monday through Saturday. Two of those days will include evening hours. If you're unable to accommodate this schedule adjustment, let me know after the staff meeting Monday and I'll find someone else for your position. Two of the pages look promising.*

*Dick B.*

BLIND TO THE BEAUTIFUL MORNING, and deaf to the tech girl's "See you, California," Cali walked back to the house. George had said they'd need to leave by ten. She wished she had another ride to the airport. But if she couldn't sit for a few hours in the limo Piers had hired, she'd have a tough time living in a city where his name was in the news every week.

She hugged Jane good-bye, thanked Harry and Mark again for showing her the priceless copy of *Pride and Prejudice,* and climbed into the limousine. Soon familiar reality would be hers again. It was far past time.

# CHAPTER
# THIRTEEN

*The Fifty-Eighth Floor*

P iers didn't knock. Putting his hand to the knob, he opened the thick black door and strode into his grandfather's office. Jacob Taylor Vaughan Prescott commanded the fifty-eighth floor of the Prescott building, alone at the top of his empire except for his secretary's office, the boardroom, a party room, a private gymnasium, and a track that ran along half the building. Seventy-five and still fit, with silvery white hair and an arresting profile that J.T.—his intended heir—had inherited, he sat behind a desk topped with black granite before a flat-screen computer.

Piers waited. His grandfather had taught him that silence was often more powerful than words. And he hadn't yet managed to control his temper.

Eyes on the screen, his grandfather said, "I assume you've had enough of this foolish little rebellion and are ready to return to work."

A shaft of icy chill went through Piers. His grandfather sounded remarkably like the emperor in *Star Wars*. How hadn't he noticed that before?

He didn't answer.

Finally his grandfather's hands retreated from the keyboard, and he sat back in his chair. He lifted a brow. "Well?"

"You shouldn't have done it. It was petulant, the act of an angry child rather than a man of business. You're already being criticized for it."

"When I care what the idiot liberals at the *City Paper* have to say about me, I will make certain to inform you. Now, if you have useful information to impart to me, do so. If not, leave me to my work."

"I'm leaving."

"Don't be a fool."

"I'm leaving, Grandfather." His sense of relief was so profound that for an instant he could only breathe in and out slowly, and deeper with each inhalation. *Freedom*. For the first time in a decade, he felt free. "I had hoped to go without bad feelings. But your recommendation to the foundation regarding the *America's Heroes* exhibition convinced me that I don't need to worry about your feelings. Or your scruples. Nevertheless, I wanted to tell you in person that I'm leaving. I'll be gone from the building tonight. After she's wrapped up some tasks, Mrs. Crowley will be leaving as well."

"To go where?" His grandfather spoke tightly. "Will you have one of the best assistants in the city ladling stew at a soup kitchen?"

Piers laughed. He'd been through the worst already—thirty-six hours of nonstop meetings with board members, lawyers, journalists, and the library's director. But he'd made it out the other side of this mess, and his grandfather hadn't won.

"Good-bye, Grandfather. If you can bear to dine with a family of failures, I'll see you at Mom's at Thanksgiving."

He left the office of the CEO of Prescott Global for the last time and went down to his office a floor below. He'd called his secretary in on a Sunday to help put things in order, and she'd greeted him more cheerfully than in years.

"Mr. Prescott, your mother called and asked—"

"Insisted."

"—that you come for dinner tonight. Your lawyer, Mr. Charlotte, called as well. The funds have been transferred from the account in the Netherlands and will be available for use at the start of the business day tomorrow through Deutsche Bank. And the reporter at the *City Paper* has several follow-up questions. I've forwarded those to you. *Philadelphia in the Morning* is requesting a ten-minute spot tomorrow. Should I accept or decline?"

"Accept. Then let's finish the Bingley Industries report so you can pack that away with the rest. And please tell my mother I'd very much like to see her, but later this week would work better."

"I'm sure she'll understand, sir, given the circumstances."

"Mrs. Crowley, we've got a long night ahead of us here."

"But a good one, sir."

"I'm glad you're happy with the change."

"Honestly, I'd gotten awfully impatient for it." She shook her head and marched into the meeting room and the stacks of file boxes there, leaving him staring bemusedly. But he understood impatience well enough. California's plane was due to land in an hour.

That battle wasn't yet won. She had walls fifty miles high. But her family's tragedies hadn't made her cold or withdrawn. Instead, she poured her passion into service to others. And she'd shown him that even when he intended the best, he still operated just like his grandfather. She'd been right about him. But he could change. He'd changed already.

If he could change, she could too. Just enough to let him through the wall. After that, life was going to get pretty damn good.

CALI HEAVED her suitcase through the apartment door, thinking of Mark and the helpful staff at Brampton, then firmly archiving the memory. Dropping her stuff, she went into the kitchen and switched on the burner under the teakettle.

"Zoe?" she called. No answer. Sleeping probably.

She dragged the suitcase to her room, plugged in her dead phone, and returned to the kitchen to make tea. Leaving it to steep, she went to unpack.

Her phone blinked to life. The text message bell trilled, and messages leaped onto the screen one after another. Below an unidentified number was a message with a time stamp from right before her plane landed: *Crazy woman who doesn't have an international plan. Hope your trip back was smooth. I want to see you tonight.*

An hour later: *Call me, Cali.*

Then fifteen minutes ago: *I'll wait. - Piers*

She scrolled through the list of calls she'd missed during the week: Work. Landlord. Medicaid rep. Zoe's OT. At the end of the list was a message from Piers. Her finger hovered over the Play button. She clicked Delete.

He didn't get it. He didn't get that she couldn't even afford *regular* phone service. And he didn't get that when he disappeared without explanation she would feel like someone had punched her repeatedly in the stomach. He didn't get that she wasn't the kind of woman he'd dated before. He was so completely in another world from her, he would never get it.

Setting her phone on her half-unpacked suitcase, she sat down on the edge of the bed and tears ran down her cheeks. Zoe wheeled into the doorway.

Cali swiped her hand across her face. "I'm back." She tried to laugh it off.

Zoe gave her a sympathetic face. "Wedding envy or jet lag?"

"Exhaustion." Partial truth. She picked up her phone, turned it off and tossed it on the bed table, then hugged her sister for a full minute. "Did you have fun with Nurse Marcia?"

"Best week of my life. We watched *All My Children* reruns for ten hours every day."

This time Cali laughed honestly, but it came out burbled with tears she'd suppressed since she'd woken up to find Piers gone and realized she'd fallen for him despite everything. She bent to her suitcase and pulled out one of the sexy shirts Roxanna gave her that had made him want her.

Zoe's lips pinched. "What happened, Cal?"

"I took your advice." She tossed the shirt and her jeans into the overflowing hamper. Fantasy over. Back to reality with a hard shove.

"What advice?"

"I hooked up with a hot, rich guy and had mind-blowing wedding party sex in a garden. Also in a stairwell and in both of our bedrooms." She bent to remove her shoes from the suitcase, but instead hung there with her face pressed into her knees. "There was some very fine making out in a limo, too, and in a stable," she said, her voice muffled by her jeans. "Oh, and at the pool. Then he left without saying good-bye, and now my heart hurts like hell and it's all your fault."

"Bull," Zoe said. "You wouldn't have done it if you hadn't wanted to."

"I know. I said that to try to make myself laugh, but it didn't work."

"Has he called?"

"Yes."

"Then what's the problem?"

Cali raised her face, damp with tears. "I can't do it, Zoe. I just can't."

Zoe pushed up out of her wheelchair and moved onto the bed beside her. Wrapping her arms around Cali, she stroked her hair. "I'm so sorry you're hurting, sweetie. So, so sorry."

"You're comforting me," she mumbled into Zoe's shoulder.

"Is that okay?"

"That you're well enough to comfort someone else? It's the answer to every one of my prayers."

"Who is he, Cali?"

"Who *was* he." Cali pulled back. "Piers Prescott."

Zoe blinked. "Big money Piers Prescott?"

"Yes."

"Wow. When I said hot and rich, I didn't think you'd really go after *hot* and *rich*."

"I didn't know I wasn't supposed to take you literally."

"Wait." Zoe's eyes widened. "He's the one who funded the bookmobile."

A sick feeling twined through Cali's stomach. "How do you know that?"

"It's been all over the local news this weekend." She slid back into her chair and spun away. "I've got the paper right here," she shouted from the other room. Cali followed.

Zoe waved the paper at her. "The lefties at the *City Paper* are so excited that for once a Prescott is doing something good for the masses, they did a huge spread on it."

Cali opened the paper with shaking hands. He'd said his grandfather would never find out. So he lied about that too. She should have expected it. She should have known.

"Apparently Jacob Prescott found out about the bookmobile and threatened to pull the money for that big exhibition, *America's Heroes*, that the Prescott Foundation is funding at the library," Zoe said, "plus three other cultural projects in the city. So Piers came out with it all to get support. I guess it worked. The morning news today said that if the Prescott Foundation walked, both the Barnes Foundation and the Pierpont Morgan in New York would step up to fund *America's Heroes*. And Piers and his uncle—some doctor, I think—set up a new trust for the bookmobile, so that's safe too. The editorial in today's *Inquirer* is less gushing than the *City Paper*, but still seemed impressed. The *Star* was all about Piers at Jane and Duke's wedding, of course. Apparently that's where the paparazzi got the news about the bookmobile." Her eyes went wide. "Holy crap, Cali. You knew he was the donor, didn't you?"

"I found out accidentally, after he slept with me a few times." She folded up the *City Paper*, dropped it in the recycling bin, and went back into the bedroom to finish unpacking. Inside the black silk pumps she'd worn to the rehearsal dinner she found a folded sheet of Brampton monogrammed paper.

*California, I have to fly back this morning. My grandfather learned about my donation to the library from the paps chasing Duke and Jane. He's angry with me, and threatening to take board action against the library. I've got to go head off disaster. You're so incredibly beautiful sleeping now, I can't bear to wake you. And I hope you're dreaming of me, so there's some self-interest here too. Enjoy the wedding. I'll see you at home tomorrow. Call as soon as you land. – P*

WHEN SHE LOOKED UP, Zoe was in the doorway. "Accidentally?"

"Yes." Cali crumpled up the note and threw it in the wastebasket.

"What was that?"

"Oh, just a letter from Mom reminding me not to get involved with guys with whom I have absolutely nothing in common." Paparazzi. Private jets. Million-dollar donations. Foundations that could cripple a library in one blow. Titans battling it out, using mountains as weapons while the little people below got crushed by the resulting boulders.

Thank God for the paparazzi. She'd gotten a lucky break. The quicker the hit came, the quicker the bruise healed.

"Cali—"

"I'm really wiped out, and it's 3 a.m. in England now. Are you okay for the night?"

Zoe nodded.

Cali kissed her sister's cheek. "Night. And thanks for the comfort, little sis. You're the best." She closed the door, climbed under the sheets, and cried. Tomorrow she would put her head back on straight. No malingering misery. No dramatic ups and downs while he strung her along. No endless weeping. A clean break now and in no time she'd be fine.

But just for tonight, she let herself cry.

# CHAPTER
# FOURTEEN

*Philadelphia*

The next morning at the staff meeting, Dick spoke to everyone professionally, exactly as he always did in a group. Afterward in his office, Cali confirmed with him that since the bookmobile's funding had been secured again, she would be taking out the van as usual.

He tapped his pen on the desk.

"Since it's gotten such high-profile press lately," he said, "Cara is considering assigning it to someone with more experience. Miller, possibly. Or Brown."

"I've been here six years, Dick. I have experience. Cara knows that."

"Deborah Miller has a master's degree. She's a librarian."

But Cali knew that Dick was finally making her pay.

"Did you recommend this to Cara?"

"She thinks your skills are better suited to the main branch." He folded his hands around the pen. "But, listen. I'll do what I can to help you keep the bookmobile, Cali. If you'll do your best for me."

She walked to Security to retrieve the van's keys with a sick stomach.

Everyone on her Monday stops seemed really glad to see her. Some mentioned the press coverage and the Prescott family's fight. But mostly they just checked out books and chatted cheerfully, and she felt a little better and tried to settle back into the rhythm of her job without thinking about what Piers had said to her while they were making love. He called and left another voice mail message that she deleted without listening to it.

That night as she was washing dinner dishes, the doorbell buzzed. She wiped her hands on a towel and went to look through the peep-hole. Her heart did a 360. She opened the door.

"How did you get into the building?"

"One of your neighbors let me in," Piers said without smiling. "And it's nice to see you too."

Seeing him here, in the dingy hallway of her apartment building, still looking like he'd just stepped out of a magazine, was unreal.

"What are you doing here?"

"Why are you the only person in the country—and abroad, I'll add —who doesn't answer her phone?"

"I do answer my phone."

"Right. Just not when I call."

He understood. And he was angry. But if she closed the door on him now, if she ran away without explaining, she'd be just like her father.

"I got your note." She wouldn't tell him when. It didn't matter anyway. "Thank you for not leaving me wondering where you'd disappeared to."

"Once again offering you a consideration you didn't think to offer me in return."

"Piers." She had to do this now. "I told you it was just a kind of one-night stand. I made that clear."

"You did." His jaw looked like rock. "And you were wrong."

"I wasn't wrong. Don't you see? It's not going to work. This, between us, it's just not... *there*."

"It's not there?" He shook his head. "You, California Blake, are a flat-out liar. I know you want me."

"Even if I did in England, there's no way anything will ever come of it here." She tried to lighten her words with a shrug. "Why can't we just leave it as a great fling and go our own merry ways now?"

He didn't laugh. "Didn't you hear me the other night?"

She couldn't pretend to not know what he was talking about.

"We were having sex. Men say a lot of things they don't mean in those circumstances."

"Yeah?"

"Yes."

"I'm falling in love with you, California. No. Correction: It's a done deal. We're not having sex right now—unfortunately. So how are you going to explain it away this time?"

"I don't know." Panic was creeping up her throat. "Lust? Infatuation, maybe?"

"Right. Okay. How long do we need to see each other before you'll believe it's not just lust or infatuation?"

"What?"

"How long?"

"I don't know. Six months, maybe."

"Six months? Are you certain?"

"I don't know! Piers, come on. Be reasonable. This just isn't going to work. Why can't you accept that?"

"What in the hell are you afraid of?"

That she was already in love with him. But the sooner she ended this, the sooner she'd get over the heartbreak. Because whether he believed it now or not, it was going to end. And it wouldn't end prettily. It would start with her spending every dime she could spare on clothes and makeup so she wouldn't feel like she was embarrassing him when they went out. She'd struggle to keep up with his glittering lifestyle and she'd get resentful, and he'd get frustrated that she couldn't afford ski chalet wear or a new sexy dress for every gala. When his lust started to cool, he'd realize that slumming wasn't so much fun after all. He'd pull away, slowly and gently because he wasn't a jerk, bit by bit becoming less available. And she'd turn into the pathetic woman her mother had been, begging him to care about her, making scenes while he drifted farther back into his world of wealth and privilege.

She respected herself too much to do that. And she couldn't afford to descend into emotional ruin. Zoe needed her to be strong and capable.

"What's going through that brain?" he said. "I know you're trying to come up with an argument I can't refute."

She gripped the door and started to pull it closed. "I'd like you to go now."

"What if I don't?"

"I'll call the police. There've got to be one or two officers in this city who aren't on the Prescott family payroll."

"Nice. Really nice. Listen, tell yourself whatever you have to. I can't stop you from doing it. But I know you're too smart to actually believe it."

"I'm too smart to be as stupid as you expect me to be."

"Right." His hands flexed at his sides and she thought he was about to touch her, but he fisted them. "Okay. Bye, California." He turned away and went toward the elevator.

Hot, sticky panic swept through her.

"Piers."

He looked around. "Yeah?" His voice was tight.

"Will you stop funding the bookmobile now?"

"No," he said tonelessly. "I won't. But that you thought for even a moment that I might, I guess proves you right. At least on your part, there clearly isn't anything here." Without waiting for her response, he bypassed the elevator, pushed open the door to the stairs, and disappeared.

Numb, Cali went into the living room.

"Holy crap," Zoe said from the hallway, her eyes wide. "He's even hotter in person than in pictures."

Cali slumped onto the couch and covered her face with her hands. "Thanks. That really helps right now."

"Did I just hear you break up with him?"

"In order to break up with someone, you first have to be together with him."

"It sure sounded like he thinks you're together. Or were," Zoe amended.

"Did you listen to the entire conversation?"

"Like the part where he said, 'What in the hell are you afraid of?' Yes, I might have heard that."

Cali sucked back tears. Oh, God, it was happening. Crying again. Pain overtaking the numbness. The urge to run after him and beg him to want her, not just now but forever.

"Cali?"

"What?"

"What in the hell *are* you afraid of?"

She pressed the heels of her palms into her eyes. "Becoming Mom."

"But you're not Mom. You're strong and independent and much smarter than she was. And here's an idea: maybe Piers Prescott isn't Dad."

"I can't know that for sure." He'd said that she could never know for certain if he was playing her.

After a silence, Zoe said, "I'm going back to school. Online. Mrs. Fletcher's goddaughter gave her a computer and Wi-Fi for her birthday. She never uses it and says she wants me to. I'm starting the fall semester next week."

Cali sat straight up. "For counseling?"

Zoe nodded. "My PT says I have eighty-five percent mobility in my hands now, and I'm strong everywhere else too. Really strong."

"I know. But I didn't know if you knew."

"I'm so ready to get back to work. You're my inspiration." She cracked a grin. "If you can throw yourself into a tumultuous affair with a corporate shark for a week, I can reclaim my life."

"You're going to make a great high-school counselor, Zoe."

"Who better to give advice to screw-ups than somebody who's got plenty of screw-ups in her family? My sister excepted, of course."

*Not excepted.* "I screwed up this time." Hugely. She just didn't know if she'd screwed up worse nine days ago in England, when she'd decided to have a fling with Piers, or a few minutes ago in the hallway.

"Cali, while you were gone, I visited Dad."

No words. Disbelief.

"A few weeks ago he wrote and asked me to do a program with him for schools and community groups about addiction," Zoe said. "It's a special prison outreach project. I met with the organizers when I was there. They say that given how articulate he is, and how successful he once was, he's the ideal spokesperson—that he and I would be perfect together. And you know him. He thrives on attention, so he's excited about it."

"Zoe…"

"I want to do it, Cali." She took her hand and squeezed it. "I need to do it."

Cali looked into her sister's brutally scarred face and understood. Neither of them were their parents. They'd been through the fire. And they were stronger.

CALI CONSIDERED SENDING Piers a letter of apology about how she'd asked if he would cancel funding for the bookmobile. But she didn't. The cleaner the break, the better. If he thought badly of her, so be it.

The next morning she collected the van's keys from Security and set off. She made all the usual Tuesday stops, and tried not to wonder who exactly were his closest friends, and at which places he bought coffee or the paper.

At the end of the day, in the employee room, Dick mentioned almost casually that he was considering recommending to Cara that they keep Cali on the bookmobile. Then he put his hand on her ass. She kicked him in the shin and ran. But she was through with running, from herself or anyone else, including her mother's shadow.

Getting to work an hour before everybody else on Wednesday morning, she signed out a handheld video camera from the AV office and set it up in a locker in the employee lounge. After work, alone in the lounge, she swiftly turned on the camera then grabbed her purse, signed the bookmobile log, and tried to slip out quickly. Dick appeared at the door and blocked her exit. Then he jostled her against a locker and grabbed her breast. She pepper-sprayed him. Miraculously, it worked. He howled. Then he called her a nasty word and said he'd do her whether she wanted it or not.

She ran, vomited in a trashcan at the bus stop, and had to shower twice when she got home to get the feeling of him off her.

Early Thursday morning, she retrieved the camera from the locker and took it to the police station. She sat silently as a young woman officer and her older, male partner watched it. They handed her a box of Kleenex and a cup of coffee and took her statement.

By the end of the day, Dick had been arrested. And fired, Cara said the next morning when she called Cali into her office to apologize for not taking serious action against him before. Cara gave her a raise for protecting herself as well as the rest of the library's female staff, and she recommended that Cali get to work on a master's degree so she could move up to the position of librarian. Cali almost broke into hysterical laughter. She didn't. No reason to make a scene when she'd gotten what she wanted: Dick was gone.

But Piers wasn't.

When she pulled up to Green Park she nearly didn't get out of the van. She had to, of course. The meeting with Cara had gotten her off to a late start, and the kids from the daycare were already waiting. But her limbs wouldn't function.

Wearing the same hat, jeans, and half-laced work boots as usual, but without the chamois shirt over a T-shirt that now revealed his arms, Piers sat on his usual bench reading a paper. He didn't look up or acknowledge in any way that she had arrived.

She climbed out of the driver's seat on wobbly legs and went through the motions of chatting with the kids and their teachers and exchanging their books. They were extra excited to see her since she'd been gone the week before—in England making love to the multimillionaire sitting nearby, looking like a drug dealer. They gave her tight little hugs around her knees.

When Roy and Maggie appeared, Maggie gave her a cozy squeeze and Roy kissed the back of her hand. Masala showed up a few minutes later.

"Cali girl, did you meet Prince Charming and dance the night away on that trip like I told you to?"

She simply could not answer. She stared at Piers's hands holding the newspaper and had no rational thoughts. She told them about Jane's gown, the wedding ceremony, the cake, the band, and even the sumptuous breakfast on Sunday morning. She told them all about the party *after* Piers had flown away in his private jet. She couldn't manage to tell them anything else while he was within earshot.

At eleven o'clock, he folded his paper and left the park, as always— as always, before he'd doctored a rash on her butt with designer vodka and told her he was falling in love with her.

He didn't call or text.

By the following week, the leaves on the little tree in the center of Green Park had begun to turn gold. Piers was there again, still without his chamois shirt. She should never have admired his arms. He was doing this to torture her. For vengeance, probably. At eleven o'clock, again, he left without looking at her or speaking to her.

The temperature dropped abruptly and the next week the little tree was bare. So were Piers's biceps, despite the cold. Cali averted her gaze. She was dying to apologize to him for thinking he'd cut the bookmobile's funding. But she didn't understand the game he was playing now and she'd already cried over him plenty.

At five minutes before eleven she took a book from the front seat of the van and put it in Roy's hands.

"Would you please go over there and give this to him?" She pointed.

Roy's bushy gray brows flew up under his fedora. "You want me to give this book to *Junior*?" he practically shouted.

No movement of the *New York Times* in Piers's hands. But she didn't need him to react. Whatever he felt about her, whatever game he was playing, this time she was doing what she knew was right.

She nodded.

Roy looked down at the book. "But this here's a children's book." He frowned. "Men like Junior and me don't read children's books."

"Well, maybe he won't read it. But I'd still like you to give it to him."

Roy harrumphed, then started across the park. Cali jumped into the van and drove away. She knew she'd done the right thing, but that didn't mean she had the courage to see how he would take it.

The next week Piers was at the park when she arrived. He wore a faded Stanford sweatshirt and read the *Guardian Weekly*. On the bench beside him was the book she'd given Roy to give to him. Its broad, bright orange cover glowed in the autumn sunshine.

The start of the school year brought a teacher and her class from the nearby middle school to visit the bookmobile. Helping the daycare kids and a handful of other patrons, Cali kept busy. When eleven o'clock came and she looked around, Piers had already gone. He'd left the book she'd given him on the bench.

For the first time in the months that she'd been bringing the van to Green Park, she walked over to his bench and looked down. *Wild About Books* by Judy Sierra. A story about a mobile librarian's successful venture into uncharted territory.

She picked it up and turned to the final page. Her note was still tucked there.

*To the Anonymous Donor of the Bookmobile,*
*I'd forgotten to say it before: Thank you.*
*Very sincerely,*
*California Blake*

He'd left the book and the note. She didn't understand his game, but it clearly wasn't the one she'd half-hoped, half-feared he was playing.

She withdrew her note from the crease. Its opposite side was scrawled with his handwriting:

*Great book. A little beneath my reading level, though I appreciated the themes. Maybe something more sophisticated next time?*
*P.S. One month down. Five to go.*

One month down? What was happening in six months?
Her heartbeats jolted.
He couldn't... He *couldn't* mean what he'd said, what she'd said,

how in six months she would believe it wasn't only infatuation or lust between them. He couldn't possibly still be pursuing her, not from silently across the park once a week. That would be insane.

But everything about his pursuit of her from the start had been insane. And he liked to win. He was like no other man she'd ever met, and he made her smile and feel hot and tingly without even getting near her now.

She thought about the bookshelf in the library at Brampton, how she'd been so eager to touch an original edition of *Pride and Prejudice* that she'd gone against what she'd known—that it wouldn't even be on that shelf—and pressed her nose up against the clear plastic. Then everything had come falling down on top of her.

She'd survived that catastrophe. She'd gotten bruised, but eventually she'd touched that precious volume. She'd held it in her hands. Maybe to get what she wanted she had to learn to not fear catastrophes. She had to trust that maybe touching something wonderful was worth the potential for hurt.

The next week, in a whisper, she told her friends at Green Park who he was.

"Well, I coulda told you that," Roy scoffed. "I *said* he had the same name as his father, didn't I?"

Again, Piers didn't look at her or acknowledge her. Before she left the park she gave Roy another book for him, this time at his reading level: *The Grapes of Wrath* by John Steinbeck.

The note he left in it the following week read:

*Intriguing. Moving. Grim. The wrong guys won, clearly. Now, give me a good comedy...*

The next week she brought him Shakespeare's *Much Ado About Nothing*, which he returned with no note, instead adding a DVD of Joss Whedon's modern film version of it.

The next week, via Roy, she gave him Tolstoy's tragic romance *Anna Karenina*. Piers's reply the following week was succinct:

*I know this is considered one of the greatest novels of all time. But just no. And no.*

Cali rolled her eyes but she couldn't stop smiling.

The next week, she sent Roy to him with Milton's *Paradise Lost*. Seven days later, she sat on the bench in the spot Piers had just vacated and read his ten-page analysis on the themes of the idolatry of materialism and power, and the dangers of both hubris and the acquisition of forbidden knowledge. She was late for her second stop that day.

The next week, she put Paulo Coelho's *The Alchemist* into Roy's waiting hands. The Friday after that, on the piece of paper tucked into its final page, Piers had copied two lines from the book.

*She smiled, and that was certainly an omen — the omen he had been awaiting, without even knowing he was, for all his life.*
*"Don't give in to your fears," said the alchemist, in a strangely gentle voice. "If you do, you won't be able to talk to your heart."*

At home that night, she slipped the paper into her bed table drawer with the others.

A week later, she sent Roy to him with two nonfiction books: a book about burn victims and one about the children of alcoholics. The note Piers left on the bench with the books the following week made her eyes blur with tears.

*I understand. And I'm not him.*

The next week she handed Roy *Pride and Prejudice*. Not a library copy, but her own paperback with her name written on the title page in round teenager's script. The copy she'd read a dozen times.

As Roy walked over to Piers and Cali quickly locked up the back of the van, Masala said, "Cali girl, this is gettin' crazy."

"Why don't you just go over there and talk to the boy?" Maggie said.

Because he wasn't a boy and she really was in love with him now. If he was playing with her, the heartbreak was going to be worse than anything she had imagined.

On Monday, Piers appeared in the *Star* in a photo spread of a big society party he'd attended over the weekend. On his arm in the pictures was a beautiful professional tennis player. The captions speculated, "Gorgeous Piers Prescott and his new leading lady. Could our favorite native son have finally found The One?" Aching, Cali clutched the paper in numb fingers and knew that he wouldn't be at Green Park on Friday.

She went through the week distracted, her mind out of focus. But by Thursday she was already tired of that haze. Pining away didn't work for her. On Friday morning she styled her hair, put on a pair of skinny jeans, and dabbed on lip gloss. If Piers didn't want her, after work she'd go out somewhere fun and start looking for someone who did.

But when she reached the park and her sexy hat guy wasn't there, the ache returned ferociously. She told herself this was okay, natural. But she'd thought they would at least part on friendly terms. She'd never imagined he would just disappear.

Masala and Maggie met her the moment she stepped onto the sidewalk.

"Girl, you look good." Under canary yellow bangs, Masala's brow was worried.

Maggie wrung her hands. "Where is that boy today?"

"You both saw the pictures in the *Star*, too, didn't you?"

They nodded gravely, like they were at a funeral. Hers.

"How you doing, girl?" she thought Masala said, but demolition vehicles tearing down an abandoned crack house across the street drowned her out. A biplane engine overhead added to the clamor.

"Not great." *Devastated*. But not forever. She would get over him. Someday. And when her heart stopped hurting she would look on this little interval as a learning experience. Or something. Eventually. Maybe by the time she was eighty. "What's going on over there?"

"They're building a garden." Maggie tried to sound cheerful, but she darted another glance at Piers's empty bench.

A sign wired to the new chain link fence around the lot proclaimed

COMMUNITY GARDEN - COMING SOON, with an address two blocks away and a website where people could apply for a free plot. In smaller letters at the bottom was *P&P Enterprises, Inc.*

P&P Enterprises?

Cali shook her head. It was another sign, like the limo driver's sign at the airport, but this time a mystical one rather than a literal one. A sign that she'd gone too far in giving him *Pride and Prejudice*. It had finally woken him up to reality.

"It wasn't meant to be," she said.

Masala squinted and cupped her hand over her ear. A guy with a jackhammer was going at it on the demolition lot. A wrecking ball swung from its long chain toward one of the three remaining walls of the ruined building and crashed into it.

"That is a wrecking ball," Cali said dumbly.

"What's that, dear?" Maggie shouted above the biplane's engine.

"That building is like my love life. But I think that's all right."

"What's all right, girl?"

"Ugly old things like fear and doubt must come down"—a tractor revved up its engine—"in order for beautiful new things to grow," she shouted. "Like a garden." She pointed to the sign.

"What, dear?" Maggie called over the biplane.

"Oh, hell." Cali choked between a laugh and a sob. "I can't even hear myself trying to talk myself into forgetting that I'm in love with a man who's not in love with me after all."

Roy came to her side. "I got somethin' here for you," he called over the noise. "From Junior."

Cali's stomach turned over. It must be a final good-bye note. Things with his new girlfriend must be serious. Probably he figured it'd be less uncomfortable for them both if he ended this in writing rather than in person.

As if in sympathy with the funereal tenor of the moment, the construction noises abruptly stopped. Overhead, the biplane engine seemed farther away. She braced herself for the good-bye and looked down.

It wasn't a letter. It was a folded page of the *Wall Street Journal*. The heading across the top of the page read:

### Crown Prince of Prescott Global Resigns

Holding her breath, she read.

Piers had left his family's company, but he would continue on the board and still maintained a hefty share in the company that he'd held since his father went rogue and gave his shares to his son a decade earlier. The heir to the Prescott empire was, instead, turning his considerable business acumen to nonprofit urban renewal, starting with establishing community gardens and offering social services and job skills training in the neighborhoods where the people who needed them most lived. In six months, building would also begin on a second branch of Dr. John Vaughan Prescott's free medical clinic. The new nonprofit organization under which this work would be accomplished was P&P Enterprises.

Beneath the article were two words in Piers' handwriting: *Look up.*

"Look up?" she whispered. "Look up what?"

Roy tilted his head back. "Uh, Cali?" Maggie's eyes went round. Masala's lips split into a toothy smile.

Cali followed their attention upward. High above the Philadelphia skyline, on a backing of brilliant blue, a biplane was spelling out huge block letters in white smoke.

I CAN'T WAIT 6 MONTHS
  I LOVE YOU, CALIFORNIA BLAKE
  MARRY M

"The E's coming, girl."

But she didn't need the E, because Piers was walking across the street toward her. She put the paper in Maggie's hand and went to him.

"I know there's a lot to say," he said, coming close, his gaze scanning her face. "But it's been three unbearably long months of seeing you without being able to touch you. So first you've got to say I can kiss you."

"You can ki—"

Their mouths joined and fused together. He lifted her off her feet and held her tight.

"But—the pictures—in the *Star*—" she stuttered through kisses. "What about your girlfriend?"

"In my arms now, finally." He kissed her like he'd never stop.

She tore her lips away. "In the *Philadelphia Star*. The party you went to last weekend. Your date?"

He cupped a hand around her face. "My sister's roommate got dumped right before her big birthday bash. She's like a little sister to me. I did it as a favor. One last favor before I checked out of that scene forever." He kissed her again, fully and hard, reclaiming her entirely. "I have missed you unbelievably a lot."

"You've seen me every week." She smiled beneath his lips, running her hands down his back. "Just like before England."

"It was torture then too. But then I didn't know this flavor." He covered her lips with his and her need for him filled every part of her body. Her fingertips brushed a paperback sticking out of the back pocket of his jeans. He surrounded her hand, pulled the book out, and pressed it into her palm.

"*Pride and Prejudice.*"

"Good book." He nuzzled beneath her ear. "The guy got the girl he wanted in the end. That's my kind of story."

"She fell in love with him," she said. "She got rid of her prejudices."

"Seemed to me like she changed her mind after she saw that big-ass house of his."

She laughed. "I've never seen your house."

"I live in an apartment."

"P and P Enterprises?"

He smiled. "Has a nice ring to it, doesn't it?"

"It doesn't by any chance stand for Piers Prescott?"

"No, ma'am."

"You didn't just name your new company this week, after I gave you that book, did you?"

He shook his head.

Cali's throat was thick. "I don't know what to say."

He wrapped his arms around her. "The moment you gave me that speech in the rain, I knew I had to be the man you want."

"At the gazebo? When I thrashed your family for elitism?"

"Yeah."

"You're insane."

"I'm crazy about you, California. And I'm willing to do whatever it takes to make this work."

"Quitting Greed Incorporated is a good start."

"I've wanted to quit since my first day on the job. But I wouldn't have done it without your inspiration. Your contempt gave me the push I needed. Your honesty sealed the deal."

"I wasn't honest with how I felt about you. I was afraid of it."

"Not now?"

"Not now." Never again. "But there is something I need to tell you." A smile pulled at the corners of her mouth. "Before England, back when I didn't know you were you, I had a crush on the guy on the bench."

He laughed. "Not on Piers Prescott, though?"

"No. I thought he was a jerk."

"So it would've been better if I'd just come over one day and asked you out?"

"Yup."

"Damn. The time we lost. And all that money I could have saved on sending you to Jane and Duke's wedding."

He was teasing her. She loved him for laughing about it—at her, at himself, and at them together. Instead of pain and blame, all she felt was happiness.

"You could afford it, millionaire," she said.

He glanced up at the skywriting. "Minus what's currently floating away in smoke. I'd no idea how expensive hiring one of those is." He looked back down at her. "But it's no joke. I haven't lived on a fixed income in years."

"I have. A lot smaller than anything you'll ever have to worry about. You can hire me as your financial manager."

He kissed the tip of her nose. "I'll look forward to that."

Her cheeks ached from smiling. "Why the skywriting?"

"I know how you feel about the written word. And I didn't want you to doubt my intentions." His arms tightened around her. "When do I get an answer?"

"Hm…" She fiddled with the top button of his shirt. "Given that you didn't tell me who you were for three months, should I make you wait?"

His face got very sober. "You can make me wait as long as you need, California, as long as in the meantime you let me in."

"You're already in," she whispered.

He bent his head. "Come again? I didn't quite hear that," he said with a smile of thorough confidence. But his heartbeat beneath her palm was hard and very fast.

"I love you." Her eyes were misty. "Do you want me to write it in the sky now?"

"It's already written in the only place I need it." He touched the low neckline of her T-shirt. Right over her heart.

THAT NIGHT IN HIS APARTMENT, Piers undressed her and showed her again where and how he needed her love. He showed her with kisses and caresses and words, and Cali thought that maybe—just maybe—there was something better than books after all.

# AFTERWORD

The building in which Prescott Global occupies the top several floors doesn't exist, nor does Green Park. I loosely based the building on the tallest building in Philadelphia at the time of writing this novella, the fifty-eight-floor Comcast Center. The library at which Cali works is also fictional. With fifty-four branches, Philadelphia's actual public library, the Free Library of Philadelphia, is a wonderfully accessible institution with programs that serve the city's population in many ways, including a Homebound Service for patrons who can't leave their houses and a Tech Mobile unit that offers digital literacy training off-site.

For you sticklers, Christopher, patron saint of travelers, has been retired from the official calendar of saints venerated in the Catholic Church. But many people (Catholic and not) still look to him for comfort during difficult journeys.

I offer heartfelt thanks for assistance with this story to Georgie C. Brophy, Noah Redstone Brophy, Mariana Eyster, Jennifer Lohmann, Mary Brophy Marcus, Bob Steeger, Martha Trachtenberg, and my coauthors of this anthology, Caroline Linden, Miranda Neville, and Maya Rodale. Any mistakes in this novella are all me.

Stay tuned! Sexy ex-Marine J.T. Prescott's story is coming soon. For news of upcoming books, a free short story, and other fun stuff, sign up for my e-newsletter at www.katharineashe.com.

# ABOUT THE AUTHOR

Award-winning Katharine Ashe is the author of *How To Be a Proper Lady*, one of Amazon's 10 Best Books of 2012 in Romance, and eight more intensely lush romances set in the era of the British Empire and laced with adventure. Upon her debut in 2010 Katharine was honored with a spot among the American Library Association's "New Stars of Historical Romance," in 2011 she won the coveted Reviewers' Choice Award for Best Historical Romantic Adventure, and she has been nominated for the 2013 Library of Virginia Literary Award in Fiction.

Katharine lives in the wonderfully warm Southeast with her beloved husband, son, dog and a garden she likes to call romantic rather than unkempt. A professor of European History, she has made her home in California, Italy, France, and the northern United States. For more about her books and to read excerpts, please visit her at www.KatharineAshe.com.

# ALSO BY KATHARINE ASHE

# THAT MOMENT WHEN YOU FALL IN LOVE

MAYA RODALE

# CHAPTER
## ONE

*That moment when your date to the wedding of the year asks you to sell out the bride, who happens to be your best friend.*

*Brampton House, England*

O h, he did not just ask her that.

Roxanna Lane dropped her heavy suitcase with a thud on the gravel drive outside of the fancy old ancestral house. Mansion or castle could be fitting descriptions. Towering and imposing hunk of stone would work too.

She stared up a grand stone staircase to the grand stone castle. Jane would certainly be getting married in style.

They had only just arrived after a day of hellish, albeit first-class, travel. They hadn't even crossed the flipping threshold when the oh-so-dashing Damien Knightly, her sort-of date for the wedding, ruined everything. Everything.

"I hope you brought your laptop," he had murmured in his devastatingly sexy British accent.

"Never leave home without it," she replied "Why?"

"Just think of the stories you'll get for Jezebel from the events this week," he said with a sidelong glance and a spark in his eye. Bastard.

Roxanna wrote for Jezebel.com, a snarky website that combined feminist news with celebrity gossip and videos of cute baby animals. Damien Knightly, a roguish British aristocrat, owned the website, along with dozens of others, and some ancient newspapers, a TV station, and God only knew what else.

Their relationship ought to have been strictly professional. It was anything but.

Roxanna glanced at her Gentleman Friend. Manfriend. Boyfriend was too boyish a word for Knightly. Lover was too serious, though she sometimes thought he was too serious. Whatever he was or they were, the man made her tremble, feel girly, feel something like butterflies when no one else ever had. She wasn't sure how she felt about it.

At the moment, however, he was annoying her.

"I wasn't planning on writing any stories about the wedding," Roxanna told him.

He turned to face her, all of his noble, chiseled, gorgeous features assembled into an inscrutable expression. Then he merely lifted one brow. With just that, the question was conveyed perfectly: *I beg your pardon?*

Or, to translate into her own vernacular: *What the fuck?*

Roxanna could have been sly and lifted one brow back herself—it was a talent of hers that she employed to great effect. But she was tired. And hungry. And in no mood to talk business.

They had just flown from New York City to London for a few meetings, after which they had traveled for hours along windy, backcountry roads in his Aston Martin to get to Brampton House, scene of the epic wedding between her best friend and her billionaire tech entrepreneur fiancé.

On the way, they had stopped to help an old woman whose car had run out of "petrol." There hadn't been cell service, so Damien drove to the nearest town for help, leaving Roxanna to make small talk with the strange old woman for what seemed like an eternity. Finally, Damien had returned, saved the day, etc., etc. She had never admired him more than in that moment. But now she was more than ready to relax.

She turned to face him, eyes blazing.

"Do you honestly think I'm going to do gossipy, snarky stories on my best friend's wedding?"

"Have you known me to be the sort to jest?"

Roxanna might have cracked a smile had she been in a better mood. Her whatever-he-was was so aloof and broody. She *delighted* in acting outrageously to get a reaction out of him. But right now, she really wanted to get into their room, shower and change, then relax with a cocktail.

*Where was the concierge? Or bellhop? A footman? Anyone?*

"I have not known you to jest," she said, mimicking his accent. "I can't imagine you would ask me to sell out my best friend and her fiancé. Honestly. I just couldn't fathom what kind of heartless bastard would do such a thing."

"Who else will have access to the bachelorette party stories and photographs?" Damien asked, missing the point entirely.

"You are so uninvited to that," she mumbled. "If you were ever invited to that."

*Where was a staff member?*

Finally, Roxanna picked up her suitcase, stomped up the stairs, and pushed open the front door. The foyer was vast and rocking a ton of marble and gold leaf. It was also empty. There was no one to show them to their room. Maybe they could just bunk up in the first one they came across?

Roxanna started toward the grand staircase.

Damien caught up with her and took her suitcase like a gentleman.

"It's just a story," Damien said. For some reason he was still talking about this.

Before she could answer, another voice cut in.

"Can I help you?" Roxanna turned and saw an Armani model strolling across the foyer. *Yes you can,* she thought, with a wicked upturn of her lips. "I'm Mark, the manager of Brampton."

"We're here for the wedding," Damien said and he smoothly handled all the check-in details and small talk.

"Is it five o'clock yet?" Roxanna asked no one in particular. "Because I could use a drink."

"What sort of drink would you fancy?" asked Handsome Mark. She decided she liked him.

"Perhaps you might show us to our rooms and we'll freshen up first," Damien said. "Then this spitfire of a woman would like a tumbler of your most expensive whiskey."

"Charge it to this guy," she said sarcastically, with a nod in Damien's direction, even though Jane and Duke were paying for everything. "That's why I brought him."

THEY WERE SHOWN to a room that had been recently renovated and had the fresh paint smell to prove it. Jane had been a super stressed-out bride, wanting everything to be perfect for her big wedding. It didn't help that she chose Brampton House, which was still under renovation, while she was trying to plan every last detail … or that she'd been planning from another continent while trying to write books on deadline and keep up with her job at the New York Public Library.

Thank God she had Arwen Kilpatrick as her wedding planner to coordinate all the logistics and to act interested when Jane waffled over floral arrangements, cake styles, seating arrangements, and a billion other little details that strengthened Roxanna's intention to elope, if she ever married.

Damien began to unpack while she started stripping off her clothes, first kicking off her Charlotte Olympia flats and tossing her whisper-thin cashmere scarf on the bed.

"I mean it, Damien. I won't sell out my friend," Roxanna said, pulling her silky soft gray James Perse T-shirt off and tossing it on the floor. He glanced at it, obviously dying to pick it up—he was such a neat freak—but then his gaze settled on her breasts, clad in a pink lace bra that was a naughty mixture of debauchery with a hint of innocence.

"Is that so? Tell me why," he said.

"She's my *friend*."

Roxanna wriggled out of her skinny jeans. A grin tugged at his lips. He was not focusing on their conversation at all.

"Your point being …"

"You don't have friends, do you?" Roxanna said, standing before him in just her bra and undies. He was obviously distracted by her *lack of attire*, as Jane might say in one of her delicately worded historical novels. Roxanna would say tits and ass. Either way, she was having a freaking insight about her Gentleman Friend / Lover / Boss and she was never shy about sharing. "You have business associates, contacts, a network, you never lack for company for drinks or dinner. But you don't have a guy who you can just kick back, have a beer, watch the game, and bitch about women with."

"With *whom* you can kick back, have a beer, watch the game, and bitch about women," Damien corrected.

"Whatever."

"Said the writer. None of those activities appeal to me," he said with a shrug. "Except for one."

"Bitching about women."

"Beer."

Roxanna laughed and strolled into the bathroom. She turned the shower on, stripped off her lingerie and stepped into the steaming hot water, careful not to get her hair wet and ruin her blow-out. Ahhh. Bliss.

Damien followed her in, watching her. God, she loved his eyes on her. He was not at all aloof or inscrutable when he was looking at her. His expression had darkened considerably. The man's gaze positively set her on fire in a really, really good way.

"I understand," he said. "I do. But something has come up and let's just say if it weren't for this one reason, I would never ask this of you."

"What is this mysterious serious reason?"

"I can't say," he said softly.

"Then I can't do it."

"What if this is an order from your boss?"

She did, often, enjoy orders from her boss. Just not at work. And not for this. Not when it involved Jane, who was so freaking sensitive, and would be devastated by a betrayal from her maid of honor.

"Jane is my friend. She's had enough of her romance splashed across the Internet. This is her big day and she doesn't need grainy iPhone photos of her puking at her bachelorette party all over the interwebs."

"And why was her romance splashed across the Internet to begin with?"

"Touché."

On that high note, Damien returned to the bedroom.

Roxanna might have launched Duke and Jane's entire relationship with a prank post to Jane's Facebook page declaring that she and the guy she'd met but once were engaged. A sham engagement ensued (naturally), followed by real love ... and now this wedding. Because so much of their relationship had been conducted online—as will happen when you fall in love with a famous tech entrepreneur—Jane was desperate to keep their wedding as offline as possible. Guests would be asked to leave their phones in their rooms for the events this week and it was requested that guests keep the location and all details secret.

No way could Roxanna be the one to share intimate details of the wedding. Not for her boss, or her boyfriend, or whatever he was.

She turned off the shower, dried off, and started rummaging through her luggage for underthings and a dress. She slipped on a matching bra and undies made of an insanely delicate black lace under a slinky navy blue wrap dress. Damien was frowning at his computer and glaring at his phone.

"There's no bloody Internet or cell reception."

"Oh God, that's terrible." In this, she was not jesting. Jane was marrying Duke Austen, a billionaire tech entrepreneur who lived and breathed via the World Wide Web. Thus, so did many of the guests. Including her. And Damien. There would be a swarm of angry people suffering from Twitter and e-mail withdrawal. Hardly festive.

There was one plus to this, though ...

"Guess I can't do the story, then! Wah wah!"

"What about the dress?" Damien asked.

"I am not leaking pictures of the dress!" God, she wanted to smack some sense into the man. "Duke will see and everyone knows that's bad luck."

"No, I mean *your* dress," he said. "Off with it."

"Gawd, listen to you. All haughty British aristocrat, giving orders," she retorted, but there wasn't much fire in her reply. The man made her positively weak in the knees when he did that.

"That's right," he murmured. "Impertinent American."

He had that look in his eye: like he had all sorts of wicked intentions and Would Not Be Stopped from executing his plans. She never thought she was the nervous, feeling butterflies kind of girl. But when he looked at her like that ...

When he crossed the room, all towering male and totally determined ...

When he slid his arm around her waist and gave her the most devastating smile that promised all sorts of trouble ...

"I know you happen to have a thing for impertinent Americans," she murmured, wrapping her arms around him and savoring the feeling of his hard body against hers.

"I also have a thing for providing exclusive and original content to millions of readers, to whom I also deliver millions of dollars in advertising, all for a nice, big bottom line."

His hand playfully swatted her ass. She scowled.

"I love it when you talk business to me," she said dryly.

"This isn't some new facet of my personality, Roxanna. I believe it's been widely reported. In fact, I know you're intimately acquainted with my ... personality."

"You don't need this story," she protested. "Your sites are performing well. You have money to burn. So why?"

He turned away, glancing out the window at the green lawns and blue skies beyond. This was a man who always looked you in the eye, who never shied away from anything. She had once seen him face down a would-be mugger on the Lower East Side with nothing more than his steely gaze.

"I can't tell you," he said.

"Oh?" And now she did lift one brow. "The plot thickens."

"There's no plot," he said, pushing his fingers through his hair. "There you go with your imagination again."

"My friend is the one who has the imagination. I just detect bullshit. You are up to no good, Knightly. Spill."

"To a known gossip like you?"

"I've kept *our* secret. So far."

What with him being the owner and CEO of the company for which she was just a writer, she supposed she ought to think of him as her *secret* Gentleman Friend or *secret* Manfriend or *secret* lover.

"I can't tell you this. But I need stories on Jane and Duke's wedding. With pictures."

"Why don't you take them?"

"Because I'm not as close to Jane and Duke as you are, which means I can't get as close. But if I have to, I will. I'll send awful iPhone photos to that woman in your office with whom you have a rivalry. What was her name …?"

"That Bitch Karen."

Not That Bitch or Karen but *That Bitch Karen*. She had once published a story outing Jane as the author of her novels, and insinuating that they were based on Duke (which they were), which caused tons of trouble for him, since his investors wanted news of his private life *out* of the media and reports of his company on the front pages. The whole thing almost broke them up.

Damien paced around the room, loosening his tie, and rolling up his sleeves. She could see that he was coming undone.

There was a haunted look in his eye. Her smooth, debonair man was *troubled* by something and she felt out of her depth, not knowing what to say or do.

"I am desperate, Roxanna. I need the story."

"Or else?"

"Or else …"

He strode toward her and pulled her close, flush up against his hard abs and chest. Her face tilted up to his as he lowered his mouth to hers for the sort of kiss that was an intimate promise of more for later.

*God, is it later yet?*

It wasn't. And he was just avoiding all her questions. She couldn't help him if he wouldn't confide in her. She wouldn't expose her friend for the guy she was just dating.

They were just dating. On the DL. Secretly. Nothing serious.

For the first time that irked her.

"I won't do it," she said, breaking away. Jane had made her

promise *no more meddling*. No more online shit. No more borrowing phones, or surprise Facebook updates. No Tweets, or Pins, or Instagrams. She didn't want the details of her special day leaked all over the world for strangers and crazy ex-boyfriends to find out about. This was Jane's wedding to her real-life romance hero, and she wanted it to be private.

Damien frowned. "I'm sorry Roxanna, but then I'll have to find someone else who will."

"Are you joking?" She had to ask, anyway. Again.

"You keep asking me that," he said half impatiently, half laughing.

She wasn't finding this funny at all. To demonstrate it, she grabbed his loosened tie in her fist and growled, "I won't let you publish anything about this wedding."

"Is that a challenge, Ms. Lane?"

She gave him her most seductive smile and said, breathlessly, "Oh, yes it is, Mr. Knightly."

# CHAPTER
## TWO

*That moment when you want to rip off your girlfriend's dress and make love
to her, but have to make small talk with strangers.*

*On the terrace*

Roxanna had put on some slinky blue dress that made him deeply
regret the need to socialize with the other guests on the terrace.
He wanted to take her back to the room, strip the dress off, lay
her down on the bed, and make love to her until they were completely and
utterly spent in a tangle of sweaty limbs and gasping for breath.

Damien schooled his features into the sort of cool, aloof expression
befitting a ridiculously wealthy aristocrat, but inside he was churning.
He wanted her intensely, but she was angry with him. Without this
story, he was screwed.

It occurred to him, as he sipped a much-needed drink, that he'd
been counting on her to save him from the stupid, catastrophic situation he found himself in. But it seemed now that he would lose her if
he went ahead with the story, somehow. Or he would lose the only
other thing he cared about in the world.

Damien Knightly was not accustomed to losing.

He watched her slink across the terrace— pausing to toss a coy smile over her shoulder at him. She accepted a glass of champagne from a passing waiter and went off to greet Jane. They did their girlish hellos—lots of hugs and laughter as if they'd been parted for months instead of days.

Damien hardly knew Jane. She was Roxanna's best friend, roommate and a novelist who wrote some sort of smutty books about English lords and whatnot. He was better friends with the groom, Duke Austen. Although *friends* might be a stretch. They did business together and socialized together frequently, though they never kicked back with beers to watch a game and bitch about women. Still, Damien entertained the idea of reporting on his wedding. He had to.

The story of the billionaire tech guy and the romance novelist who based her books on him was too rich for any news outlet to resist. Someone was going to do it. Might as well be someone who could control the story and images instead of some scummy paparazzo taking grainy shots from the bushes on behalf of, say, *The Daily Post*, which was the most tawdry, salacious publication, barely a step above the rubbish handed out free in the Underground.

Damien's brooding was interrupted by another guest—a gentleman he could identify with, given the man's expensive suit.

"How do you know the couple?" the expensive suit asked him.

"I'm an acquaintance of the groom," Damien replied. Then he added, so that Expensive Suit wouldn't get any ideas about her, "And I'm with the maid of honor."

He didn't know what he and Roxanna were. Girlfriend wasn't quite the right word. It was *too girly* for her. He was embarrassed that the phrase *woman friend* even crossed his mind. He was probably physically incapable of uttering such rubbish. *Lover* was just too ridiculous. She was just … his *Something*.

The bride would probably have the perfect phrase, but he would die a thousand deaths before asking her. Obviously.

"Friend of the groom as well," the Suit replied. "We were roommates at Stanford before Duke dropped out."

"The stories you must have to tell," Damien said, with a grin. Maybe he would get this story even if she wouldn't.

"You wouldn't believe what that guy got up to," he said with a laugh. "Let's just say they didn't call him the bad boy billionaire for nothing. I can't sell out a friend, though. At least, not without more to drink." Damien was about to offer to get them both another round when he introduced himself. "I'm Piers Prescott, by the way."

"Knightly. Damien Knightly."

"You don't sound American—British?"

"Yes. I divide my time between London and New York. Where are you traveling from?"

"Philadelphia."

Damien noted that his gaze settled on one of the girls standing in a circle with Jane and Roxanna. He probably had plans to sleep with her, because that is what one did at weddings—drank excessive quantities of champagne and sought out someone for a one-night stand to regret in the morning.

Such a bracing lack of romanticism was required as an antidote to the sappiness of weddings.

Like any British gentleman, he had a severe aversion to the sentimental, emotional, or anything that might be deemed a feeling.

Like gentlemen, he and Piers made the rounds on the terrace, chatting with all the other guests. They met Duke's lawyer, Archer Quinn, who mentioned having work to do on the trip. Another guest asked if it was about the *People* magazine deal, to which Archer replied, "No comment."

If it was what Damien suspected it to be, a deal with a magazine could only complicate things for him more. He just sipped his drink, feeling the slow, hot burn of regret as the whiskey went down. He didn't want to sell out his friends or wreck his *Something* with Roxanna. But he wasn't keen to lose a precious family heirloom either.

The conversations continued with other wedding guests—there were lots of young, severely underdressed software developers and the pretty young women they were ogling.

But he only had eyes for Roxanna. That minx was slowly threading her way through the crowd toward him. Their gazes locked. His drifted to her perfect pout of a mouth, then lower. He had perfected the cool exterior. But he had not been able to tamp down the flames he felt inside whenever she was near.

Roxanna leaned in close to whisper in his ear, a rush of air stealing across his skin as she spoke: "I won't put out unless you tell me why you need this story."

He breathed in deeply, inhaling that scent that was just *her* and that went to his head. And he said in a low rumble: "And I will not 'put out' as you Americans so crudely put it, until you write the story."

"This is going to be a long week," she lamented, tracing her fingertips down the lapel of his bespoke suit. In her other hand, a nearly empty champagne glass dangled precariously.

"Do we need separate rooms?" He didn't mean it.

"Oh hell no," she said in a low, throaty voice that made him aroused. "Keep your friends close and your enemies closer. You may retire to the floor if you find you are unable to restrain yourself from my gorgeous self."

Roxanna Lane was everything he wanted in a woman: beautiful and bold, passionate, fiercely intelligent, outspoken, and not cowed by his aloof demeanor.

They had met when they were stuck in an elevator together at the Jezebel offices. Instead of spending the time fuming about being late for a meeting, or taking the opportunity to return calls and answer e-mails, Roxanna had had him laughing, sparring, and regretting the installation of security cameras.

A series of "accidental" encounters and casual invitations ensued. Then he began to pursue her in earnest.

She made him break all his rules about separating business and pleasure and about separating pleasure and emotions.

Which is why he hated to ask her to do this story. But there was only one thing that mattered to him more than *anything* and it was on the line.

# CHAPTER
# THREE

*That moment when you admit you like a boy.*

*The bride's bedchamber*
*Two days later*

The bride twirled around in her utterly gorgeous and obscenely expensive wedding gown, with layers of chiffon and lace and pure loveliness swirling all around her. Roxanna lounged on the bed, drumming her red manicured nails on her lips as she watched Jane admire her own reflection in the mirror: a young woman in a rapturously perfect Monique Lhuillier dress … with her hair in a sloppy ponytail and a seamstress named Abby at her feet, making the final alterations to the hem—or trying to.

"I just love this dress," Jane gushed.

"It is the perfect dress," Roxanna agreed. It wasn't her style, but it fit Jane to perfection, with all the delicate layers and romantic flourishes.

"I can't wait for everyone to see it," Jane gushed with a dreamy look in her eye. "Especially Duke."

"About that …" Roxanna began, sitting up. She'd been walking around for two days wondering why Damien needed the story, what he wasn't telling her, and what the hell she was going to do about it. She'd thought about confiding in Jane, but she seemed so happy and busy with wedding things. So Roxanna had kept it a secret. If there was a greater torture, she couldn't imagine it. Now she couldn't hold it in any longer.

In the mirror, Jane looked nervous.

"So my mysterious millionaire lover wants me to sell you out. He wants me to write up snarky stories on your wedding and leak all kinds of pictures of your dress and you barfing at your bachelorette party."

Jane looked horrified. And then solemn.

"If you agreed to this, you will no longer be my maid of honor."

"Way to give me a reason to do it, Jane. Jeez," Roxanna said sarcastically. She wasn't exactly the bridal party type of girl, especially after being a bridesmaid in her sister's wedding. But Jane was different and Roxanna was happy to be her maid of honor.

"Roxanna!"

"Of course I refused."

"You're the best." Jane beamed.

"I know," she replied, a bit morosely.

"But …" Jane prompted, as if sensing *more*. And indeed there was more.

"He says he *needs* the stories for a reason that he will not share. I'm going crazy imagining why he could possibly need a picture of you barfing at your bachelorette party."

"Can we please stop talking about me casting up my accounts?" Jane said, slipping into what she called "Regency-speak," aka the language of the historical romance novels she wrote. "And if that's what you have planned for my hen party, then we need to have a serious conversation."

Roxanna stared at her blankly: "I was supposed to plan your hen party?"

"Roxanna!"

"I'm kidding!" she said, laughing. "Of course I have something fabulous planned."

"No strippers! Swear to me on your iPhone."

"By the way, what's with having no cell or Internet service here? WTF? I'm going crazy without it and exhausted from walking up to the gazebo for cell service every time I want to check my email."

"I am *well* aware," Jane huffed, her cheeks turning bright pink. "Duke suggested relocating the wedding back to New York, after all the planning and everyone flying in!" A nerve. This had obviously hit a nerve. The lack of Internet was all anyone could talk about so far, including Jane. "It's not that there isn't any Internet. You can get online at the gazebo. It's just slow. And frankly, I don't see why people cannot put down their phones for a few days and enjoy this beautiful house and grounds and *my wedding day*."

"Take a deep breath, Jane."

"Besides, you know we don't want word to get out about the wedding location, especially any pictures. I'm quite happy if people aren't able to Instagram or whatever the kids do these days."

There was no way in hell Roxanna was going to do the story Damien requested.

"Well, it's just like your novels," Roxanna said diplomatically, even though she was dying to check Twitter.

"That's what I said. It's romantic." Jane smiled happily at herself in the mirror.

"Anyway, this lack of Internet is buying me some time with this story, which I am *not* doing. But Damien has some Secret Reason. Aren't you just dying of curiosity?"

"No. I'm worried about a video of me getting a lap dance from a hulking male stripper showing up online."

"I promise I won't let that happen."

"Thank you."

"At least, I won't record it," she said with a grin.

"Roxanna!"

"Just kidding, Bridezilla!" Roxanna said. "But seriously, what am I going to do, Jane?"

This time Roxanna sighed dramatically. For extra emphasis, she flung herself back on the supremely comfortable bed and stared at the detailed crown molding on the ceiling.

"Well, I'm wondering if I should confiscate your phone," Jane said, looking nervous again.

"That will not be necessary. Hos before bros."

"That is so crass."

"But the sentiment is sweet," Roxanna replied. "At any rate, I'm *not* selling out my friend for my whatever-he-is."

"Your mysterious millionaire lover. Dashing paramour. Sinfully seductive Rogue. Lord of Your Heart." Jane went on and on with her names while Roxanna made gagging noises. But then she said something that made Roxanna's heart stop for a second. "But if you love him, you have to do it."

"Um, what are you talking about?"

She tried to sound all confused and sarcastic. But jeez, her insides had a violent reaction to the L-Word. All quivering with excitement, or something like that. How embarrassing.

"If your *Whatever* with him is going to become *Something*, then you have to show that you love him above anyone else. Including me."

"I'm not giving up my dignity and selling out my best friend to show him that I lo—have romantic inclinations in his general direction."

"You need to find a way for you both to win. And me. I don't want wedding pictures leaked. We're working on a deal to sell them to *People* in exchange for a donation to Little Paws Rescue. Think of the puppies and kittens, Roxanna."

She did think of the puppies and kittens: little warm, soft, and squirmy balls of fluff that would never ask you to sell out your best friend and would snuggle up and lick your face.

"OMG, this is torture. *Torture.*" Roxanna smacked the mattress. "The question is: do we think his Secret Reason is more deserving than homeless puppies and kittens?"

"If he thinks it's a valid reason, then it probably is. I've only met the man for, like, ten minutes but he doesn't seem the kind to care about stupid, frivolous stuff. We have to find a win-win situation."

"You are such a hopelessly optimistic romantic," Roxanna said. "I don't know how we're friends."

"And yet we are *the best* of friends."

"The very bestest," Roxanna said.

Jane didn't reply for a moment. She bit her lip and scrunched up her face as she did when she was deep in thought. Finally, the bride spoke.

"Abby, is there a bridal shop nearby?"

"Are you having second thoughts about this beautiful dress? You certainly won't find anything this fine around here. There's Oldwart's Bridal Shoppe in Melbury, but … Well, it's not Monique Lhuillier."

"Jane, have you finally gone mad?"

"No," she said, with a wide grin and a mischievous sparkle in her eyes. "I have just come up with a scheme for everyone to have their happily ever after."

*A top-secret meeting in the butler's pantry (with the door closed)*

"WE NEED to stage fake wedding dress photos," Jane told the impossibly handsome and outrageously gay concierge, Mark. She, Roxanna, Cali—the other bridesmaid and Jane's best friend from college—and he were packed into the small space to have a confidential conversation.

To his credit, Mark didn't even bat one of his ridiculously long eyelashes.

"Of course," he murmured.

"Roxanna must do a story on our wedding, leaking all the details or else Something Bad Will Happen to Damien Knightly," Jane said in a grave tone.

"Oh my God, what?" Cali asked in a whisper.

"We don't know," Jane answered gravely. "But we believe that Damien is not the sort of man who would do something like this without an excellent reason."

"He isn't. And there is an excellent reason, he just won't tell me what it is," Roxanna said.

There were things he talked about: business, his family, what he was thinking, books, movies, and all that sort of thing. They did not talk about feelings, or their "relationship," or This Big Secret Reason. Yet.

Perhaps she would get him drunk and seduce the answer out of him.

Or hold the story hostage until he confided in her.

Or just go ahead with Jane's insane plan.

"Knightly, the impossibly handsome and distinguished and actual peer of the realm with whom you have arrived?"

He never used his title, saying they were outmoded, but Knightly was actually Lord Northbourne, which delighted Jane endlessly but wasn't a huge deal for Roxanna.

"Yeah, that guy," Roxanna said.

"You must like him," Mark said. "I don't see how anyone could resist him."

"Whatever," Roxanna said with a shrug.

"He makes you feel *whatever?*" Cali asked incredulously.

"You want me to help stage fake wedding dress pictures just four days before the real wedding for a guy who makes you feel *whatever?*" Mark chided, not quite believing that she cared so little.

"Roxanna has a very colorful vocabulary," Jane explained. "But it is woefully deficient in words and phrases with which one might communicate their innermost feelings, particularly of the romantic variety."

Everyone crammed into the butler's pantry looked at Roxanna expectantly.

There was nowhere to hide, but she looked anyway. Nope, no way out.

"Fine!" Roxanna exclaimed. "He makes me feel all the feelings."

"It's also for the puppies and the kittens," Jane added.

"So we need photographs of the bride in a fake wedding dress and holding a fake bouquet so you can leak the fake pictures just days before your actual, already-planned wedding while there is essentially no Internet access," Mark said. "This shouldn't be a problem at all."

"Thank you, Mark!"

"Of course. I know exactly where to begin. Don't worry, Jane. This is your day."

"And now it's my *days!*" Jane exclaimed.

Roxanna and Cali shared pained smiles.

*Up to no good in Oldwart's Bridal Shoppe*

GETTING to Oldwart's Bridal Shoppe was almost more difficult than getting to Brampton House from New York City. After their conversation with Mark, they had to escape a conversation with Jane's mom, who was already asking about grandchildren, Duke wanted to talk about "the Wi-Fi situation," and one of Jane's aunts couldn't find her daughter, Kimberly, who was probably out hooking up with one of the developers.

Everyone wanted to chat with the bride. They also wanted to know why the three of them had ensconced themselves in the butler's pantry when there was a whole house of properly sized rooms.

"Just planning a little surprise for Duke," Jane said, smiling.

"A secret surprise," Roxanna said.

"One that isn't an outrageous last-minute request at all," Cali said.

"I can't wait," Duke said.

"You can tell me, darling!" Jane's mom, Miranda, exclaimed. "Especially if it's about grandbabies!"

"Not right now, Mom. You'll see!" Jane said. "Mark, could you bring a car around for us?"

"Anything for the bride," he murmured. "I'll have George come around with the Rolls-Royce."

"I'll never tire of hearing that," Jane sighed, smiling.

Roxanna and Cali exchanged tight smiles.

The car slowly cruised out of the gates of Brampton House.

"No paparazzi! Phew!" Jane exclaimed. "I heard rumors some guy with a camera was lurking around. It's been a nightmare keeping the location secret from the media."

"The things you do for the puppies and kittens," Cali said. "It's so sweet."

George took the back way and drove slowly down the insanely narrow, winding roads.

Finally, they arrived at a small shop on the High Street of a town that could be best described as Ye Olde English Village.

Oldwart's Bridal Shoppe was exactly as one might imagine it: small, dusty, and lit with the kind of fluorescent lighting that would make a supermodel look bad. Dresses—dozens and dozens of hideous dresses—were stuffed on racks lining the walls. It was a far cry from the sleek, Spartan boutique in Manhattan where Jane had bought her actual dress.

"I don't suppose this place is going to serve champagne while you try on dresses," Roxanna murmured, as a surly teenage girl with loads of heavy black eyeliner gazed up at them from her perch behind the counter.

"Doubtful," Jane agreed.

"You need *this* dress," Cali said, pulling one off the rack. "It's just like the one you taped on the mirror in your freshman year dorm room."

"Let's just say my tastes have changed," Jane said, eyeing the white poof with something like horror. "In both men and dresses."

"Let's just say thank God for that. That thing is the epitome of awful."

"If you think that's bad, wait until you see this one," the salesgirl said, reaching for a champagne-colored gown with a lot of lace and beadwork and ruffles. A lot.

"What are you waiting for, Bride? Go try some dresses on!"

Jane disappeared into the dressing room and emerged a few moments later in an explosion of satin ruffles and sequins.

"Oh no, you can't laugh," Roxanna said. "We need pictures of you beaming because you have finally found The One Dress."

"I'm dying. I need to laugh."

Cali just shook her head no. "This is serious, Jane. Even though you look like a cupcake, you cannot laugh."

"A cupcake who is also is a stripper in Vegas."

"OMG I can't even breathe," Jane said in a strangled trying-to-suppress-laughter voice.

"Smile for the cameras, Jane," Roxanna chirped as she pulled out her iPhone and started clicking away.

"I think I need another dress," Jane said.

"Try this," Cali said, grinning as she handed over another fashion disaster. Masses of white feathers covered a full, A-line skirt. The bodice was swathed in lace and decked in sequins. It was a bit excessive.

"You were not kidding about your ugly decoy wedding dress," Roxanna said, eyeing the dress that was not only ugly, but unflattering on Jane. "These pictures are going to be something else."

"I will not have my big day ruined. I will not have it," Jane said, quite possibly stamping her foot underneath that voluminous mass of fabric and feathers. A few feathers floated off the skirt, into the air, swaying gently to the floor. "But I have also never seen you so into a guy who is actually worthy of you."

*Ah, back to that.*

"He asked me to report on your wedding," Roxanna said. "Is that really worthy?"

"But he said he had a good reason," Jane replied.

"That's what he *said* ..."

"And I've seen that he's made you super happy for the past few months. Taking you on proper dates instead of just meeting up for drinks. He invites you over to spend the night at his grown-up apartment, not to crash at a place he shares with a bunch of guys in some far-flung neighborhood of Brooklyn that is only accessible by the G train."

So that's what made an eligible bachelor these days. Dinner dates and a grown-up apartment near the subway.

"It's just the sex," Roxanna replied. She suddenly developed an intense interest in the collection of veils on display. Who knew there were so many different styles? Who knew they could all be so ugly?

"It's never just the sex," Jane insisted. "I've caught you whistling merry tunes while you do your makeup before work."

"I do not whistle merry tunes," Roxanna muttered. Wow, this veil was lined in white satin and this one was studded with little rhinestones.

"It's okay to like a guy, you know," Jane said.

"Said the romance novelist. And bride."

"Her mind has always been clouded with romance," Cali chimed in. "She's been insufferable about it since forever."

"One of us has to be romantic!" Jane protested adorably.

She was just so nice, and proper and optimistic about everything. At first, Roxanna wasn't sure they would make good roommates when Jane answered her Craigslist ad, but now she couldn't imagine the apartment without her. Fuck, she would be leaving soon!

"I do like him. I *really* like him. He does make me feel all the feelings. But I also like things just the way they are. Not too serious. Not too much pressure."

"He's not like Josh," Jane said softly.

Josh was her college boyfriend who had somehow managed to slowly smother her spark, which was remarkable, given that she was a pretty sparky girl. But once she broke up with him and moved to New York City, Roxanna became downright fiery. She had vowed never to let another person dull her spark again. To her, that meant never letting anyone get close enough to do so.

"I know," Roxanna sighed. "Damien is different."

"You should fight for your true love," Jane said earnestly.

*True love?* Jeez, she'd only been having a thing with the guy for a few months now.

"I think you've been reading too many romance novels again," Roxanna said. But there it was again: that weird flutter in her stomach at the thought of the L-word.

"If you don't love him, tell me now. This fabric is starting to itch and I want to take this hideous dress off. But if you do love him, get your phone out and start taking pictures."

Roxanna exchanged a glance with Cali. Then she got out her phone.

They had a hysterical time trying on a few more dresses and taking pictures that were purposely askew, as if they'd been taken surreptitiously. Then Jane bought one to carry out so they could also take pictures of the bride picking up her dress and so they could get more pictures of her wearing it at the house. It was perfect: Damien would get his story, Jane would keep her privacy, and the puppies and kittens wouldn't be deprived of their donation from *People* magazine.

On the way back to Brampton, Roxanna whistled a merry tune and thought perhaps there was such a thing as happily-ever-after.

# CHAPTER
## FOUR

*That moment when your plan goes totally wrong.*

*At the gazebo*
*Later that afternoon*

Roxanna found Damien at the gazebo, the one place on the estate that had cell reception. As a result, many of the guests had congregated there to make phone calls and check their e-mail, Twitter, and whatever else they were desperate to do online. The wedding planner had thoughtfully provided places to sit, small bites, and splits of champagne.

There was a faint Wi-Fi signal emanating from someplace at the edge of the property. Archer Quinn, Duke's lawyer, had gone to investigate and hadn't been heard from in some time. He was either dead or had found Wi-Fi and Damien thought it was worth risking the former for the latter.

Damien leaned against the balustrade of the gazebo, gazed at his phone and fixated on the weak cell service quite a few people were all trying to use. Going through his e-mails was slow, painfully so, and made him almost want to give up and chuck his phone off into the bushes.

Not one of his e-mails was from Roxanna, explaining what she had been doing all day. He had woken up alone and annoyed to be alone. It was almost worrying that he hadn't seen her here until this late in the day. The sun was just setting when he saw her strolling up the path, hips swaying with every step.

"Fancy meeting you here," Roxanna said coyly upon arrival. "How has your day been?"

"A vicious fight for Internet access and a ruthless battle with the contents of my inbox."

"I'm so bummed to have missed that," she said, affectionately stroking his arm. It was the sort of little intimate gesture that couples did. Real couples. Not just "having a thing at work" couples. Good God, he liked it.

"What trouble have you been into this morning?"

"Oh … just the usual maid of honor duties. Helping the bride with dress alterations, checking out the flowers, the cake. All the stupid little wedding details only girls want to hear about."

"I am appalled that I am curious." Truly, he was—and he hoped all the stupid little wedding details were documented. His birthright kind of depended upon it.

"For all the wrong reasons, I bet," she retorted and he winced at the word *bet*. He wouldn't be making any more bets anytime soon. "Let me show you," she said, pulling her iPhone from her back pocket. "But you have to promise me something."

"Whatever you want," he said.

"Remember that," she said with a mischievous smile. She was up to no good and he didn't mind.

"Show me," he murmured, leaning forward and breathing her in. It was only then that he realized that something had felt off, missing, all day and that it was her. That was hardly compatible with their previous arrangement of discretion at work, indiscretion at night. But all of a sudden that plan didn't seem to be what he wanted. He wanted to pull her close, listen to her talk about the trouble she'd gotten into that day—knowing her, there would be some sort of "misunderstanding" with authorities, or an audacious scheme, or someone's feathers ruffled. Then, a kiss. And then the kind of lovemaking that left one's mind blank and heart pounding.

"She's having second thoughts about her dress," Roxanna said, showing him a picture of Jane in the sort of dress that made him want to run in the opposite direction. She looked like a bird in that dress stuck with feathers.

"I encourage her to have third or fourth thoughts about that dress," he said.

"Oh! And these are the flowers and some pictures of the Gold Saloon. But you don't care about all that."

"You are amazing," he said, pressing a kiss on her cheek.

"I haven't published these yet," she warned.

There was a tense moment between them. She stared brazenly into his eyes. He bit back a growl. She didn't blink.

"You want to know why I need this story so badly," he said finally.

"Your intelligence is one thing I find so sexy about you."

He was about to tell her. There was no reason not to, other than that it had been such a stupid move on his part and she just said his intelligence turned her on. But then there was a rustling in the bushes—too big to be a squirrel or some other little rodent. It was possibly a deer or a fox. But the unmistakable sound of a soft *click click click click click click* told him exactly what kind of rodent was lurking in the bushes.

Species: paparazzi. Habitat: wherever famous people go, especially if the masses are excluded, and especially if there is a wedding.

Known Predators: people who value their privacy, the law, and Damien Knightly.

He leapt over the balustrade, dropping into the bushes, while Roxanna shouted after him.

"Damien! What the hell are you doing?"

He quickly spied the bastard: a trim, ginger-haired man with a Canon camera bearing a huge, extra long lens around his neck. He knew that bastard. It was Snooper MacBracken, infamous and reviled freelance paparazzo and gossip. Damien had no doubt that Algernon Gardner at *The Daily Post* had hired him.

Then Snooper, the bastard, spied him and started running away, clutching the camera and shielding his face from all the branches. Damien sprinted after him. And then, good God, Roxanna was dashing after them both. For a few moments, the only sounds were of footsteps pounding against the earth, brush and foliage being shoved aside, and heavy breathing.

And then a thud. Followed by a certain four-letter word.

Roxanna had tripped over a root and sprawled on the ground. His heart clenched—was she all right?

"Roxanna! Are you okay?"

Her iPhone, which she'd been holding in her hand, went flying in the air toward … oh bloody hell.

"Get the phone!" she screamed.

Damien dove for it, colliding with Snooper. They both hit the ground and wrestled for it.

Snooper MacBracken did not fight like a gentleman. Damien wasn't sure why he expected he would. He took a fist to the face. Stunned, he released his grip on the iPhone for just a second. Just one little second as his hand instinctively went to the pain.

Snooper grabbed it, and tried to push Damien off. After some scuffling, the wiry bastard succeeded in scrabbling to his feet—phone in hand—and he ran helter-skelter through the woods.

"Oh no you don't," Damien panted. He leapt to his feet and took off at a sprint.

Armani loafers were not ideal for running. Neither were bespoke suits from Savile Row. It didn't matter. Especially when he saw a clearing looming ahead—and a road. With a motorcycle. The man had an escape plan, and in his hand, pictures that would destroy a friendship and pictures that could cause him to lose his most treasured possession.

"Damien hurry!" Roxanna shouted.

His lungs were burning. Muscles, screaming. He dug down deep for every shred of strength and force he possessed. Sprinting faster now, he was Just. Behind. The. Bastard. He launched himself forward, grabbing the paparazzo and taking them both down to the ground. They hit the earth with a thud.

The phone flew from MacBracken's hand. Roxanna dashed over to snatch it up with a ferocious scowl.

"Bugger off," Damien growled, gripping the man's T-shirt in his fist and twisting hard until it was a little too tight around the neck. Snooper's face started to turn red.

"Damien, darling …" Roxanna's voice gently reminded him not to go too far.

"Fuck off," he spat at the pap. Then he stood, watching his foe shuffle to his feet and sloppily run toward his motorcycle. With a roar of the engine, he was gone.

He heard Roxanna approaching behind him. Every fiber of his being was attuned to her, and how she alone possessed the ability to ruin him or save him.

He wasn't just thinking about the story.

"You have a very rakish James Bond thing happening right now," she said, eyeing him hungrily. He glanced down at his gray suit and white shirt, all rumpled and askew, with dirt and sweat stains, possibly even some blood.

She reached out and lightly touched his cheekbone where he'd been hit. He flinched, slightly.

"I hope you're okay. But for what it's worth, I like it," she murmured.

"Not the time, darling," he said. His heart was hammering. And he glanced down at the phone in her hand with pictures of the wedding of the year—and the pictures he needed to win the bet, save his family birthright, and not be the one to lose a two-hundred-year-old family treasure.

He hated that he was torn between business and pleasure. He took a long lusty look at Roxanna and thought about tumbling her right here, right now.

"I can see that you are in the throes of a major crisis," Roxanna continued casually. "Anytime you want to, you know, confide in your … whatever the word is for what we are … Or should I just say *me*. Anytime you want to confide in me … Go for it."

He stared at her for a moment, trying to tease out all the things contained in that rambling speech while there was limited flow of oxygen to his brain.

She had, perhaps inadvertently, started the "What are we? How serious is this?" conversation. There was something about how he didn't confide in her. And then there was the way this normally bold and brash woman suddenly became ever-so-slightly shy and uncertain.

There was one thing to say: the truth.

"I bet Algernon Gardner of *The Daily Post* that I would be the first to publish pictures of the wedding."

"What did you bet him?"

"I wagered *The London Weekly.*"

He winced, remembering the one night when he had had one whiskey too many and, so certain of Roxanna and their access to the bride and groom, agreed to a wager that he thought he couldn't lose.

He thought he knew her, and that she was like him: emotionless, driven to succeed in business at all costs. He didn't know her. She was loyal, devoted, and caring to her friends.

"Oh wow," she said dramatically, eyes widening. "That is horrible, Damien. That is a disaster. That is the worst possible thing, isn't it? It's like stabbing you and twisting the knife right in your heart."

He started walking back to the house. God, he hurt.

"Thank you for reminding me why I don't make a habit of confiding in people."

She followed behind him.

"I'm sorry. Apologies for not reminding you why people don't usually confide in me." He smiled a bit, but she didn't see it. "Fortunately for you, I have a devious mind."

"Splendid."

"For example, you might be interested to know that those pictures were fake."

He stopped, turned around. She was serious.

"Fake? That looked just like Jane in that ghastly dress."

"But it was *a ghastly dress.*" She repeated this and mimicked his accent, too. "Obviously she would never wear it. We spent the morning at Oldwart's Bridal Shoppe in the village."

"And the flowers and other things?"

"The work of Mark, the most amazing hotel concierge who didn't bat an eyelash when Jane told him we needed to stage fake photographs of the bride."

"Why?"

"Because selling out my friend is not an option," Roxanna said. And biting her lip, she added. "But I wanted to do this for you too. I figured you would have a good reason."

"Thank you," he said. And then because he was so grateful he said it again. "Thank you."

Roxanna Lane was amazing. He knew in that moment that she was the woman he wanted on his side, by his side. Always.

He swept her into his arms and kissed her passionately.

Then he set her back on her feet and said, "We need to publish. Immediately."

# CHAPTER
## FIVE

*That moment when things get serious.*

Roxanna had left her bag with her laptop at the gazebo, where the other guests of the wedding had kept an eye on it while reveling in this one little patch of cellular access.

"What was that all about?" Piers asked, leaning against a pillar and glancing up from his phone.

"Nothing," they said at the same time

"Really?" Duke asked, glancing up quizzically from his iPhone.

"Damien was just chasing off a paparazzo," Roxanna said.

"Thanks, dude," Duke said, even though Damien was so not a dude. He was too posh for that. "Jane is obsessed with making sure nothing about this wedding shows up online."

"Oh, I know," Roxanna said. Then she proceeded to spend the next hour making sure the fake wedding pictures were posted online. On Jezebel.com.

THE BAD BOY BILLIONAIRE'S BRIDE
*They're the wedding pictures I know you all have been waiting for: one of tech's most debauched dudes is getting hitched. Who is the woman who*

*managed to reform this bad boy billionaire when so many others have failed?*
*Jane Sparks, the future Mrs. Jane Austen, who publishes romance novels*
*under the pseudonym Maya Rodale. Jezebel—and only Jezebel—has scored*
*exclusive photos of the bride getting the final fitting for her wedding gown.*
*The groom should stop reading now, but the rest of y'all should take a look and*
*try to guess the designer!*

Writing snarky articles, uploading the pictures, and formatting everything was something she did every day. But there was something different about it when Damien was beside her, watching as she corrected typos, rewrote a phrase, or tweaked the HTML. She was acutely aware of her every move, and acutely aware of *him*.

Usually, their workplace interactions consisted of him striding around glass-walled conference rooms, dominating meetings, issuing orders, and bossing people around while she snuck glances from behind her monitor.

Then there were all the little illicit moments: walking too closely in the hall and accidentally brushing up against one another, a stolen kiss in the stairwell, sending sexy text messages when she knew he was in budget meetings, or when he knew she was on deadline.

She finished tweaking the article for SEO, added a few links to previous stories on Jane and Duke, and did one last preview.

"Time to publish!"

Within seconds it was live on the website.

Moments after she sent in her post, there was a ping from someone's phone. Duke's iPhone. He looked at it, followed the link, then looked over at them with a really lethal glare.

"What the *fuck?*"

"Darling, I think we'd better run," Damien murmured.

Roxanna laughed as they dashed along the path to the house, Duke chasing angrily behind them. Her heart didn't stop pounding for the trip back—because of the running, she told herself. But then it didn't stop once they got back to their room and locked the door behind them.

Anticipation, that.

They laughed over their adventures. They kissed. Lips against lips, imperfectly but perfectly wonderful. Her back up against the door, his weight leaning into her. She threaded her fingers through his hair and kissed him deeply.

There was a knock on the door.

"Shhh. It could be Duke."

"Just a sec!"

"Just wanted to see if you were ready for dinner." It was Cali.

"I need a few minutes," Roxanna called out. "We have to get ready," she whispered reluctantly.

"Then we'll finish this later," Damien murmured, pressing a kiss on the hollow of her throat.

And they began to get ready for dinner.

It should have been so unremarkable. Off with the skinny jeans and into the slinky dress. Off with his disheveled and dirty suit, then into another sexy black suit from Savile Row. Putting clothing on shouldn't be so sexy. Though they had undressed each other dozens of times, they had never really put on clothes together.

They had spent nights and days together, lying in bed, tangled in sheets. They had spent Hurricane Geoffrey delightfully ensconced in his apartment, watching the rain by candlelight. There were long lunches marked with "do not book" on the calendars. There were sexy late nights. There were dinners at the most intimate and exclusive restaurants where they had the most discreet tables, the best wine, obsessively attentive service. There were gifts of lingerie and expensive bouquets of flowers. There was something secretive and illicit about them, not because there was anyone else—there was no one—but because they worked together. Though, while it wouldn't be ideal to find themselves the subject of office gossip, it wouldn't be the end of the world or their careers.

They were not a "we" or an "us" couple. They didn't do events together. The bathroom door was always closed. Neither kept a drawer of toiletries and such at the other's place. They were all about the romance and not at all about the day-to-day. It went without saying that Roxanna had never thought of them as a "couple who attends formal events together." But Jane had insisted she bring her mysterious millionaire lover as her date and in this moment, Roxanna wasn't sorry at all.

She liked him. Maybe even more. Maybe she could even enjoy this intimacy.

Because there was something about this—dressing together for a formal dinner at a house party wedding—that felt more intimate. It felt downright seriously romantic. Like they were a couple. A serious couple with joint bank accounts, arguments over who remembered to pay the maintenance bill (oh shit! She already missed living with Jane, who took care of that stuff), and who said "we" at every opportunity.

The kind of couple she had no interest in being ever again after Josh.

But here and now and worlds away, Roxanna lounged on the bed, wearing her favorite underthings from La Perla, debating whether she wanted to keep this slinky dress on or change into something else and watching him tie his tie. As grown-up, fabulous, and chic as it all was, she still managed to feel like an angsty teenager again. There were all these questions she wanted to ask him. About the bet, and *them*. Us. Whatever.

They were not the sort of people that made a big thing about relationships. They liked their freedom, being beholden to no one. Having only the beautiful, sexy parts of being together with none of the day-to-day drudgery. They were not people who had "the talk."

But here they were, a couple at a wedding—was there a more "couple" activity? Perhaps this … watching him button his shirt instead of unbutton it. Learning that he pulled on his trousers one leg at a time, like any other man. Having Damien instead of Jane zip up the back of the little black dress she had decided to wear.

"So about *The London Weekly* …" she began as he oh-so-slowly pulled the zipper up when she wanted him to yank it *down*.

He stepped away and started fastening his cuff links.

"It is my family's pride and joy. The newspaper that made the Knightly family fortune and which launched our media empire. All the way back in 1816."

"*Media empire*." She couldn't resist whispering the words under her breath, mimicking his accent.

"My family has a business, too," she said.

"I didn't know that."

"It's a contracting business back home in Jersey. My dad does all the heavy lifting and my mom manages the business."

"Makes one wonder how you ended up a journalist in New York City."

"I was always nosy and meddling and bored to tears back home. I got out as soon as I could," Roxanna said. "But we've saved your paper, right?"

"As long as it doesn't come out that those pictures are fake, yes. But if it's discovered that we knowingly posted staged photographs, I'll have not only lost the paper, but jeopardized the reputation of my websites."

"Oh fantastic. And my byline is on that. There goes my career."

He gazed at her. "I promise you won't be fired."

"You bet I won't be," she retorted. He could not fire her after this. She would sue the pants right off of him before he even considered it. "So why did you make the bet?"

"Because I was sure that I would win."

"You were counting on me to sell out my friend for you," Roxanna stated, slightly shocked, slightly bitter. "That speaks volumes, doesn't it? You think that I am that infatuated with you. Or that I don't care that much about my friend. Haven't you ever heard the phrase hos before bros?"

It was the sort of crass American saying that made him wince, which is why she *had* to say it. She was gratified by the expected reaction.

"Honestly—I wasn't thinking about your friendship with Jane. Or our relationship. Only that we would have unrestricted access to the event that the whole world is dying to know more about."

After taking a moment to consider all the information—and decide on a pair of strappy black satin Sarah James stilettos—Roxanna asked: "Well, what did you stand to win?"

"It doesn't signify."

"Way to make me way more interested," she replied, sitting on the bed, slipping on the shoes, and watching his gaze darken.

"What a way with speech you have, Roxanna."

"Oh, shut up, you stuffy old aristocrat," she said, tossing a pillow his way.

"I am not old. Or stuffy," he said, sounding awfully stiff.

"Whatever you say, *your lordship*." But he wasn't old. Or stuffy. He was young and hot and reserved, which she found incredibly alluring, all the more so in a world where most guys shared way too much online. But he did need to be teased, for he was far too serious.

"So, do you want to talk about ..." He paused, delicately. Her heart pounded. Then, in his insanely sexy accent he said the one word that set off the butterflies in her stomach: "Us."

Oh, God. The talk. She had brought it up, but now she wished she hadn't. Things could just go on, all sexy and casual forever, right? Of course. There was no reason for her heart to be beating so hard.

"Us?"

"You mentioned it twice today."

"Did I?" She feigned ignorance.

"You did."

"Do *you* want to talk about us?"

"I'd rather show you," he said.

She had been sitting on the edge of the bed. He stood before her, then eased her back until she was flat on the mattress and he was lowering himself onto her. He pushed up her very little black dress, his open palm possessively skimming her thigh.

Roxanna gazed into his eyes. Dark. Mysterious. Mischievous. Then she closed her eyes and surrendered to just feeling ... his mouth, possessively claiming her from her lips to her neck to lower down to her breasts. That dress she had just put on moments ago was already being pushed out of the way. She felt the hot, hard length of him against her. God, did she want him now.

They had to go to dinner.

To hell with dinner.

His mouth crashed down on hers. Then she was lost in the taste of him, the feeling of him. His weight upon her, pinning her to the mattress, not that she wanted to be anywhere else in the world. His hands, skimming all of her as if he couldn't get enough of her long legs, or her breasts, or her belly or any inch of skin that was *hers*. The way he so plainly wanted *her* turned her on so much. Almost as much as how she just plainly, desperately wanted *him*. All of him.

She started to undo all those buttons he'd just done because she needed to feel him, too, feel his hot skin under her palm. The beat of his heart was faint, but she could feel it.

"Take off this dress," he whispered urgently.

"Yes, boss," she whispered. Then she stood and pulled it off.

He playfully swatted her bottom. "Don't you forget it," he murmured.

She just smiled—and rolled her eyes. Because in the bedroom—and, well, everywhere—she acted however she damn well pleased and they both liked it.

"Keep the shoes on," Damien ordered.

"Obviously."

Her stilettos were crisscrossed across his back, gently digging into his bare skin. A growl at the back of his throat; a purr from her.

"These trousers have to go."

"Your wish is my command."

And like that, they were gone and he was hard, straining against her.

They were going to be late for dinner.

The rest was ... The rest was rough, urgent, kisses. Deep breaths, quick breaths, can't-get-enough-air-this-pleasure-is-going-to-my-head breaths. She felt them steal across her skin. Soft sounds of pleasure.

The rest was ... feelings. Her fingers wove through his soft hair or her nails down along his back. His weight upon her. His cock hard and full inside of her, in and out, in and out, until she thought she'd scream. Every inch of her skin tingling with desire.

The rest was ... the taste of salt on his skin, the intense pressure building within until she couldn't help but cry out. His mouth on hers, his fingers sinking into her hair, and his own sounds of climax.

The rest was ... For Damien, there was no more. This was it. She was it. The only one. The only woman for him.

His heart was still pounding from their lovemaking and it didn't slow down at the realization that this was it. She was it. He was done.

. . .

WHEN THEY DESCENDED the stairs to dinner—with her in a slightly wrinkled dress and he with his tie askew—he clasped her hand in his. When they entered the saloon for cocktails, he didn't let go.

Roxanna watched Jane and Duke, so utterly, radiantly happy, while she and Damien drank champagne, chatted with other guests, and held hands all the while. She started to wonder … What if they never let go?

What if—gulp—she and Damien weren't just two lovers or *whatever*. What if they weren't just something but *Something*. Or even, the one thing.

Roxanna Lane was not the kind of girl to freak out or panic or indulge in debates of *what does this mean*, either with others or in her own head. Except, she was now panicking. Because, heart thudding, she suspected she knew what this meant.

# CHAPTER
## SIX

*That moment when you're surrounded by a mob of armed and angry men.*

*The stag party*

T hanks to Roxanna and Jane's scheme, *The London Weekly*—and his birthright—were secure. That is, as long as word didn't get out that the pictures were staged. That is, as long as no one else got real photographs of the wedding. Relieved as he was—and appreciative—it occurred to Damien that these staged photographs didn't quite solve his problem. Once the issue of *People* magazine hit the newsstands, everyone would know that his were fakes. He couldn't quite bring himself to mention it to Roxanna and he wasn't certain what he would do.

In the meantime, everybody assumed they were real and unfortunately, Damien had to keep up the charade—even while joining the stag party for a day of shooting with the armed and angry groom and all of his friends.

Duke's stag party was made up of a bizarre group, including a bunch of geeky developers, an assortment of billionaires and millionaires, and, oddly, an English lord or two.

Duke had stubbornly worn his uniform of jeans and a free T-shirt, though he conceded to fashion and tradition by adding a hunting jacket. Some of his friends dressed like him, but others—the hipsters, Damien thought with a cringe—took this opportunity to layer themselves in tweed trousers and flat caps, Barbour hunting jackets, and Hunter boots.

Someone—perhaps the best man, his assistant, or the wedding planner—ensured that everyone was gifted with a flask engraved with their initials and brimming with whiskey.

The drinking began immediately.

It was eight o'clock in the morning.

Damien had been born and raised an English country gentleman. He'd been hunting and shooting since the age of four. He wanted very badly to comment on how adorable it was to see them all dressed up and pretending to know what they were doing.

But the loaded guns.

And the whiskey.

And the pictures that were not supposed to be public.

Damien was more than capable of defending himself against them. But as a gentleman "in the wrong" he was obliged to let them take their shots—in a manner of speaking. That didn't mean it was agreeable to him.

He took a swig from his flask and thought of Roxanna. If she were here, she would probably best them all. For some reason, he was sure she was a terrific shot. If she were here, he would have the perfect person to whisper snarky comments to. She would diffuse any tension with a sarcastic remark, or twenty. She was, in short, the kind of woman a man wanted by his side. Badly. Always.

He took another swig of his whiskey.

*Us. We. The talk.*

They had almost had that conversation yesterday, but he sensed that she was just as skittish as he. Things were perfect; why ruin it with labels?

Damien lounged against a tree, shotgun at his side, taking occasional swigs of whiskey and brooding over a woman. What a start to the day. This stag party couldn't start fast enough.

After a basic shooting demonstration for the novices, presented by Jacobs, the gamekeeper, they all set out for a day of adventure, but most likely danger in spite of taking all the necessary precautions.

"I don't know about you, but giving these guys loaded shotguns and whiskey seems like a terrible combination," Piers said, after strolling over to Damien.

"Someone is going to shoot their eye out," Damien cracked. "At least they are not angry with you for ruining the wedding."

The two of them were clearly the grown-ups in this group—as well as the only ones who had grown up shooting.

"I'm surprised to see you here," Kyle said, coming up to Damien and Piers. He had been introduced earlier as one of Duke's developers, and Damien would have guessed as such. Kyle was in his mid-twenties and wore a hunting vest over his plaid shirt, and a pair of heavy boots. "I thought you'd be out at the hen party."

Damien stared at him coldly. Kyle hastily added, "To take pictures. For the Internet."

"Or are you here to take pictures of us to leak online?" some other guy, Dave, with thick, black-rimmed glasses, asked. He was decked out in tweed breeks, a vest, and a flat cap.

"He's here so we can keep an eye on him," Duke said, glaring mightily at him. Damien stifled a sigh. "Also, he was invited."

"Is he the reason we had to leave our phones behind?" asked Rupert, another one of Duke's developers. "I feel bereft."

Everyone adopted tragic expressions. Damien bit back laughter.

"Yeah, and he's the reason I had to spend an hour consoling my fiancée and her mother. They were both upset about the photos being leaked and it fucks up our deal with *People* magazine. They wanted exclusive pictures in exchange for a donation to Little Paws Rescue. Archer might be able to save it. But if not ..." Duke turned away from his group of friends to level an accusatory stare at Damien. "You have deprived the puppies and kittens."

If it weren't for the shotgun in Duke's hands, Damien would have laughed. But that was why he wanted to laugh. It was a bit rich, championing the animals while embarking on a day of shooting.

"I wasn't the one to post the pictures," Damien said, pointing out a minor technicality.

"But it was you who threatened Roxanna with being fired if she didn't. What was she supposed to do?"

Given that he had done no such thing, and had no idea how that rumor started, he wasn't sure how to answer that. Nor was he clear on what stories Jane and Roxanna had concocted, or why. He'd do best to keep his mouth shut and let them think whatever they wanted.

His newspaper depended on it.

But Damien wasn't thinking of that now. His thoughts were drifting to Roxanna, and marveling at the efforts she made in order to protect her best friend. And him.

"Those poor puppies and kittens," someone muttered.

"I might find that more upsetting if we weren't literally loading shotguns in preparation to go hunting more small, defenseless animals," Damien pointed out. Everyone looked sheepishly at the shotguns they carried. He made a note to make a sizable donation to an animal-friendly charity.

"What are we hunting, anyway?" Duke asked.

"Foxes," Rupert answered resolutely.

"Foxhunting was banned in 2005," Damien informed them. His father had not been pleased with the passage of that law. "And even then no one ever shot foxes."

"Stags," Kyle said. "We're hunting stags."

"No."

"I thought this was a stag party."

"The term 'stag party' is the British equivalent of what you deem a bachelor party," Damien informed him in what Roxanna would probably deem his "haughty, oh-so-posh aristocrat accent." The woman was working her way into his brain. If he wasn't careful, she'd end up sneaking her way into his heart. Or had it already happened?

Now was not the time to ponder his feelings. Not with a batch of armed and angry and increasingly intoxicated men milling about.

"Are we hunting posh aristocrats who ruin weddings?" Kyle asked.

"No," he answered. "We didn't secure the necessary permits."

"And who gives those out?"

"Posh aristocrats," Damien drawled. "Gentlemen, we're shooting grouse. Since you don't have your phones and thus cannot Google it, I'll tell you what that is. A grouse is a type of bird. It has brownish feathers and is slightly larger than a pigeon. They live in moorland areas, such as the one we are about to traverse. You are to point your shotgun at the bird *and only at the bird* and pull the trigger. "

The day progressed. Whiskey was drunk, even though—or perhaps, because—it was an ungodly early hour.

Shots were fired. Thankfully, no one was hit. In fact, their shooting was deplorable. As the day was winding down only Damien, Piers, Duke, and a few others had been successful in downing a few birds in spite of all the shots fired by the rest of the bachelor shooting party.

"Man, I'm so much better at Big Buck Hunter," Kyle muttered as they trudged back. The group was tired, hungry, drunk, and perhaps even hungover from drinking steadily throughout the day.

But then, a noise—a rustling in the foliage. They had been primed all day to listen for birds, or other creatures.

"Guys ... that sounds like something big," Rupert whispered.

"Get ready," Duke ordered.

All the guys lifted their shotguns and aimed them at whatever was in the bushes. They crept closer. Uneasy glances were exchanged: *what could it be? A deer? A bear? Did they have bears in England? Why couldn't they Google it right now?!*

Closer and closer still they crept, visions of monsters and aliens in their heads. Damien had a sneaking suspicion he knew what was hiding there—and what was in for a nasty surprise. He felt no pity.

Finally, whatever was mucking about in the foliage emerged, revealing itself to be that same damned paparazzo from the day before. He froze at the sight of nearly a dozen armed men with shotguns aimed right at every one of his vital parts.

"You," Damien seethed, eyes narrowed. It was none other than Snooper MacBracken, in all his smirking, meddling, ginger glory. That bastard hadn't learned his lesson about spying on this wedding. Damien lifted his shotgun and held it steady, poised to shoot.

Snooper screamed like a girl in a horror film, his face turning as red as his hair.

"Hand over the camera," Duke ordered.

The man dropped his camera and ran.

Damien breathed a sigh of relief. Duke did as well.

But it was too soon and their relief was short-lived. A few hours later—after a big, hot meal at the hunting lodge—they were all en route in a Mercedes passenger van to a different pub. Every one of them had their heads bent over phones, the glow of the screens lighting up their faces and showing eyes widening in shock over something.

There were more than a few whispered swear words.

Duke took a phone call.

His expression became concerned, then gravely serious, then fucking furious.

"So the *People* magazine deal might be off," he said angrily. "Jane is going to be pissed. And/or heartbroken. Fuck. I promised her this one thing. *One thing.*"

"Might be off or is definitely off?" Piers inquired.

"Might be."

"Why?"

"This is why," Rupert said, holding out his phone, showing a picture of them all traipsing through the countryside in full hunting attire with shotguns held aloft … and aimed at the paparazzo.

"What a shot," Piers said with a low whistle. "No pun intended though."

"That damned photographer must have had a friend with him," Damien said. "They're like vermin. You get rid of one only to find ten more."

"I'll have to get Archer on it. So he's going to be pissed," Duke said.

"*People* magazine issued a statement. They don't condone hunting anything or anyone," Rupert said, shaking his head forlornly as he read the news article online. "Those poor puppies and kittens. They'll all starve and die without *People*'s big donation."

"I'll make a damned donation myself," both Duke and Damien muttered at the same time.

"My donation will be bigger," Duke said to which Damien replied, "Fine."

"But first, let's not forget that we're at a bachelor party," Kyle said, snatching Duke's phone. "We are going to get wasted."

"I hope someone planned for strippers," Dave said.

"Or girls, at least," Kyle added.

Damien was thinking only of one girl. Roxanna. They'd been apart for too long today and he missed her. My God, what she would make of the day's events. He would have loved her company on a day when everyone was against him. As long as she was on his side, what did the rest of it matter?

Really, though. There it was again: the woman he lo—had an inordinately strong fondness for. Or some old newspaper that had been in the family for ages. Newspapers were dying, anyway. Everyone knew that. But then he thought of all the previous Lord Northbournes who managed to keep the paper and true love and Damien knew he couldn't be the one that didn't have both.

"Here we are," the driver said as the car stopped before a small, old pub in the village near Brampton House. All the young bucks spilled out of the car, shouting, "Time to crash the bachelorette party!"

# CHAPTER
## SEVEN

*That moment when you mistake an officer of the law for a stripper. As one does.*

*The hen party*

Roxanna went all out when it came to planning Jane's bachelorette party. Or rather her hen party, if one wanted to be all properly English about it. Jane had requested something elegant and tasteful. As her maid of honor, Roxanna delivered just that ... though she did have some tricks up her sleeve and had planned an amazing day that her friend would love.

And, speaking of love, Roxanna thought she might just be falling in love herself. Or allowing herself to admit that she'd been in love with Damien Knightly since that first moment they met in the elevator. The damned thing had gotten stuck and they both swore at the same time. Then she cracked a joke, he laughed, and it was all over.

Love. That.

She caught herself whistling a merry tune. Then stopped. This was Jane's day and she had to make sure everything went off without a hitch. She could not be distracted by her own romance.

The day began properly, with a big breakfast buffet just for the ladies. Very well, there was a hint of impropriety in the mimosas (or Buck's Fizz in England, which she thought sounded so dirty) that were served. Then Jane was gifted with a gorgeous hand-embroidered sash (thank you, Etsy) declaring her "The future Mrs. Jane Austen."

"I'll never take it off!" she exclaimed.

Then everyone had to laugh and chatter about a modern-day romance novelist being named Jane Austen. *What were the odds? How perfect! Will you change your name?!* All the other girls were given similar sashes with the words "Lady's Maid."

"I've always wanted a lady's maid!" Jane gushed. "Now I have lots!"

"Just for one day," they all muttered.

After breakfast, Roxanna ushered all the ladies outside. There was the bride, of course, and her bridesmaids. Her cousins Cassidy and Kimberly came along, as well as two of Duke's best developers, Amy and Jessica.

"Ooooh," Jane sighed when she saw a fleet of horse-drawn carriages waiting, along with very handsome footmen and drivers dressed in full livery and Mark holding a tray bearing glasses of lemonade.

As the girls climbed into the carriages—aided by handsome footmen, of course—Mark handed each girl a glass of lemonade. Roxanna had spiked it herself.

"It's too bad we can't Instagram this!" Jessica exclaimed. "It's all so perfect!"

"Think of the puppies and kittens," Roxanna said as she reminded everyone of the "no phones" policy. "We don't want to deprive the cute little puppies and kittens, now, do we?"

"Is the driver a stripper?" Jane asked in a low voice. "A sort of modern-day playboy stripper dressed in the attire of a Regency carriage driver?"

"Any chance his very fitted breeches are hiding Velcro seams so that they can be ripped off in one fluid movement, much to the delight of this bachelorette party?" Jane's other cousin, Kimberly, asked.

"I thought you didn't want any strippers," Roxanna said, smiling sweetly.

"I don't," Jane replied, with a longing glance at the footman. "But I don't trust you for a minute."

"I do," Kimberly said. "I want strippers."

"I'm afraid he's just a pretty face I hired for the day," Roxanna said. Then, kicking off a drinking game that would last for the rest of the day, she declared: "Never have I ever been driven in a horse-drawn carriage by a stripper in disguise."

"That would be a first for all of us! Drink!" Cassidy declared.

"It's even a first for me!" Kimberly exclaimed.

And so the bachelorette party began in earnest.

A SIMILAR CONVERSATION was had at Edgeworth Park, a nearby National Trust property, where the bachelorette party arrived for a private tour. The bride, being a historical romance novelist, did love visiting ancestral homes and it was livened up for the rest of the party by the ongoing game of "never have I ever" and ogling the tour guide.

Their guide bore a striking resemblance to Colin Firth as Mr. Darcy (with a dry shirt, alas), especially since he wore traditional Regency era attire.

"Roxanna, are you sure *he* is not a stripper?" Jane asked in a very low voice as "Darcy" the tour guide lectured the group at length on the origins of the wallpaper in the yellow drawing room.

"Do you really think a male stripper has this much to say about nineteenth-century wallpaper patterns?"

"I should be paying attention to this for my books," Jane groaned. "But I'm tipsy and imagining him in wet clothes murmuring how ardently he loves and admires me."

Cali leaned in and asked, "Are you sure you don't *want* him to be a stripper, Jane?"

"No," Jane said, blushing furiously.

"If you wanted a stripper, you only had to say so," Roxanna whispered. Jane blushed even more.

"Is something the matter, Ms. Sparks?" Cali inquired. "Or shall I say the future Mrs. Jane Austen?"

"Nothing is the matter. Thank you. Everything is lovely."

"Do you ladies have a question?" asked Colin-Firth-Darcy-Tour-Guide-Not-A-Stripper.

"Never have I ever hooked up with a guy in reenactor attire," Kimberly murmured.

They all drank to that, except for Cassidy, which surprised everyone.

"What?" she said, when everyone gave her very strange looks. "I spent one summer working at Colonial Williamsburg."


OVER A PICNIC LUNCH on the grounds of Edgeworth Park, Jane was certain all the waiters were strippers. Kimberly threatened to test her theory, Cassidy told her to behave herself *for once*, the two sisters started bickering, and the rest of the bachelorette party started flirting with all the hot men in uniform bringing them food and drink. Just in case.

All the while, the game of "never have I ever" continued until the girls were quite tipsy, especially the bride.

Later that afternoon, they toured the gardens and Jane got excited about all the ideas this was giving her for her books. When they returned to the ballroom for a brief waltzing lesson with the oh-so-handsome waiters (strippers?), it was discovered that Kimberly had gone missing. She turned up later with a smile and bits of foliage in her hair.

The group enjoyed High Tea in the Orangery.

"I could get used to this," Jane sighed.

"Me too," Roxanna replied. "I see the appeal of days of yore. We just don't live like we used to."

It was back to the modern day after that. A fleet of cars with drivers was waiting to take the girls to their next destination.


*The Bull's Head Pub*

By the time the girls arrived at the final stop of the hen party, they had been playing "never have I ever" all day. There was great confusion over when one was supposed to drink (or not) as part of the game, with the result that all the girls were in an advanced state of intoxication and it was no longer clear who had done what (or not) with whom (or not).

It had to be noted that The Bull's Head pub was the only pub near Brampton. The Pineapple of Perfection, a restaurant run by vegan lesbians, did not count, obviously. Here, the locals—old guys hunched over pints at the bar and families enjoying quiet dinners of fish and chips—were obviously wary when a bunch of drunk girls spilled into their dark, quiet pub.

"It's so quaint! And charming," Cassidy exclaimed.

"It's very Ye Olde English Pub," Jane remarked.

"And it's been here since 1782," Cali pointed out, having read the plaque outside the door. "Perhaps you can set a scene from one of your novels here."

Jane looked around, taking it all in. "Maybe if one of my characters has fallen on hard times and found themselves stranded in the countryside, desperate for a place to stay."

"Drinks?" Roxanna asked the pack of inebriated girls who were about to become way drunker. She paused, imagining how Damien would roll his eyes and despair of her use of phrases like "way drunker." But then he would kiss her and it would be "way hot" and there wouldn't be much talking at all after that.

She and Jane sidled up to the bar.

"Oh! They have Prosecco on tap," Jane exclaimed. "Is that even possible?"

"It's so real," Roxanna said. She had requested it specially. She had also made a playlist and ordered cupcakes decorated with little marzipan versions of the male anatomy. Jane had been adamant about having a "classy" bachelorette event. But Roxanna thought a little trashy fun—and penis swag—was required at this point of the party.

"Just look at that bartender ..." Kimberly sighed, leaning against the bar, twisting a lock of her blond hair around her finger as she made eyes at the hunk who bore a striking resemblance to Colin Farrell.

It had to be noted that his shirt had only two buttons fastened and one had to wonder why he even bothered.

"Is he a stripper?" Jane asked, nervously, again. But this time, she'd already had some drinks and she wasn't speaking as quietly as she thought. Colin-Farrell-The-Bartender overheard and flashed a sexy grin suggesting that 1) he was a stripper or 2) he could be one, for her.

"Never have I ever hooked up with a bartender—" Cassidy started to say, but Roxanna cut her off: "—said no girl ever."

"I haven't!" Jane exclaimed.

"Drink!" all the girls shouted. All the girls drank.

"Or make out with him," Cali suggested with a sly grin.

"No! I'm getting married!" Jane cried out happily. All the girls cheered, and the music started blaring. The playlist started with Beyoncé, then a little Lady Gaga and classic Madonna.

"Hey! I love this song!" Jane shouted when "Drunk in Love" started playing.

"I know!" Roxanna shouted back.

Then there wasn't much talking as all their favorite songs played, and all the girls danced, and drank Prosecco from the tap, and turned this Ye Olde English Pub into a wild ladies' night dance party. The locals were not amused.

And then the guys rolled in, still dressed in their hunting outfits, right down to the muddy boots.

"Wait, we're supposed to have separate parties," Jane said loudly, her face flushed from all the dancing. And the drinking. She might have stumbled a little bit. Roxanna held her arm to steady her, but she was a bit wobbly on her heels too. It had been a long day.

"Good to see you, too, future wife," Duke said, pulling her close for a kiss.

"Hey," she sighed. "Hiiii."

"Break the rules, Jane," Roxanna told her. These guys weren't going anywhere and this party was only just beginning. She saw the drunk bachelors and bachelorettes start to pair off for some dirty dancing and making out in the dark corners of the pub.

"You're right. About something," Jane said, draping herself across Duke, who held her close.

"Also, drink some water," Roxanna said, handing her a full pint glass.

"I'm fine," Jane said. "I feel fantastic."

"Remember how you don't want pictures on the Internet of you vomiting?"

"Nooo." Jane shook her head slowly. And stopped, wincing. "Bad idea, the headshaking."

"Drink water," Roxanna insisted. "Or go home."

Roxanna watched Jane glance around the pub and see that all their closest friends were dancing, drinking, making merry, and generally having a ball. Was that Cassidy with one of the developers? That was indeed Kimberly making out with the bartender. Jane wouldn't want to miss any of it.

"Pass the water," Jane demanded before chugging the glass Roxanna gave her. Then off she went to dance with Duke.

With the bride in good spirits and happily with her groom, Roxanna sought out her own guy. She'd been wanting to text him all day with little comments or inside jokes or just to see how he was getting along with a bunch of angry tech guys holding loaded shotguns. Jane used to be her person for stuff like that, but now ... Now she just wanted him.

She wandered through the crowd until she found him leaning against the bar. Wrapping her arms around him, Roxanna pressed herself against him, savoring the feeling of his body against hers. She breathed him in.

Damien slipped his hands down to her waist and like that they started to dance. Slow. Oh so slow. Somehow they ended up in a darkened corner of Ye Olde Pub. Damien's back was against the wall and he held her close.

"How was your day, darling?" she purred, peering up at him. "Did you get shot?"

"I did not, but there were many close calls," he said, claiming her mouth for a quick kiss. "And how was your day?"

"Girly," she replied, laughing softly. "Want me to tell you all about it?"

"Tell me anything. Even if it's terrifying."

For a second Roxanna paused. He meant that girly things were terrifying and he wanted to hear about her day. But it occurred to her alcohol-addled brain that that was the perfect opportunity to say *I love you*.

Where did *that* come from? All the Prosecco she had been drinking. Drunk logic suggested that she confess her love for him now, when she could easily laugh it off if he didn't say it back. But that was idiotic and immature. She ought to take her own advice and drink some water.

But really, this wasn't the moment to say those three little words. *If* she said them—when she said them, it shouldn't be while drunk in the pub.

So instead, she said, "Jane didn't want any strippers."

"Pity, that."

"So I hired a ton of male strippers to drive the carriages, give the tour at the Edgeworth Park, and to serve tea. You name it. Now she's convinced every hot guy she sees is a stripper."

Damien grinned and said, "Well, that explains why she's manhandling that police officer."

Roxanna whirled around.

"OMG. Oh. My. God."

Jane was indeed manhandling the police officer. He was cute in the boyish, small town cop kind of way. He was not hot in the male-model-hired-for-the-day kind of way, like all the others. But Jane's vision was probably seriously impaired by all the alcohol she'd been drinking since breakfast. Thus, she was obviously flirting with the cop, feeling his biceps, asking to touch his nightstick, and giggling uncontrollably. Duke was unsuccessfully trying to stop her.

"I have to go deal with this," Roxanna said, pressing a kiss on Damien's lips and heading toward her friend. "Jane! Wait!"

"This one is the stripper, isn't he?" Jane said loudly. Then, to the not-a-stripper police officer she cooed, "Hello, you. It's my special night."

"Congratulations, ma'am. But I'm not a stripper. I'm an officer of the law."

"That's what they all say," Jane said, giggling. Roxanna was hard-pressed to restrain her own laughter.

"I'm just going to take her to get some water," Roxanna said, trying to pull her friend away from the cop.

"An excellent idea," he said.

But Jane wouldn't budge. No, she leaned heavily on Roxanna, and seriously considered the officer.

"I bet your shirt just ... rips right open," Jane said thoughtfully. Then, in a serious voice, she added, "Because of the Velcro. Or maybe snaps."

"There's no—" Roxanna started to say. But Jane, good God, just reached over for the officer's shirt, fisted the fabric, and tried to yank it right open.

The buttons did not oblige.

Jane stood there awkwardly, gripping fistfuls of the officer's shirt.

"Babe ..." Duke was there, by her side. "You're confused. *I'm* your male stripper for the evening."

"Well, show me what you got," she said matter-of-factly, hands on her hips.

Duke bit back laughter and said something about a private performance back at the house. It took a moment, but the bride-to-be was persuaded to leave her bachelorette party.

"Aaand this party has been a success," Roxanna declared. "Aaand we're done."

DAMIEN WATCHED the entire exchange from the corner of the pub. Jane and Roxanna loved each other, that was abundantly clear. And even Roxanna and Duke acted as if they had acknowledged that they were, for better or for worse, now life partners when it came to Jane. Together, they gathered her things, gave her water, and escorted her out to the car waiting to drive them back.

Damien grabbed Roxanna's things and pushed through the dance floor, intent on a ride back to the house with them. God forbid he be left at that pub with all the drunk girls. God forbid he miss out on Roxanna. They all squeezed into a black car.

Jane nestled up against Duke, who wrapped his arms around her and held her close even though she muttered something about not feeling well. He made a crack about happily ever after including vomit.

Roxanna offered a sheepish sorry-not-sorry kind of apology. Then she handed him "a hair thing" for when Jane was inevitably puking later. Duke seemed a bit perplexed, but accepting of this, and Damien did not envy what was in store for him later this evening.

Or did he?

There was love all around. It wasn't complicated; it just was. Jane loved them both, and they loved her, so they had all bonded in the way that only a chosen family can. It didn't have to be a big thing. It. Just. Was. Like air and water and Mondays and Saturdays.

It made him rethink his rules about the L-word and avoiding dramatics, complications, and messy emotional entanglements. He wanted, fiercely, to be a part of that. Maybe even more than he wanted to hold on to a two-hundred-year-old newspaper.

# CHAPTER
# EIGHT

*That moment when you have to give a heartfelt speech and realize you
actually mean it.*

The following day—the day before the wedding—was spent
recovering from the night before. All of the women indulged
in manicures, pedicures, facials, and massages. Most of the
guests spent a significant portion of the day lounging around the pool,
soaking up the sunshine, sipping cold beverages, and taking a dip in
the cool water.

Jane and Roxanna reclined on chaise lounges, sunglasses on and
giant glasses of water in hand. Kimberly was nearby, making an effort
to ensure that the maximum amount of skin was exposed so she'd
have as few tan lines as possible. No one complained—especially the
male guests. Cassidy was in the shade reading *War and Peace*.

"Do you think he's a stripper, Jane?" Roxanna asked. It was clear to
whom she was referring: the hot hunk of man in very small, fitted
shorts tending to the swimming pool.

"Shut up," Jane mumbled. "Just shut up."

All the girls lowered their sunglasses and gazed at the pool boy. Or,
more to the point, at all the tan, exposed, muscles of the pool boy. Oh,

and his gorgeous smile and that dimple on his left cheek. He was totally aware that all the girls in bikinis were ogling him and he was totally okay with it.

"Is it his chiseled abs that make you think so?" Roxanna asked. "Or his amazing ass?"

"Or that sexy, smoldering look he's giving me?" Kimberly added.

Jane reluctantly pulled down her sunglasses and gave the pool boy a glance. Then she pushed her glasses back up and said, "He doesn't compare to Duke."

"Doesn't compare to Damien," Roxanna murmured to herself. "And speak of the devil."

Roxanna took a turn ogling him as he walked toward her. He was tall, dark, and fucking gorgeous. He could have been a model, but he was too smart for that, which only made him sexier.

He stopped before her, blocking the sun. Then he grinned and said, "I know you were pining away for me and now here I am, making all your dreams come true."

"Your modesty is what I find sexiest about you," she retorted.

"That's what all the girls say," he said with a grin. He turned to address Jane. "Ms. Sparks, I'm wondering if you would spare your maid of honor for the day."

"What for?" they both asked at the same time.

"It's a surprise," he said.

"A romantic one?" Jane asked suspiciously.

"I hate surprises," Roxanna interjected.

"Ignore her," Jane said.

"As if I could. Yes, it's romantic. I think. Or a disaster that will be the end of our relationship."

"You may take her," Jane said, waving her hand dismissively. "But I want to hear *everything* at the end of the day."


AFTER ROXANNA HAD SHOWERED and dressed, she followed Damien to his Aston Martin convertible parked in front of the house. Damien went ahead and opened the door for her as if chivalry wasn't dead.

"I can't believe you just negotiated my release with the bride," she said, sliding into the seat and buckling up. "I'm free!"

"You make yourself sound like a convicted felon serving a life sentence," he said, slipping on his sunglasses and starting the engine. The car roared to life, then started purring.

"You've obviously never been in a bridal party," Roxanna informed him.

"I have not had the pleasure."

"Where are we going?"

"You'll see."

"Are you so desperate for Internet access that you're driving us into London?"

"No." Was that the faintest of smiles on his lips? She thought yes. He was up to something and it would drive her crazy not knowing.

"One thing you should know about me is that I hate surprises," Roxanna said.

"I know," he replied.

She glanced out the window at the lush countryside as they sped by. Were they a thing or were they not a thing? Why was she suddenly dying/terrified to know? Everything had been so chill and easy in NYC and now … It must be the wedding. She had wedding brain. Ugh.

"We're going to see a house," he said, which shocked her into momentary speechlessness.

"One with Internet, I presume?"

"Of course," he murmured. She got the sense that wasn't it at all, but why else would they go see a house? He didn't seem like the sort who enjoyed touring National Trust properties—or was he, and she was too sex-addled to discover other facets of his personality? Did she not know him at all? Funny, that, when she thought she was falling in lo—finding herself increasingly emotionally invested in him.

He obviously wasn't going to show her a house for sale. But OMG what if he was? She sunk into her seat, overwhelmed by all the ridiculous thoughts in her brain, which had clearly been warped by the wedding.

Damien drove his sporty little car along tiny, windy country roads.

It was all beautiful. Eventually he pulled into one of those discreetly fabulous driveways. The entryway itself wasn't very remarkable, but then there was a long gravel drive flanked by ancient, gnarled trees forming a canopy over the road. Up ahead loomed the very definition of a Stately Ancestral Home.

He parked the car in front of the house. Which was massive.

"This is my home," Damien said, turning the car off. They both remained in their seats, staring at the ancient mansion.

"Did you grow up at the National Trust?"

"Unlike most ancestral homes owned by members of the peerage, we've never had to open the place up to the public," Damien said. "Thanks to the profitability of our media holdings."

"Does anyone actually live here?" As far as Roxanna was concerned, people didn't actually live in houses like this. They were places where history buffs toured with notebooks and cameras or that children were dragged to on school field trips. They were Days of Yore houses, not anyone's actual home. She couldn't imagine coming home to a place like this.

"My mother lives here."

Roxanna made the sound of an explosion.

"Am I about to meet your mother? Is that the romantic, possibly relationship-ending surprise?"

"I'm afraid so," he said softly. She glanced over and couldn't read him.

Roxanna leaned back against the seat and exhaled.

"This just got real. Really real."

"You say that as if it's a bad thing," Damien said. Because she heard the faintest bit of nervousness in his usually very posh and self-assured voice, she was totally, utterly, plainly honest.

"I'm just … scared."

For a moment he was silent. Then he laced his fingers with hers and said, "Me too."

"So we are both scared. But we're both into this. Can we pretend we never had this conversation?" Roxanna asked.

"Please," he said. They sealed it with a kiss.

"Oh, and best not to mention that stupid business with *The London Weekly*. My mother will kill me."

It turned out Roxanna was going to meet his mother immediately. A tall woman with blond hair strolled out of the house and up to them as they exited the car.

"Darling! I wasn't expecting you! Why didn't you call?" she asked in a very fancy accent. Air kisses ensued.

Roxanna did not come from an air-kissing family. Her father would gruffly say something resembling a hello, hold out a big burly paw and go back to watching the game. Her mom would be all nervous and talk about making a casserole or something awful. In short, her family was not oh-so-glamorous like Damien and his mother, who would probably be played by Meryl Streep in a movie.

"There's no phone reception where we're staying."

"You can't expect me to believe such rubbish. Why didn't you call from the road? Send a text?"

"I believe most mothers admonish their children not to text and drive."

"Yes … yes," she said, patting his cheek and turning to Roxanna. "And who is this?"

"This is Roxanna Lane. Roxanna, my mother."

"Call me Cassandra," she said. Then, turning back to her obviously beloved and favored son, she said, "So is she a friend? Or a girlfriend?" Then, quickly, she turned back to Roxanna. "Apologies, darling. He's just never brought a woman home before."

"And now I am reminded exactly why," Damien said.

Never brought another woman home? Roxanna caught his eye and lifted one brow. He just grinned and shrugged. She reached out and clasped his hand in hers.

Okay, this had definitely got real. This was a bigger deal than the talk because this visit spoke volumes. He was inviting her into his life, his childhood home. Or maybe his brain was addled by the wedding too. But she didn't think so. Roxanna exhaled, trying to still the tingling nerves and the fluttering in her belly.

"Do come in. Let's have some tea and a chat," Cassandra said breezily. As they entered the house and passed the butler, she said, "Some tea, please, Jeffries."

"Do you actually have a butler?" Roxanna whispered.

"Of course."

"Even Jane couldn't make you up," she replied.

The three of them took tea in a sundrenched parlor looking out over extensive rolling lawns dotted with sheep.

"Purely decorative," Cassandra explained.

"Pet sheep. We don't have that in New York."

Cassandra laughed and asked them about the wedding, their visit, how they met ...

Meeting the parents was supposed to be a super awkward occasion. But they bantered easily and Roxanna found that she could just be herself. Damien also seemed more at ease as the visit progressed and everything was fine. Weird.

After tea, Damien gave her a tour of the house, but one that wasn't at all like the boring school field trip tours. She was shown the room where they celebrated Christmas, the room where the dog had been sick after eating all the Christmas chocolates, the formal dining room, the less formal dining room, the dining room they actually used, the butler's pantry, and the servants' quarters in the attics, which were a good place for sneaking a smoke when at home on school holidays.

In the upstairs corridor he showed her the collection of framed front pages of early editions of *The London Weekly*.

"We keep a complete collection in the family archives and there is another collection at the Colindale branch of the British Library."

"How fancy," she murmured as she peered at the very first issue—all yellowed with age. There were a few other framed pages of a column called "Dear Annabelle."

"What's this?"

"The love story between the first Lord and Lady Northbourne started in the pages of the paper. She wrote an advice column for him in the 1820s. He was just mere Mr. Knightly then, and was later awarded the title based on the success of his publishing empire."

"Oh, wow."

"So you see, it's not just a newspaper."

"It's your family history," she said. "How could you wager this?"

"I had lost sight of what really matters," he said softly. "But now I know."

She turned to face him. In the darkened corridor, their gazes locked. And she knew. This was really real. And it was good. Really good.

Next he showed her his childhood bedroom. She barely noticed anything before he shut the door behind them and pushed her up against the door. She laughed, and said, "Hey!"

He kissed her. She kissed him back. Then she had to stop and ask, "What's so funny?"

"I have a girl in my bedroom."

"You are supposed to be this debonair gentleman. You are a mysterious millionaire CEO. And you are laughing about having a girl in your childhood bedroom."

"Oh, like the chic, clever, stylish Roxanna Lane won't feel a little bit thrilled to have a hot, successful businessman with a sexy accent in her childhood bedroom when she brings me to her home in New Jersey."

"So we're meeting the parents? Is that what we're doing now?"

"I've only ever driven through New Jersey. Never stopped."

"For a reason. It's the most boring place on the planet."

"Not if you're there," he said softly.

There was only one response to that. She wrapped her arms around him and kissed him.

She kissed him like she was a schoolgirl again, with her heart unabashedly bursting with feelings. *The cute boy liked her!* Her crush returned the sentiments. Some feelings never got old. And some feelings made a girl feel downright new again.

His lips on hers were firm, then yielding, as if he, too, couldn't help but surrender to the simple joy of a good kiss with the girl who liked him back. This knowing that they had romantic feelings for each other made her soften... but it didn't dull her spark at all. Oh no. This was a just a kiss, a sweet, innocent, in-his-childhood-bedroom kiss ...

... and damn she could feel the sparks starting, then catching, and the fire in her belly starting to smolder.

They were interrupted by a text message from Arwen, the wedding planner. Followed by a text from Jane.

411

Arwen Kilpatrick: *We could use your advice, if you have a minute.*
Jane Sparks: *OMG come back ASAP. Disaster!*

"We have to get back for the rehearsal," Roxanna said reluctantly. She pressed one more kiss on his lips. "And, crap, I have to write a speech."

"You haven't written it yet?"

"I'm an impulsive, last-minute kind of girl," she said with a grin.

"We don't want to upset the bride any more than we have already," he said. They said their good-byes to his mum, got in the car, and buckled up. But Damien didn't start the car. He just looked at her. She just looked at him.

God, she lo—had the feelings for this man. For the first time she realized that if they stopped having this thing, she'd be devastated.

"Me too," he said, replying to the thoughts in her head. Then he started the car and they were off to the wedding rehearsal—and, apparently, disaster.

### Scheming with the bride and groom

A SHORT WHILE LATER, Roxanna and Damien breezed into the small sitting room at Brampton house and encountered a tense scene with the wedding planner, Arwen, the owner of the place, Harry, and the bride and groom.

"What did we miss?" Roxanna asked.

"There is a paparazzo lurking on the grounds and we can't get rid of him. But Arwen and Harry have a plan so that he spies on the wrong wedding," Jane explained.

"Well, that sounds like one of your books," Roxanna said, taking a seat on the couch.

"I know. God forbid anyone gets married and it's easy," Duke grumbled.

"The happily-ever-after is sweeter when there are obstacles," Jane said. Presently, no one shared her romanticism. There were more practical matters to consider.

"We're planning a second, decoy wedding," Arwen told them.

"Naturally," Roxanna replied.

"We can't let Snooper get a picture of the real wedding; otherwise, the *People* magazine deal will be off. They're already pissed about those hunting photos, and the ones on Jezebel," Duke explained, with a dark look at Roxanna and Damien. Jane and Roxanna had the same reply.

"But the puppies! The kittens!"

The mood in the room was tense, in spite of Jane's efforts to keep things cheerful. Something wasn't adding up. Damien knew what it was, but there was no way in hell he would say it. A few days ago, he would have without a second thought. But things had changed now. He slipped his hand over Roxanna's.

"What about Damien's ... deal?" Roxanna asked. "If Snooper gets pictures and runs them in *The Daily Post* and everyone thinks they're real, Damien will be screwed. Once the *People* magazine pictures run, they'll know ours were fake. Oh no!"

Roxanna looked up at him, eyes full of concern. His heart slammed in his chest. He knew what he had to do.

"It's fine," he said softly.

"What?" she exclaimed, not at all softly. Out of the corner of his eye, he saw Jane and the others watching them avidly.

"If Snooper runs wedding pictures, the *People* deal will be off *and* you'll lose your newspaper," Roxanna exclaimed. There was a sharp intake of breath from someone, a gasp of shock. He could feel the intensity of Duke's angry gaze. Roxanna looked around at everyone. "We all have an interest in keeping him out."

"It's fine," he repeated. "If Snooper runs those fake pictures, *People*'s pictures will be much more valuable for being authentic," Damien explained. "And I'll deal with *The Daily Post*. Neither of us can win if we've both published fakes." Then, clearing his throat, he added. "But for what it's worth, I am prepared to lose *The London Weekly*. I will do whatever I can to help with the decoy wedding and to preserve the privacy of the real wedding."

"But ..."

"I have figured out what matters more," he said, gazing into Roxanna's eyes and squeezing her hand.

"Oh," Jane sighed, dabbing at her teary eyes with a tissue. "It's so romantic."

*At the rehearsal dinner*

FOR THE REHEARSAL dinner in the State Dining Room, Roxanna put on another sexy dress that Damien wanted to strip off, to reveal the even sexier lingerie underneath, which he also wanted to strip off to reveal the sexiest thing of all: that girl, her bare skin, in his bed.

But what he felt for her was not just lust.

He suspected there were very few women to whom he could admit being scared ... and even fewer who would respond perfectly, as Roxanna had done. They were not emotional, demonstrative people. That didn't mean they didn't feel deeply.

He had never really felt this deeply before, to be honest. And now ...

As he said, he was scared. He was scared of the intensity of his feelings for her. Scared that he might lose his family's prized possession, yet resolute in putting Roxanna and her friends first. He had been a presumptuous idiot to make that wager. And who knew—perhaps he could win or buy it back. Perhaps if they both published fakes, the wager could be deemed a draw. He'd worry about it later. But he now knew what was most important.

But Damien had not been raised to sulk with his feelings. Men in his family put on their suits and strolled out as if they owned the world.

So he did, with one gorgeous redhead on his arm.

They were more affectionate and demonstrative than usual that evening. It was as if the wedding was affecting them. Or now that he'd started to acknowledge the intensity of his feelings for her, he couldn't help but express them with a kiss on her cheek, his palm on her lower back, or a suggestive gaze and wicked smile.

Did the other guests notice? He didn't care.

Damien was thinking seriously romantic thoughts when Roxanna stood up to make a speech. He was glad to have this time to just gaze at her and appreciate how hot she looked in that black dress. He was lucky to have this glimpse into her heart and mind. And, frankly, he was damned curious to hear what she, a woman of more sass than sap, had to say in a speech at a wedding rehearsal dinner.

"Hello everyone," Roxanna started. "Jane asked me to say a few words, which is a request she is going to regret in a few minutes."

Everyone laughed, including the bride.

"I first met Jane when she propositioned me on the Internet," Roxanna began. "Craigslist, to be specific. I was looking for a room-mate who wouldn't stiff me on rent or murder me in my sleep, so I was incredibly lucky to find Jane, who is the kindest, nicest, most trust-worthy girl I know. We're an unlikely couple, but we hit it off right away. Fortunately for me, she made sure that all our bills were paid and that I didn't subsist exclusively on bourbon and popcorn, which is the only thing I know how to cook."

That didn't surprise him in the slightest, knowing her as he did. But why didn't he know that about her? They would have to hire a chef when they moved in together or got married.

He straightened in his chair. Where had that thought come from?

He braced himself for the wave of discomfort that would come from even considering sharing his flat with a woman, or binding himself for life to another person. It didn't come. So they would have a chef. He certainly wasn't going to cook—he couldn't—and a chef was an expense he could afford.

"Jane has been a terrific friend and has taken such great care of me," she continued. "Which is why I decided to return the favor by announcing her engagement to Duke. Before they even met. I have been forbidden, upon pain of death, from telling any more of *that* story. Sorry, kids."

Everyone in the crowd laughed and called out demands for that story.

"While I have given her romance a little nudge forward, she's also done the same for me. Living with a romance novelist will make you start believing in all this romance stuff."

She paused to take a long sip of champagne, which made him grin.

*All this romance stuff.* He wanted to share in *all this romance stuff* with her.

"When she asked me to read her first book, I did it as a friend. And I should point out that by ask, I mean that I might have taken a printed version of the manuscript off her desk without permission. Because really, there are only so many reruns of the Kardashians a girl can watch. But as I read the love stories she wrote and watched her own love story unfold, Jane kind of sort of maybe made me believe in love."

"That's her equivalent of shouting her undying everlasting love from the rooftops, by the way," Jane added, to everyone's amusement.

"Or maybe I've been reading too many of her novels about haughty, devastatingly sexy, undeniably romantic English lords," Roxanna said with a wink at him.

"Hey, I thought those books were about me," Duke interjected.

*No, she's talking about me,* Damien thought.

"So I'd like to propose a toast, because after being so publicly emotional I'm just dying for a drink. Here's to Jane, and Duke, and romance when we least expect it, and being smart enough and open-hearted enough to realize a good thing when it's announced on Face-book. Or ... whatever. Wherever. To Jane, Duke, and happily ever after!"

# CHAPTER
# NINE

*That moment when you declare your love.*

Damien found her at the bar outside on the terrace shortly after the speeches concluded. She was sipping champagne and looking impossibly gorgeous. But now he saw the vulnerability there. She kept it hidden behind a mass of red hair, a bold stare, and a willingness to say anything—so long as she didn't have to talk about her innermost feelings.

"Nice speech," he said, leaning against the bar next to her.

"Nice speech?" she echoed. "That's all?"

"Are you asking me to talk about my feelings?"

"I know. I met your mother this afternoon. One shouldn't ask for too much in one day."

She said it flippantly. But he was feeling honest and straightforward and like speaking from—he cringed, but couldn't deny the truth—his heart.

"Roxanna, if anyone else said that, I would think that it was a nervous way of not wanting to ask for too much. But with you, I think you get me. Us. We are not Hallmark people. We cannot meet one another's parents and engage in a heart-to-heart conversation all in one day."

"It'd be too much."

"For the record, I think your speech might top an introduction to my mother," he said. He still wasn't sure he had processed all the feelings—yes, feelings—he had experienced watching her, listening to her be so emotional and honest in front of a room full of strangers.

"Are we competing over who can demonstrate their feelings the most?" Her eyes lit up. His girl did love competition.

"Some would say that's a bad thing," he murmured. "But perhaps not for us."

"Us," she echoed softly. And then, with a coy smile, she added, "So we're a thing?"

"We are definitely something," Damien confirmed, gazing down at her. He'd never meant words more.

To that they clinked their champagne glasses together and took a small sip.

"Let's get out of here?"

"I thought you'd never ask," she said. A moment later, she added, "I've always wanted to say that, BTW."

He laughed and what he said next came easily. "I love you."

"Well, you sure know how to make a girl feel special," she replied in her Roxanna way. But then she stood on her tiptoes and whispered into his ear, "I love you too."

Hand in hand, they left the dining room and strolled out to the gardens, away from the party. After a while, they slowly began making their way back to the house. They took the long way, enjoying the warm summer night, and holding hands, and the fact that they were A Thing now and it hadn't taken a long, awkward and emotional conversation. It hadn't been a big deal at all. It just *was*.

When they'd had enough of the romantic moonlit stroll, they proceeded at a brisk, New Yorker pace back to their bedroom.

Once inside, he pulled her into his arms for a kiss.

"About that dress …" he started.

"This dress?"

"Off. I beg of you."

The dress was off in a moment, a bunch of silk fluttering to the floor at her feet. She wore sexy lingerie—something with scraps of black lace and satin—and some killer heels.

"That's much better," he said, with an appreciative gaze. "Or much worse. I am tortured."

"You are far too clothed."

She started to loosen his tie and unbutton his shirt as he shrugged his jacket off.

They could hear some of the music from the rehearsal reception filtering in through the open window. The only other sounds were of rushed, deep breaths or of various articles of clothing being removed and dropped to the floor. He kissed her deeply, as if he could not ever have enough—even though after this evening he knew she wouldn't be scarce. She kissed him back with all her fiery passion.

They were a tangle of limbs, kissing, stepping, stumbling, and more kissing across the hotel room until they finally collapsed on the bed.

Her shoes, however, stayed.

He kissed her mouth. Then he paid lavish attention to her breasts, then lower. Then lower still. Her fingers wove through his hair and her long legs wrapped around him as he brought her to dizzying heights of pleasure with just his mouth, his hands. She cried out loud and long, as if she didn't care who heard that she was in the throes of an insanely intense climax. His heart slammed in his chest.

That was just the beginning.

There was more kissing.

There was a wicked grin from Roxanna as they switched positions and she slowly, torturously licked him from his chest down to his rock-hard cock. She took him in her mouth. He groaned. She may have been the one on her knees, but he was the one completely at her mercy. The things she did with her hands … her tongue …

"Stop." His voice was hoarse.

"Stop?"

"If you want more."

"Oh, I always want more."

She wasn't just talking about sex. Well, she was. But she wasn't. There was a marked lack of blood to his brain at the moment, but one thing was crystal clear: this woman was his match. He loved her, deeply and completely. And then he gave her more.

# CHAPTER
# TEN

*That moment when you live happily ever after.*

*The day of the wedding*

The wedding day dawned, bright, warm, sunny, and perfect. Jane was downright giddy as the hair and makeup team took over her bedroom and her wedding party piled in to get all done up. They played everyone's favorite pop songs and fervently discussed eyeliner and hair styles as if they were the most important things in the world. But mainly they gathered around to celebrate that their Jane was getting married. She had found true love.

She hadn't lost her ability to be aware of other people, though. While having her hair curled and styled, she fixed her gaze on Roxanna.

"*You* are whistling a merry tune."

"I am not whistling a merry tune," Roxanna replied. Even though she was indeed whistling a merry freaking tune.

"You and Damien left the rehearsal reception early last night."

"I was tired," she said, making no effort to even pretend to tell the truth. Her ridiculously happy grin was answer enough.

"Pfft." Jane expressed her disbelief. And when Roxanna didn't respond she said, "OMG."

"Shut up."

"You said you loved him!" Jane exclaimed to the entire room. Somehow, she just knew. "Did he say it back?"

Roxanna thought about protesting. But really … She was whistling a merry tune and she had said it. "He said it first."

Jane shrieked with glee. All the other bridesmaids did too.

"That is the best wedding present I could ask for!"

"I'll just return that crockpot then," Roxanna said. But she was smiling. Because love.


THE WEDDING WENT off without a hitch. Well, a few guests got confused and went to the decoy wedding at the gazebo, but they made it back in time to witness the real one. Jane looked radiantly beautiful in her Monique Lhuillier gown. Duke got teary. Hell, even Roxanna got teary. They promised to love, cherish, and keep their arguments off social media.

Afterward, the bride and groom took a selfie with Duke's phone. Then Jane called Roxanna and Damien over.

"Here," Jane said, thrusting the phone into Roxanna's hand. "Go post that picture to *The London Weekly*'s Twitter account."

Damien and Roxanna just stared at her.

"You'll have to go up to the gazebo. There still isn't any reception down here. *Alas*." But she was smiling, as if she had masterminded the entire Internet/cell service blackout herself.

"But the puppies," Roxanna said.

"And the kittens," Damien added.

"Will be fine," Jane said. "Poor Archer and Duke. I had them add a clause to the contract allowing this one shot before the others are released."

"Why?"

"What she means is, that is extraordinarily generous and thoughtful of you," Damien said.

"No really, you don't have to go to all that trouble," Roxanna said. "Why?"

"Because it's romantic," Jane explained, pushing her veil back from her face. "Because I can. Because it's my day and I want you both to live happily ever after with your newspaper. Now go!"

"Yes, Bride!"

After a hug from Roxanna and a kiss on the cheek from Damien, Jane turned back to the official photographer and her wedding guests. They dashed off to the gazebo.

"And don't post anything else!" Jane shouted after them. Then she was swept off by her groom and the rest of the wedding party for even more photographs, and the first dance, and the rest of the celebration.

Roxanna paused, halfway up the hill to the gazebo, looking back at the festivities. She had always thought, "ugh, weddings," but now she saw how rare, delicate, and wonderful it was for two people to find each other and fall in love, for better or for worse, flaws and all. That deserved one hell of a celebration.

"The sooner we post this picture, the sooner we can get back and join everyone," Damien said, as if he knew just what she was thinking, which was weird and wonderful all at once. Funny, that.

Up at the gazebo, the music drifted up from the reception tent down below. The decorations from the decoy wedding were still there —lots of garlands and a smattering of chairs.

Damien got to work posting the picture on *The London Weekly*'s social media accounts. It being a selfie, it was just their faces—they looked outrageously happy—and a bit of the dress. There wasn't enough detail to show for certain that the earlier pictures were fake. Not that it mattered anymore—they had scored the first picture of the bride and groom. They could maybe, just maybe, breathe a sigh of relief.

Before he sent the tweet, Roxanna took the phone from his hand. She dared to add the hashtag #HappilyEverAfter.

"Happily ever after?" Damien murmured, looking over her shoulder.

"It's something Jane would say," Roxanna said softly, turning to face him.

"And what about you?"

"I would just kiss you," she said, wrapping her arms around him and pressing herself up against him. God, she loved the feel of this man. His mouth claimed hers for a sweet, slow kiss.

"This works too," he murmured.

She just smiled and went back to kissing him because … kisses, and love, and happily ever after.

"I love you, Roxanna Lane," he said softly. "I don't think I'll ever love anyone else like this."

"So don't," she said, as if it were that simple. But what if it was?

"Maybe I won't," he said, and she thought it was maybe the most romantic thing she'd ever heard.

"You've ruined me for any other man," she told him.

"Is that so?"

"It is so."

"We should probably stay together then. Forever."

"For once I find myself speechless," she murmured.

"Just say yes," he said softly. There was emotion and nervousness and all of the feelings in his voice. Her debonair, aristocratic, perfect man wanted her now and forever and he was worried that she would say no.

Her heart was pounding, her knees were weak, but her mind was clear when she said, "Oh, hell yes."

# AFTERWORD

I would like to thank the Lady Authors and Martha Trachtenberg for their help in crafting and editing this story. Any remaining mistakes are my own.

I am also thankful to Megan Mulry for allowing my character to dress in the shoes designed by her character (Sarah James of the excellent novel *If the Shoe Fits*).

# ABOUT THE AUTHOR

Maya Rodale began reading romance novels in college at her mother's insistence and is now the author of numerous smart and sassy romances. A champion of the romance genre and its readers, she is also the author of the non-fiction book *Dangerous Books For Girls: The Bad Reputation Of Romance Novels, Explained* and a co-founder of Lady Jane's Salon, a national reading series devoted to romantic fiction. Maya lives in New York City with her darling dog and a rogue of her own. To discover more of her books, visit her on the web at www. MayaRodale.com.

# ALSO BY MAYA RODALE

THREE SCHEMES AND A SCANDAL

**NOVELLAS AND COLLECTIONS**

THAT ROGUE JACK IN AT THE DUKE'S WEDDING

HOT ROGUE ON A COLD NIGHT IN AT THE CHRISTMAS WEDDING

THAT MOMENT WHEN YOU FALL IN LOVE IN AT THE SUMMER WEDDING

SEDUCING THE SINGLE LADY

**YOUNG ADULT**

ALICE AND GABBY'S EXCELLENT ADVENTURE

**NON-FICTION**

DANGEROUS BOOKS FOR GIRLS

**CHILDREN'S**

LADY MISS PENNY GOES TO LUNCH

# EPILOGUE

*Dear Arwen,*

*I'm looking at the gorgeous Regency snuff box you gave me over cocktails last week. Thank you again—I'm so glad you found it in the Melbury antique shop. Since you're going be in England so much, I shall send you off on research trips whenever I need accessories for my characters. Duke is threatening to take up snuff—I never give my heroes such a disgusting habit—so I've decided to use the box to store Advil.*

*As for the wedding, I loved everything you planned and didn't plan. It was perfect. I'll tell everyone and you can give me as a reference anytime.*

*Yours,*
*Jane Austen (finally!)*

———

*Dear Harry,*

*I will never regret that my wedding ended up at Brampton House. Thank you and all your staff for your hard work getting it ready in time. And special secret thanks to you for not turning on the Wi-Fi, even when the Internet came back the day after we arrived. I'll never tell Duke. Probably. You were a prince for putting up with the complaints from Duke and his techies so that I could enjoy an entire week with my husband's almost undivided attention. It was the best wedding present you could have given me.*

*Thank you also for the wonderful book* Erotic and Romantic Frescoes in English Houses. *The pictures will inspire many scenes in future books and those of the Gold Saloon will always remind me of the happiest week of my life.*

*Arwen must have told you we had cocktails at the Delaville Hotel last week before she flew back to England. She tells me you are very romantic but I knew that – only a romantic would have agreed to a bride's request for an unplugged wedding. I'm going to persuade Duke to return to Brampton for vacation next year and I expect you to turn off the Internet, again. JK. I look forward to hanging with you and Arwen. Also, Arwen and I think we should find a nice man for Mark.*

*Best wishes,*
*Mrs. Jane Austen*

———

*Archer-*

*Great seeing you at the wedding; thanks for making the trip. Thank you also for the donation in our honor to Little Paws Rescue. Jane and I really appreciate your help in saving the magazine photo deal.*

*Duke*

*PS: Nice work with the pastry chef. Totally a babe.*
*PPS: Jane is enclosing another autographed book. For your "assistant."*

———

*Dear Natalie,*

*I can't thank you enough for stepping in to help save the rehearsal dinner dessert at our wedding. Arwen told me—in confidence—that your cakes were even better than the ones she originally ordered. The bride cake especially was stunning and amazing and I plan to force Duke to take me to Boston to eat at Cuisine du Jude sometime (assuming we can get a table!).*

*Sincerely,*
*Jane Austen (I will never get tired of signing that name ...)*

---

*Dear Cali,*

*Thank you for coming to England and being my bridesmaid. And thank you for my wedding gift. I LOVE it! I hung it over my desk. Duke walked into my office and said, "Why do you have a poster of Colin Firth mounted on a horse and reading?" I just said, "Research." He said, "Right. Research." He understands me. He's perfect.*

*I'm crossing my fingers that your Mr. Perfect comes through for you too. He's one of the good ones, you know. Duke swears by it. Maybe this time next year we'll be heading off to your wedding. Here's hoping!*

*Big hugs,*
*Jane*

---

*Piers-*

*Thanks for making the trip for the wedding, and for the antique twin-barrel Manton. Very funny. Jane said she'd make me mount it above the fireplace if we had one. She's determined to learn how to load it. I usually enjoy her book research, but I'm keeping this research out of the bedroom.*

*Duke*

*P.S. Best of luck with Cali. Trust me, it'll be worth it. Librarians make the best lovers. I should totally put that on a T-shirt…*

————

*Dear Roxanna,*

*What can I say? Thank you for everything—from introducing me to life in the big city to introducing me to my husband (though I continue to be appalled by your methods). You are the best friend and maid of honor a girl could ask for.*

*Also, thank you for the crockpot. I honestly thought you were joking about that.*

*Love,*
*Mrs. Jane Austen (can you believe that's my name!?)*

————

*Dear Lord Northbourne\*,*

*You have succeeded where I have not: turning Roxanna into a romantic. For that I shall forgive you for wagering about my wedding photographs. Duke and I look forward to seeing you more with Roxanna, but we should warn you—no sharing baby pictures when the time comes!\*\**

*Best wishes,*
*Mrs. Jane Austen*

*\*You know how thrilled I am to have an actual lord among my acquaintances.*

*\*\*Which may be sooner than you think!*

# THANK YOU!

Thank you for reading! If you enjoyed *At the Summer Wedding*, please consider posting a review of it online to help other readers.

The Lady Authors invite you to visit them online at TheLadyAuthors.com for behind-the-scenes glimpses into the making of this anthology and more about their other books.

**Books by The Lady Authors**
available in print, digital, and audio

AT THE DUKE'S WEDDING
AT THE CHRISTMAS WEDDING
AT THE SUMMER WEDDING
A WEDDING FOR ALL SEASONS (A BOXED SET INCLUDING
AT THE DUKE'S WEDDING AND AT THE CHRISTMAS WEDDING)

Lightning Source UK Ltd.
Milton Keynes UK
UKHW020304080223
416610UK00016B/1894